Praise for the works of Cheryl Sawyer

The Chase

"[W]ill have readers enthralled with its complex characters, intricate plot, and richly detailed setting." —*Booklist*

"Fine Regency romantic suspense starring an intrepid heroine . . . a tense historical intrigue." —The Best Reviews

Siren

"With its lavish use of history, boldly passionate story, and vividly detailed settings, Australian author Sawyer's American debut is a grand and glorious delight for fans of the classic love stories of Kathleen Woodiwiss and Rosemary Rogers."
—*Booklist*

"[A] sweeping epic tale . . . wonderfully brings to life a bygone era." —*Midwest Book Review*

"From the very first pages of this impressive novel, the reader is treated to a colorful tapestry of sights and impressions set amongst the vivid streets of New Orleans to the colorful beaches of the Caribbean. . . . A high-seas adventure."
—Historical Romance Writers

continued . . .

The Code
of Love

Cheryl Sawyer

A SIGNET ECLIPSE BOOK

SIGNET ECLIPSE
Published by New American Library, a division of
Penguin Group (USA) Inc., 375 Hudson Street, New York, New York 10014, USA
Penguin Group (Canada), 90 Eglinton Avenue East, Suite 700, Toronto, Ontario,
Canada M4P 2Y3 (a division of Pearson Penguin Canada Inc.)
Penguin Books Ltd., 80 Strand, London WC2R 0RL, England
Penguin Ireland, 25 St. Stephen's Green, Dublin 2,
Ireland (a division of Penguin Books Ltd.)
Penguin Group (Australia), 250 Camberwell Road, Camberwell, Victoria 3124,
Australia (a division of Pearson Australia Group Pty. Ltd.)
Penguin Books India Pvt. Ltd., 11 Community Centre, Panchsheel Park,
New Delhi - 110 017, India
Penguin Group (NZ), cnr Airborne and Rosedale Roads, Albany,
Auckland 1310, New Zealand (a division of Pearson New Zealand Ltd.)
Penguin Books (South Africa) (Pty.) Ltd., 24 Sturdee Avenue,
Rosebank, Johannesburg 2196, South Africa

Penguin Books Ltd., Registered Offices: 80 Strand, London WC2R 0RL, England

First published by Signet Eclipse, an imprint of New American Library,
a division of Penguin Group (USA) Inc.

First Printing, May 2006
10 9 8 7 6 5 4 3 2 1

SIGNET ECLIPSE and logo are trademarks of Penguin Group (USA) Inc.

LIBRARY OF CONGRESS CATALOGING-IN-PUBLICATION DATA:
Sawyer, Cheryl, 1947–
    The code of love / by Cheryl Sawyer.
        p. cm.
    ISBN 0-451-21838-8 (trade pbk.)
    1. Peninsular War, 1807–1814—Fiction I. Title.

PR9639.4.S29C63 2006
823'.92—dc22   2006001305

Printed in the United States of America

To Rosemary, with love

The Garden Prison

"Escaped prisoner!" On a hot night in July 1810, the news sped around the capital of Mauritius and sent a frisson through the veins of its inhabitants. Captain General Decaën might well run the island as though it were the tightest ship in the Indian Ocean, but this was a time of war, and the English fleets hovering over the horizon created a powerful sense of menace around the remote Bonapartist stronghold. Rodriguez was already occupied by the British, Bourbon had fallen only a week before, and it was to one of these islands that the prisoner must have been aiming, for having silenced two sentries he reached the port unseen and swam out to snatch one of the French navy pinnaces in the harbor.

Delphine Dalgleish, at her family plantation of Saint-Amour, received a hasty note from a neighbor about the escape, and read it with consternation. The prisoner was English, an enemy, so she should not care—but she did. It was too close to home. The soldiers of the legion had been just in time to retake him, he had been mauled by four men-at-arms and he was already in solitary confinement by the time society rose and took its chocolate and sweet rolls in the warm light of the next morning, but the shock of it stayed in the mind. With one dramatic gesture, this young British officer had shown how different he was from the other prisoners of war, most of whom lived amongst the French colonists in a spirit of understanding. He had acted with a violence and speed that ran counter to the ordered island ways, which was why his treatment by the legion had been so vicious.

It was three days before he was brought back to the Maison Despeaux, the Garden Prison from which he had broken out. He was scarcely able to walk. He had not spoken a word under interrogation, nor a syllable since. Only Delphine Dalgleish knew who had betrayed him to the legion, and she told just one other person, so no one else knew what to think. Which made a visit to the Garden Prison de rigueur at the earliest opportunity.

It was set on a low hill a mile or so out of town, a spacious, two-story mansion now used to detain British officers captured by the French navy. Despite the guardhouse and sentries, and the surrounding dry-stone wall, it looked less like a place of confinement than like the residence of a nobleman. The five-acre grounds were graced with luxuriant tropical vegetation and offered views of a wooded valley and steep hills behind, and to the west the harbor and the ocean. Prisoners were even allowed by day up to a flat part of the roof, to gaze at the passing naval scene. The Maison Despeaux also allowed visitors, French officers and island sophisticates who valued variety in their social round.

So it happened that, on the very evening of the prisoner's return, he was making ready to walk down from his suite on the upper floor to join seven fellow officers at a reception in the salon below.

"La Générale is expected this evening, sir."

Gideon Landor, seated before a cheval glass while his manservant's hands flickered around his head, did not reply.

"Madame Julie Dalgleish, accompanied by her daughter, Mademoiselle Delphine." Ellis held the scissors still. "The idol, they say, of the island."

"Thank you; that will do."

Ellis hesitated. The trim was done, but he had another duty—to keep the lieutenant abreast of what had transpired while he was under lock and key in town. But his master's glacial green eyes met his in the glass, so he busied himself removing the towel, brushing down the wide-shouldered coat and banishing the bright, fallen hair from the floor. As he set the room to rights, he shrugged and reflected that the facts spoke for themselves. La Générale, so nicknamed because she was the widow of one of France's most brilliant revolutionary generals, was a Bonapartist through and through; she even maintained a friendship with the former empress, Joséphine, whom she visited every summer when she and her young daughter went to Paris. They were also friends of Captain General Decaën, who governed the island. Sir Gideon looked as warm as an iceberg over the prospect of the soirée, and who could blame him?

Eventually Ellis finished fussing about and held out Gideon's cane for him. Grimacing, Gideon took it, then got up and limped to the window. He looked down on the garden, so lush, so extravagantly green, the glittering crown of what must be the most beautiful prison in the world. He took a deep breath, then held it with an inward curse as pain clamped around his bruised ribs.

Ellis was by the door, his misgivings hidden under the bluff air he always adopted on board ship. "You don't think it might be prudent, sir, to have the physician call again?"

Gideon smiled cynically and shook his head. "The damage is public enough."

The merest crease showed in Ellis's weatherbeaten cheeks. This evening, nothing mattered more than appearances, and no one knew that better than Ellis.

"I shan't need you until midnight," Gideon said. "You know what to do."

"Certainly, sir." Ellis withdrew.

Later, in the elegant salon of the Maison Despeaux, Gideon found the reception more tolerable than he had foreseen. He was surrounded at first, and he despised the open curiosity of some of the citizens who approached, but amongst the French military he detected some sympathy, and they drew the attention away from him after an hour or so. He sat in a corner, leaving untouched the refreshments that had been thoughtfully ordered by one of the younger demoiselles, and observed the crowded room while trying to control his restlessness and impatience.

It was colorful, the officers in dress uniform, the ladies in Parisian gowns of light-colored fabrics that went with their pale skin—they never allowed themselves to tan, despite the relentless sun of the southern tropics. They afforded a pretty picture that he might have appreciated on another occasion, but he wasn't here for the chatter—he was waiting for just one person. A friend, or so he had come to think of him: Armand de Belfort, planter, militia officer and aristocrat of intelligence and ability. Gideon looked forward to the regular visits that Belfort paid from an estate some miles south of town, the stewardship of which he had held since the death of an uncle, General Dalgleish, or D'Alglice, as his name was pronounced on the island. The general had left his widow a generous endowment and the right to continue living on the plantation, which was named Saint-Amour. Gideon had not met the ladies, since they had been in France for the last few months, but they would be here tonight.

Mademoiselle Delphine D'Alglice was pointed out to him by an English officer the instant she walked in. Very slender, a little above middle height, and so blond that the glow of the chandeliers seemed to surround her forehead with silver, she entered like lightning and arrested every conversation. It was amusing to see people align themselves differently, the influential ladies gliding forward to welcome the widow, who made a handsome though sober figure beside the daughter, and the gentlemen joining in a murmur that traveled around the walls to Gideon.

She threw a dart of blue across the room and looked straight at him. Then she turned away to greet someone, revealing a delicate neck above fine shoulders, and bringing a smile to the person's face.

There was nothing else about the scene to attract Gideon. He might have been less critical if over the last three months he had been able to adapt to imprisonment on this paradisal island, but he was aching to get back to sea. He might have been more at ease if his surroundings had afforded less of a contrast to the filthy cell in which he had been interrogated under duress three nights before. He might have viewed this crowd with less hostility if he could have been sure that none of them had betrayed his escape to his captors.

Meanwhile Mademoiselle D'Alglice, despite her divine beauty, behaved with no less frivolity than the other young gentlewomen disposed about the room. She was clearly a habitué of such evenings. She had the knack of focusing attention wherever she moved, and all the verve in the place seemed to spring from her. She had sparkling eyes, and a quickness of expression that did not lack grace. She shone—he granted that—but from his viewpoint the brightness seemed a reflection only, coming from no fire of passion or intellect within. She might be a colonial, but she looked like a pure product of Paris—exquisitely dressed, and as empty as a piece of porcelain.

The time came when they must meet. The French visitors in the room were wondering why he had not walked forward to pay his respects already, some saying that his injuries prevented him and others that if he opened his mouth he might well utter something disobliging, given what he had just gone through.

As Delphine crossed the floor with her mother and an acquaintance who had offered to present Landor to them, she wondered how to keep her countenance. She knew enmity when she saw it, and having it directed at her from afar for the last half hour was made worse by the knowledge that it was more or less justified. For it had been one of her own servants, sent to the docks to fetch home the last of her baggage from France, who hastened to the *gens d'armes* and told them what was going forward in the bay.

Landor rose as she approached, and apart from a slight compression of his well-shaped mouth, there was no sign of discomfort in his stance. On the contrary, he loomed, being tall, straight and strongly made. He watched her with a stare that was sea green and pale, as though he were raking her from across a windswept deck with the sun in his eyes.

The introductions were made, and Delphine's curtsy was answered by a stiff nod. Perhaps his injuries prevented a deeper bow. She tried not to feel guilty about that.

"We have heard much about you from my nephew Armand de Belfort," her mother said in English. "I would say, 'How delightful to meet you at last,' but I'm aware the delight is not necessarily returned. Given the unhappy circumstances." She received only a dry smile in response to this opener. Delphine thanked fate that at least one of them could be natural before Sir Gideon—she had forbidden the servant to talk, so only her cousin so far knew who exactly had given the alarm.

It would help if Armand were here too; he reckoned himself a friend of Sir Gideon Landor and considered him a capital fellow, even charming when in the mood. Armand should know, being loaded with charm himself. But the mood required his presence tonight.

The colossus spoke, however. "Am I to look forward to seeing your nephew?"

"We hope so. He's at supper with the captain general, but he promised to join us and escort us home. Did he not, my dear?"

Delphine said, "Maman, we are keeping Sir Gideon standing. Let us sit down." She was watching the clear, somewhat frightening eyes, and noticed no gratitude for her consideration. He had not used his cane as he stood up, but when he sat he took his weight rather carefully on the padded armrests and bent forward for a moment so that she could see only the top of his head. Cropped rather too short for fashion, his hair was fair—gold at the roots and bleached at the tips by the East India sun. Then he straightened and turned to her.

Delphine had been cheerful and flirtatious all evening, perhaps more so than usual in order to arm herself for this encounter, but she now found flirtation quite out of the question. "We consider your treatment barbarous, sir. Have you thought of lodging a protest?"

"No. The right person would go unpunished."

Maman said, "Scandalous, that it should have happened to an officer and a gentleman . . ."

"Scandalous," he murmured, and Delphine had the distinct idea that this was sarcasm.

She said, "You apprehend that the orders to . . . question you . . . came from higher up? That would be more than scandal. It would be a breach of honor."

"Yes, but I cannot prove that from here, mademoiselle. And until I can, I should prefer not to have four brutes from the lower ranks thrashed in another man's place."

He meant it; he was convinced that the order came from above.

Was he looking as high as Captain General Decaën? Disturbed, she said, "Surely the culprits have already been punished. Ile de France has always treated its prisoners with justice, sir, and cared for their comfort and safety. You have only to look around you."

"You will forgive me, mademoiselle, for being less than enthusiastic about the Maison Despeaux. Despite its affording me your most interesting company."

Sarcasm, without a doubt.

Her mother intervened. "If the Maison is not to your taste, have you considered giving your parole and allowing the captain general to place you on an estate? We have a friend who agreed to do just that, and lodged with the D'Arifats at Wilhelms Plains. He obtained his release and sailed home only last month. The D'Arifats are quite heartbroken!"

"Ah. Captain Matthew Flinders, I collect."

There was the faintest sneer as he said the name, and Delphine had to set him right. "A most amiable commander. He longed to go back to England, but while he was here he was a wonderful boon to good company."

"For six and a half years. His eagerness for home evidently had limits."

"He was held as a spy. Once that kind of mud has stuck, clearing one's name takes some doing."

"You thought him innocent?" For the first time Landor looked interested.

"Unlucky. When he arrived, he had no idea France was at war with England again, and by the time he was in custody it was too late."

"If he were no spy, he should have been detained as a prisoner and exchanged."

Delphine's mother said, "There were some quite foolish mistakes. At the very beginning, Captain Flinders was invited to a reception, where someone asked him whether he knew anything about the explorer 'Fleendare.' He denied it." She gave a melancholy shake of the head. "He didn't recognize his own name. These things happen. As you may know, our name is Dalgleish, but on this island it bears another accent."

He said, "Not a grave enough error to damn him, surely. If he was reconnoitering the coast, he would have had maps, drawings—he's a surveyor, is he not?"

Delphine said, "In his cabin there were sealed letters to the Admiralty from the governor of New South Wales, recommending a close investigation of our defenses." Landor raised an eyebrow. "Of course, he ought to have destroyed the papers the moment he was challenged. But he didn't know what was in them."

"He was caught," her mother observed sadly, "in a game where he was unaware of the rules. Indeed, he hardly knew that he was in a game until . . ."

Landor said, "Naval instructions are to send all such dispatches to the bottom when at risk. War is no game; if he'd done his duty then, we should not be discussing him now. However *aimable* you may have found him, Mademoiselle D'Alglice." He spoke the French word, and the French version of her surname, with flippant precision, as though her language were also a kind of game.

She flinched. "We didn't believe Captain Flinders because he was well mannered and clever, though he was both. We believed him because he was an honest man."

Gideon saw a blush across her fine cheekbones as she said it, and decided there was a fondness for the complaisant Flinders. They were extraordinary, these women, with their patronizing visits to young men whose dearest wish was to be half the world away—captives whom they condescended to make pets of, for as long as it suited them. But he was curious on another point. "How is it that you managed to pass the blockade when you arrived?"

The demoiselle answered. "We weren't intercepted. If we had been, your fleet would have learned that our vessel carried nothing more than a few families returning home before the summer in France." She caught his look and said with meaning, "Our captain assured us that he had no contraband on board—nothing that could relieve any of the dreadful shortages imposed upon us by your navy."

He changed the subject. "General Dalgleish . . . Your father was a Scot, I believe?"

"Yes, from Edinburgh."

"That explains your remarkable English."

From a flicker of her eyelashes, he realized she had taken his compliment as a slight. He should have chosen a more definitive word—"fluent," or "skillful." She was alive to nuances in a way that suggested more sensitivity than he had bargained for under that stylish exterior.

And her voice! It was low, with a vibration in it that made every statement sound like an intimacy. There was humor in it too; it reminded him of the amusing delivery used by female wits of London high society. Usually he disliked that kind of studied cleverness, but there was nothing studied about Mademoiselle Dalgleish; indeed, she seemed only too free with her opinions.

She said lightly, "My cousin has a great admiration for your French, monsieur. Pray, how did you come by it? I must hope that it doesn't all spring from *captivity*. That would be too cruel."

"I was lucky in the French tutor I had as a child. He was an émigré who came to England after the Revolution: highly educated, and a most entertaining friend. Better still, he introduced me to his family, for they lived in London. He's now in America, but we still correspond."

"If you speak our language so well, why don't you leave the Maison and live with a family? Or have you refused to give your parole?"

"It's not consistent with my duty."

Which was to escape, if he could. But he wouldn't be going anywhere after what her own countrymen had lately put him through. They had spared his face, though. The well-defined, regular features were as composed as if he were on the deck of his ship giving orders. She wondered, looking into the light green eyes, whether the interrogation had been about what the English navy was doing in these waters.

"You don't care for Ile de France." She felt a pang as she said it. She had come to the island as a little child, when her father purchased their estate, and her love for it was so profound, so physical, that she felt wounded by any thought of its being threatened, or even disparaged.

He examined her face, and his deep voice was thoughtful as he said, "Let's say I'm not overfond of captivity, mademoiselle. Something I have in common with your slaves, I imagine."

"We keep none. Our fields are worked by laborers. They came here to settle of their own free will. From India."

"Under my late husband's encouragement," her mother said, almost as though she were apologizing. "In the spirit of the republic. Liberty, you know."

"I wish I did." He grinned suddenly, a wide, wolfish grin that showed perfect teeth. He was tickled by Maman, as people frequently were. They found her pleasant and easygoing and were disarmed by her soft brown eyes and the way she sometimes failed to finish her sentences. It could take them some time to see beyond the good humor to the sagacious woman she really was.

"Liberty!" said a voice behind her, and Armand was with them, greeting Delphine and her mother and then putting a hand on Landor's shoulder as he continued, "It is good to see a smile on your face as you speak the name of freedom."

"Laughter being my sole option." But Landor's grin disappeared as he rose and shook hands.

Armand murmured, "My dear fellow. When I heard what you've endured . . ."

"Not worth discussing." Landor gestured for Armand to take the chair beside him. "Your aunt and I were talking about agriculture."

"Indeed!" Armand gave a disbelieving chuckle and sat down, flipping the tails of his black evening coat to each side and disposing himself comfortably with one silk-clad lower leg advanced a little in front of the other. From the top of his dark head to his neat evening shoes, his lean form looked as elegant as a fashion plate in the *Assemblée* magazine, but at the same time it was poised with alertness. "Our own or the neighbors'? The Dufours are selling up, you know, and going back to France. I heard it tonight at supper."

Delphine shivered. She could guess why the Dufours were going: they were in flight, to the safety of the homeland. While the others talked on of local news and gossip, she thought for the thousandth time of invasion. If the English took Port Napoleon, they would snatch everything to themselves: the reins of government, command of the island's trade and resources, the rule of law. Even land, perhaps.

Sir Gideon glanced at her now and then but more often at Armand, and Delphine could see that he wanted to talk to her cousin alone. She sat in impatient silence, twisting her bracelet around her wrist. It was the only jewelry she wore, her mother having quietly remarked that if she were going to wear diamonds, it should be just one piece. Prisoners, even if they had the kind of wealth that allowed them luxuries such as Sir Gideon enjoyed at the Maison, felt another kind of poverty in their confinement. It was ill-bred to remind them of it.

Eventually Delphine made her mother walk away with her to take coffee. Sir Gideon rose as they did and favored them with another stiff nod.

Her mother said with a lovely smile, "So gracious of you, sir, to put up with our ramblings. Now, you must not let Armand go on and tire you completely."

"No fear of that, madame; I always find his conversation stimulating."

And that, thought Delphine as she walked off, could well be a nice underhand piece of sarcasm too.

Alone with Armand de Belfort, Gideon took one second to ascertain that no one else was in earshot, then said, "Thank you for coming."

"You thought I might not?" Belfort's cheeks glowed, making his blue eyes glitter. His accent sounded stronger in his distress. "And good reason too. *Jésu*, what a damned 'orrible *cursed* disaster. And to think it was my—"

"No, my doing altogether. There was nothing wrong with the plan."

"I still don't believe it. What went *wrong?*"

Gideon began, "Ellis helped take care of the sentries and we got down to the port undetected. I found the dinghy and the oars just where you said they would be."

"*Dieu merci* for that at least. So?"

"The moon came out—the whole shoreline was awash with light. Where you had it moored, the dinghy was too exposed. I decided the only inconspicuous way was to swim for the pinnace. I told Ellis to leg it."

"Why on earth?"

"Able Seaman Ellis can't swim. He had orders to get back here on the double before the sentries came to and raised the alarm, but he hung about until he knew the whole thing had gone to blazes, and only just got back in time."

"And you?" Armand spoke with deep concern and a tinge of fear for what was to come.

"It was choppy, the clouds were moving and there was plenty of shadow on the way out amongst the ships—there didn't seem to be a soul on shore at the time. I've no idea who spied me."

"You—" Armand stopped and took a long breath. With Gideon watching him intently, he said, "You'll know soon enough. Servants can never keep quiet. It was one of ours."

Something inside Gideon froze, but he said calmly enough, "How?"

"Apparently he was down at the docks collecting some of my cousin's baggage."

"At two in the morning?"

"He'd been sent down that evening, but when he got to the inn where the trunks were being held he lingered on. So that's how he happened to be lounging about the dockside. He saw you, realized something was wrong and went straight to the town major. He thought this was a good excuse for half a day's idleness, but my cousin was furious when she heard. She dismissed him on the spot. It took all my persuasion to make her keep him on and keep his mouth shut."

"So she knows who turned me in," Gideon said. He could not help looking over to where she stood in a little circle of ladies, but she had her back to him. Hiding the fine, deceptively angelic face.

"Yes. She was nervous about coming here tonight, poor thing. As was I, if you want the truth."

Gideon heard the tremor in his friend's voice, but he went on. "Well, unaware of these enthralling events, I succeeded in getting on board the pinnace. I should have reconnoitered her at once, but you'd told me she was unguarded, and there was no dinghy beside her, nothing to indicate anyone was aboard. I was making ready to hoist sail when the whole blessed shoreline sprang to life. A platoon of legionnaires, naval officers running hither and yon; then they put a boat in the water with four marines. Far too quickly for me to do a thing but stand and take it."

"You couldn't have tried slipping overboard? Evasion?"

Gideon said sardonically, "Not with a pistol jammed into my spine."

Armand gasped, which made a few bystanders look his way. "There was a man on board?"

"Indeed." Gideon shifted a little so that Armand would have to turn farther from the crowd to speak to him, and so hide his face. His own felt as cold as marble. "The world knows the rest."

"What did they want from you?"

Gideon shrugged, then winced. "You don't need to know. You were helping a friend; it was a favor from one gentleman to another. It went awry, that's all."

"It won't next time, I promise you. In a few weeks—"

"No. You've done enough."

"If only you'd allowed me to let you take my yacht."

Gideon shook his head. "Too suspicious by half. You'd have been questioned and forced to lie. I couldn't put you in that position."

"I'd as soon tell Decaën the truth! That he has no right to keep you here and refuse ever to exchange you. It's to his own dishonor that he does so, and none to mine if I give you the means to go free."

"Noble sentiments, my good fellow. I appreciate them."

Armand shook his head. "You were so close. But for one idle servant, and a soldier lurking where he shouldn't have been . . ." Gideon shifted in his chair and Armand went on, "*Diable*, this evening must be a torment to you. Look, take my advice and retire. We'll speak of this again."

The two men rose and Gideon looked down at Armand de Belfort for what he cordially hoped would be the very last time. But one. They shook hands, and he managed to say with composure, "Kindly give my compliments to Madame and Mademoiselle Dalgleish." He took up his cane and then, trusting himself no further, turned toward the stairs.

Gideon strode into his apartment, stopped and hurled the cane across the room. It smashed into the wall and clattered to the floor, and a second later Ellis burst in from the bedchamber, his eyes wide with alarm.

Grinding his teeth, Gideon said, "I know who turned me in."

"So do I, sir. I heard it tonight, from the cook's boy. It was a servant of the D'Alglices that—"

"Yes, primed by Armand de Belfort himself."

Ellis stared and finally said, "You have me stumped, sir. Why, it was he who helped you in the first place!"

"Yes." Gideon walked to the window and looked up at the night sky. It was cloudy and the waning moon was invisible. "My escape allowed Decaën's men any method they liked to question me. Because they could justify it by saying I resisted. They must have been hand in glove; it's the only explanation. With Belfort to lure me there and Decaën's men to close the trap." He leaned against the embrasure of the window as the recollection made him shudder.

Ellis said, "I can hardly believe it of Monsieur de Belfort. Are you sure, sir?"

"No one else knew the plan. Yet there was a man on the pinnace. I've been wondering about that ever since. Belfort tried to look surprised tonight when I told him, but for once that smooth face of his gave him away. He knew all right. He placed him there. And how do I know?" His voice came out as a low growl that made Ellis take a step back. "He rightly named him as a soldier. Now, you'd expect Belfort to assume he was a sailor, for it was a French naval vessel. But no. I never said the bastard was army."

Ellis seldom heard Sir Gideon swear, and rarely did himself, except for the night when his master was returned to him, bruised and half conscious, from the guardhouse in town. He said, "By God, I wish I had him in my sights now."

There was a long silence. Sir Gideon began pacing, without a hint of a limp, back and forth before the window, his hands clasped behind his back and his head up, chin forward, as he was wont to do on the quarterdeck. Ellis, who had served with him for two years and never regretted a day, waited in confident expectation.

Finally his master turned, his eyes alight. "You have everything ready?"

"Yes, sir."

"We leave in an hour."

"Pardon me, sir, but what are we going to do? The harbor is as full of uniforms as Portsmouth on parade."

"We're going to take Belfort's bloody yacht."

The Gazebo

O n the way back to the plantation, Delphine and her mother quizzed Armand, but he could say only that Landor was exhausted and unwilling to discuss the treatment he'd received on the captain general's orders.

"That won't stop me from bringing it up myself," he said. "I'm going to pay Decaën a visit tomorrow and give him my views. I said nothing tonight—I could hardly broach it in company."

"Do you really think he could have stooped to such a thing?" Delphine asked.

"I shan't know until I tackle him, shall I?"

"Can you persuade him to ask Sir Gideon to give his parole?"

He shook his head. "All parole was revoked months ago."

"Oh. He failed to explain that to me."

Her mother said to Armand, "Are things so very bad, my dear?"

"We've no idea. We can only wait for the English to make the first move." His voice was bitter. "For all we know, there'll be an English flag flying over Port Napoleon by the time Landor's recovered."

The women took this in silence, since they could see Armand wasn't in spirits. When they got home the others soon said their good nights, and Delphine found herself alone. Despite a promise that she was retiring, she went upstairs to fetch a shawl and dismiss her maid, and then walked out across the verandah and down into the parterre garden to look at the stars.

It was a ritual of hers to take relief from the heat of the night in the sea breeze that sailed over the slope above the beach and drifted up across the grounds to the plantation house. As she tipped her head back to look at the sky, she felt the cooler air touching her like a welcoming caress. She let the shawl hang from the crooks of her arms—it was for form's sake only, a concession to her mother, who never quite approved of her midnight star watching.

Tonight clouds were moving across the sky, and she could spy her favorite constellations only in the deep blue gaps between. The half-moon was up, and eventually the bank of cloud at the zenith moved away and allowed light to spill around her.

She left the parterre and strolled down the lawn, one end of her shawl brushing the manicured grass. The shrill sound of frogs singing in the casuarinas at either side, the warm earth under her silk indoor shoes, caught her senses anew, as they always did when she returned home from France. But there was a poignancy about them tonight, for her island life was threatened. Armand was right—for all they knew, Landor need only wait a few weeks for his countrymen to sweep in and give him back his liberty. But he was a man of action, hating idleness, and hating those who forced him into it. Was it resentment against the French that caused his stern, icy response whenever she spoke? Perhaps, though he was ready enough to be agreeable to Armand, who was pure French, while she was half Scots!

She turned and looked back at the plantation house. The graceful facade with its verandah and elaborate shingled roof looked peaceful in the moonlight. If there happened to be anyone looking out from amongst the double rows of windows, they could see her at every step of her lone walk. Besides, halfway down the garden were overseers' houses, hidden in guava orchards on each side. With others so near, she felt no unease in this familiar landscape.

At the end of the grounds she passed the gazebo, a pretty structure with a six-sided roof fringed by white fretwork, and lianas twining up the pillars. Farther on she came to halt and took in the expanse of ocean, where the moon traced a path across the waves toward her. She was looking out above the tops of acacia trees that clung to a steep seaward slope; there were rocks and bushes all the way down, and the only descent was by narrow steps that led to the beach and jetty, where Armand's yacht, *Aphrodite*, was moored.

The breeze flicking along the coast brought to her ears the sound of waves on the coral sand below. The moon swam behind another cloud. Then she heard a different sound amongst ebony trees to her right—a snap, as though a heavy beast had stepped on a twig. She started and stared into the shadows. The dairy cattle were in fields much farther off, but a bull could have strayed through a fence. She began a slow retreat, her senses straining for another clue.

There was a thump, as though something had fallen, and distinct on the night air came a sharp outlet of breath.

"Who's there?" she cried, and then caught sight of a man's shape, black between dark gray tree trunks.

She turned and ran, driven by panic, her arms flying, her legs tangling in her gown. Her fear was so great that at first she could hear nothing—she could only see the house far up the slope and feel at her back an unknown menace surging up over the strip of land where she never should have ventured.

She got just a few paces before he was upon her; she was swept backward, one of his arms clamped around her waist and the other hand across her mouth. Her slippers skidded on the ground, then he hoisted her up against him so that her ear was on a level with his mouth.

"For God's sake, be still. I shan't hurt you." He spoke in French. The deep voice reverberated through her head and his arm pressed, fierce and strong, around her waist.

He lowered her so that her feet touched the grass again. She struggled, uttering a shrill moan against his hand. "Mademoiselle. It's I, Landor. I haven't come to harm you." He bent over her so that she could see his pale eyes, staring at her as though he were as appalled as she. "Forgive me. Please; don't cry out. Don't cry out, and I'll let you go."

Landor. She wasn't being attacked by a runaway slave. She forced her body to go still, and with care he released her and moved to stand before her, his chest rising and falling as though he had run a mile, his eyes locked on hers with a look of supplication. He said in English, "This is shocking; I beg your forgiveness. You have nothing to fear from me, I swear. Another moment and I'll be gone." He stepped toward her, but she cringed away. He ran a hand through his hair, then suddenly turned aside and growled, "Ellis! Come here."

A second man came out of the bushes, short and square-shaped, carrying a knapsack and with a large bag slung over one shoulder.

"Where's the other pack?" Landor demanded.

"Down the slope a bit, sir, it landed there when I—"

"Retrieve it, and get down that track at the double. There's a stream running somewhere below; I can hear it. Fill every container you can find and then prepare to make sail. Go."

The man obeyed. Hearing him crashing through the bushes, Delphine realized it must have been he who had made the telltale noises before, when the two were hiding in the trees, waiting for her to go back to the house, exposed and unsuspecting. She shivered.

Landor flung a keen glance around him, then strode back a few paces and swept up her shawl. "Allow me," he said and held it out in both hands.

"No!" she said. She was so angry with him that she was close to tears. "How *dare* you frighten me like that!"

"I'm sorry."

She held out her hand. "My shawl, if you please." He put it in her fingers and she snatched it away and flung it around her shoulders.

He said, "What in heaven's name are you doing here?"

"That, sir, is *my* question!"

He gave a helpless laugh. "I'm leaving, on your cousin's yacht."

She gasped. "Then you're a thief."

"On the contrary. He proposed it once before. Now I'm taking up his offer."

"And a liar." The amusement left his face and she added with scorn, "You're lying about Armand. And you've been deceiving us for days. There's nothing the least wrong with you. No one laid a finger on you, for all your calumnies against the *gens d'armes*."

He said softly, "Doubt anything else you like, mademoiselle, but accept this for a truth—your cousin has done what he could to assist my escape. That's why I'm taking the yacht. Would you be good enough to tell him that I shall pay him back one day?"

She stared at him, baffled. Armand? He was about to have the beautiful *Aphrodite* taken from him, his most prized possession. It was outrageous . . . She turned and looked back toward the plantation house. No lights burned in the windows or around the overseers' quarters.

She swung back to confront Landor. "Armand is your friend! What kind of loyalty is this, to someone who's been good to you?!" He said nothing, so she went on, "You say he *helped you escape* four days ago?"

He avoided her eye, looking instead across the gentle curve of the coast, studying the sea. And he was listening. Faint sounds came from the jetty; the knock of wood on wood, the rattle of a tin canister. His profile was hard against the returning brilliance of the moon on the waves. He was ready to go. But he lingered to pursue this bizarre dialogue. She realized at that moment that she no longer feared him. Instead she was filled with horrified curiosity; she had to know whether his extraordinary statement about Armand was true.

He turned and said, "Will you allow me to explain, mademoiselle? Pray sit down a moment." He gestured toward the gazebo. He was ushering her into the shadows, for if they stayed on the lawn the moonlight would pick them out, two silhouettes against the silver sea.

She preceded him, the hem of her gown brushing dry leaves across the timber floor as she went to sit down. To her desolation, they were the only figures moving in the ordered landscape.

He sat on the same bench, a foot or so away, his back to one of the pillars. He rested his head against it, and she noticed that the vines made a somber backdrop behind his light hair. In that position, no one could see him from the house.

"Your cousin, mademoiselle, has a scrupulous sense of justice. He confided in me very early on that he considers Decaën a fanatic."

"If patriotism makes someone a fanatic, Sir Gideon, then you must also count me as one."

"As you wish." He gave a little mock bow and leaned back again with a taut smile. She remembered what Armand had said, and suddenly she could see signs of exhaustion in Landor—the rigid way he held his body, the muted voice, a heaviness in his pale eyelids. He wasn't here just to stay out of sight, but to gather his strength for a moment. He went on, "Decaën is a diehard Bonapartist and what matters most to him is his reputation in Paris. Everything here remains in his power, including the rights of certain prisoners of war. The persecution of these gentlemen is arbitrary; he selects them on personal whim, and no appeal is possible."

She had to admit that he was right. Captain Matthew Flinders had been allowed to see Decaën only once in six and a half years. The interview had been frigid, formal and of absolutely no avail to the Englishman. "Nevertheless," she said, "for my cousin to go so far . . . to help an enemy officer escape . . . it's traitorous. It's dishonorable. That's not the Armand I know."

"Perhaps not, mademoiselle." He leaned toward her. "I regret opening your eyes in this fashion. It hurts, I see. I'm sorry."

She wouldn't look at him; she gazed straight ahead at the ocean. What mysteries were still to be discovered under the gentle surface of her life? What a dreadful homecoming this had turned out to be: ruined by war, deception and treachery. Ile de France, the paradise of her childhood, was altering before her eyes. "I wish I hadn't come home."

"Then I wouldn't have had the pleasure of meeting you."

It was said lightly, as though inviting her to smile. Instead it made tears rush into her eyes. This was cruel. She would much rather he were cold and severe.

He ignored the tears. Or perhaps he could not see them, for she stayed quite still, looking down, her fingers wound into the shawl. "So your cousin confided nothing of all this, to you or your mother?"

She shook her head.

He said very quietly, "But you knew who raised the alarm and called the *gens d'armes*, did you not?"

After a painful hesitation, she said, "Yes. One of my servants."

"Ah."

She raised one end of the shawl and pressed it against her eyes.

He said, "Then why did you come to the Maison tonight?"

He was very close to her and he had a look of great attention as he waited for her answer. She said, "Because I was determined not to be afraid of you."

"And are you?"

There was a long silence. Gideon could see tears trembling on her lower eyelashes. He would spare telling her any more about Belfort; he had only come out with the first retort because she called him a liar. Thank goodness he had not hurt her physically as well, for she had felt so light and breakable as she flailed about—like a determined butterfly. His lips twitched at the thought.

She shot off her seat and rounded on him. "You find this very amusing, sir. You think me naive."

"Not at all—"

"I'll have you know, loving my country is not naïveté. Nor is loyalty to my family's honor."

He bit his lip—she made a splendid figure, poised as though to strike him, her eyes flashing, the moon's reflection off the water shining through the fine silk of her gown and outlining her pliant form.

"If this indignation is genuine, mademoiselle, then I grant you, your sense of honor is more delicate than your cousin's."

"You're prepared to filch his property and mock him into the bargain? Congratulations. There's little to choose between you."

He laughed, but inwardly this time. He could never have suspected her to respond like a trained duelist. And her emotions surprised him: anguish and disillusionment. A moment ago, he had felt the strongest impulse to reach out and take her hand, to console her.

She retreated to the seaward side of the gazebo. The moonlight fell across the point of her shoulder and illuminated her arm as she curved one small hand across the balustrade. Her face was in shadow, with her hair a shining crown behind it, as she moved her head and shoulders in a contemptuous gesture. "No doubt your escape will be applauded in London, if you ever get so far, but I shall always know that it was achieved by the basest deceit."

He smiled. She wasn't beyond deception herself, for if there were any watchers in the darkened mansion they could not fail to read her body movements, which signaled that she was not alone, and she was defying the person she confronted. She swept the shawl closer around her and shrank back against the railing, and as she did so the fine diamond bracelet on her wrist caught the moonlight like a shower of sparks.

He rose. "You will oblige me, mademoiselle, by stepping this way."

"So you can assault me again?"

"So I can restrain you. I apologize, but I cannot have you running off to sound the alarm."

Delphine hesitated. She could make a dash for it, and at least flush him out into the open where he might be seen more clearly. She could scream, and hope that the sound would carry far enough to be heard, but it was a very long shot. And it would lack dignity. If she wanted this overbearing man to fully take in her contempt, shrieking like a girl was not the way to behave.

So she stayed where she was, to make him come to her.

He was a thief, a liar and a bully, and he believed that his hatred of France justified everything he did, but now she could feel him falter.

He said, "I regret this as much as you. May I make a suggestion? That you give your word to remain where you are for fifteen minutes, no more, and then do as your wisdom dictates?"

"This is war, sir. You refused to give your parole—I most assuredly will not give mine."

He smiled grimly and advanced, and despite herself she flinched, expecting him to grab her and haul her into the shadows with those violent hands. But she kept her back straight, one hand gripping the railing, directing an outraged stare at his face as he stopped inches from her trembling body.

He took one end of her shawl and it slithered from her shoulders and across her arms into his possession. Avoiding her eye, he reached behind her and brought her hands together on the railing. He held her wrists fast with one hand while with the other he flicked the shawl in a spiral, the fringes spinning in the air as the fine fabric was twisted into a rope.

The desire to fight him set the blood pounding in her ears. But she had achieved one important victory—he was manhandling her in full sight. She didn't dare scan the moonlit gardens, but he did frequently, glancing over his shoulder with those watchful green eyes. Never at her.

Her other victory was more subtle: now that he was touching her again, leaning so close that she could feel his uneven breath on her cheek, she could tell how disturbed he was. This was not the gentleman who had surveyed her so coldly from his high moral position at the Maison Despeaux. This was a thief in the night who had crashed straight through her defenses and by doing so had opened a breach in his own. They were man and woman now, in intimate opposition, and she wanted him to walk away from her as confused and ashamed and furious with himself as a man could be.

As the silken rope tightened around her wrists, crushing the bracelet into her skin, she studied him. His lips were pressed together and his eyes were narrowed as he yanked the knots firm. He continued to avoid her gaze, but looking up into his face she read much more about him than he could wish her to know. He had felt superior to her at their first meeting; he was by no means so sure of that now. He considered himself a resourceful man, but he was completely unprepared for this. She made him nervous. She made him wish they had never met. And he would remember their meeting forever.

When he stepped back, his skin was flushed and his eyes glittered with a strange expression as they met hers at last. "I calculate it will take you about a quarter of an hour to free yourself."

"How considerate. And what if you're wrong, and I'm trapped until dawn?"

"I know knots. You forget I'm a sailor, mademoiselle."

"Oh, I shall *never* forget what you are."

Her bitter shaft glanced off him. "Nor I you," he said and bowed. It was a gesture of the correct depth and due respect, and when he straightened she could see that it caused him pain. The color drained from his cheeks and there was a deep, straight line between his brows.

It was a shock to see him move rapidly to the steps of the gazebo, where he paused for a second, murmured, "Adieu, mademoiselle," then leaped down and disappeared at a run, over the edge of the slope and into the trees below.

He was too spent to go quietly; she could hear his heavy footsteps all the way to the bottom of the path.

Then, with tears of rage coursing down her cheeks, she bent forward and fought to tug her hands through the bindings that held her.

Orders

～

Gideon didn't stumble until he reached the foot of the steps, and he was able to catch hold of a bollard. The little cove was deserted, apart from Ellis, who was poised at the stern of the vessel, using both hands to hold it to the jetty, and the mainsail of the yacht was at half mast.

Gideon staggered to the yacht. "Get forward and cast off."

Ellis extended a hand to help his master on board, leaped onto the jetty, tore along to the bow and untied the second mooring rope, then gave the yacht a great shove and jumped aboard again.

Gideon bent over the tiller, gasping, every breath an agony. It was impossible to give orders, but the heavy sail creaked rhythmically into place and was set to catch the coastal breeze, and Ellis came aft and without a word took a firm hold of the tiller.

"We'll only have to tack once to get out of here, sir. All quiet up top?"

Gideon gave a short laugh, then lowered himself to the deck out of Ellis's way. "Any weapons below?"

"Yes, sir, as a matter of fact. Interesting."

"Have you primed any of them?"

"Yes, sir. There's two muskets each to play with, if anyone shows their face on the ridge."

Gideon examined the skyline. The moon had gone behind clouds again, and trees made cover for any pursuers. There would be shouts and a challenge, then a volley of bullets spraying down across the water.

Ellis handled the sleek yacht like the expert he was. Gideon took over the tiller and the seaman managed the lines as they picked up a steadier breeze at the middle of the bay that would take them out to sea. Gideon leaned his forehead on his wrist and closed his eyes. This was it; he had done it.

Then came a high, piercing cry onshore. And another. Galvanized, he let go of the tiller and stood up to listen, his heart in his mouth.

Ellis grabbed the bar and let out a soft curse.

"It's she," Gideon said. "Something's happened!"

He caught an odd look from Ellis. "How did you . . . leave her, sir?"

Delphine Dalgleish screamed again, and Gideon tried to tell himself she was farther away this time, running up the lawn. He'd seen her glance more than once at places nearer the gazebo, looking for help. It would have been madness not to catch and restrain her. But each cry raised the hairs on the back of his neck: he had left her bound and alone—what if she were being attacked? "I tied her up. With knots it would take time to undo." He groaned, battling a crazy impulse to go back.

Ellis spoke his mind. "Then she's got free. I know the tone of a lady who's being molested, sir, and that's not it."

"Do you, by Lucifer," Gideon growled.

Then came shouts; a man's voice, joined quickly by many others, followed by the wild clanging of a bell, no doubt the one used to call the laborers to work.

"And the devil's in it now," Ellis murmured, but cheerfully, for the yacht was cutting a smooth path between the heads of the cove.

However many marksmen the plantation could summon, and however fast they could run, none could get to either point before their master's vessel sailed through. They tried hard, though. The parties streamed out along the curves of the bay, torches in some hands and weapons only too evident in others.

"May I suggest you go below, sir, and I'll crouch down here as I may?"

It was time that Gideon made it clear who was in command. He took the tiller, keeping low, and positioned Ellis where he could not be seen. The weapons remained below—he wasn't going to fire on civilians. When the shooting began, he could see darts of red in the gloom but the reports followed at a reassuring interval and the only sound in their own vicinity was the slap of waves against the hull.

"Belfort will have sent word straight down to the port. They'll choose a frigate for the pursuit. What are our chances of outrunning her?"

"Excellent, sir. She's a sweet mover, this *Aphrodite.* Once I put the jib up, I beg to wager you may kiss the Frenchies good-bye."

Gideon sucked in his breath, still scanning the hazy shore. Belfort, if present, would be on horseback, but the scattered figures he could make out were all on foot. And all male. So she must be back in the house. Safe, and shuddering with resentment at what he had dealt to her. What on earth had she been *doing,* strolling down after midnight to a deserted shore? As he had frozen, astounded, on seeing her walk down the garden, he at once decided she must be heading for an assignation. But no partner had shown up for the rendezvous, or if he had, he had been too much of poltroon to show himself. The whole time, Gideon had half expected to be confronted by a dangerous young blood in the style of Armand de Belfort, brandishing a dress sword and shouting French imprecations. But she really had been alone, and defenseless.

At this distance from shore, he could take a last look at the grandeur of the island: the soaring central peaks, the long, palm-clad ridges stretching toward the sea, the coastal farmland, lined in the foreground by trees. The plantation house wasn't visible, but no doubt all lights were ablaze and Mademoiselle Delphine Dalgleish was within, being comforted by la Générale.

Ellis said, "Course to Rodriguez, sir?"

"No, south."

Gideon's voyage on the *Revenge* had been his last as a lieutenant. His commander had written to the Admiralty recommending him for a captaincy, and the Admiralty in reply had ordered him back to London. But a sea battle had intervened, resulting in the loss of the *Revenge* and his capture. There had been sufficient clues in the directive for him to guess that the Admi-

ralty had other things in mind for him besides his first command. He wondered whether he was to be admitted into naval
intelligence—a development he had been dreaming about for
some time. He grinned to himself: after this experience, he could
scarcely wait. If he was going to risk being shot for a secret agent,
he might as well be one.

Ellis got up and stretched, satisfied that they were making for
Bourbon to rejoin the fleet. The cool, bracing atmosphere of life
at sea settled around Gideon's aching body like a mantle. "You've
done a magnificent job, Ellis. My orders, if anything happened to
the *Revenge*, were to report back to London. You'll be glad to
know we're heading for the Cape, then home."

Delphine was miserable and Armand was in a temper. Whenever
Armand was descending into one of his black moods, she tended
to avoid him. Tonight, however, she persuaded her mother to go
back to bed, then followed Armand into his study and insisted on
some straight talk. She did it with some trepidation; she hoped
never again to see such an expression as the one on Armand's
face when she told him his yacht was gone. He was transfixed,
seized with such fury that she had a very disloyal sense of relief
that the Englishman was not on hand to meet it.

When he returned from the pursuit, he had told the ladies it
was up to the navy to catch the scoundrel now, and shoot him on
the deck of the frigate when they did so.

Delphine's mother exclaimed against such a conclusion, but
Armand said cuttingly, "Do you demur, madame, after what he
did to your daughter?"

Madame Dalgleish had put a soothing hand on Delphine's
arm. "Thank God, she has come to no harm. And in the interests
of delicacy, no one need know about that hideous encounter. You
will please corroborate what Delphine told the stewards—she saw
the *Aphrodite* being stolen and raised the alarm. I should prefer
her name and Landor's not to be linked in any way."

He had bowed and said with a grimace, "Agreed, madame.
The humiliation is quite sufficient without that."

Now Delphine was poised just inside the closed door of the

study while he stood by his desk. He said, "Cousin, this has been a fiendish night. Surely you ought to retire?"

"Thank you, I shall. As soon as you tell me what has been going on between you and Landor." She said in a lower voice, "I think I have a right to know. Considering what it has exposed me to."

Suddenly he said, "Pray sit down." When she took the little sofa close to the door, he pulled out the chair before his desk and sat just as he had in the Maison Despeaux, while they were all talking to Landor, only hours ago. After staring at the desktop for a while, he looked up with something of his usual self-assurance. "What did he tell you?"

"He said you thought the captain general wasn't acting justly toward him. That you believed he should not be in prison. So you helped him escape to the port."

"And?" he said softly.

"You don't think that's enough? Armand, how *could* you?"

"Landor is an officer and a gentleman, and he wasn't being treated like one. I had strong objections to that. There is a kind of understanding between men of breeding, Cousin, that I don't expect you to comprehend."

"I certainly don't, if it leads to what happened tonight!"

He put an elbow on the desk and leaned his forehead on his fist so she could not see his expression for a moment. "Don't remind me."

She went on, "I'm so—Armand, I'm disappointed—devastated. This is a family matter, and I must speak. My father was a great commander. Our family's military reputation has always been glorious. Our honor was unimpeachable—until tonight. I never thought that I might be living with a traitor."

He looked up then, in alarm, and she saw how shallowly he had examined his own actions.

She went on, "If there is an explanation, you must give it to me. *Tell me* why I should not mention this to my mother and insist that you leave this house!"

He looked at her for a long time, and by the light of the candle in the sconce above the desk she could see surprise, fury and self-reproach in the piercing blue eyes. At last he said, "You don't know what you're asking."

"You must understand that honor in my family is as dear to the women as to the men." If Armand's behavior was dubious, she had a duty to speak to her mother, who was the widow of one of France's most respected generals and as fervent a patriot as he had been. And behind her mother stood Joséphine de Beauharnais, the widow of another brave general, and Napoleon's former empress. From Saint-Amour there was a direct line of communication back to Paris. Captain General Decaën knew that well. So, surely, must Armand.

He rose and slowly began to pace the floor, controlling himself. Then he shook his head and faced her, leaning easily with one hand on the chair back and his legs crossed at the ankles. "No one else could drag this out of me. Have I your solemn word that it will rest in your bosom alone?"

She nodded. He sounded more like the cousin she knew, not the treacherous creature that Landor had painted.

Armand said, "I can't bear you to think so badly of me. If you doubted my probity, my life wouldn't be worth living." He paused, then went on, "I did assist Landor to escape from the Maison Despeaux." She started and went cold, but he smiled for the first time. "Remember, you have just promised never to divulge my reasons. Cousin, I'm telling you a state secret. Landor is a spy. A double agent. Recruited by the Foreign Office in London and ostensibly working for England, but acting for France."

It was like having her face slapped. "Impossible! Since when?"

"I have no authority to tell you that. But he has furnished us with a great deal of intelligence while he has been on Ile de France. And I'm proud to say that I was the gentleman selected to communicate with him."

She stared at him. "And then the captain general arranged for him to escape back to the English and continue spying for France?"

He nodded.

"But he was *arrested*!"

"By sheer accident, when your servant raised the alert. You

don't suppose the town major is entrusted with those sorts of secrets, do you? All the major knew was his duty: he performed it, and Landor was put through hell before I got word of the arrest. I at once informed Decaën and he called the interrogation off. None too soon." He shrugged. "After that, it was back to prison, and as you saw, I visited Landor at the earliest opportunity. To reassure him that we'd have him out of there before too long—and make a proper job of it this time."

"A spy." Delphine got to her feet. "On his own countrymen." She put her hands over her face. "Great God, this is horrible!" She lowered her hands. "I thought he was lying to me when he told me you helped him. Then somehow he convinced me he was sincere. But if he's a double agent, then all the rest of it, everything he pretends to stand for, is just cynical lies. He's despicable."

Armand looked at her quizzically. "Come now, Cousin; he is on our side! And to operate at his level takes an inordinate amount of courage and ingenuity. Plus a radical gift for surprise."

She thought of Armand's helpless anger. "You didn't know he was going to take your yacht, did you?"

He said ruefully, "No, I didn't. Like everyone else, I thought he was incapacitated. He took matters into his own hands and surprised us. I suppose I should be grateful, as a patriot, that it's my vessel he commandeered. But I do feel its loss, I confess." His expression darkened further. "And if I *ever* see him again, whatever his usefulness may be to France, he will suffer at my hands for what he did to you."

"He said he would repay you," she said. "He told me to tell you that, especially. What did he mean by it?"

Armand shrugged. "He is the best source that France controls in the English navy. He knows that whatever he offers us is a thousand times more valuable than anything he may choose to take away from us. That was his meaning. You're right," he said, smiling at her sympathetically, "Landor is perfidious, and doubledealing, and arrogant into the bargain. But he works for Bonaparte, and we must be glad that he has gone about his business, despite the damage he has done to us both."

He stepped forward and took her hand, and Delphine looked down at their clasped fingers. She felt desolate.

"May I trust," he said gently, "that you think no less of me for serving our country in this way?"

"Yes," she said. Then, realizing her response lacked enthusiasm, she went on, "Thank you for confiding in me. It's a heavy secret."

"You would rather not have heard it?" He was trying to read her face. "You would prefer to think me a treacherous rascal and Landor as sound and shipshape as a British man-of-war?"

She raised her head and smiled at him. "No, I'm glad you told me. Now I know the truth, I'm sure when I look back on tonight it will explain a great many things. Just now, I'm too tired to think."

She began to draw her hand from his, but he raised it and kissed it before letting her go. "Good night, Cousin," he said, "and God bless you."

Upstairs in her chamber, she undressed, put on her nightgown and then opened the casement for a while to look out at the ocean, which was now a black expanse beyond the gray, deserted gardens. She could tell that Armand expected her to hate Landor less on discovering he was working for France. Not so. She resented the man so much it was painful. Despite all his mouthings about duty, he was a traitor to his own countrymen. He had been gathering information about British forces and selling it to the French military, perhaps for years. At sea, he had served alongside brave men whom he was ready to betray at a moment's notice. As a result of his own undercover actions, many of his compatriots must have died while he went scatheless.

She recalled the story of his capture at sea, which had stirred her admiration when she first heard it. He had been first lieutenant on the *Revenge*, part of a flotilla surprised by the French navy in the Indian Ocean east of the Seychelles. Three of the English men-of-war escaped the engagement, but the *Revenge* was smashed to pieces and sank, so quickly that most of the gunners and crew belowdecks perished. When the survivors were pulled from the water, Landor was one of the last, for he was supporting two men who could not swim—a midshipman and an able seaman.

Now Delphine knew the reality behind that kind of bravery: whatever the situation, he had made certain that *he* would always survive.

"This is war," he had said to her. But he was no warrior. He was a cheat and a liar, and he played the loyal Englishman to serve his own hidden purposes.

Landor had begun to tell her about Armand . . . why did he not go on to explain the full reason for the help he'd been given?

She sighed, closed the window and leaned her forehead against the cool pane. No doubt he considered espionage to be an affair of men; no woman, even if she were caught in the net of such an intrigue, was to be entrusted with the truth. So he had continued lying to her, even smiling at some of her reactions, without ever explaining what his sly mockery meant.

She lay down on her bed and drew the thin white coverlet over her, lying with her face turned to the window, toward the west, and the invisible ocean, and Africa. During their weird encounter she had had glimpses of the kind of man he might be under different circumstances, when he was not forced to treat every person he met as an enemy. For the briefest of instants she had been able to imagine him more attentive, more considerate. When they were sitting together, he had seen her distress and turned to her with compassion. When he had come close, in the moonlight, even in her rage she had wondered just for a split second what it would be like to exert a woman's power over him—an influence more open and direct than the one he seemed to feel as he tied her bonds. And more tender.

What folly. The best she could hope for was never to meet Sir Gideon Landor again.

Charles Matthieu Isidore Decaën was a master of discipline, and for that very reason he wasn't looking forward to the meeting with Armand de Belfort on this busy afternoon. There was little to be said—his most troublesome prisoner was gone, and there was an end to it.

He sent his aide out into the anteroom to fetch the young man, and remained at his desk, tapping one shoe against the brass-bound foot of one of the legs. Belfort was of an old line of Burgundian aristocrats who had weathered the Revolution slightly impoverished but otherwise unharmed. Like many young men of his generation, Belfort felt the need to demonstrate loyalty to the new regime; he had joined the armed forces and fought in Spain for two years. He was granted indefinite leave from the army on the death of his uncle by marriage, General Dalgleish, for the general had named him executor of his will and appointed him protector to the widow and daughter. Thus Belfort had come to Ile de France—still burning with zeal, and quickly disappointed at the lack of opportunities afforded by island life. But he was clever and energetic and showed a flattering deference to Decaën's judgment, which made the older man open to finding a task for him.

Landor had been the perfect challenge. A number of English officers held at the Maison Despeaux over the years had divulged handy pieces of information about English strategy. Landor, however, was like a stone wall on all things military. Decaën had given him to Belfort as a private project, and the results had been spectacular. And, to Decaën's chagrin, quite out of control.

When Belfort was announced, Decaën glanced up for a second, then looked down at the papers on his desk while the young man advanced. Belfort, undiscouraged, stopped a foot away from the desk and spoke at once. "Good day, Governor. May I ask whether my yacht has been recovered?"

"I'm afraid not," Decaën said, signing a document with deliberate flourishes.

Belfort must already know the pursuit had been called off—his hard tone betrayed it. "Why?"

Decaën, scattering sand over the page, looked up at last. "Pray take a seat. I ordered a frigate to make sail but told the captain not to waste time in pursuit if he rated his chances too low. After an hour at sea he had to accept the *Aphrodite* had too much of a head start. And he could not guess which way Landor had sailed."

Belfort snapped, "He would have been heading for Bourbon!"

"Or Rodriguez. One could not expect a lone frigate to chase him right into the blockade."

Belfort crossed his legs abruptly, the chair legs scraping on the parquet floor. "I demand reparation for my yacht."

"Not possible, I'm afraid. It's unfortunate that Landor took it, but reparation is up to the English navy. I shall lodge a claim on your behalf."

"We're supposed to be fighting the devils, not treating with them."

Decaën stiffened. "I regret to say we shall be fighting them, and very soon." He tipped his head back and looked along his sharp nose at the younger man. "And what if we are forced to capitulate? It's my responsibility, and mine alone, to negotiate the best settlement for our troops and the people of Ile de France. How would they prefer me to behave when I parley with the English? As a red-handed zealot or as a gentleman?"

"I wonder you don't release all the prisoners at once, then," Belfort said. "The way you did Flinders."

"The permission to let Flinders go came from the emperor. If the same order were issued tomorrow with respect to the others, I should execute it."

Belfort was still looking mutinous. Decaën debated putting the fear of God into him about the English—the same fear he woke up with every morning. Belfort was incapable of thinking beyond the immediate issue. All he looked forward to was battling the invasion, and he saw it in highly colored terms—you thrust the English off or you died fighting. Meanwhile, anything was permissible if it put off that evil day.

"There is a strong chance we shall be occupied, Monsieur de Belfort. And unless we behave correctly during hostilities, we shall not be trusted when it comes to establishing terms of peace. There are acts I will not countenance, even in a state of war." He held Belfort's eye. "As you well know."

Belfort said with contempt, "You'd rather Landor got away!"

"I'd certainly rather not see a prisoner of war beaten to death under *my jurisdiction!*" Belfort didn't reply, so he went on, "Your actions were shameful, monsieur. I asked you to get what you could out of that gentleman. I did *not* ask you to concoct a nefarious scheme to get him captured and interrogated. If I hadn't heard about it in time, I would even now be trying to explain to the English how one of their officers died in my custody."

"I'm certain he was in intelligence. Cornering him was the only way to make him cough up. And if he had, you'd be commending me."

"Don't expect me ever to commend such actions! When he wouldn't talk, you told the *gens d'armes* to finish him off."

Belfort tried to shrug the accusation away. "Nonsense. Is it my fault they exceeded their duty?"

Decaën rose quickly. "It's you who exceeded your duty."

The other man also got to his feet. "I am an officer in the legion."

"Indeed. Under my orders." Decaën thought quickly. It was inconceivable to have this unprincipled young gentleman racketing around if and when the English turned up. Yet Belfort would fail to comprehend if he were disciplined, and so would the rest of his kind on the island. "I have a mission for you, monsieur. If you consider it beyond your capabilities, please tell me so at once."

Hauteur spread over Belfort's handsome features. "Proceed, Governor, if you please."

"We are faced with a grave state of affairs on Ile de France. My next dispatches to France are crucial. They must run the blockade and I must have a gentleman I can trust to carry them to the emperor. Are you fit to perform that service?"

"Perfectly fit, and more than willing," came the prompt answer.

"Thank you. Then I must ask you to put your affairs in order, for departure in three days. Your destination is Paris."

Battle Stations

~◦~

Before Armand de Belfort set sail for France, he told Delphine and la Générale that he was being sent as a secret envoy to the emperor, aboard one of the corsair ships that operated stealthily out of Port Napoleon. Delphine knew that the task would have its dangers, and she had a suspicion that her cousin was so eager to perform it—and boast about it—because it might restore his standing in her eyes, which in many ways it did. And she could scarcely reproach him for abandoning her and her mother while he had such important work in hand.

Armand had discussed the threat from the English and tried to lay any feminine fears to rest: Decaën could be trusted as a commander; he wouldn't let the island fall. And Armand himself would return as soon as possible. But it was now December, and he had not come back.

For a while, events seemed to confirm his idea that the colony wouldn't be taken by England. The navy did their part brilliantly, for there was a mighty clash at Grand Port on the other side of the island, in which an English flotilla was defeated by a French squadron.

This put heart into the island's defenders, but it proved to be their only victory. On the twenty-ninth of November, the English landed a large force on the north coast. They proved impossible to stop, and as the legion was pushed back toward Port Napoleon, the inhabitants of Ile de France, those who were not already battling the advance, were faced with a painful dilemma—whether to remain on their plantations as the victors rolled through, or seek refuge in the capital.

La Générale wavered: they had no man in the house to make

decisions, and their Indian laborers wouldn't be able to protect the plantation. Delphine had to take her mother by the hands and sit her down to make her listen. "Maman. That is precisely why we must stay here. Some of them will want to resist, but we must not allow a single man to lose his life in such an impossible cause. Think how unspeakable it would be if they opened fire on the English and the conflict came to Saint-Amour. No. When the time comes we must gather everyone in the stable courtyard, to prevent any foolhardiness. If troops cross our property we must not try to stop them."

"*Chérie,* what if they come to the house? We're totally unprotected."

"Indeed. Their commanding officer will find that this is a household of harmless gentlewomen."

"And you expect *them* to be harmless? Think of the looting and pillage and *rape* the English have committed in Spain!"

"But what they want here is possession. Maman, they want our island to be English. Not a wasteland."

"We must take what we can and go to the port before it's too late."

"And move *toward* the English? What sense would that make?"

"We must get there before they do. The captain general will defend it. Armand told us, it's well fortified, it can withstand a siege."

"We can't abandon everyone here. If we run away, who knows what might happen to the people and the house?"

Succumbing for a moment, her mother put her hands over her face. "Ah, Delphine, if only your father were here."

Delphine rose, walked to the window and looked at the peaceful park and its green borders, sweeping down to the sea. "I don't think so—he was a soldier. And thank God Armand is not here either. He would rally as many defenders as he could and ride out into disaster. *Then,* we might well face destruction. But right now, the English want it whole and entire—every field, every stick and stone."

"So you want us to watch them walk in?"

"We have no choice."

On the evening of the second day of invasion, one of the neighbors sent a devastating message: at least ten thousand enemy troops had landed, more than twice the number at Decaën's disposal. They had been brought from Rodriguez in scores of ships, and most of them were Indian army soldiers led by English officers. The legion was trying to halt them at Montagne Longue when the captain general rode north to inspect the position, came within a hundred yards of the British and was shot in the leg.

Julie was so upset that she could hardly read the rest of the message. Delphine, trying to hold the paper steady, deduced that the wound was not serious, and that the captain general had been conveyed back to the capital.

"We *must* go to him," Julie said.

"He'll have many to look after him."

"You forget his wife is my intimate friend!"

"And we must not burden her."

She sounded firm, but inside she felt everything give way. Decaën had been shot, and that one appalling detail brought the rest of the catastrophe into focus. Her world was overthrown, and fear became her constant companion. There were so many terrors to contemplate. One was the idea that the invaders might prompt the slaves into insurrection. There were twenty thousand slaves on the island, not counting the hundreds of fugitives known to be hiding in the hills. Until now, Delphine had considered the idea of black vengeance as foolish scare mongering, but half the citizens cowering in Port Napoleon probably believed it. Then there was the thought of the invading Indian troops, loyal to the British and most likely all from North India—what would happen if they were to confront the laborers of Saint-Amour, who were Tamil speakers from the south, allies of the French for more than a hundred years?

On the third day, they learned that the legion had retreated to Port Napoleon and the British were preparing to lay siege to it. For Delphine and her mother, retreat into the port was no longer an option.

Then the fourth day dawned, hot and sultry, and events began to flare up like brushfires. The first clue to disaster was an officer on horseback, seen by Delphine when she was upstairs on the southern balcony. He went by at a gallop on the main road to the port, coming from the south in a panic: a scout, with terrible news? Half an hour later, she saw a straggle of island troops rounding the same curve on the hillside. They were in disarray, retreating in the same direction as the rider she had seen earlier. Then scattered rifle fire began, as though a tribe of hunters were chasing prey through the steep mountain valleys inland. She had the workers recalled from the fields then, and the sharp-toned overseers' bell formed a weird descant to the distant firing and the pulse of approaching drums.

The English must have landed troops in the south as well. They were coming.

She mounted her mare and rode down to supervise the laborers' move to the compound within the stables, encouraging the overseers in their task. They were Indians also, men whom her father had employed when he retired from the army, left his posting near Pondicherry and selected the first team of young workers who were to develop Saint-Amour into one of the most successful plantations on Ile de France. These men, all from the same group of villages, had worked hard, sending their earnings back to India and in many cases bringing their families to the island. In their transplanted community there was already a generation of young people who, like Delphine, had spent most of their lives here. If she was afraid, what must their terrors be like? In the men she saw sullen resentment, but she knew they were capable of flying into ferocious anger against the invaders. The dark eyes of the women showed her just what she felt: a bitter disbelief.

When the first redcoats went by she was still on horseback, patrolling the sweep in front of the plantation house. The servants had shut the front door and were peeping through the jalousies. Her mother periodically opened the door a whisker and begged Delphine to come inside, but she felt compelled to be here, at the end of the long avenue that stretched between the mansion and the lower road into Port Napoleon.

When the troops came into view, she urged her mount into the shade of an ancient ebony tree that grew in the center of the gravel sweep. Her lips trembled as she whispered, "They're here, they're here."

They were marching several abreast to the beat of drums, rifles shouldered but bayonets fixed. They were too far away for her to see whether their heads in the black shakos turned to scan the plantation as they passed. The coffee fields along the road held only seedlings, and the other fields with mature trees were farther back, but she caught the vigilance of the officers on horseback who rode along the sides of the columns, keeping a keen eye open in case of enemy fire from the nearest cover. Their scouts, nonetheless, must by now have let them know that all resistance was over. She could feel it herself in the hot, heavy air, hear it in the dull tramp of boots on the dusty road: the certainty of defeat.

One man only turned aside to look along the avenue of screwpines to where she waited in the shade of the ebony. Had he seen her? Mounted on a black horse, with a bicorne hat that kept his eyes in shadow, he made a stark figure. Was it her own hatred and horror that made his lingering glance seem like one of possession?

Then he wheeled his horse and rode on. The troops took a long time to pass by, but eventually the plantation and its neighbors fell into an eerie silence. No more messengers came running from nearby properties, and Delphine began to think that the owners had fled into town. Well, then, they would be present to witness the captain general's capitulation to the commander of the invasion force. It was a privilege she could do without.

The night was arduous. The workers returned to their village, where the overseers took turns on watch. For comfort, Delphine slept with her mother in the vast canopied marriage bed, stirring at intervals and nervous at every sound. They awoke weary and without appetite, but Delphine made sure everything went on as usual in the village—except that no one was sent into the fields.

In midmorning the ladies received a visitor, a man in uniform. As he rode down the avenue, Delphine went out under the portico to observe him and noted that he was the officer on the black

horse of the day before. Behind him marched six English redcoats bearing rifles. The bayonets were not fixed; they hung in
black scabbards at the soldiers' sides. When the party halted, the
officer gave her a smart salute, then dismounted, took off his
gloves and came up the steps. He said nothing to the soldiers,
who remained at attention while one man stepped forward to
hold the horse's reins.

"Mademoiselle Dalgleish," he said in a firm, pleasant voice. "May
I introduce myself?" He bowed and said, "Captain Melbray Arkwright. May I hope to have a word with you and your lady mother?"

He wasn't a tall man, so as she rose from her curtsy she was
looking directly into his brown eyes, which were ringed with thick
black lashes. He had a short, straight nose and a mouth that in re-
pose was pursed rather like a woman's, but there was manly decision in his voice and bearing. He seemed at ease in a way that
shocked her. But perhaps all conquerors behaved thus.

Arkwright felt considerable surprise. He had been told that
Delphine Dalgleish was a beauty, but no one had prepared him
for this ethereal young woman. With her light hair and blue eyes,
and the exquisite body clothed in a white dress of some soft, float-
ing fabric, she looked more like a heavenly being than the daughter of this very substantial homestead.

To his relief, she spoke, her voice low and musical. "Good day,
monsieur. And what do you intend your soldiers to be doing
while we converse indoors?"

"Absolutely nothing, mademoiselle. They won't even breathe
unless I bid them to." He smiled at her.

She turned quickly away and said, *"Robert, ouvrez!"* A servant
pulled the door open at once, and she marched into the reception hall without glancing back. Within a few moments she was introducing Arkwright to her mother.

Delphine ordered refreshments and they sat in the spacious
salon, with the morning light slanting in between silk drapes, and
drank tea and ate little cakes, while Captain Arkwright informed
them, succinctly and in English, of what was going forward in
Port Napoleon—or Port Louis, as he called it, for the English
knew it by its old royalist name.

Delphine was proud of her mother, for now that the blow had fallen, she was calm and stoical. It was she who posed the questions, while Delphine sat in silence, taking in the worst of the facts like so many doses of numbing poison.

Ile de France was now English. The captain general had surrendered at three o'clock that morning, on a very full series of conditions, almost all of which had been agreed to. Decaën, having handed over all powers, his mansion and the administration of the island's affairs, was to be allowed to quit Ile de France "with the honors of war." The island's legion were now prisoners, but its officers would leave for France with Decaën within the month. Arkwright suavely explained that any civilians who also decided to return would be free to accompany Decaën, with whatever possessions they wished to take, and to put their properties up for sale. Those remaining on the island would be required to take an oath of allegiance to the British Crown, which would be administered by the new governor, Sir Robert Townsend Farquhar, who was expected to arrive shortly from the island of Bourbon.

Delphine remembered Arkwright's proprietorial air as he had sat assessing Saint-Amour from the saddle the day before. Did he have some vested interest in this part of the grand English plan for Ile de France? "Will there be any confiscation of land?" she asked abruptly.

Arkwright was taken off guard but shook his head. "England's intention is to govern this territory, not to annex property. The aim is to improve agriculture and restore your commerce. The governor looks forward to meeting with landowners and merchants as soon as possible."

"I'm sure we're much obliged to him."

The man's fleshy mouth pursed again at this sarcasm, but his eyes met hers with a surprising hint of sympathy. She could not help being aware that he was attracted to her, but there was something else in his manner also. Something almost protective. "I'm here under orders, and it's time I explained them. The governor has been aware for some time that Saint-Amour is unusual amongst the plantations around Port Louis."

Delphine interrupted. *"For some time?"*

"Allow me to continue. There are two issues. One: unfortunate circumstances have deprived you of the head of your household. Monsieur Armand de Belfort is still in France, we are told."

"Or possibly on his way home," said la Générale, her voice faltering on the last word. "We rather expected him . . ." She failed to finish the sentence, and Arkwright took the chance to go on.

"Two: Saint-Amour has a highly productive market garden close to the capital where our troops will be garrisoned. You also have a fine dairy herd. At this stage, supplying the garrison is of paramount importance. In short, ladies, I'm charged with the task. I shall be billeted in this house for the foreseeable future." Into the stunned silence he said, "Given the size of your residence, I'm sure you'll be able to find me a suitable corner to lodge in. Shall we say five this evening for my arrival?"

Delphine's voice shook. "Are any other places to be *occupied* in this way, or have we been specially singled out?"

"I can't tell you that. My orders refer only to Saint-Amour."

"So you come to dispossess us," la Générale said.

He rose. "No, madame, this property remains in the hands of your family. But from now on its administration rests in mine."

Delphine got up too, so hastily that he took a step back. Yet she could still see in his eyes a glow of something like pity, or at least male condescension. Good God, did he imagine he was doing them a *favor* by marching in and taking over? "Five o'clock, then, monsieur. We shall be ready for you."

He bowed, they nodded and he wisely elected to say no more. Delphine summoned a servant and he was shown out.

When he was gone the two women remained where they were—Delphine frozen in the middle of the room and her mother still seated. Neither spoke, fearful of the other's reaction. Delphine ached for her mother, who in the space of two years had lost her husband, a great measure of her independence, and now the freedom of her own home. Meanwhile, Julie Dalgleish looked at her daughter with a mixture of grief and self-reproach. She should have insisted that they spend the anxious days of waiting in Port Napoleon, to protect their interest with Decaën. Delphine had not yet developed an aptitude for diplomacy—she was self-reliant, like her father, in a way that completely contradicted her appearance. Only her intimate family knew how stubborn Delphine could be once she got a notion in her mind.

Julie burst out, "I can't believe the captain general allowed this to happen. He's always been such a friend to us."

Delphine turned, and the hurt in her eyes made the tears prickle in Julie's. "You still think we should have fussed around him in town? Maybe—who knows? Whichever way, he is crippled, and so are we."

"It's atrocious!" Julie rose. "I'm going in to speak to him."

"We'd be better occupied putting our records in order."

"*Chérie,* ever since Armand left, you have been telling me the estate is well in train. What do you mean?"

"I mean that when that man walks in here tonight, he will sequester all the books and make an inventory of our possessions. If you have anything of worth that can be concealed, Maman, I suggest you hide it now. Whilst I do what I can for Saint-Amour."

Julie caught her breath. "You're going to falsify the records?"

Delphine gave a short, ironical laugh. "There's no time. All I can do is ratify those two grants of land to workers that Armand was supposed to sign before he left. As for the rest, what's the point? The English know how wealthy Saint-Amour is. They have known, so Arkwright says, *for some time.*"

Julie had the miserable feeling that she was somehow under attack. But Delphine, in her sensitive way, suddenly changed expression and came over to put her hands on her mother's shoulders. "It'll do us no good to fret. Decaën had no choice. The English have the whip hand—it's so important that they are not driven to abuse it."

"That's very true, my dear." Julie Dalgleish drew her daughter to her. "We must try not to overreact."

They embraced, and for the first time Delphine began to cry. With her cheek against her mother's soft face, she felt their tears mingle. She squeezed her eyelids together, trying to stop the flow. "We will endure this, Maman." She drew back and tenderly wiped her mother's eyes with her handkerchief. "I'll let Arkwright inspect whatever he wishes, and in return I'll try to make him tell me just what he has in mind."

Julie Dalgleish sighed. "He has come well primed for action. And their information about us is excellent." She looked at Delphine in sudden consternation. "You don't think Decaën . . . ?"

"No!" Delphine hesitated but chose not to reveal the suspicion in her mind. If Gideon Landor had managed to rejoin the English fleet in July, who better to inform the invaders about the usefulness of Saint-Amour? Especially when he had a cover to maintain and would be expected to give a host of details about the island. He merely had to double-cross a friend—and betrayal was, after all, his stock in trade.

Gideon enjoyed his visits to the family estate in Wiltshire, but there always came a moment when he began itching to get away. It made him think of the time when he had come home after just a year at Cambridge and told his parents that he was joining the navy. They had been devastated; their only son, giving up his brilliant university studies and even more promising political prospects for a hazardous career. But the sameness of Cambridge and the predictability of rural life were too much for a young man who had his eye on adventure and achievements that would be his alone, owing nothing to his family's wealth and position. As for any aspirations toward politics, he could think of nothing that compared with sailing the oceans of the world. His father had been angry and his mother deeply upset, and he still remembered their faces when he told them he was leaving England to fight in the war against Bonaparte.

Today he stood in the same room, looking out over the familiar countryside. Buff House, the family's Stuart mansion, stood on one side of a long, open valley that descended from higher ground and curved in a majestic sweep toward Salisbury plain. On this winter's day the pastures on the opposite side looked hard and brittle, and the bare hedgerows stretched across them in spindly lines as though scratched by an etcher's hand. But in the wide valley bottom, where a stream ran, the view was enlivened by color and movement: a yellow haze of willow branches along the banks, the gray stone of farm buildings, a bunch of brindled pigs being driven along a road, streamers of blue smoke wavering up from cottage chimney pots. He knew all the men and many of the women of his age in those cottages, for they had been his companions in times gone by. On his return, he'd had no difficulty taking up some of the old ties again, at least with the men. They still shared the same territory—the copses, waterways and coverts that they had explored in childhood. His father was happiest charging through them on the hunt, but Gideon enjoyed simply walking or riding far and wide along the public paths, talking with people as he went.

Nearer at hand, on the great stretch of land before him, there was much activity to observe, in the home farm, the park and the walled and terraced gardens below the house.

His father appeared at his elbow. "What's your guess—shall we have our usual snow at January's end?"

Gideon shook his head. "I doubt it, sir; the clouds give no sign."

"Snow at *sea*, now," the Earl of Tracey said, "must create a dashed peculiar effect?"

"It does. Especially in the North Atlantic. A hellish inconvenient place when the visibility's so reduced." Then he cursed himself because his mother had just then entered the room; he tried to stay off the risks of life at sea when she was present.

She said in her unhurried way, "But it must have a certain beauty? Does it decorate the spars as it does the ash branches here—or are you obliged to clean it off at once?"

Gideon smiled at the thought of jacktars being ordered aloft to scrape down the yardarms, but replied, "We pray for a thaw to lighten the ship, Mother. Snow makes her sluggish." He pondered a moment and came up with an image. "I do remember one morning, though, after we'd had a fall in the night, and when I came up on deck the *Revenge* looked prettier than Tisbury Wood at Epiphany."

Her mouth curved in her slow smile, and her hazel eyes twinkled. Tall, elegant and outwardly serene, the countess rarely made demands on anyone, and scarcely needed to—it always seemed the most natural thing in the world to try to please her. Gideon knew, however, that hearing about the loss of the *Revenge* and his capture and imprisonment had caused her terrible anxiety. And he now stood in a position where he could cause the same agonies all over again.

"May I ask, sir, if it's possible for me to open up the town house? I think of going up to London shortly."

His father beamed. "No need to ask! Excellent idea—why hang about in the country to be dull? London, now, nothing like it!"

Gideon smiled. Neither of his parents cared in the least for the capital, and it was extremely rare these days for his mother to think of abandoning her gardening and her watercolors, or for his father to stir from his domain. He teased them, "Shall you be coming up with me, then?"

His father looked startled. "As to that, I can't see my way clear to anything until this business with the kennels is over to my satisfaction."

The countess said with placid good humor, "Tracey, the hounds can do very well without your fussing over them." She turned to Gideon, her eyes bright. "I'm so glad you're not to miss *all* the season."

He grinned at her. "And why is that, ma'am, when you take so little interest in it yourself?"

"Well, naturally it's tedious for the gray-haired and addled—"

"On the contrary, that was the only sort of person I seemed to meet when I passed through. I should have much preferred your clever company."

She gave her characteristic low chuckle. "Oh, if you're inclined to flatter, I'd be happier if you found a suitable listener in London. I hear there are some quite lovely young women out this season."

Gideon moved away from the window and across to a side table, absently picking up a book he had left there earlier. He knew just what this enthusiasm meant. On his return to England he had been made captain, as promised, and given a command. It was a signal honor that his ship was to be a new frigate—in fact it wasn't yet completed, and his duties at present consisted of making an occasional visit to the Greenwich shipyard and planning for the frigate's maiden voyage in nine months. Meanwhile, he was on half pay, almost a man of leisure. His parents had been relieved and delighted; he knew they were hoping for an end to the war before his next voyage. And this was the very time, they considered, for him to marry.

He was the only child of a long noble line, and the earl deserved to feel sure that he would be handing the patrimony on to a worthy heir. The countess's method of persuasion was more subtle; having no daughter, she sometimes mentioned how much she looked forward to Gideon bringing his future wife down to Buff House. After the wedding, she said, they must stay there for a time so that she could enjoy hearing a woman's voice about the place and sharing a woman's concerns and enjoyments; and only when the young wife was ready should she and Gideon move to Landor, the handsome dwelling on the neighboring property that came to him with the baronetcy held by the heir to the earldom.

He put down the book and looked across the room to where his mother sat by the fire, and she said, "Do you remember Georgiana Howland? I hear she has turned out quite exceptional."

Gideon said, "Indeed she has. She's taking her time to marry, though. Lady Howland has nothing less than a duke in mind."

"Nonsense—it's Georgiana who'll make that decision. They dote on her."

"With prizes like that lovely gel," his father put in, "direct action is required. In your case, you'll merely need to walk into the room. You've been away too long, but it's to your benefit, you see? Novelty. That's all anyone wants nowadays."

"Tracey," his wife said, "our son is not some new piece of clockwork." She said to Gideon with fondness, "You are a very proper man, my dear, and you may marry just exactly where you choose."

"If anyone will take me."

The earl snorted. "You have every advantage!"

"And some serious drawbacks. I'm scarcely home, for one." He shook his head. "London's all very well, but I've never lived there for long. What if I find I can't stand it for more than a month at a time? As you say, entertainment is all any young woman wants nowadays, so I'd be depriving her. And I shouldn't think she'd enjoy being buried in the country any more than—" He stopped abruptly.

His mother said, "This self-deprecation is charming, Gideon, but may I understand you another way? You are not at all sure that *you* will be entertained by the young ladies at present amusing themselves in London."

He gave a rueful laugh, which was answer enough.

She sat back. "In that case, I've only one remedy to suggest. You must go straight up to London and judge for yourself."

He bowed. "Thank you, ma'am, I shall." He went over and stood at the end of the mantelpiece, one boot on the marble slab before it and his shoulder against the chimney piece. "But I have to tell you: marriage at the moment is a complication I cannot afford."

"Complication?" the earl said.

"I may have time up my sleeve, but I haven't yet left the service. When I came back I was offered a secret mission. They seemed to think I was the officer for the task and . . . well, I thought it over and I found I couldn't turn it down."

"Who are *they*, and where are you going?" his mother said with deceptive calm.

"The Aliens Office. And I can't tell you."

"Out of uniform?" she said in alarm. "That makes you a spy."

"For this purpose, it's important that I'm seen to have settled back into civilian life. Spending time on the usual things, in town, down here, on country visits and so on. Meanwhile, on occasions I'll in fact be gone from England." He looked at his mother's face and made himself see the hurt and consternation that she was trying to hide. "Each time, you will be the only people apart from the secret service who know that I've left the country."

"Really? Why tell us?"

He ignored the sarcasm in his father's voice. "Because I'm about to ask you a favor. If it's ever noticed that I've slipped away from London, people will naturally assume I'm at Greenwich, or I've come down to Landor. If you don't deny it, that would be a great help."

"You wish us to lie for you," his mother said.

"Not if it's against your principles. Or if you think any the less of mine." There was a long pause. "I had to be frank with you. If it's a burden, I'm sorry."

"We wanted you home," she said, folding her hands tightly in her lap. "And all we'll have is the pretence of it."

"It's not as though you'll never see me again!" He smiled, but the words cut through the room like a chilly draft of air.

"I hope," his father said gravely, "that you've considered all the implications of this?"

"I have, sir."

"There's nothing to be done, then, is there?" The old man looked down at his wife. At times like this his age showed, and Gideon became more aware of the fifteen years' difference between his parents. The countess raised her eyes, then put out a hand. The earl took it and said to Gideon, "I honor your choice. And I speak for your mother as well when I say, I wish you had not made it."

The countess rose and transferred her hand to her husband's wrist, ready to leave the room with him. She said to Gideon. "You have our support. As always." Then with silent dignity they walked out.

They were disappointed and miserable, and they had gone to console themselves as best they might.

He felt guilty, angry and excluded.

He went to sit where his mother had been, with his face to the fire, and leaned his elbows on his thighs.

Perhaps it would have been more diplomatic and respectful if he had approached them separately. But he hadn't had the courage to break the thing to his mother alone—how was that for a truth? And if he had gone to his father for advice, he knew what it would be: stay on fighting at sea or beg leave to serve his country at Westminster. There was nothing to boast of with a son who went skulking about Europe behind enemy lines.

No, it had seemed right to tell them when they were together, for that was how they always appeared to him: a truly united couple. He grimaced. With such an example before him, he should surely be kinder to the thought of marriage! He sat up, his palms on his knees, and looked into the fire. No, there had been a great deal of luck in such a union, and he could hardly hope for fortune to smile that way on him. Certainly he had never met a young woman who gave him cause to even imagine it.

Marriage was impossible just now, anyway, for he had no time or attention to spare on a wife. His sense of fairness rebelled against the idea of finding some perfectly raised, biddable chit, getting her with child and then neglecting her. If he took on someone else like Georgiana Howland, destined to become a society leader, he could scarcely expect to incarcerate her in Wiltshire, and leaving her to entertain half of London would mean expenditure that would dismay his parents, however generous the young lady's dowry. Choosing a gentlewoman for her attractions alone would be even more disastrous. Imagine a wife like the volatile Delphine Dalgleish, divinely beautiful and as full of stratagems as a high-bred filly, left to kick her heels in London in his absence.

He gave a sardonic grin. She must be well and truly married by now. The only explanation for her having returned to Ile de France unbetrothed after her last visit to Paris was that she must have been extremely choosy. She'd no doubt been bent on an illustrious marriage, and she had the looks and spirit to hold out for it. With the island doomed, she was most likely back in France again, for he understood what she felt about the English: a hatred he had done nothing to diminish by his own behavior.

He could picture her exercising her considerable powers in the magnificent Paris salons. He had been there only once, in 1802, during the peace of Amiens. Walking the busy thoroughfares by day, through the elegant quarters, crowded riverside slums and tree-shaded public gardens, he had been struck with the strange and poignant feeling that he somehow belonged in that stimulating city. It had beckoned to him ever since.

Perhaps that was why he had said yes with so little hesitation to the mission he was about to undertake. For it was to Paris.

The Governor

Delphine and her mother were driving through Port Louis on their way to the governor's mansion, as Delphine looked out at the sunlit colonial buildings and rehearsed in her mind the petition that they were about to make to Sir Robert Townsend Farquhar. She got on well with him, but that didn't mean she could make him change his policies. Still, he always found a great deal to say to her, and he seemed to enjoy their sparring.

Her mother said, "My dear, you did well to secure us this audience, but don't depend too much on it."

Delphine said, "The governor likes us."

Her mother smiled. "So does Captain Arkwright, but that doesn't mean he listens to us about Saint-Amour. Think of it from Farquhar's point of view. Arkwright is selling all our produce to the British army and navy at rates we can scarcely afford. Is there any reason why Farquhar would wish to change that? Arkwright won't approve the land grants that your father promised to our workers in their fifteenth year of service. Can you imagine why Farquhar would interfere over such an issue?"

"I managed to put through the grants to Pragassa and Arékion!"

"Only by forging Armand's signature."

At this Delphine blushed and fell silent. It was true: at Saint-Amour she was thwarted at every turn, and any small victories she achieved were behind Arkwright's back. He was impregnable to direct opposition and, unlike the Frenchmen she knew, he could not be swayed by charm—she had tried to flirt with him once and regretted it instantly, for he seemed to think she was making fun of him.

Julie Dalgleish gave a small sigh. "*Chérie,* if we cannot move Farquhar, we may have to bring stronger forces into play. Don't be surprised at anything I say in this meeting. I must ask you to follow my lead."

Sir Robert Farquhar, meanwhile, looked forward to the Dalgleish ladies' afternoon call at Le Réduit, the beautiful residence that he had taken over from Decaën. It provided another signal that the English had done nothing to undermine the prosperous and civilized way of life that the islanders considered their birthright. He was bent on managing a smooth transition from French to British rule, and it had gone well so far. When he joined the East India Company as a youth, he could scarcely have predicted that he would find himself governor of the island of Bourbon at the age of thirty-four, and to be governing Ile de France was an even greater astonishment—but he had not let the advancement turn him into an autocrat. There was a whole section of the population here that had resented Decaën's Bonapartist energy for improvement; they were languid and conservative, if not royalist, and the prospect of existing under a monarchy, even if it was English, was not unpalatable—as long as he let certain things lie. Slavery, for one. And simply taking possession of the island had already achieved most of what England desired. William Pitt once said, "As long as France holds the Ile de France, the British will never be masters of India." Now, at last, the French fleets and corsairs had no haven in the Indian Ocean, and Port Louis provided a safe harbor and victualing port between the Cape of Good Hope and India. It was in England's best interests that Ile de France flourish now as never before. The wealthiest and most cultivated of the islanders more or less understood this, and amongst them, until recently, he had counted Madame Dalgleish and her ravishing daughter.

There seemed to be a female mutiny brewing, however, at Saint-Amour. At a reception the day before, Mademoiselle Dalgleish had asked for a private conference to discuss Captain Arkwright's administration of the property. This was awkward, for Arkwright was making an excellent job of running Saint-Amour and would not relish criticism. Thinking fast, Farquhar had asked him for the same visit, but without her knowledge.

When the ladies entered, Farquhar greeted them and Arkwright rose and bowed. As they sat down, Mademoiselle Dalgleish looked dashed and disappointed, and Farquhar felt a small pang of self-reproach.

La Générale, however, seemed rather to come into her own, saying to Arkwright with gentle humor, "We wondered why we didn't see you at breakfast, monsieur—but you were reserving that pleasure for this afternoon!"

"I rode down to the village early. Someone has to ensure order there."

"And the overseers don't? There must be some misunderstanding. Allow me to speak to them, monsieur. They are my husband's old friends."

Arkwright looked as though he had a quelling reply to this, but the tea arrived, and there was a little bustle as la Générale offered to pour it, moving to the low ottoman to perform the task.

Farquhar rather enjoyed the picture they all made in the finely furnished room, the ladies delicate as flowers but with that rare glow that seemed to come only from Paris, flanked by two young men in the prime of life—the vanquished and their conquerors, destined by breeding and policy to share a relationship that had every chance of being pleasant. If only Arkwright would take the ramrod out of his back.

But he showed no sign of it yet. "The overseers are too lenient. Production has gone down lately—"

"Since your arrival," la Générale said sweetly. "Lemon?"

"No, thank you," Arkwright said, and leaned forward to take the Sèvres cup and saucer from her hand.

"You find the overseers uncooperative?" Farquhar said.

"They have no idea of discipline. Last week a worker was caught out in theft and he went unpunished until I stepped in."

Delphine meanwhile was chastising herself for not having guessed that Farquhar would drag Arkwright into this. The gentlemen were in league to direct the conversation; she would just have to counter where she could. "Captain Arkwright is referring to a man called Chavrymoutou," she said to Farquhar brightly. "He is Brahmin."

"He's a *Christian*," Arkwright said.

"Nominally. He is Brahmin first. He and the other Brahmins eat special food, and the kitchens have always provided it. Lately, that food has been denied him. Unbeknown to my mother, Chavrymoutou and his relatives were starving. As the head of the family, he acted, and stole food from the stores. If he had come to us, we would have prevented such a situation. But he was forbidden to do so."

She could tell it was hopeless; Captain Arkwright would never take proper care of the people on whom the plantation depended. Her defense of Chavrymoutou had been in vain; the captain listened to her with rigid politeness, then went his own way.

There was frustration in Arkwright's black eyes as he said, "This all comes of having hired labor. These Indians have a ludicrous idea of their own station, and without vigilance there would be no governing them."

"They are free men, monsieur," la Générale remarked mildly.

"Free to make an unnatural nuisance of themselves. They are also free to leave—with my blessing."

Farquhar raised his eyebrows. "Where would you suggest they go?"

"The Malabar Camp, Governor."

Farquhar nodded. The Camp des Malabars, the Indian suburb of Port Louis, was in a thriving state.

Delphine explained in a pleasant tone, "Some of our people *do* move to Malabar, but only once they have land of their own. Malabar is a place for merchants and tradesmen. Our workers depend on farming; they have no other skill. Turning them off would ruin them and do nothing for Saint-Amour."

Farquhar said cheerfully, "I'm sure Captain Arkwright has no thought of that. We are very gratified by the contribution that Saint-Amour makes to Port Louis. And you must be more than happy with the return." He smiled at Delphine's mother. "Your prosperity and that of the island are very fittingly linked."

"Thank you for saying so. In that case, it's my duty to tell you of two great threats to our *mutual* prosperity." She turned to Ark-wright. "The first, Captain, is the price at which you sell our pro-duce to the military; it's far too low. The second is your intention to replace the workers with slaves."

Farquhar stared at Arkwright, and Delphine thought she saw annoyance in his eyes, for slavery was the most inflammatory sub-ject on Mauritius. He was probably in no mood to debate it here, so he fell upon the other subject at once. "Madame, the prices that the army and navy pay for victuals are not under my juris-diction; they are negotiated between Captain Arkwright and the catering corps. Rest assured, there is nothing amiss; the military makes purchases here in much the same way as at the Cape and in India."

"Really?" Delphine cut in. "You mean there are suppliers in the Cape and India who are forced to sell their produce exclu-sively to the British army and navy?"

Farquhar was searching for an answer when Arkwright chimed in again. "With respect, mademoiselle, to whom else could you sell it?"

"I preferred the French navy, sir—they paid half as much again as your English pursers! And we used to export our coffee. But you are turning our plantations over to sugar."

"In short," la Générale said, "I must regretfully point out, Monsieur le Gouverneur, that your government is in breach of its agreement with the landowners of Mauritius. I request you to rec-tify the situation."

Farquhar didn't even pause to think. "Saint-Amour is under the supervision of Captain Arkwright. He decides on all such matters."

Delphine said aside to Arkwright, "Oh, I well remember the day that you arrived and began telling us what to do. But then, Ile de France was under martial law. That is no longer the case. We are under British rule, and Britain has pledged to honor the terms under which Captain General Decaën surrendered this colony."

Her mother turned to Farquhar. "We hereby lodge an official complaint with you, sir. May we hope you will deal with it yourself, or must I address it to London?"

Julie Dalgleish was appealing to his sense of self-sufficiency; during the short time that he had been running Ile de France, Farquhar had been ready to listen to the islanders' concerns and cautious in his decision making. But he was giving nothing away yet. "What are your precise wishes, madame?"

"Saint-Amour must be run by the family. And we will not accept a change to slave labor."

Farquhar raised his eyebrows. "The head of the family is in France, I believe—Monsieur Armand de Belfort."

"He will return. In the meantime my daughter is perfectly capable of running Saint-Amour."

Farquhar said, "I agree it's in your interests for Monsieur de Belfort to come back. All Frenchmen of Mauritius are required to sign a pledge of allegiance and he has less than two years to comply. If he does not, Saint-Amour passes to the Crown."

Delphine gasped. Her mother said, thin lipped, "We are prepared to consider giving that pledge ourselves, monsieur."

"Not possible, I'm afraid."

"You deny our right to make decisions about our own property?" Delphine said.

"We must follow due process," the governor said smoothly.

"Your processes are illegal," Delphine said.

"I regret to remind you—French law, even if you imagine it supports your case, no longer decides land ownership in these islands."

"I'm talking about the agreement between France and England that was ratified in December. The situation at Saint-Amour is not within the letter or the spirit of that agreement. If you do nothing to rectify it, our family has no choice but to take our case further."

Farquhar said, as though to humor her, "Where, mademoiselle?"

Her mother took over. "To Paris. Where the emperor will decide on how it's to be settled with London."

Astonishment kept him silent for a moment, then he said, "It's hardly a matter for high diplomacy!"

Julie held his eye. "That lies in your hands."

Arkwright gave a satirical laugh at this, but the governor looked in no humorous mood. He reflected for a moment. "Madame, this administration cannot accede to either of your requests. If you are contemplating a visit to France, you are free to go. It may even benefit you—I suggest you lose no time in persuading Monsieur de Belfort to return and sign the pledge of allegiance."

Delphine's mother rose and drew a piece of paper from her reticule. "Here are my requests, monsieur. I expect a reply from you in writing by tomorrow afternoon. If I'm not satisfied, my daughter and I sail for Europe on the *Peacock*."

As Delphine rose too, she saw Farquhar's eyes flicker at this. The *Peacock* was carrying the governor's own dispatches back to London, where he must hope good things would be said of him in the coming months. It was not easy for a gentleman to protect his reputation for competence when he acted in a far-flung territory unfamiliar to the rulers back home—something that Decaën had always been acutely aware of.

Delphine gave Farquhar a sweet smile. "The captain of the *Peacock* has agreed to find us a means of sailing to France when we reach the Channel. If we do go, would you like us to convey your compliments to General Decaën when we get to Paris?"

Farquhar smiled ruefully back at her and said, "I should like you to tell him that our loss is his gain. I know I speak for Captain Arkwright, indeed for all of Port Louis, when I say how much we should regret your departure. Please, mademoiselle, tell me you are not about to leave us?"

He was good at this; he made it sound like nothing more than a gallant plea from a gentleman to a lady. The corners of her lips twitched, for though he might treat her mother and herself as powerless women, they had a strong chance of commanding the ear of an emperor. How nervous did that make him?

She looked at him under her lashes. "Monsieur le Gouverneur, my going or staying depends on you."

"So my wish is your command? Oh, mademoiselle, what a paradise this island would be, if that were so."

It was a paradise, until you came. For a moment, it was all she could do not to cry out the words. Then her mother began her courteous farewells and the visit was over.

Delphine felt faint and cold. They had failed; Farquhar would not act, and Arkwright would remain in control. In the end, Saint-Amour would be ruined—and if Armand didn't return it might even be taken from them.

Farquhar bowed over her hand. "I beg you to reconsider; what can you achieve by suing to Bonaparte? Even if he listened to you, London wouldn't listen to *him*. We cannot escape it, mademoiselle. This is war."

"Indeed, monsieur. As I too well know."

After they had gone, Farquhar began pacing up and down in front of the windows, looking down at the Dalgleish carriage as it swept away from the steps. He was annoyed with Arkwright, who was clearly incapable of managing the women of Saint-Amour. What was wrong with the fellow? He was well bred, personable and not without intelligence. A sidelong look at his face suggested where the weakness might lie—he was in love with the demoiselle, and it had put him seriously off his stride.

"Sir," said Arkwright, "do you really think they'll leave?"

"It rather looks that way. Unless you can give them some incentive to stay, what?"

Arkwright drew himself up, stung. "*I*, sir? Are you referring to the way I run the plantation?"

Farquhar gave a chuckle. "Not at all. I'm referring to the 'idol of the island,' Captain. And I have just one recommendation where she's concerned. You may count on my unqualified blessing if you follow my advice."

"And what is that, sir?"

"Marry her, my dear fellow. Marry her."

The Emperor

It was midnight at the Tuileries Palace. Armand de Belfort, standing at a casement above the place du Carrousel, watched carriages flowing to the foot of the great steps and scanned the privileged guests who alighted, his breath misting the window, which was closed against the chilly March air. Delphine and her mother were later than expected.

What if the friendship with Joséphine held la Générale back? No, tonight, as everyone waited in the royal palace for the birth of the emperor's heir, was hardly the time to take Joséphine into account—the woman whom Napoleon had divorced precisely because she had not been able to give him a child. The new empress, Marie-Louise, was closeted away, tended by her most devoted ladies and a little group of physicians. Meanwhile, the emperor, gathering around him a host of solicitous guests, had mentioned that he would also welcome the attendance of Madame Dalgleish and her daughter.

This notice reflected well on Armand. He had been in Napoleon's presence only twice, a silent bystander during brief meetings concerning the war in Spain. As a member of the Bureau of Codes in the Ministry of Marine and War, he was rarely seen at the palace. But Napoleon had an unerring memory, and noticing Armand hurry past the end of a long corridor at around seven o'clock, he had sent an aide after him with an order: Monsieur de Belfort was to make it known to Madame Dalgleish that their little family party would be welcome at the palace tonight.

There! La Générale and Delphine were being handed down from a handsome equipage by a footman. Armand savored the sight: the women's natural elegance and Delphine's rare beauty, which at this distance caught the eye like a graceful marble figure in a rich setting, the light from the footmen's torches giving a glow to her pale cheeks, as though she had just been roused from a stony sleep and was stepping into the warm world of the flesh. When he had first met Delphine he had considered marrying her, for her manifest charms as well as her valuable plantation. But he had not given himself time to contrive it, and now he was relieved, for he had his eye on an heiress in Paris who could give him something even Delphine could not arrange—a very promising entrée into politics, through the lady's brother, a powerful deputy.

He went to the head of the grand staircase to greet his distinguished relatives. He had given some thought to escorting them to the palace himself, but they were coming directly from Malmaison, Joséphine's residence outside town. He had decided against attending on them there; Joséphine's influence on the emperor had died with the divorce. It would be the wrong association for him and would do nothing for his ambitions in the ministry. Since coming to Paris he had traded on his overseas experience to create a reputation for himself in foreign intelligence, using Decaën's name without having to call on the gentleman himself for confirmation, since the general on his recovery had been given a command that took him away from Paris. The capital suited Armand; he had important responsibilities in the bureau that handled Napoleon's military codes, and he found he had an aptitude for the work.

The ladies were gliding toward him ahead of a small group of other guests, and their eyes lit up to see him. When the greetings were over, la Générale murmured, "What does this mean, Armand? Am I to hope that he has read my petition?"

Armand shook his head. "You had it delivered when? Monday? Madame, his mind must be far from such matters tonight."

"Then why does he do Maman this honor?" Delphine said. "It can't be on my account. The last time I saw him I was twelve years old; he has no notion I exist."

Armand indicated the way to the salons and walked between

them, one on each arm. "It's perhaps in tribute to the memory of your husband," he said to la Générale.

"It's all so bizarre," Delphine said, looking around her. "Here is a poor young woman in childbirth, and half Paris is camped outside her door!"

"But it's natural, don't you think, for the emperor to want friendly faces around?" When Delphine threw him a satirical look he went on, "I must tell you, his devotion to the empress has been touching. He has scarcely left her side since they were married, and he never stirs far from Paris, with or without her. No campaigns, no grand plans, none of the old restlessness. Not even a sign that he's going to take part in the Spanish war—he's positively domesticated!"

"His mother," la Générale said, "must be in her element. Letizia's dream has come true: he's married royalty at last. Far better an Austrian archduchess than Joséphine de Beauharnais, the colonial widow."

"His lady mother," Armand said, ignoring the ironical tone, "is not in Paris just now. I think he misses her. He is in a tender state, they say, and feels the need of women's counsel."

Delphine raised her eyebrows but saw her mother's face soften. La Générale's friendship with Napoleon had not been a shallow one, and despite the estrangement once he divorced Joséphine, Delphine had never heard her mother pronounce a harsh word about the emperor. There had been great sadness but no blame. All resentment was reserved for others: his insanely ambitious family; the subtle politicians in Paris who were so much less to be trusted than his generals in the field; the plotters angling for power who had made him desperate to ensure the succession and provide an heir to the imperial throne.

Besides, Joséphine still loved him, in her way. And la Générale suspected in her heart of hearts that Napoleon still loved Joséphine. Which made mother and daughter curious about how their host would behave, should he deign to notice them.

It took hours. The vast salons of the palace were filled with noisy, incoherent movement, but none of the colorful eddies of figures produced the emperor. Armand would have been happy to dash off, find him and come back to fetch them nearer his presence, but it was beneath la Générale's dignity to allow this maneuver. So they lingered by the enormous tables of refreshments and passed the time chatting with friends, while everyone wondered how the nineteen-year-old empress was faring. Bets were mounting, for Napoleon had confidently predicted a son: the odds were ten to one. Hearing one gentleman wager a thousand, Delphine turned away in disgust; it seemed an offense against womanhood to continue this public show of concern and this private indifference to anything but opportunity.

At six a.m. an announcement was read out: Her Majesty was "in excellent health" and still anticipating the happy event. By now people had begun to give up and depart, but Delphine's party instead happened upon Napoleon when he entered a small anteroom at the same moment as they did from the other side. The short, beautifully attired figure and haggard face caught them by surprise, and he threw them all a startled look—he was in distress and fleeing the crowd. Then he recognized la Générale and halted.

She cried, "My God, Sire, she is not in danger?"

His expression changed, and Delphine saw tears spring to his dark gray eyes. "Madame—generous as ever. No, I'm told there is nothing to fear. But it's so *long*." He took her hand and Julie Dalgleish curtsied, murmuring words of reassurance. Meanwhile the people behind the emperor were catching up. He raked the three of them in with a glance and said, "Will you accompany me?" Taking their amazed looks for consent, he drew Julie's arm through his, and saying "This way!" turned and set out through the next room.

Hurrying along beside Armand, Delphine could hear disgruntled voices behind her and soon detected the pursuit falter and then stop. Napoleon was headed for his own apartments, where no one else would dare to bother him. She marveled at how she felt for him. The splendor of his presence that she recalled from her childhood had vanished in his disarray. He was a tired little man worried about his wife, and she could not help feeling a spark of sympathy.

When they reached the apartments his attendants came forward at once, but the emperor ignored them, turning instead to greet Armand with a formal word, then begging Julie Dalgleish to present her daughter.

Delphine curtsied low and he took her hand. "Forgive this reception; what can I say, but that your mother and I may be said to be old friends? The past"—he looked away with a sad smile—"has ties that no one with a heart may forget."

Then he asked them to be seated, and when Julie was settled on the sofa he sat down beside her.

"Sire," Julie said in her gentle way, "you are concerned for Her Majesty. May I help?" She gestured toward rooms below them where Delphine guessed the empress must be.

Napoleon said, "You are very good. Madame de Montesquiou and her ladies are doing everything possible. No, I . . ." He hesitated, then repeated, "It's so *long*. Doctor Dubois tells me it's normal. But can I trust a man? What would a woman tell me?" He looked at her pleadingly.

"Labor has lasted twelve hours?" He nodded. "This is not at all unusual, Sire. Heed their advice." She went on with a smile, "Every baby chooses its own time to come into the world."

This operated on Napoleon at once. He gave a relieved sigh and sat back on the sofa, his chin on his chest and eyes fixed on the floor. There was a pause, which to the other three was most awkward. He had asked them there on impulse, and at any moment must wish them gone. But he turned again to Julie. "What am I to do?"

She thought for a moment, then said, "It's after six in the morning, Sire. What would you normally be doing at this hour?"

"Taking my bath," he said and smiled for the first time, with a glance at the doorway to his rooms, where a manservant was standing ready.

"May I suggest you continue as usual?" Julie said with an answering smile. "And meanwhile we must cease to incommode . . ."

He rose at once. "No, madame, you are to stay. All of you. Pray do not stir." He moved energetically to the doorway, then half turned to look back at Julie. "I have read your petition. I shall discuss it with Mademoiselle Delphine alone. In my study, in three days' time. You will receive a note as to the hour." He gave Delphine one piercing, peremptory look, then disappeared.

Julie gasped and Armand muttered, "Good God! I wish I knew what's going on."

"Nothing out of the ordinary," Julie said. "He wants a hand to hold, and we provide it. But if you are squeamish about coming too near the birth, dear Armand, do say so at once."

"I don't mean *that*. Surely he'll not ask us there." He shifted impatiently on the hard, brocaded chair. "I mean over the plantation."

"That lies in Delphine's hands," Julie said, looking at her daughter. "Have no fear, *chérie*, he is no satyr, especially at a time like this. Armand will escort you there and back."

"But what does he mean?" Delphine asked.

"Business," Julie said. "He will let you know. Don't try to bring it up until then; he is beside himself, poor man, over this baby."

They waited, and waited. They were provided with refreshments, but the servants who brought them had a distracted air. Finally a man rushed in, his lean face alive with urgency, and at the servants' cry Napoleon reappeared in his bathrobe, his sparse hairs plastered to his scalp and his eyes large with alarm. "Well, Dubois?" he said in a strangled voice. "What is it? She's not dead?!"

"The waters have broken, Sire. It will be a breech birth. There's nothing we can do about it."

"What?" The emperor stared at the obstetrician, but no explanation was forthcoming, so he threw a haunted look at Julie Dalgleish. "What?"

"It happens, Sire." She rose. "I feel Her Majesty will need your support."

Napoleon seemed to rally. Taking a step toward Dubois, he said in a firmer tone, "Calm down: pretend she's just a little shopgirl from the rue Saint-Denis . . . forget she's the empress."

"But Sire, forceps will be required."

"Oh, God! Is it dangerous?"

Dubois said, his voice trembling, "We may need to make a choice: the mother or the child."

Napoleon took a great shuddering breath, then swept his arms toward the doorway. "Come! We must go. There is not a moment to lose." Four people leaped to obey. "There, there, downstairs," he cried. As they bolted to the floor below, Delphine heard him say, "Come along, now, Dubois. Don't panic. Save the mother; I am behind you."

The little corridor at the top of Napoleon's private staircase was crammed with people, but the party rushed by as though they were invisible, Napoleon's manservant darting comically downstairs trying to dry the emperor's hair in their flight.

They reached the rooms below far too soon for Delphine. The scene was terrible, at least to her unprepared senses, and Armand went pale and beat a hasty retreat. The room was hot and stuffy and seemed packed with people, and all eyes were fixed on the rumpled bed where the young mother lay in dire pain. They had heard screams as they approached; now with a wild sob she let her head fall back on the pillow, her hands in her tousled hair.

Delphine felt her mother's hand on her arm, and halted just inside the door, seized by pity and a fierce yearning for escape. A few venomous looks from across the room showed how little they were welcomed by the ladies, and Madame de Montesquiou, who was acquainted with Julie Dalgleish, met Julie's eye with a look that said, *Things are bad here; for heaven's sake, avoid making them worse.* Meanwhile, the covey of physicians fixed terrified eyes on Napoleon.

He made a soft and unhurried approach to his wife's bedside and took her hand. She clasped it and looked up at him, tears spilling down her hot cheeks. With a tender smile, he kissed her cheek. "*Ma mie,* I am here. All will be well."

But no matter how the poor, exhausted girl pushed, the baby wouldn't come. All the physicians moved to the foot of the bed, and forceps were produced. Julie took Delphine by the hand. "*Chérie,* you are not obliged to stay." At that moment, Napoleon glanced their way, his eyes full of tears that his tortured wife could not see. Delphine remained.

Julie moved closer so that she could see what the men were doing. It required muscle, in horrible disproportion to the tender flesh they were invading. Delphine admired her mother's courage.

At last there was another great scream, then an outlet of breath from the people around the bed. Delphine, paralyzed by horror, saw a small scrap of bloodied flesh being carried away by Madame de Montesquiou. The whisper went around the room: "What is it?"

But there was no answer. Whether it was a boy or girl was irrelevant; it wasn't moving. Put on a linen-covered table, it lay like a small butchered animal. Madame de Montesquiou cleaned the floppy limbs and put drops of brandy into the tiny mouth, but the baby didn't stir.

Delphine saw her mother turn and murmur something to the ladies, and they took towels warmed by the fire and wrapped the child up. The physicians continued active at the bed until the whole messy, terrifying process of birth was over. All this while Napoleon kept his head averted from his still child and spoke gently to his wife, caressing her brow.

Minutes passed like hours. No one dared approach the emperor and empress, and the ladies around the baby seemed frozen. It was Julie Dalgleish who acted at last. She walked up to the table, murmured two words of apology to Madame de Montesquiou and continued more audibly, "You may massage its body. Pray examine it, at least!"

She reached forward to draw back the top layer of towels and all the ladies said in awe and sadness, "A boy!"

Then he moved. A little arm flailed, and the stifling room was pierced by a thin cry. The parents' heads turned in disbelief, and Madame de Montesquiou burst into tears, flung the towels over the baby and scooped him to her.

Napoleon rushed around the bed and stood looking at the red face of his son. Mute, he held out his hands, and Madame de Montesquiou placed the bundle in them. Delphine had never seen such wonder on a man's face before; relief, pride and every other emotion were swallowed up by it.

Then he went to the main door of the room and people scrambled to open it for him. From where Delphine stood, he was a stark figure against the giant screen of color and light beyond, where the last tired but loyal crowd of partygoers, clad in their crumpled finery, were surging in from the outer salon.

Into the avid silence, Napoleon said, "Here he is! The King of Rome." And carefully stretched out his arms.

The Spy

Gideon was sitting in the place de la Bastille with a pretty serving girl perched on his knee who was using her considerable wiles to coax out of him the name of the mysterious woman he was in Paris to pursue, while he laughed and stuck to his story that he was only there with dispatches from his Normandy regiment.

Mélanie tugged at the buttons of his blue coat, stroked his mustache with a fingertip and declined to believe him. "She is married, faith. Oh, but then you could see her during the day, when the husband's occupied. And you're sitting here like a lamb at my table! You're ready to be unfaithful to her? Poor woman!"

None of her clients in the cabaret could distract her from the cheeky interrogation, so Gideon smiled and lifted one of her dark curls off the nape of her neck. "Here's a truth; since I came to Paris I've seen no one more delectable than you. Or more curious."

She laughed. "Oh, no, *everyone's* curious. The boss especially— 'Why isn't he gone, with these dispatches?' So I told him what Ellis said, and don't try to deny it, for soldiers can never keep secrets. 'He thinks he's in love,' I said, 'with a pasty-faced Normandy girl, and she's in Paris. *That's* why.'"

One of Mélanie's regulars growled at her for some service and she pouted and slid off Gideon's knee, leaving him to watch her neat figure bustling about among the tables and meanwhile to wonder how well Ellis was reconnoitering the principal building of the Ministry of Marine and War, some distance away across the city. He had never meant to bring Ellis into the mission to Paris, but he had changed his mind when the manservant, taking an accurate stab at his destination, had pleaded familiarity with the city from visits in peacetime when he was young. Ellis spoke French well because he was a Channel Islander from Guernsey and thus bilingual from the time he could talk. Gideon had seen the possibilities: Ellis could easily have decided to seek his fortune in the French military and would have no difficulty playing the part of batman to a Normandy brigadier.

So here they were, with a foothold in Paris that left them independent of the only other secret agent stationed there—an Anglo-Irish Catholic priest going under the name of Durand, who was there to report on Irish activity against England. Other contacts, Gideon was told, operated just outside Paris or in the provinces, in league with the royalists of the clandestine Chevaliers de la Foi, whom he intended to avoid. Getting to the coast, bagging the right uniform and leaving the theft and the injured officer undetected behind him had not been easy, and it lent a certain tingling suspense to his stay in Paris.

Gideon looked around the busy square, taking in the looming, pockmarked walls of the grand prison that had fallen when the French claimed their republic. These people were doomed now to the legacy of those days of violence, saddled with a despot who invoked the republic with studied rhetoric but bent the state to his own purposes. When Gideon saw Ellis return and take the stairs to the back rooms, he rose and walked through the inner room and up to his modest lodgings. Whatever information Ellis had brought back, the deed must be done tonight. He shut the door and spoke in French, to prevent unfamiliar murmurs being heard through the thick stone and plaster walls. "The guards?"

"At every entrance. You'd never force any doors, day or night."

"The courtyards?"

"There's a troop assigned. And they might well patrol inside the building after dark—I was in no position to ask."

"Well, where do I get in?"

"Buggered if I know," Ellis said in English, but under Gideon's quelling stare he realized he had overstepped the limits of tolerance. "Meaning, sir," he ground out, "like you saw last night, all the windows are too high. Even standing on a man's shoulders, forget it. It's a ladder or nothing. There's one window that stands out from the frame, even when they try to latch it at the end of the day, and it's the only weak point I could see."

"You made a sketch?"

Ellis fished a piece of paper out and made to spread it on the table by the window. "May I know what it is you're looking for, sir?"

Gideon sighed. "Ellis, what you've done so far is well beyond the call of duty. I'll not implicate you further. You'll stay here tonight to give us a cover, and we leave in due form, after breakfast."

"I've heard that tune before, sir. But I always knew why I was whistling along."

Gideon hesitated, but only for a second. What Ellis had done was already fatal—they were British military, their target was the French headquarters of war and they were after top secret documents. The less he knew, the better. "Permission denied. The drawing, if you please."

To complete his preparations for the night, Gideon needed to buy a pair of gloves. Not something to match the workman's clothes that he would don later in the evening, but a gentleman's gloves, suitable for a delicate task. The officials whose documents he hoped to examine were expert cryptographers, versed in the use of chemicals, including invisible inks. The touch of his skin might leave marks on the papers, and gloves would avoid at least one risk of betraying his secret visit.

The best place to buy a pair of fine calfskin gloves was in the elegant quarter of the rue Saint-Honoré. He remembered the street from his earlier visits—the ground-floor shops kept by haberdashers, tailors, coffee merchants and mercers, and the recherché apartments above, rented in the main by wealthy single men.

He and his money were well received there, and the young woman who eventually supplied just the right pair of gloves wrapped them with such care, and so many winning glances, that he concluded the military were still as welcome in Paris as they were in wartime London. When her lips curved they even reminded him, in a less enchanting way, of Mademoiselle Dalgleish's radiant smile.

His purchase made, he strolled back toward the place de la Bastille. It was his last afternoon in Paris and, secretly regretting the fact, he watched the traffic and tried to guess who might be rattling by in the well-sprung coaches that conveyed Napoleon's elite to their favorite shops.

Ahead of him he saw a young woman descend alone from an opulent equipage. She was the epitome of the Parisienne—slender, exquisitely turned out—and had that suppleness of figure that he loved to see in a woman. As he approached she was hidden by people on the pavement, and when she came into sight again she was looking into a shop doorway. Then she changed her mind and turned, and Gideon found himself face to face with Delphine Dalgleish.

The world shrank to one narrow, breathless space. Astonishment and pleasure hit him, the greatest shock coming not from surprise but from the thrill of seeing her when he had been thinking of her only moments before. The miracle of this discovery flooded over him, banishing from his mind the consequences of her having discovered *him*.

She was even more beautiful than his memory of her: more delicate, the blue eyes wide in disbelief, her lips trembling. But she didn't speak.

Dazed, he pulled off his shako and bowed. "Mademoiselle!"

"Monsieur." She didn't curtsy.

Her muffled, neutral tone, in such contrast to the amazement on her face, acted upon Gideon at last, and with brutal clarity he recognized the disaster of this meeting. He felt a wrench in his heart that of all the women he might have seen in Paris, he had come upon his most particular enemy.

As he replaced his headgear, she took in his uniform and sword in a sweeping glance, and then her eyes rose again to his face, brimming with condemnation. But she said no more.

He finally said, in French, "You don't ask what I'm doing here."

She shuddered. "There is no need."

"Perhaps not." They were still face to face while passersby stepped around them. It was absurd: Bonapartist and spy, trapped in this encounter, might have been nothing more than two acquaintances exchanging news.

She said, with peculiar passion, "I know what you are!" She gave him a look of contempt, but there was a kind of pain in it.

Baffled, he waited a moment, then said, "Whom will you tell? Your mother, your cousin . . . ?"

Meanwhile Delphine gazed at him, a hollow feeling in her stomach. She said at once, very low, "No one."

Landor's sea green eyes widened. "Good God! Why not?"

Why not? Because I hate what you are, but you work for France. Why not? Because no one from my family will ever give you assistance if I can prevent it. She burst out: "I wish I had never met you!"

"Yet . . . you spare me." There was a hint of color on his cheeks and his voice was hesitant. "This is the last thing I would have expected from you."

"Ah, you know yourself there, monsieur!"

"True. How can I call for mercy when I showed none to you? I've reproached myself a thousand times for what happened at Saint-Amour. I beg you to forgive me."

"You dare to speak of Saint-Amour to me?"

He grimaced. "I regret my behavior. And I'm sorry you won't accept my apology." Then he frowned, as though he suddenly guessed where her greatest resentment lay. "What happened under the occupation? You have not suffered, I hope?"

She stared at him in outrage.

"Come," he said, "I may have treated you abominably, but I was in England by the time the invasion took place. You regard me as your enemy, mademoiselle, but there at least I've done you no personal harm. Nor would I—ever—if I could help it."

There was emotion in the last words, but she could not interpret it. "I don't understand," she said. "You gave no information about Saint-Amour to your commanders on Bourbon or Rodriguez?"

"About Saint-Amour? No! Why would I? The invasion plan was in place for months before I even came to Ile de France. Good God, mademoiselle, don't tell me you have cast me as your nemesis!"

"So you don't know what's happened to us?"

He shook his head. "Not unless you tell me."

She looked at the invitation in his eyes and knew he was telling the truth. All at once her anger fell away and she felt overwhelmed and defenseless. "There is little to say. Saint-Amour is being run by the British army. I'm about to make my home in France."

Watching her tragic expression, Gideon was tempted to say something kind—but what words of sympathy would be tolerated from an invader? Then the full significance of her last words sank in: she had found a place for herself in France. She was about to marry, or was married already. It was only in this moment that he realized how much he disliked the idea. "I see. Am I to congratulate you?"

"On what?" she said sharply.

"I thought, perhaps . . . you were intending to marry."

Her cheeks turned pink and her blue eyes glistened as though he had done her an injury. "I have no such plans at present." She looked at once furious and hurt, and he dared not say more. It was she who ended it. "I shall, as you say, spare you. And I hope never to see you again." She turned aside and beckoned to her coachman, who at once backed the horses to bring the carriage up beside her and leaped down to arrange the steps.

Gideon was at a loss. The relief of knowing she would not denounce him as a spy was obliterated by what he felt at this parting. It was like a lovers' quarrel, where the passions were so deep that neither had the slightest hope of understanding the other. Certainly, he didn't understand *her*. Why, why on earth, was she letting him walk away free?

He must allow her to go, of course. Every moment in his company compromised her more—a loyal Bonapartist who, incredibly, was not going to reveal his presence in Paris. He should let her leave, though he had a dangerous urge to take her arm and beg her to remain.

Delphine shrank away from Landor's hand, and her coachman helped her into the carriage instead. She had completely forgotten what she had meant to buy in the rue Saint-Honoré, and she gave no destination to the driver as he closed the half door of the coach and climbed to his post again. All she wanted was to escape. This was only the third time she had seen Landor, but it was as though he had been put on earth especially to torment her, and each meeting was worse than the one before.

He said nothing, and through the open window she could not read his expression; he was schooling himself to give her a polite farewell. His appearance was so at odds with his double-dealing! Even in the plain regimentals of a French soldier he looked the perfect officer and gentleman, his fine figure and strong features a match for the inner integrity that one could swear he possessed. How the surface belied the man.

He moved closer, but she had to put her gloved hand on the top of the half door and lean forward to hear his quiet words.

"How can I thank you enough, mademoiselle? Why I should owe this to you . . ." He paused, a flicker of hope in his eyes, but she could not speak. He continued in an even tone, "I have no right to ask." He slipped his fingers under hers, drew them to his lips and kissed the tips. His thumb exerted a warm pressure across the back of her hand. She suddenly had no desire to break the bond, but with a last questing look into her eyes he let her go and stepped back.

"Drive on!" he said to the coachman, and when the coach jerked forward he swept off his shako and made Delphine a bow of farewell. As she drove away, she could see only the top of his fair head.

The Grand Cypher

Much later, Gideon stood concealed in a lane outside the ministry, while a troop of guards settled in for the night in one of the vast courtyards that he could glimpse through a double gate across the street. None could suspect that he had come here after curfew to take up his vigil, and no guards patrolled outside; the city watch instead took the building in on their march through the streets, passing along two sides every half hour as they swung in from the place de Grève.

Despite the tension of waiting, he found it hard to think about the task ahead; his mind was riveted on Delphine Dalgleish. What would happen once she had time to reconsider her rash promise of the afternoon? She would speak to someone in authority, and he would be tracked down and arrested. Paris was crawling with police and informers, and no one, even the meanest visitor to this wide-awake city, went unrecorded. The smallest conspiracy, the merest flicker of intrigue, was exposed and stamped out, and the police prided themselves on their speed and efficiency in the chase. This was the most perilous city in the world for any Frenchman of the wrong persuasion—and it spelled death to an Englishman. Gideon had ordered Ellis to smuggle their gear out of the cabaret and await him with fresh horses in a separate rendezvous.

Yet she had said she would not denounce him. What reason had come to her mind? Was she squeamish, unable to hand a man over to torture and certain death? But consider what she would achieve for her family if she did—revenge for her own mistreatment and the loss of Armand de Belfort's yacht, and praise for a singular act of patriotism.

He passed his hand over his face, his palm grating on the stubble he had allowed to grow since the morning. Was she afraid of him? Perhaps, though he had seen no fear in her enchanting face, only anger. She should have made sure he was hunted down, but something prevented her—something that went against all her principles and was strong enough to lead her to the edge of treason. She had allowed him to walk free in her city whilst knowing he was a spy.

His heart thudded. Had she felt a momentary sympathy for him? Her effect on him was still powerful enough for a glow to steal through his body. Then he shook his head, banishing the ridiculous speculation, and wrenched his mind to the task at hand.

He was after one of Napoleon's codes. For years now, the emperor had taken no part in the war in Spain, but it was a territory of his empire and he had no intention of letting the English invade it from Portugal. On the contrary, his plan was that the French generals in the Peninsula would push the English back into the sea. Napoleon never went to Madrid in person, but he continued to direct his commanders, since his brother Joseph, the king of Spain, had no military gifts, and the French armies were deployed over an immense terrain and required solid coordination.

Orders between Paris and Madrid were sent in a series of codes, a number of which the English had succeeded in decyphering from captured dispatches. Lately, however, the French seemed to have created an impregnable form of communication. Sir Arthur Wellesley, commander of the British forces in the Peninsula, stood to lose much vital intelligence that interception of French envoys had previously given him. He had his agents in Spanish towns, his exploring parties and the keen eyes of the Spanish guerrillas to aid him, but Napoleon's own dispositions for war were being turned into a set of garbled instructions that the English code breakers could not fathom. The French had created a cypher whose complexity stood unmatched in the history of war. It might take years for it to be understood, and the British in the Peninsula did not have that time to spare.

Gideon had been told of his mission in a dusty little office in a crowded building, not too different in some ways from the ministry he hoped to penetrate in the next half hour. His interlocutor from the Aliens Office claimed to be a functionary acting for a higher authority. Gideon, used to the clear hierarchy of the navy, was ready to balk at such a briefing, until he read the gentleman's subtle expression and realized he was in fact talking to the person who had conceived of the mission in the first place. So he listened.

The Peninsular army was desperate to crack Napoleon's great code, and there was only one sure method—to penetrate to its source, and in such a way that the French would continue to use it, unsuspecting.

"You have no infiltrators in Paris?" Gideon had asked.

The only answer was an ironical laugh.

"Am I the first to attempt this?"

There was no answer.

With the conviction that he had been preceded by at least one failure, Gideon said, "Do we know who created this grand cypher?"

"Napoleon's diplomatic codes are supplied to him by Hugues Maret, the secretary of state; it's reasonable to suppose the same bureaus are creating the military codes. Some time last year, Maret made an important new appointment, a renowned mathematician named Alphonse Dauriac. We believe Dauriac and the members of his bureau in the Ministry of Marine and War are responsible for the *grand chiffre*. For safety, there is probably one copy only, kept in Dauriac's desk and used on the premises by whoever is encoding each dispatch. It must consist of a very large number of sheets—it's a numerical cypher, and there are more numbers in it than any of our cryptographers has ever seen before. One sheet alone would be of enormous service to intelligence. It might even win us a war."

Now, at last, Gideon judged that the moment for action had come. Moving out of the lane and away from the guards' line of sight, he pressed his back into a doorway. Against the door behind him stood a long pole that he had carried through the streets hours before.

On cue, the city watch clattered past at one end of the street, the hooves of four horses awaking echoes in the deserted thoroughfares, the dark uniforms of the Paris legion scarcely distinguishable in the moonless night. When they were gone, Gideon ran swiftly forward on supple, silent shoes, and flattened himself against the wall on the other side. High above him was the window Ellis had spied—the only one in the whole huge edifice that didn't appear to latch. Though pulled to, it stood out very slightly from its frame. It was the single hope of entry.

Pulling a coiled rope ladder from the front of his jacket, Gideon attached it to one end of the pole and raised it to the level of the windowsill so that it snaked down and hung against the wall. It wasn't difficult to jam the pole into place, settling it into a groove above and forcing the other end against two paving stones at his feet. Then he made sure the bag over his shoulder hung at his back, and climbed up the ladder. It was, he thought wryly, perhaps the only seaman's skill that he would have the chance to use tonight.

The next part was difficult; he was exposed to the view of anyone who might step around the corner of the street, and he had to stand on the uppermost loop of the ladder while trying his luck with the window. He inserted the tips of his fingers behind the frame and gave a heave. No result. He pulled a knife from the sheath at his waist and slid it into the gap, applying pressure upward. With a squeak the brass latch suddenly gave way and the window jerked toward him. The knife flew from his hand and clattered onto the floor inside, and he grabbed the central part of the frame. Having announced his presence to anyone who might be patrolling inside or out, he made no effort to be quiet while entering the building. Speed was the key—in a matter of seconds he was in and had hauled pole and ladder over the sill.

Yanking the window in again, he paused to listen. The thick silence of the old building descended around him. He propped the pole and ladder behind the drapes at one side of the window, picked up and sheathed the knife and then looked around the room, trying to accustom his eyes to the gloom.

It was a reception hall or salon, high ceilinged and capacious,

furnished with stiff-backed chairs around the walls and a few polished tables. This second floor of the ministry would be where
dignitaries were received, where conferences and military courts
were held. The grandest rooms would be on the other side, overlooking the place de Grève, but even this one had a majesty about
it. From the walls, historic commanders glowered down at him
from within massive gilded picture frames. When his eyes were
sharp enough, he struck out for the center of the building, following Ellis's plan in his mind's eye, and made for the grand staircase to the story above.

It was too dark away from the windows, so he unhitched the
bag from his shoulder, took out a box and crouched on the floor
to make a light. From it he lit a candle within a small, dark
lantern, which he was careful to direct into the interior of the
building. If the guards patrolled in here at night, they must use
just such a lantern, for he had never seen a light in his evening
reconnaissance.

He reached the principal staircase and was halfway up it when
the pole crashed to the parquet floor in the room he had entered. He came to a halt, his feet on separate treads, one hand
gripping the banister. Devil take it! The din was enough to bring
the whole troop pouring in from the courtyard.

He ran lightly to the next floor, urgency sizzling up his spine
as he gazed around for somewhere to hide. But these rooms were
just as uncluttered as the ones below. The staircases, however,
were narrower, indicating that a more humble sort of functionary
toiled in the floor above. The stillness pressed around him once
more. He could hear only his own breathing and the soft pad of
his footsteps as he crossed to the opposite wing of the building
and crept up the last flight of stairs. He paused to put on his
gloves.

The great achievement, as Gideon had known right at the beginning of this insane exercise, was to come across Dauriac's
desk. Given the vastness of the building and the complete lack of
intelligence about what went on inside it, this had seemed a
pretty hopeless task. He had narrowed the odds, therefore, by
sending Ellis on a small expedition that very day.

Walking up to a guard at one of the gates, Ellis had held out a folded and sealed piece of paper. "For Monsieur Dauriac."

"Give it here."

Ellis drew back. "Only Monsieur Dauriac, third floor, place de Grève."

"That's fourth floor to you, but it makes no difference; you can't go up." The guard showed suspicion. "What is it?"

"A bill, unless I'm much mistaken. From my boss, gentleman's outfitter. Overdue, I should say. Judging by the language my master used." A wink. "I'm not to go back until I can say it's been delivered."

The guard frowned, not insensible to the humor of a superior gentleman's being inconvenienced, but alive to regimental pride. "Give it here. It'll be on his desk in five minutes. Be off with you."

Ellis left, satisfied—and short on cheek for once, or so he informed Gideon. What Ellis didn't know was that the seal on the document was spread with a substance invisible in daylight, but which glowed like phosphorus in the dark. Dauriac, when he opened the paper in the afternoon, would have found that it was addressed to the wrong Monsieur Dauriac, and either handed it back to the guard or thrown it away. Meanwhile, for some hours his fingertips would have left on everything he touched a film of luminescence that Gideon could now pick up with a special slide on one side of the dark lantern. Among the warren of desks, Gideon had provided himself with a clue as to which one belonged to Dauriac.

When he reached the right area, he found a long interconnecting line of bureaus, some with one desk, others with several. He examined them all, halting briefly at each desk. Where incoming papers lay on the tops he picked them up and ascertained the addressee's name by the light of the lantern. If he took nothing else back to London, he could at least furnish a list of some of the people involved in Napoleon's codes.

The names multiplied. Monsieur B. Morvan, who smoked a pipe at his window; there were ashes along the sill inside. Robert Couvier, who smoked at his desk. Martin Barfleur, who cleaned and trimmed his dirty fingernails with his penknife. Armand de

Belfort—Gideon gazed at the opened letter in disbelief. He let the sheet drop out of the tiny rectangle of light, picked up another and looked at the outside. The same addressee. At the upper edge of the desk, beside the ink bottle, was a seal ring that showed a swan against a background of reeds: the device of Belfort's family crest that had appeared on the stern of Armand's graceful yacht, *Aphrodite*.

Delphine Dalgleish's cousin was here in Paris. And not only present, but closely concerned in the strategy of the war. One word in his ear, and the dogs would be on the hunt throughout the city.

Propelled by a new sense of forboding, Gideon strode forward into the next room—and came upon Dauriac's bureau. The large desk was piled with documents and spotted here and there with traces of reflective ink, greenish against the mahogany surface. Today's revealing bill lay crumpled on the floor amongst other scattered papers; Monsieur Dauriac had menials to pick up after him.

Gideon must make sure that nothing of his touched the contaminated areas. Crushing the bill carefully in another piece of paper, he put it in his bag. Then he tried the drawers. All were locked. He extracted a set of keys and unbound the strip of cloth that had stopped them from jangling together. The man at the Aliens Office had been encouraging about their use: one key was bound to do the trick, for furniture makers across Europe were sadly conventional.

The seventh key worked; the drawer slid open and he shivered. This was it. He scarcely had to touch the papers to believe it. The top sheet was ruled in a grid, with more painstaking accuracy than a schoolboy grammar, with more meticulous care than a page of important accounts. It was all here: line after line of numbers with their equivalents catalogued beside them—whole words or names, syllables, single letters, and now and then a blank, representative of those random, meaningless numbers that were the despair of the English code breakers.

Napoleon's great cypher was here under Gideon's hands. The temptation to sweep it into the bag at his feet was almost overwhelming. But that would be catastrophic; he must leave it apparently untouched.

He lifted out the papers and saw that they could be divided into two. The large sheets on top were the decryption tables. Below these were the encryption tables; there were no grids on them, and they contained an alphabetical list of letters, words and syllables with a code number or numbers written against each: *abandon . . . 1035; able . . . 185, 808.* Which pile should he copy from? To avoid disturbing the desktop he laid both piles on the floor, his temples pounding. He had been told to choose the decryption tables. That made sense, didn't it? The *numbers* were what faced the English code breakers in Portugal every day.

Gideon flicked through the decryption sheets, right to the end. They were in numerical order, ruled off by heavy lines into groups of ten. He had paper, pen and ink; he might copy one big sheet, perhaps two. As he began to do so, despite his concentration he felt the menace of the vast building all around him, as though it were full of silent watchers. He listened for sounds in the bureaus, dark and hollow tonight, but home during the day to some of the cleverest men in France, who had the best reasons in the world to hold on to their precious secrets. He counteracted the threat that gathered behind his back by carefully transcribing the words, and parts of words, that each number represented.

651 mieux
652 protest, e, ations
653 intention, ne, s
654 terrain, s
655 E
656 quel, lle, s
657 persuade, sions
658 pla
659 Q
660 seul, es, ment

Whole words and their permutations, intermixed with syllables and single letters . . . the sophistication of it stunned him even as he wrote. Strangely, it was the solitary letters that thrilled him the most. To nail "E" and "Q," both so frequent in French, was a terrifying triumph; it was only as the letters formed under his pen that he recognized the power of life and death that resided in each stroke.

For a moment he was tempted to thumb through the other pile of papers and see whether "E" was represented by more than one number—another cryptographer's ruse that could turn code breaking into a nightmare. But he gritted his teeth and went on filling in the paper that he had ruled up that day at the cabaret. Even to have been caught with the blank sheet in the street outside the ministry would have sealed his doom—and probably set Monsieur Dauriac to the creation of a completely new *grand chiffre*. Gideon gave a sardonic grin. He was saving that gentleman a great deal of trouble by keeping this subtle invasion a secret.

Then the guards found the pole and ladder.

There was a shout, and Gideon leaped to his feet, his ears ringing. With his training of vigilance at sea, he had no difficulty pinpointing the direction—there were men in the room he had entered. There must be a night patrol after all, and they had been much more quiet and circumspect than he could have imagined.

He cursed as there was another shout and a distant thump of boots. Two men, soon to be joined by the troop. Time to retreat.

He bent, picked up the papers and with a grimace of reluctance put them back in Dauriac's drawer just as he had found them. He locked the desk and gathered up his gear. Doors crashed below and the inner courtyard sprang to life. Poised to leave, he examined the floor and the bureau for the last time, then froze. *The phosphorescence!* It was due to fade in about twelve hours, but what if the guards' lanterns somehow picked it out? He unwrapped the bunch of keys and used the cloth to rub at a luminescent spot. No result; it required some kind of liquid, which he didn't have. Ordinary ink would be disastrous—Dauriac would notice any spills at once.

His brain drumming with the tumult two floors below, he noticed two bottles and snatched them with his gloved hands. One held a dark ink; the other was full but clear. He unscrewed it, praying this was invisible ink, which was readable only if heat were applied. Wetting the cloth with a fingertip, he rubbed it across one of the least obvious spots, on the side of Dauriac's chair. The glimmer disappeared at once.

With speed he got rid of all other traces, replaced the bottle and crept out into the corridor. Boots were pounding about, and shouts came from where the guards were combing the rooms below. He took one long look down the line of rooms ahead, quenched the lantern, and ran blindly for the end of the building, praying he would find a servants' stair before guards erupted onto this floor.

He slowed and began a stealthy search. In a majestic edifice like this, servants' doors were discreet: narrow and constructed to blend with the paneling or plaster. He looped the handle of the lamp in the crook of his arm to leave his gloved hands free. The first door he opened led into a cupboard full of papers and equipment for the clerks. He paused to put the cooled lantern in his bag. Then he pushed on, his eyesight growing sharper, so that he was aware of flickers of light darting up the central stairs.

It was bizarre, but he suddenly thought of Delphine Dalgleish. If they caught up with him, the investigation would involve Belfort, who would at once identify him. The snake wouldn't be able to resist telling her. How would she react to his ignominious death—shot in the back while robbing the Ministry of Marine? For he would not let them take him alive.

Then he felt the small cup shape of a latch under his hands, pressed down and pushed inward, and stepped into a space filled with a chilly, different air that welled up from below. He let the little bar fall into place with a click, just as a shaft of light flashed down the corridor on the other side. Then he was flying down the stairs.

The noise above intensified, but they had not seen him go; they were still searching. As he passed the next floor, he could tell there were men there too. He plunged on down, his mind racing before his feet. He must pause and take something that a thief might plausibly have been sent to purloin from these sumptuous rooms. And he had to get away from this wing, for an exit onto the place de Grève was suicide; one rapid glance through a window was enough to show him men in uniform pacing about the square.

Reaching the floor where he had first entered, he opened the door a crack and peered through. No light, no voices nearby, but there were still men on this level, calling to one another as they ferreted through the reception rooms. He found the servants' stair in the far corner and made himself go past it, then stop in a large, grand room. He drew his knife.

The task accomplished, he darted down the last flight of service stairs. With every step his heart plummeted—this went too deep for safety, below street level. When he emerged into a grand maze of storerooms, sculleries, cool rooms and kitchens, his instinct was to find a place to hole up. But he knew the guards would begin a more extensive search, looking in every cranny. They had the rest of the night, because the troop—and by now, the watch—had the place surrounded.

He lit the lantern and went on with its tiny light bouncing before him, furious at being backed into a corner at this crucial point. At last he found he was stuck in a cellar, with wine barrels and racks of bottles on every side. Barrels . . . which had to be delivered at some point. Were they rolled from another stairwell, or down a ramp from the courtyard above? He explored and found the ramp, which sloped up to a solid trapdoor that fastened from the inside. He stood looking at it, his heartbeat pounding in his ears. Was there even the slimmest chance that this trapdoor might open up onto the street, against an outside wall? There was only one way to find out.

He extinguished the lantern and blew on it to cool it before putting it in his bag, then crawled up the ramp. The trapdoor had iron bolts, which he carefully slid back. On his knees, he put palms and head against the trapdoor and listened. He could hear nothing above. He lifted it slightly.

A pair of black eyes gleamed back at him, inches away.

Rigid with shock, Gideon felt his heart stop. Then he managed to take a breath, and expelled it on a string of curses that would have made the toughest quartermaster recoil.

Able Seaman Ellis, however, was made of hardier stuff. He whispered, "You took your time, sir, if I may say so," and put a large hand to the edge of the trapdoor to help Gideon heave it back.

"I told you to keep your damned hide out of here." Next second he was standing with Ellis in an alcove in the outer wall that led out into a back street. "Where the hell are we?"

"Not far from your point of entry," Ellis said softly as he lowered the trapdoor back into place. "There was a guard at the corner"—he gestured briefly in the dark—"but not anymore. Leastways he's there, but not in any state to take a line of sight on us. Might we belay this now, sir?"

Gideon grunted, moved to the edge of the pavement and looked up and down the street. No one. "Come," he said and ran straight across into the lane opposite.

When the way became wider, Gideon gestured Ellis past him and followed him through the sleeping city to the place of rendezvous. It was eerie, running across cobblestones that sent the sound echoing up stone walls as they dashed by. The ministry behind them, crawling with avid guards, was the only point of light and life in Paris. The watch, all eyes and ears at the place de Grève, had not penetrated this warren on the edge of the grand district that they patrolled every night.

At the stables their horses waited, unattended by the groom, who had been well bribed to stay asleep in the next-door loft. Gideon changed back into blue regimentals and stuffed all the night's gear into his pack roll.

Gideon was trying to find a place for a long cylinder of canvas when Ellis burst out, "What's *that*, then?"

Gideon partly unfurled it and held it up near their one tallow candle. It was a painting of Napoleon, conveying not only the palatial setting of the portrait and the glorious detail of the sitter's imperial garments but the powerful intelligence behind the pale, lofty brow.

"Boney!" Ellis searched Gideon's face. "What—is it valuable or something?"

Gideon examined the signature in the bottom left corner: *EUG de* and then a swiftly painted black cross. He said, "I damned well hope so. Mount up."

A New Recruit

~~~~~~~

Delphine was not made to wait when she kept her appointment with Napoleon. She was ushered up the stairs to the study while Armand remained below, and she spent less than a minute in the anteroom before the door opened and the previous visitor was escorted out. The door was open, and at a few words from within she was shown into the room alone.

Not surprisingly, the emperor looked somewhat different from the other night, and she was relieved—memories of him in his bathrobe had returned since to alarm her. He received her kindly and seated himself on her side of the splendid brass-bound desk, while she made inquiries about the queen. He beamed as he answered: there were no fears for mother or child.

He soon came to the point. "Mademoiselle, I've considered the matter that your mother laid before me. In times of peace, negotiation with England might produce the results you want. But we are at war. You comprehend me so far?"

"Indeed, Sire."

He gave an amused smile. "Ah, I remember that look. Do you recall a conversation, years ago, when you lectured me on the Austrian campaign?"

"Good heavens!" Delphine said. "Even if I had the audacity then, shouldn't I deny it now?"

He chuckled. "You were standing in the garden at . . ." He stopped, and the smile disappeared. But he went on, "I asked you whether you thought I should beat the archduke in the summer. And you declared, 'Papa says, as long as you retain your genius, the high ground will always fall to you.'"

Delphine stared at him. What an innocent she must have been at twelve years old!

His smile returned, gentle, reminiscent and self-indulgent. "I was deeply fond of your father. And it struck me then that you were his very image." He caught her eye and added, "In spirit."

"Thank you, Sire." She would have liked to keep the emotion out of her eyes, but she could not, and his own misted over too. He got up, went to the window and looked out on the leaden afternoon.

Not a word was said. The days to which he referred would never come again. La Générale had said to Delphine before she left Malmaison that day, "He will always be remorseful—and God knows what else he feels—about Joséphine. I think, in his mind, a kindness to us means some paltry amends toward her. But he will never mention her."

After a while he returned and sat down, his face intent. "There is but one solution, and it lies in your hands. You must go to London." He saw her amazement and said, "Hear me out, mademoiselle; it's important, not just for you but for France. A few weeks ago I permitted an English delegation to come to Paris to discuss an exchange of prisoners. I gave them five minutes of my time, which was wasted on them; they all had titles of some sort, but no notion of diplomacy—if they're a sample of the English nobility, I wonder we deign to make war on them. When they were gone I discovered they had stooped even lower than I predicted. One of them, Lord Ferron, violated diplomatic immunity so far as to try and bribe a clerk in the Ministry of Marine and War. But I didn't lodge a protest with England or make an international issue out of it. I've not so much as hinted that we know of this outrage. Because," he said, holding her gaze, "I don't know whether Lord Ferron obtained any of our secrets or not. He may have made approaches to other officials and been more successful. The possibility is too perilous to ignore."

"The clerk?" she ventured.

"Dead." She felt instantly cold at the way he said it, but he went on in the same dry tone, "He became ill and died while assisting the police." He said with solemnity, "I'm speaking to the daughter of General D'Alglice. You will not utter a word to anyone, even your mother or your cousin, of what I'm about to say."

As though she had a choice! "No, Sire."

"Lord Ferron wanted to buy copies of a document that is of the utmost importance to the war in Spain. A code, written on large sheets of paper that contain words and letters together—I shall allow you a glance at a simulated page today, so you'll know what you are looking for. I wish you to find out whether Lord Ferron got what he wanted. If so, you will let me know, by courier, in a prearranged note, and I'll take appropriate measures."

Delphine exclaimed, "How could I possibly do that? And what—?"

"By wooing him. By getting so close to him that he will reveal his secrets to you—wittingly or unwittingly."

She was so taken aback, she laughed.

He shook his head. "Lord Ferron is wealthy, he has a fine estate—by English standards—he is a very personable man and he is unmarried. He is also a noted connoisseur of everything beautiful. He added a number of treasures to his collection during the time he was in Paris." By the gleam in the emperor's eye, Delphine realized the list included women, and she hoped he was delicate enough to refrain from saying so. Napoleon wasn't above risqué talk with ladies.

"I'm not accustomed to wooing men, Your Majesty. It's up to them to woo me."

"And so he will! Mademoiselle, trust me. You will come to know him well and he will seek your company, he will be unable to resist you, and in time he may even seek your hand in marriage. And that is how you will accomplish your mission. I'm convinced that only a dear friend—or better still, a fiancée or a wife—could get close enough to find out what we need to know."

Her voice quivered. "What makes you think I'm capable of such a proceeding, Sire?"

"My dear mademoiselle," he riposted, "have you looked in the mirror today? You have only to travel to London, with a touching story about my indifference to your family concerns, and England will gather you in. You are an extraordinary beauty, you have

youth, pedigree and a handsome fortune—you will have every
gentleman at your feet."

Her lip curled at this mercenary catalog. "My fortune, Sire, is
debatable. Saint-Amour is in English hands."

"Yes, in those of the governor and his what—his catering officer? My dear young lady, Ferron wields all the power you could
wish in foreign affairs. He will reverse your inconvenient situation with a wave of his hand. Even better, if you promise to tie the
knot with him, Saint-Amour will be yours to govern as you please."

"His, you mean. Supposing I should *ever* consent to marry
him!"

He chuckled. "Oh, dear. You really think I'm sending you defenseless into the wolf's mouth? *Nella bocca del lupo?* Would I
dream of doing that to my little childhood friend? Mademoiselle,
I have total confidence Lord Ferron will come to trust you. Who
knows, you may even find yourself ready to step with him to the
altar. How you conduct the friendship, the engagement—or the
marriage—is up to you. My one desire is for you to gain access to
his affairs as soon as possible and ascertain what he took away
from Paris. Whatever the result—whether he stole the code or
not—your next action will be as follows: in noble indignation, you
will announce to his superiors that you have discovered what he
tried to perpetrate in Paris. As a French gentlewoman, you will
express your disgust at the degradation of being associated with
such a man. And in return for not revealing his shameful secret
to the world, you will break off the relationship. Or, supposing
you are his wife, you will insist on an annulment of the marriage.
In either case, you will demand perpetual rights to Saint-Amour."

She gazed at him, her lips parted. But it was beyond her to
speak.

"The British would do anything to prevent being humiliated
before Europe for such a breach of statesmanship. Ferron will be
professionally ruined, but the public will know nothing of it unless you denounce him in the press. He will be as eager to settle
with you as the government could be, just to make sure the scandal doesn't come out. England's good name will be at stake, and
they will do anything to protect it. You will have your freedom,

and Saint-Amour, and my eternal gratitude. I swear it to you, on the memory of your father."

For a breathless moment his voice and manner moved her so much she could almost imagine herself doing what he asked. But she said, "And what if I get to London and decide such an attempt is beyond my power?"

He stood up and looked at her in a way she remembered from the far-off happy days at Malmaison. Then he bent and did something he rarely did, even then; he pulled her earlobe affectionately between finger and thumb. "You will not fail." He turned away and walked to the window again.

She looked at his rounded back in dismay. *Good God. He is ready to sell me, to buy back his secrets.* Then she recollected what she had just said: *If I get to London . . .* She had practically agreed to go.

For a second, she wished her mother or Armand were there to help her. Then the thought rushed to her brain: *He has chosen me. Only me.* He had just shared a vital state secret with her. He relied on her. If she refused him this service, would he ever trust her or her family again?

"Sire, have you considered how badly I should be received in London? I'm the daughter of one of your bravest generals. Everyone on Ile de France, and the most important people in London—they all know we are patriots. Wouldn't my every move be doubted?"

He turned slightly, his hands clasped behind his back, and looked at her sidelong. "You have a most pitiful story to tell. You have come to Paris with your worries about Saint-Amour, but I've refused to help. Heartbroken and disaffected, you see no alternative but London. There you look for friends and supporters, who will not be wanting, I assure you. Your innocent plea is to find security and peace in Ile de France—or England, if such an opportunity presents itself. My dear mademoiselle, you will be the most touching, the most fascinating young lady in London."

"How could anyone believe that I would turn my back on France?"

He smiled and came to stand closer beside her. "Lord Ferron will believe it. The idea will be irresistible to him."

"It . . . the whole scheme is dreadful to *me*."

Instead of getting angry at this dangerous statement, he sat down in the chair opposite and, sinking his chin on his chest, looked at the floor for a while. Then he sighed and raised his face. "I've not been frank. I have a second motive. There is another mission for you in England, and nothing but *past* love and loyalty makes me ask it of you."

Her heart jumped. Joséphine? But what on earth had she to do with England? Out of her depth, she allowed him to continue. Glancing at him now and then during their exchange, she could see feelings that altered his expression as he spoke, so that he seemed by turns vulnerable and furious, vengeful and bereft. For this matter did indeed spring from the past—from a time long before Joséphine, when the Bonaparte family followed their brightest star from Corsica to France, and one by one took their places within the mighty Bonaparte constellation that came to preside over the countries he conquered.

"You have met my brother, Count Lucien Bonaparte?"

"I've not had that privilege."

He gave a heavy frown. "You know what he has done?"

"I've heard that he's in custody in England, Sire."

"Traitor! Yes." Napoleon's lips quivered.

Delphine waited for him to go on, too wary to commit herself, for the situation was complicated. Lucien Bonaparte, Napoleon's second brother, once a beloved favorite, had according to the emperor married beneath him, and his wife, formerly his mistress, had borne him several children. When Napoleon decreed that Lucien should divorce this nobody and marry into royalty, Lucien refused, and went with his little family into virtual exile in Italy.

"He rejected every overture from the most generous brother—endowed with the finest, the wisest vision for his future! Ah! Be thankful, mademoiselle, that you have no brothers to repudiate your noblest sentiments and tear you apart as mine has done to me."

There was nothing Delphine could say. She was not inclined to make loud protests against a man whose first loyalty was to his wife and children. She felt sorrow rather than antipathy for Lucien Bonaparte.

"He ignored every advice I gave him in Italy, but I never guessed what his ingratitude was until he made the perfidious threat that he would go to the United States."

Lucien Bonaparte had been ready to exchange a "republican" empire for a republic—a true one. With this thought in her mind, Delphine didn't dare look up.

"It sickens me to repeat the infamous details. He was captured by the English off Sardinia and they forcibly offered him *asylum.*" His mouth twisted on the word. "From me! From France, the country to which my family have dedicated our lives, our future, our children."

His distress was so deep that Delphine said gently, "And he is living where?"

"In Worcestershire." He pronounced the difficult word as though the place were a cesspit.

"The English allowed him to retain all his possessions, I hear."

"To injure me, they would do anything."

"But he is not allowed to leave his estate." She shook her head. "In a sense, he is no better off than when he lived in Italy."

He gave her a grateful look, then said, with more self-knowledge than she had given him credit for: "Ah, but in England he is safe from my persecution." He got up suddenly. "I've abandoned any hope of making him accept my plans for him. He is hurt, and he has grown obdurate." He shrugged and looked down at her with sorrowful irony. "I have a confession to make, mademoiselle. Think the less of me if you will—I'm sure the world would do so, if they knew."

She looked at him in perplexity as he paced the room, the heels of his boots digging soundlessly into the thick rectangle of carpet. "I've written a letter to my brother. It's not a diplomatic note, nor is it a decree under the grand seal. It's a simple message, so simple that few would believe me capable of writing it. I wish you to put it in his hands."

Her heart sank. For all she knew, this second mission was even more fraught with peril than the first, for everything depended on what Napoleon had written.

He gave her a quizzical look, then sat down again and made an attempt to speak humorously. "Have no fear. No international incident can erupt from this document. If it were intercepted, or if my brother published it, no heads would fall in Europe. Certain people might smile; that is all. Let them." His voice changed. "I have no shame in speaking the language of the heart. Mademoiselle, my brother is lost to me unless I make a gesture that even he will appreciate. I must forgive him in order for him to understand me." He regarded Delphine tragically. "He has exiled himself and betrayed me, but whatever I may say in public, I cannot banish him from my affections. He is my brother still, whatever he has done. That is the message, mademoiselle; no more, no less. Will you take it to him?"

Arrested by the dark gray gaze, Delphine felt his whole being reach out to lay hold of her will. With a corner of her free consciousness, she reproached her mother for taking their family problem so high, for it had projected her into a sphere in which she had no training or experience. And escape was impossible; looking into the glowing eyes of the man before her, Delphine knew that whatever means were required to accomplish the hallucinatory tasks he had just proposed, he would provide them. He had raised her to a plateau from which her world took on a different, dizzying perspective. For a second, she shared his vision; she saw how she might serve Saint-Amour, France and the emperor. And she pledged herself to the attempt.

In the carriage on the way back to Malmaison, Delphine underwent her first apprenticeship in duplicity, under an interrogation by Armand. "Well, then, what did he say?"

"He seemed to want to talk about the past. He was altogether disarming at times; quite sweet and sentimental. He mentioned Papa, and he said he felt sorry for Maman, and spoke very kindly about our troubles."

"And? What's he going to do about Saint-Amour?"

"He thinks we should apply to London. In person."

"He's not serious! What, send us packing to England!"

"Well, Maman and me."

Armand reddened. "And what about me?" Delphine could see he was still mortified that he had not been invited into the emperor's confidence—or even the anteroom to his study. She would have pitied him if she had not been feeling so desperately sorry for herself.

"Oh, I expect he thinks you are much too valuable here."

Armand looked a little mollified but didn't reply. He always kept a rather important silence about his work; they knew only that it was for the Ministry of Marine and War, and Delphine was almost convinced that it had to do with intelligence. She thought of saying Landor's name and watching Armand's face when she told him where she had last seen that arrogant and double-dealing Englishman. But she held her tongue. The idea of Armand having any contact with him, worse still conferring behind her back, was unpleasant, and she wanted nothing to do with Landor. The memory of his icy green eyes, assessing her as she stood with him in the street, made her spine tingle with apprehension still.

Armand frowned. "How can the emperor expect you to go to England?"

"We are civilians and may travel as we please. He is giving us passports across France and out of the country, signed by his own hand. And don't forget, we are Mauritians, therefore in a sense British. There will be no difficulty entering England."

"How can *you* agree to leave France?"

"The emperor says it's necessary for Saint-Amour. We failed with Farquhar—we must see what his superiors can do for us." She tested him, "Of course, you might fare much better with Farquhar than Maman and I if—"

"Oh, no, no. If you think I'm dashing off to Ile de France, on command, to sign their ridiculous oath of allegiance . . . No, it would take months. I can't possibly be spared."

She looked out the window to hide her disappointment. Since they had arrived back in Paris, she had become aware that Armand now put his career and interests before all others. Though he was fond of her, he was not a man to whom she could turn for comfort or protection. And she could not ask his advice over this mission: Napoleon had sworn her to total secrecy. Similarly, there was no one to whom she could turn in London. She would be contacted at some stage after her arrival in England, but the agent there was a mere courier, standing ready to take any messages from her back to France.

Armand exclaimed, "It will be expensive, this exercise!"

"We are not yet paupers, Armand. Besides, the emperor is paying."

He looked astonished and envious, and she scolded herself. So far she had not lied to Armand, but she should be equally careful not to tell him the whole truth!

"He must think a great deal of you," Armand said slowly.

It was time for humility. "Goodness knows why. I can hardly imagine how we shall go about this. I must sort things out with Maman."

"Will she consent?"

"It's the emperor's wish. Can you imagine her doing otherwise?"

Portraits

Gideon was enjoying London, for it gave him the chance to catch up with friends, but it made him restless. He had chosen the navy for a life of adventure, and he never spent long on shore without yearning for action. Unlike many of his friends, he was not content with hunting, curricle racing, fencing or riding horses in a match. Half his acquaintance were dedicated to sports and entertainments that he found dissatisfying, and he was no keener on the preoccupations of the other half, namely, politics and power.

Abroad, in the service of his country, he had believed he was of use. Returned from France with the stolen portion of the code, he had astonished the Aliens Office and earned their gratitude, and now he attended the assemblies of London with a sense of unreality—this was not his milieu. The excitement that other gentlemen experienced on the hunt came to him only when he faced the dangers of war, far away from their tidy estates. By delivering a portion of Napoleon's grand code to the intelligence bureaus he had given them something of significance, but it was not accolades that he craved, it was something to do.

And it was being done by others. The person who would put his piece of information to use was far away with Wellesley in Portugal, fighting to free Spain. Gideon had not yet found out the man's name or his rank in the army, but he must be highly placed in Wellesley's headquarters, part of his "family." Just the thought was enough to put Gideon out of sorts with staying idle in London.

But he had an identity to keep up, that of the complacent gentleman about town. Apart from blood sports, he found another occupation of a kind—gambling. The clubs were agreeable and he possessed the kind of coolness required at the card tables. And to give himself a reason for the odd escape to the country, he decided to begin construction of a summerhouse at Landor. It was in search of ideas for the building that he one day visited the Royal Academy of Arts at Somerset House, where the designs of Britain's finest architects were held. When he arrived, there was a portrait exhibition open in the main salon of the east wing where the academy was housed. On impulse, he stepped inside.

Delphine was taking in London by degrees. When she arrived, it had a frosty look to it, the streets crooked and narrow, and the buildings a dirty gray. Foreign smells surged over the sill of the coach window, recalling the unsatisfactory inns where she had stayed on the way up from the coast, with their odors of boiled meat and sour ale. Spring was covering the countryside in green, and she had heard a cuckoo in the woods by the highway, but in the city the trees seemed shy in their light clothing of leaves, and the sheen on London's brick and stone looked suspiciously like a layering of soot.

As she and her mother approached the district where they were to stay, however, they began to pass through places that had some of the amplitude and grace she was used to in Paris. The squares that charmed her most had trees planted over lawn in the center and were surrounded by houses of very regular design that had fewer stories than Parisian mansions, thus letting more light onto the elegant facades.

"There's no grandeur here, Maman, but there is style."

"Wait before you judge, *chérie*," la Générale said. "The English are sometimes at their most grand when they're pretending to be modest."

Delphine made no answer to this, not wishing to challenge her mother's expertise. La Générale had of course never visited Britain, but ever since she had learned English following her marriage, she had carried on a correspondence with certain of her husband's relatives in Edinburgh. After Alexander Dalgleish's brilliant mathematical studies as a youth in Edinburgh, he had begged to attend the Sorbonne in Paris, and his parents had consented. He had stayed on and made his career in the French army as an engineer, and they were forced to accept that this independent spirit would find his own way on the Continent. He already had a fine career when the Revolution occurred, but his parents expected him to renounce it, and France, and return to Scotland at once. When he didn't, and they realized he had embraced the republic, they cut him off.

La Générale, much younger than him, and the daughter of freethinking aristocrats, shared his ideals when she married him in the turbulent year of 1789. Her first letter to his parents began (with some assistance from her tutor):

> It will surprise you to hear from the wife of a son who left you in order to fight for our Revolutionary armies. I hope it will not surprise you to learn that he comports himself in France with the nobility of soul that he has inherited from you. May I hope also that you will be gracious enough to receive news of him from my humble pen? Close to him as I am, I feel the courage to ask you: he has left your shores, but has he entirely left your hearts?

The Dalgleishes, wary at first, showed this letter to the rest of the family, who passed it on to others, and it caused a certain excitement in their circles. The idea of a reply, initially to expose this subtle Frenchwoman, became irresistible, and in fact the parents and Julie developed a sentimental attachment over the years, which deepened when General Dalgleish himself was prevailed upon to write. The parents didn't reverse his disinheritance, but his own fortune took the sting out of this on both sides. After the parents died, Julie continued to write to women in other branches of the family, and when Delphine broached the London visit she realized how useful this would be. One of her father's older cousins, a Mrs. Laidlaw, lived in Mayfair. The late Mr. Laidlaw, also from Edinburgh, had been a banker in London, and after his death his widow had remained, always talking of returning to Scotland but never doing so. She at once extended an invitation to Julie and Delphine "to stay for as long as I stay myself.

The place was beginning to bore me, but I feel all my curiosity revive. Pray come; the idea is enough to divert me already."

Mrs. Laidlaw proved to be a short, compact woman in her late seventies, with great acuteness and energy of mind. She was hampered by a rheumatic condition that discouraged her from going out very much, but it didn't curtail her favorite activities, which were reading, painting and keeping up with what went on in London. During her husband's ascendancy in banking, she had presided over a lively salon, and her visitors still tended to be people of influence. "I seldom have gatherings these days, so none of them can be sure whom else I'm seeing," she confided with a glint in her dark blue eyes. "In camera, it's astonishing what they let fall. They think my teeth were all pulled long ago, I dare say." She gave Delphine an appraising glance. "I shall certainly have a gathering for *you*, mademoiselle, but all in good time. You must be talked about before you are seen. We shall secure you an invitation to something of significance, so you can make a proper entry into the arena."

"You are very good, madame," Delphine murmured.

Sensing doubt, Mrs. Laidlaw gave a short laugh that lit up her face with amusement. "Fear not, I don't expect your life to be a desert in the meantime. Go forth, explore. May I suggest the Royal Academy tomorrow? I should like to see the new portraits myself, but being pushed about Somerset House in a Bath chair is not my notion of entertainment. Go, and bring me back a report. You'll be doing me a favor."

They arrived in the early afternoon, but mist was still curling about the building and stretching a canopy over the great inner courtyard, which Delphine could see through the entrance as they alighted from Mrs. Laidlaw's carriage. The four sides were lofty and graceful, built of a light-colored stone that looked even paler in the chilly atmosphere. There were people standing about on the gray paving, and at the far end men in naval uniform moved busily in and out between double glass doors leading into a reception hall overlooking the Thames.

Delphine at once thought of Sir Gideon Landor. Indeed, ever since Napoleon had given her this arduous mission, any idea about what she might do in London had been colored by the knowledge that in all likelihood she and Landor must meet again. She might have every excuse to be on his terrain, but she had a ridiculous dread of crossing his path. Here, the naval uniforms alarmed her. "Let's go in, Maman, out of the cold."

Inside, Julie Dalgleish made a careful study of what every visitor was wearing, while Delphine, aware that Mrs. Laidlaw would ask probing questions, had an even closer look at the portraits. It wasn't easy, as the windows were few and in the dim light only the faces and the lighter draperies of the sitters stood out. She received a favorable impression of English complexions, silks and laces.

The Royal Academy had included amongst the new works some portraits from its collection by Joshua Reynolds, its co-founder, and Mrs. Laidlaw, a skilled portraitist herself, recommended his work. Going in search of it, Delphine stepped up to the next floor, and in the very first room her gaze hit upon Sir Gideon Landor.

He was alone, with his back to her, looking up at a full-length image of some military subject. Delphine gasped, took a step backward and collided with her mother, who exclaimed in surprise.

The gentleman turned and Delphine saw sheer amazement cross his face, followed by embarrassment. Of course—how appallingly problematical for him. He and la Générale had met but once, on the night when he committed the outrages at Saint-Amour and stole Armand's yacht! "My goodness," she said, "Sir Gideon Landor. Let us see if he can keep his countenance." And she swept forward, la Générale at her side.

It was deliciously unfair. Delphine relished the awkwardness of the greeting he gave to her mother and his perturbed glance as he bowed to her in turn. Julie Dalgleish showed him no mercy, scarcely opening her mouth to say his name before she closed it and fixed him with a cold, regal look. Delphine wondered how soon it would be before he tried some kind of apology. When he did so, she felt with quick resentment that it was typical of his self-contained character.

"What can I say, madame? You see me in the safety and freedom that I owe in part to your family—much against your will. It would be dishonest to say I regret standing here before you. And none of my apologies have been— That is, I know none are acceptable to you."

"You must make what excuses you can to my daughter, monsieur. My nephew's yacht, however, is another matter. When can he expect restitution?"

His eyebrows, dark in comparison with the fairness of his hair, drew in above the straight nose. "Words cannot express how I feel about the injury I did to Mademoiselle Dalgleish." He was avoiding her eye. "But the yacht . . . it ended up as the spoils of war, madame, no more and no less. You may inform Monsieur de Belfort that that is my final word on the subject." He realized how trenchantly he had spoken, and continued in a quieter tone, "Is your nephew in London?"

"No. His place is in Paris. He can never set foot here while France and England are at war. And only the worst of misfortunes could have brought us here ourselves."

Delphine could see that he remembered what she had said to him in the rue Saint-Honoré. Before he could speak, she said, "We are here to reclaim our rights over Saint-Amour. The invasion of Ile de France damaged us in more ways than one. We hope against hope to find justice in London."

His eyes were riveted on hers. By this speech, she was telling him that she had kept her promise and said not a word of their Paris meeting to Armand or her mother. There was the faintest tint of color along his high cheekbones as he took this in, and she felt a warmer blush on her own. She had kept his secrets, for the sake of France, while all the time despising his activities. She had felt superior to him because he was a double agent. Now she was on the same level—she was an agent also, posing as a colonial supplicant in London whilst in the clandestine pay of Napoleon.

He turned again to la Générale. "Will you allow me to help, if I can?"

Julie was astonished, and perhaps a little moved. "May we know what influence you might bring to bear?"

"I don't know until I try. I'm on half pay, but still in the navy. I can't be sure until I know your problems better."

"Oh," said Delphine. "So you are not here today on military . . ." She trailed off, rather as her mother was wont to do.

He looked down with a touch of amusement. "I'm here, mademoiselle, to look at the collections. My interests don't always run to ravaging foreign territory."

Julie Dalgleish looked at him shrewdly. "I'm not inclined to forgive you for anything, monsieur. But we have just arrived, and you have the privilege—or misfortune—to be the only gentleman with whom we are acquainted in London. If you should choose to call and leave your card, we reside with a relative, Mrs. Laidlaw, in Berkeley Square."

He said, "Indeed? Ambrose Laidlaw, the banker?"

"Yes. His widow is my late husband's cousin."

He nodded. "Then you have fallen on your feet."

Delphine bristled; as though they needed his approval for where they stayed! It was uncomfortable having him near, and the prospect of his calling at Berkeley Square was even more so. In his presence it was hard to forget how close they had been to each other during the encounter in the gazebo on Saint-Amour, and impossible not to relive the sensation of his hands on her body. There was a hidden physical counterpoint to every exchange of words between them.

She said, "Mrs. Laidlaw is a gifted painter. She asked me to look for portraits by Joshua Reynolds. Do you know where I might find one?"

"In the next room. Allow me." He offered an arm to each and they processed through a large doorway. Thus, instead of escape, Delphine was faced with close contact. They paused before the Reynolds, a portrait of some great landowner and his wife, and her mother kept hold of Landor's arm on the other side. Delphine knew why. Julie Dalgleish was aware of the handsome picture they made: the tall, good-looking English aristocrat, totally at his ease, and the stylishly dressed French newcomers, intent on the best of British art . . . it was as though they occupied a niche in London society already. For her mother's sake, Delphine kept her fingers resting lightly on Landor's forearm. It felt warm through the superfine cloth, conveying latent strength and an absurd feeling of intimacy.

A thought occurred to her—a temptation that had been at the back of her mind ever since Napoleon named her mission. She *did* know one of Bonaparte's agents in London: Landor himself. She was not authorized to approach him, but what if he could be persuaded to help her investigate Lord Ferron? Unfortunately there were two reasons against this. One was the risk to the emperor's secrets, for surely none of the London agents could know anything about the grand code; otherwise, why send her? The other was the thought of saying to Landor, "I'm here to trap a man into friendship and then double-cross him." She had promised the emperor she would try, but she feared she could never go through with it. Other means must be found, but could she bear to ask Landor to provide them?

It was hopeless trying to take in the Reynolds, but Landor asked, "And how does it strike you, mademoiselle?"

She threw a wild glance at it. "The portrait of a lady more preoccupied with her lapdog than her husband."

He laughed, and she felt the tremor come down his arm into her fingers. She took them away.

He said lightly, "His problem is that he's an English husband, Mademoiselle Dalgleish, and a mere lieutenant colonel at that. If he were French, and a marshal, the lapdog would be put straight in the shade, I imagine?"

She rallied. "Alas, monsieur, I've met French officers—not many, I'm glad to say—who have fewer manners than a well-trained poodle."

"You astonish me. And how do you manage them?"

"I don't. With puppies, all one can do is hope they'll someday grow up."

He laughed again. "Do you like Reynolds, though? I've always thought there's something appealing about the natural look he gives his sitters."

"Yes, they breathe. The skin tones are exquisite. So transparent. It's something I've noticed today."

He nodded in reply. She took a quick look at his profile, wondering where the conversation might go next. For the moment it was more open than she could have predicted.

Then her mother's voice intervened. "If this palace is typical of English public buildings, I must say it's a little cold. Don't you find, *chérie?*"

Delphine recognized her cue to go. "I shan't keep you standing about, Maman. It's time we went back to Mrs. Laidlaw."

"Let me walk you down," Landor said in his calm, masterful way. As they negotiated the staircase, causing many a person to press themselves politely against the banisters to let them pass, Delphine felt all eyes upon their little group. They had in some measure laid claim to Landor; la Générale had ensured that he was made guilty about what he had done on Ile de France, while giving him a hint to start making amends. So he was in their debt.

His conversation as they stood waiting for the carriage was polite but unforthcoming. She gathered that he lodged in the family town house in Curzon Street and followed the usual pursuits of the season. His only open response came when la Générale asked him what amusement they might expect to find in London: he laughed. But he did not explain himself.

As the carriage was about to drive away, he stood with his hand on the half door, and Delphine was reminded of Paris, when he took her hand and kissed it in farewell. He didn't touch her this time. She could not tell whether he was struck by the same thought, but just before he bowed to them she caught the penetrating look that he had given her in the rue Saint-Honoré. Then it was over.

For his part, Gideon went back into the palace, kept his appointment to see the architectural drawings, made no headway with them at all and finally gave up and spent the afternoon and evening at one of the clubs, where for the first time he sustained consistent losses. It was impossible to think of anything else; against all the odds, Delphine Dalgleish was in London. It had been piquant, standing at her side looking at portraits. Their last two meetings had been in distinct contrast: the night when he had tried to subdue her in the gazebo at Saint-Amour; the highly charged encounter on a Paris street.

He reminded himself that she was a stranger with secrets he could not begin to penetrate. She was still a Bonapartist and he an English spy. The Dalgleishes were Mauritians by force, and here to wring what they could out of the administration, but their allegiances would never be English, in heart or mind. Any fool could see that.

Delphine was rather annoyed with herself. She had had plenty of time to think about how she would deal with Landor if she came across him, but he had somehow turned the tables on her, so that the strongest reaction she had got from him was not defensiveness but laughter. For a day or two the memory of his self-possession got under her skin and ruined her sorties about London. Meanwhile, her mother gave Mrs. Laidlaw a dramatic description of the meeting that made the Scotswoman laugh and declare it too fine a story to stay in camera. Thus London heard of it, and in very short time.

Delphine and her mother soon settled into Berkeley Square, where they were well looked after. Delphine had had to share her mother's maid on the way to England because her own took fright and wouldn't come; now she engaged a young Londoner called Molly, who proved very competent and agreeable. Delphine also came to enjoy Mrs. Laidlaw's company. Most of their conversations occurred at breakfast, their hostess's favorite meal; she stayed awake reading books until early in the morning, rose at around ten and breakfasted at eleven, when Julie and Delphine joined her. She brought some of her correspondence to the meal, and as she toyed with her food she gave a succinct account of what had happened in the high echelons of society the day before, frequently reaching for a letter to read something out, her eyes glinting beneath her lowered lids and her voice curling ironically around the words.

One morning, Delphine said, "I love the way you read. If only I spoke so well."

The dark blue eyes sparked. "They say the best English is spoken in Edinburgh. I have no idea; I've lingered in this town too long." She gave Delphine a searching look. "Your voice will do very well, young lady. Even better if you tell me exactly what it is you want here."

Julie Dalgleish said, "You know everything about our case. If you have the slightest idea whom we should approach first, I'd be most grateful."

Mrs. Laidlaw put down the letter. "Laidlaw always used to say, you don't understand a thing until you have the lie of the land. Land meaning property, *mes amies*. Now, somehow you have to find a highly placed gentleman who takes a personal interest in how Saint-Amour is administered. What rare kind of gentleman might that be? Another owner of property. You tell me people are selling up in Mauritius?" At Julie's nod she said, "Therefore others are buying. English investors, most of whom already have land elsewhere—in the British Isles, the Indies. Gentlemen with great estates and grand ideas. The news that plantation owners on Mauritius are being shabbily treated by the governor won't appeal to them. If you can make one of them aware of the issue, half your battle will be won."

"How do we find them?" Delphine said.

Mrs. Laidlaw gave a little shrug. "People who are about to invest are often about to borrow. I still know the foremost bankers in London; I shall inquire. Then we'll put you in the gentlemen's way—nothing could be easier, for you are coming with me to Lady Melbourne's tomorrow, and I'm persuaded she will invite you to her ball in a fortnight's time. She is intrigued by your plight, and on meeting you she will be even more so. I'm not saying she'll wage a crusade on your behalf, but you could not have a more influential ally. Nor," she said thoughtfully, "a more formidable enemy."

Julie said with a touch of irony, "*Vraiment?* Then how do we neutralize her?"

Mrs. Laidlaw chuckled. "No one has ever tried to neutralize Lady Melbourne. She's like mercury—it's hardly possible even to contain her."

*   *   *

Gideon always liked going to Melbourne House. He remembered it well from when he was much younger, since on his parents' London visits they had often been asked to dine there. The dinners were enormous affairs, part of Lady Melbourne's adroit politicking on behalf of her husband and the Whigs. If the Earl of Tracey was anything he was Tory, but, being indifferent to party politics, the worst he ever said of the Whigs was that they were irresponsible, at which Lady Melbourne would laugh, and then launch into a mordant account of what the Tories were lately perpetrating in Parliament. Gideon's father would raise his eyebrows and murmur, "Really, really, really?" at the right intervals, then return to Buff House and regale the neighbors with Lady Melbourne's wit and style and the excellence of her wines.

Later, Gideon had been asked for his own sake, along with some of the men he had studied with at Cambridge. Although Lady Melbourne had been a celebrated beauty, and even at sixty-one was still handsome, she demanded no tributes to her feminine powers and her manner was natural and engaging. Along with Lady Jersey, the patroness of Almack's, she more or less ruled London society, but where Lady Jersey was exclusive, Lady Melbourne handled people with tolerance backed up by a clever judgment of character.

Tonight Melbourne House was as he recalled it: crowded, glittering and filled with the eager hum of conversation. The lord and his lady were together for once to greet the guests, and they each had a quick word for him. Lady Melbourne's question was political—she wondered when his father would next be speaking in the House—but her husband said, "Heard you were promoted. What are you now—admiral?"

Gideon laughed. "Father is in excellent voice, I thank you, but it's heard loudest on the hunt these days. And there's a ship building for me at Greenwich. I'll be captain of her in a few months' time—quite enough to be going on with."

Lord Melbourne nodded and turned to the next guest, but her ladyship lifted her chin and said, "I hear you're not above *commandeering* vessels when your patience runs out."

"Ah. Am I to conclude that Madame Dalgleish has been court-martialing me to my acquaintance?"

She smiled. "Your story has gone the rounds, yes. So I should warn you—she and her daughter are invited tonight."

"I'm obliged, but the warning's unneccessary; there'll be no fracas under your roof."

"Really, really?"

People seemed to be hanging around the stairs, but Gideon forged straight up to the ballroom and was announced, his name ringing out in a lull. Heads turned and for once he felt conscious of walking in alone. He was after all something of a novelty in London, just as his father had predicted, and he attracted a special attention amongst marriageable young women and their mamas, which was entertaining in a way, for it afforded him some lovely company. He looked beyond all the familiar faces in search of Mademoiselle Dalgleish, but she was absent. He was ready for her—he had promised restraint to Lady Melbourne, but if the Dalgleishes had been painting him as a pirate to half of London, he was justified in cutting up a little rough. They were on his territory now, and he was no longer a bruised, betrayed and angry prisoner.

He fell in with a group of acquaintance and said the usual things that began such an evening, and for the hundredth time he wondered whether Armand de Belfort had ever confided to his cousin the infernal trick by which he'd drummed up the legionnaires on the night of the first escape. Everything pointed to a negative. Belfort's pride, for one: Mademoiselle Dalgleish had a keener sense of honor than that sly devil, and surely he wouldn't have wanted to lower himself in her eyes. Second, the cousins were evidently not close; otherwise the lady would have rushed to tell Belfort about Gideon's appearance in Paris. So she must have no idea that Belfort had trapped him after he first broke out of the Garden Prison. She and her mother had simply been broadcasting about town that he was a thief. But suddenly a worse possibility struck him: had they spread the tale of his attack on Mademoiselle Dalgleish?

He felt his ears growing hot, and walked away from the people he had been speaking to, earning a startled glance from one of the women as he did so. From the side of the room he scanned the crowd. The worrisome Frenchwomen were still not here. And Georgiana Howland was standing only a few yards away with her mother. There he could claim the confidence of a friend, and Georgiana was on the brink of betrothal, so singling her out at this point in the evening would set no tongues wagging. He approached and the Howlands greeted him happily, Georgiana giving him a smile that made him warm to her as always. They had known each other since childhood, and despite a slight difference in their ages they had always enjoyed each other's company. Truth to tell, he had often fancied that he might end up marrying her. Somehow, though, he had not fallen in love with Georgiana, and her feelings seemed just as disengaged. As an heiress with a splendid freedom of choice, she had been in no hurry to settle on a husband, and her manners with him had never altered.

Being promised in marriage (to a duke, as he'd predicted) suited her; she looked prettier than ever tonight, a little more womanly in her rather elaborate silk gown, while her keen hazel eyes and abundant dark curls reminded him of the child she had been. She turned aside to talk to him. "I wondered how long it would be before you noticed there were others in the room, sir. The navy has given you a habit of staring out over people's heads—it won't do in London, you know."

"Nonsense; I was aware of you the whole time. I was stranded, trying to rehearse my felicitations. How do I tell a childhood friend how very earnestly I wish for her true happiness?"

She looked conscious, so much so that she looked down to hide her expression. When she raised her face the smile had gone, but warmth still lit up her eyes. "To me, you couldn't have chosen better words. Thank you. Combrewood is very kind. It wasn't until I met him that I realized how much I value kindness."

"Kind? He's lucky—the luckiest man in England. And I hope he makes you the happiest woman."

She gave him a level glance, but realized he had spoken sincerely and looked away.

"I wonder if you'd tell me something." he said. She gave him no answer, distracted by something on the other side of the room, but he pushed on. "You know I escaped from Mauritius this last voyage?"

She was all attention again. "Of course! Everyone knows."

"Do they? But are they aware how?"

She gave him a humorous frown. "Naturally they are. We had all the details the moment you came back. You made two attempts to escape, against horrid odds, and the second time you got clean away. And you took someone's private yacht to do it, right from under their noses. Really, Gideon, you've been a legend to every young lady in London from the day you arrived. Has no one asked you about it?"

He considered. "Perhaps one or two have tried. I think it no one's business but the navy's and my own." After a pause he said, "*You* never asked me."

She was adjusting a glove. "I had no need to. When I heard the story, it sounded like you all over."

"Oh," he said. "Am I about to be categorized à la Georgiana?" He permitted himself the use of her first name, because she had just used his.

"Oh, yes," she echoed. "Ruthless, rapacious and dangerous to cross." When he laughed she looked up with a smile. "I'm very glad you got away, even if you had to purloin someone's property to do it. Though I did wonder how you'd manage if you ever came face to face with the owners. There are two French gentlewomen in London who claim you stole their yacht, and they rather justifiably want it back, now that you've finished with it. I presume you've finished with it?" She looked at him pertly and it struck him that given the slightest prompting she would take the Dalgleishes' side.

"They've said nothing more?"

"I've no idea what they've said; I've never met them. But you have, I gather, the other day. And you gave them very short shrift. Is that true?"

"Let's get this straight," he said. "The yacht belonged to the cousin, a dyed-in-the-wool Bonapartist by the name of Belfort, who called the militia out against me. If he wants his yacht he can come to England and beg for it."

"Did Lady Melbourne warn you, then? She's invited them here tonight."

He grinned at her. "Thank you; I think I can stand the excitement. Has Combrewood already claimed the first dance, or will you grant me the honor?"

She was indulgent, and he danced the whole set with her, falling into easy conversation about everything but the Dalgleishes. Combrewood was due to come later and take Georgiana in to supper, and Gideon, who knew him slightly, recalled that he wasn't fond of dancing, nor of balls and soirées in general. He was a lofty man, preoccupied with his noble estates and the management of his immense wealth, which would leave Georgiana the direction of their social life. Looking down at her face, Gideon wondered for a moment whether Combrewood's vaunted benevolence would be enough to keep her from feeling lonely on occasions. It struck him that a clean division between husbandly and wifely duties could be a great burden on both people, and one he wouldn't like to bear himself. When he married, he would want someone to share things with.

"You know I'll always be your friend," he said to Georgiana as the last strains of a polonaise faded away.

"Yes, I do," she said. Her face was turned from him, toward the arched entrance to the ballroom. "Goodness me—are those spectacular persons the ladies from Mauritius?"

Lady Melbourne's Ball

D elphine was trembling with nervousness about the evening. Her mother was full of blithe anticipation, but Delphine's secrets haunted her and made everything a trial. Establishing herself in London was only the first step; the second was to meet Lord Ferron. It was too much to expect that he would be present this evening—in fact, she was coward enough to wish the opposite—but everything she did must create the right first impression. Before stepping into the ballroom, she took herself to task. It was too late to be turning timid before a crowd! Why not behave exactly as she would in a Paris salon?

Just as she came to this bold resolve, they were announced, and she looked across the room and saw Sir Gideon Landor. Her ears rang. *Bon dieu,* to meet him here, of all people. Her hardwon courage wavered at the thought of playing a part before the very person amongst all these strangers who knew most about her.

She turned aside, pretending she had not noticed him, but while Lady Melbourne was introducing them to the nearest group, Delphine could still see his tall, dark form and the brightness of his hair. He had just been dancing with a young, very pretty woman. He had straightened, his hand still holding the lady's gloved fingers, and Delphine had seen his wide shoulders stiffen and his features freeze in an expression that she gave herself no time to read.

When she could attend to the polite talk around her, she found that one of the middle-aged gentlewomen was already speaking of him. "And what has Landor done with your cousin's yacht, Miss Dalgleish? Have you any hope of getting it back?"

Delphine smiled. "*Ma foi,* I think London knows more about the matter than we do, madame. And much more about Sir Gideon. He was a prisoner when I first met him. If fate wills, perhaps I shall see him again. If not, I doubt if either of us will much regret it."

Another lady said, "I think fate's already intervened—he's here."

A dowager dressed in embroidered silk gave a sideways nod of the head that set her ostrich plume waving. "And he's danced the whole set with Georgiana Howland. I declare, if Combrewood doesn't show his face soon he stands a good chance of being cut out."

The other said, "Not according to what I've heard. A settlement has been reached and the engagement's about to be announced."

"And what if the lady's behavior announces something else? I've always thought her besotted with Landor, poor girl, and tonight proves it." She looked past Delphine's shoulder. "But there, he's leading her back to Lady Howland. A magnificent figure of a man, Miss Dalgleish, as you'll remember, handsome estates, and the only son of a fine bloodline—and as inviting as the Arctic when it comes to taking a wife. He's the despair of the season."

Another dance was about to begin. Would Landor come her way? Delphine addressed the dowager's son, Mr. Elliott, a tall, thin young man who had been trying without success to say something in between his mother's pronouncements. "I'm afraid I can't forget that Sir Gideon is in the British navy. I hope *you* are not in the navy, sir?"

"My word, no, Miss Dalgleish!"

She smiled at him. "Goodness, what a relief." Then in mock alarm, "Nor the army, I trust?"

He smiled back. "I'm not sure I share your horror of the military, but will it set your mind at rest if I promise never to join up without your permission?"

She laughed in reply, he asked her for the next dance and they walked out onto the floor. It went very well; Elliott was agreeable and talkative, he didn't mention Landor once and Delphine never looked that gentleman's way. She discovered that a few minutes of mild flirting gave just as much amusement and pleas-

ure in London as it did in a Paris ballroom, and to her surprise it
was smartly returned. When she was handed back to her mother's
side, another gentleman begged to be introduced and asked her
to dance, and after that she was constantly engaged.

Delphine caught glimpses of Landor, but he never approached. His demeanor was nothing like the dowager's description of him: he wasn't distant with women; in fact, he spent a
great deal of time dancing, and all the evening talking, with
ladies. Once she saw him laughing, and the tilt of his head and
the flash of his teeth gave the complete lie to his arctic reputation—
he looked much more like a hunter after prey. Unfortunately, at
that very second he glanced across the room and saw her, and
above the grin his eyes signaled an instant challenge.

When Gideon walked over he had Georgiana Howland on his
arm, and Mademoiselle Dalgleish had just danced for the second
time with young Elliott. The exercise enhanced her beauty; her skin
had a becoming radiance, and having watched her graceful dancing, Gideon felt an appreciation of her supple body, clad tonight
in pale green silk. She looked like a forest sprite who had just
drifted indoors from some wooded bower. Not that he had the
least intention of telling her anything so fanciful.

She was very much at her ease; the moment the introductions
were over she returned to the topic she and her partner had been
discussing. "I'm invited to be one of a party to Vauxhall Gardens
once the weather has warmed up," she said to Georgiana. "It
sounds delightful, but how do you recommend one should
arrive—by carriage or the Thames?"

"At night, it's best to be driven. If you're anything like me, you
won't care for the river in the dark."

Gideon looked down at Georgiana with a smile. "There's not
the least danger, you know."

She said, "Perhaps not with you. But then you've never made
the offer to convey us, sir."

Mademoiselle Dalgleish said to him teasingly, "Oh, I know *your*
preference already. Boating is the natural choice for you. Tell me,
how does the *Aphrodite* handle on the Thames?"

He replied in the same light tone, "Extremely well, I'm sure.

But you'd have to ask someone at Greenwich about that. I was obliged to hand her over to the navy, as a prize."

For a just a second he saw a flash of surprise and indignation, but she rallied. "I do hope she fetched you a handsome sum?"

"None at all, so far. The French navy claims she is a civilian vessel, not a prize of war, so she remains impounded until the dispute is settled. It's a pity to see her lying useless, but short of snatching her again I have no chance of sailing her on the Thames or anywhere else."

Mademoiselle Dalgleish gave a little laugh that added a sparkling brilliance to her blue eyes. She was quite up to sparring with him, which made him wonder why she had avoided him all evening. "Ah, with the *Aphrodite,* yours was the behavior of an officer, my dear sir, but was it that of a gentleman?"

He raised one eyebrow. "I'm not the best judge. But I must say, few gentlemen have ever found themselves in quite my position."

"And when you struggle with your conscience, are you always so victorious?"

"I really can't tell you; such occasions are rare. Duty tends to loom over the horizon and I know my direction at once."

"So you are a stranger to principle, but a loyal friend to authority?"

He countered softly, "That depends on the authority. Where it's informed by principle, I think I know my course."

She brought her hands together in front of her as though about to applaud. "There speaks the officer again—true blue." Then she stopped. Was she recalling the moment when he stood before her in a Paris street, clad in blue French regimentals? "I must tell you, I should never engage you on this for my sake, or my mother's. It's my cousin's cause. If it were not for the fondness I bear him, I should let it drop."

She had found them both a way out. He grinned. "Then I admire your courage, mademoiselle. For behold, here you stand, surrounded by inveterate enemies."

Georgiana spoke up. "Really, how can you tease Miss Dalgleish so?" She went on to the lady, "You are to take no notice of him. I assure you, I seldom do."

At that moment the music started up again. Having brought Georgiana across the room, Gideon could not abandon her for this dance, but glancing around he noticed her fiancé walk into the ballroom at last. He leaned toward her and said quietly, "Combrewood is here."

He watched her face as she turned toward the entrance. When her eye met Combrewood's there was a tremulous smile that betrayed a certain affection. "Do please excuse me." She began to move off, then said, as though Gideon had spoken, "No, pray stay here and make your apologies to Miss Dalgleish, if you please," and walked away.

He turned back at once to the lady in question. "Tell me, how shall I manage that?" She tilted her head to one side, pursed her lips but gave him no answer, so he continued, "By degrees, I surmise. May I begin by begging the honor of standing up with you in the next?"

"It's the supper dance!" Elliott said. "I'm taking Miss Dalgleish in to supper."

"Then I promise to deliver her safely to you, the moment the orchestra stops." Gideon held out his arm, and after the merest hesitation she put her fingers on his wrist, gave Elliott a kind smile and walked out onto the floor.

He felt a thrill when she did so; he couldn't help it. They would be tête-à-tête for the first time since he happened upon her in the rue Saint-Honoré. "It's a waltz. You don't mind?"

She gave a laugh and paused before him, just the right distance away. "Why on earth should I?" She leaned over, grasped the tip of one panel of her gown and straightened. Then she stretched forth her other hand to place it lightly on his shoulder, and he put one hand on her waist. A sensation coursed through him that was quite out of keeping with her butterfly touch, and he had an almost irresistible urge to slide his hand farther around her body and pull her to him.

Other couples began to glide by and she said very low, "Have no fear; I do know how to waltz, monsieur."

He stepped back into a space in the crowd, then exerted pressure on her waist, and they danced for a minute without speaking. He had been wondering, ever since he had seen her at Somerset House, what they might do with an opportunity to talk uninterrupted, but now he had no wish to disturb the charged atmosphere between them. He didn't want debate or explanations; he wanted nothing but the heady closeness of her body to his.

But he eventually said, "I've had no chance to pay my respects to your mother. She is as well as she looks, I hope?"

"Thank you, yes." There was mischief in her eyes as she looked into his. "Don't be afraid to approach her; she will never be as impertinent to you as I am."

"Impertinent? I don't find you so."

She gave a self-mocking smile. "Oh, dear. Worse? A harpy?"

He considered. "Impertinence is a girlish fault. And your weapons, mademoiselle, are all womanly."

"*Tiens,*" she pondered as he guided her through a quick turn and spun her in another direction. "I'm not sure whether that's a condemnation or a compliment." She continued on a breathy laugh, "All *your* weapons, monsieur, are double-edged."

"Am I so frightening, mademoiselle?"

"Terribly."

"*Vraiment?* As I see it, of all the women of my acquaintance you have the best excuse to be afraid of me, but—and I hate to say it—you show by far the least fear."

"That is because I know you better than they do. You are a dissembler, so I dissemble in my turn."

She said it as though in fun, but it stung. He replied, "I've used no artifice with you tonight. Don't feel you need use any with me." Then, to disguise that she had gotten through to him, he said more smoothly, "There are things we neither of us care to speak of just now. Your national loyalties and mine, for instance. That is not concealment—it's consideration. One can hardly waltz at daggers drawn. But I'm game, if you wish it."

"Oh, no. There's quite enough to set us at sixes and sevens without that. Lady Melbourne, for instance. I'm sure she asked us here in the hope of seeing you and me bare our teeth at each other. Or is that unfair of me?"

He could not help laughing. "No, very astute. I hope you'll think none the less of her for that, though. She can be a powerful ally."

"So I'm told. And who are your allies in London?" He hesitated, and she went on gaily, "But how silly of me—you have the ladies, en masse. And the navy. You cannot want more."

She was mocking him, but with such a dazzling smile that he forgave her. He sighed. "You're rating my powers far too high, mademoiselle. Nothing frightens me more than ladies en masse—you may go to Almacks and judge for yourself. As for the navy, it picks me up and drops me as it pleases. I'm virtually unemployed at the moment." It seemed a good opportunity to make her believe that his spying days were over. If she thought he was still in the secret service, she might well talk about it to friends in London, and the dangers of that didn't bear thinking about. "I have nothing to do but idle about on half pay, waiting for my next vessel to be launched."

She caught his meaning at once. "So you are not—" She paused and began again, facetiously, "You are not about to sally forth against the perfidious French?"

"I have no such orders," he said. It was easy to say, since at that moment it was the truth. "May I hope that this state of affairs meets with your approval?"

She opened her eyes wide. "Do you seek my approval, monsieur?"

He said sardonically, "I seek everything that is hard-won, mademoiselle. I'm afraid it's in my nature."

"I think you're forgetting that my mother and I are the petitioners. It's we who must seek approval here, and understanding, so we can regain our rights over what is ours." A strange look of resignation crossed her fine features. "When I consider where I stand, I think that for me to hold your actions up to criticism *is* impertinent."

What was she saying? That he already had her reluctant approval—even though he was both a warrior and a spy against her countrymen? No, even in play she'd shown her claws tonight. She loved her homeland too much ever to forget that he was the enemy. Not even a waltz at Melbourne House at the height of the London season had the power to bring her any closer to him than arm's length.

As the music wound to a close, he searched for a phrase that would create an excuse for this singular dialogue to continue. But young Elliott appeared before them, and Mademoiselle Dalgleish lifted her gloved fingers from Gideon's shoulder, stepped back and gave a quick, neutral half smile. He bowed. "Mademoiselle, thank you. With great regret, I must relinquish you as promised."

With a slow curtsy, she thanked him in turn. "And now we have supper. How curious. Bon appétit."

He watched her walk away, debating with himself. Supper at the Melbournes' could take an hour—very different from the stand-up refreshment offered in the Paris salons. He could not take Georgiana Howland in to the tables and it was too late to ask someone else. He wasn't in the mood for walking in alone, so he sought out Lady Melbourne, thanked her and left.

When he got to the club he went straight into a winning streak. Later, at three in the morning, he found himself sitting with a group of friends, drinking cognac and thinking about Delphine Dalgleish. She had rolled out the guns over her cousin's yacht, but they had both navigated out of that engagement. The rest had been target practice, the more pleasurable for the genuine warfare that leaped into the exchange now and then. But there was a possibility that he had begun to disarm her—as long as she believed he was no longer a secret agent. If so, the tactical advantage lay at present with him. Breathing in the fumes from his brandy glass, he told himself not on any account to press it.

High Stakes

G oing over the ball the next day with her mother and Mrs.
Laidlaw, Delphine expressed herself very glad that Landor
had left before the end of the evening. Mrs. Laidlaw chuckled
and said that, from the sound of it, he might have met his match
in their contretemps. Delphine didn't deny this, though she was
by no means sure the victory had fallen to her; she had never
crossed swords with anyone quite so skillful. Really, though, she
had been relieved when Landor left, because it had given her
time to breathe and a chance to think in case Lord Ferron appeared. Which he had, some time after supper, and just as she
and her mother were doing the rounds bidding good night to all
la Générale's new acquaintance.

Delphine had heard his name as he was announced, and
looked over at once from the opposite side of the room. Was it
rudeness, to come this late? Not to Lady Melbourne's, it appeared, for her ladyship greeted him with a smile and he looked
all confidence. Delphine studied him as his gaze swept the room.
He had dark eyes with thick lashes, not unlike those of Captain
Melbray Arkwright, though with a predatory expression in them.
When they reached her she kept her face cool and blank, but she
took him all in. Nowhere near as tall as Landor, but not short just
the same; he had a broad, well-muscled figure that was rather too
fleshy for his age, which must be around thirty. His clothes were
fashionable, his russet hair wavy. He didn't look away; he was making his own assessment of her in return, with a pucker of appreciation at the edges of his well-shaped mouth.

She turned away to her mother and steered her in the other
direction, and a few minutes later they made their departure.

Delphine was sure he would inquire about her, for the encounter with Landor had made them both the entertainment of the evening, just as Lady Melbourne must have hoped. She knew that to most observers she had come out of it with all colors flying, and could almost feel grateful to Landor, if he had not been such an exhausting opponent to withstand.

Meanwhile, all she could assert about Ferron was that he had looked very sure of himself. Remembering the rounded contours of his face and the set of his mouth, she was prepared to wager that if he had a weakness, it might well be self-indulgence.

After they had discussed Melbourne House, Delphine said casually to Mrs. Laidlaw, "What kind of man is Lord Ferron?"

"I don't know him, though Laidlaw did. Ferron is a rake."

There was a little silence. "Pray explain," said la Générale. "I'm not familiar with the term."

"A rake is a gentleman with no respect or affection for women—those he marries, those he keeps or those he pays for."

La Générale frowned. "There are such gentlemen in France. But I don't think we have a special name for them!"

"A rake is a gentleman who flaunts his latest cyprian in public—at the theater, for instance—regardless of the feelings of his female friends and relations. The worst kind will even parade his mistress before his wife."

La Générale nodded. "Merely having a mistress does not make a man a rake, then?"

"Absolutely not. Think of one of our former prime ministers, Charles Fox. He kept a mistress for years, the beautiful Mrs. Armistead, but she lived very quietly and it was a love match—he's said to have married her in the end, in secret, of course. A true gentleman hesitates to go into society with his former mistress."

Thinking of Lucien Bonaparte, Delphine realized she could draw a contrast between the French and the English here, but she was rather more eager to hear about Ferron.

Mrs. Laidlaw was still searching for a definition. "A rake may lavish a great deal of money on women, but he maintains them like high-bred horses and often values them less than his bloodstock. Marriage makes no difference to his behavior; in fact, there

I think you have the most glaring distinction between a rake and a gentleman."

La Générale said, "It seems to me that the best of society in England go about these things just as they do in France. With discretion. Lady Melbourne, for instance—I believe she manages her own affairs, and her husband's, with tact?"

"Indeed. The Melbournes have always had an admirable understanding. You'll see no vulgar mistakes made in their company."

"Can you tell what mistakes Lord Ferron may be in the habit of making?" Delphine asked.

Mrs. Laidlaw said, "I have to disappoint you—I've heard no details. Ferron has the reputation of a rake, that's all I know. Laidlaw knew him, for the good reason that he used to lend him money. All paid back with interest, I may say, for the gentleman does not lack for income, or at least he didn't back then. He does lack a wife, however, and no one expects her life to be a pretty one when the knot's tied, no matter how rich she will be." She transferred her dark, intelligent gaze to la Générale. "And here's a final clue for you. There is a streak of cruelty in the rake, that everyone recognizes and no one can alter."

La Générale made up her mind. "We do have a name for such a man."

"*Libertin?*"

"*Salaud.*"

The two older women burst out laughing.

Gideon was seated in the same dusty office where he had once received instructions about Bonaparte's grand code. His contact was also the same, a gray-haired, middle-aged gentleman who looked as though he pored over dossiers all day. He had the bloodless, academic approach that Gideon remembered in his Greek professor at Cambridge, moderated only by a suppressed excitement when military campaigns were being discussed.

"Where am I to go this time?" Gideon said.

"You'll be glad to hear you have a task in keeping with your present circumstances. It's in London."

Gideon frowned. He had been eager to get away, for a variety
of reasons. The main one was personal: he had spent weeks without a sign of Delphine Dalgleish—he had even turned down invitations that might have put him in her way—but she had
remained in his mind the whole time. He and Mademoiselle Dalgleish didn't suit—they never would suit—and spending time in
her company might put his feelings in danger. He was not made
of granite.

Catching his cool look, the official went on, "It's the same old
issue we've been battling with since the war began. There are too
many French in England for us to keep them all under observa-
tion, and it's obvious that a great deal of information travels
across the Channel. Military secrets are virtually on a one-way
route out of London."

"You're exaggerating." Gideon was irritated: the man had
some distasteful mission in mind and was trying to tempt him
into it by making it sound like a great challenge.

"It's no exaggeration to say Bonaparte has spies in London!
We do on occasion manage to catch them out. But there seems to
be a network, headed by someone with the background and the
means to gather and transmit this information—in other words,
a French aristocrat. He is most likely to be part of the émigré
community, passing himself off as a royalist, or at least as a critic
of the empire. We should like to discover who he is, and you are
ideally fitted to do so."

"Why?"

"You move in the highest social circles. Your French is faultless
and I hear that you already number some French amongst your acquaintance. The more you mix with them, the more you'll learn."

"This is ridiculous. You're forgetting Mauritius. What makes
you think any Bonapartist would trust me for a moment?"

"It will take time; we realize that. But friendship and familiarity will eventually work their influence. It may need only one slip
of the tongue, and someone's careless conversation will lead you
to the center of the network."

"I find it hard to credit that any Bonapartist would be prepared to regale *me* with his secrets."

The other said quietly, "He might if you led him to think you had some of ours to sell in return."

There was a stunned pause, then Gideon's disbelief turned to icy anger. He rose. "I've always done my duty. It has never included compromising my name. If the service asks me to do what you just suggested, I must refuse. If they don't like it, let them court-martial me."

The other got to his feet too, in haste. "Good heavens. No one is . . . that is, I . . . no, I quite see what you mean."

"Do you? Let me be very clear, just in case you don't. I'm prepared to investigate the French in London. I'm not prepared to creep about town giving the impression I'd sell my country's secrets for my own gain. If you want someone to play double agent, you have the wrong man. I'll not have the name 'traitor' within a thousand miles of mine!"

"I apologize, Sir Gideon. I gave quite the wrong picture of . . . Allow me to explain. The investigation will go forward according to whatever plan you adopt. If you think surveillance is required, for instance, you'll need personnel. The men, the expenses, will be supplied by the office. Simply let me know what you need and—"

"I shall," Gideon said curtly. "You'll have a message tomorrow at the usual address. Now you'll excuse me."

His fury was stifling him—he had to get out. Downstairs he set off walking into the streets without any idea where he was heading. He took long strides, breathing deeply. At the corner of a square he stopped and leaned against the railings, facing the passing traffic. He felt sick. What had he gotten himself into? During his long, perilous training, in the thick of the war, through the hot engagements at sea, under captivity, he had been sustained by a belief that he had made the right choice when he put on a naval uniform. He had a purpose to perform, and he had stayed true to it. But after Mauritius he had agreed to become a spy, and what if in doing so he had passed some moral crossroads without realizing it?

His ears were assaulted by the din of vehicles on the road, and people passed close by him, their voices and footsteps surrounding him, but he had never felt so alone. He wished to God he could go back to sea and take on the clean responsibilities of command, where the enemy defined himself with blatant aggression and an equal assumption of risk. He closed his eyes and put up a hand to pinch the bridge of his nose, trying to banish this nauseating confusion.

He was due in Greenwich tomorrow to see how the new frigate was coming along. He must put things back in perspective and figure out a way forward. Wherever it led, he would not let it take him to dishonor.

Vauxhall Gardens

⟨⟩

It was time Delphine achieved something for Saint-Amour, but in the last month she had seen nothing of either Lord Ferron or Sir Gideon Landor. She heard about Ferron from time to time, for acquaintances let on that he had inquired about her. All well and good—luck would bring him to her. But Landor's neglect weighed on her. Her mother was disappointed, for she had believed his promise at Somerset House to do what he could for them. Delphine, knowing him to be a man of deceit, did not expect him to do a thing in that direction. Somehow, nonetheless, it rankled that the false pledge had been forgotten.

Much to her surprise, she was beginning to enjoy London, but nothing so far had come up to the stimulation and suspense of Lady Melbourne's ball. Dancing with Landor, she had been kept on edge at every second by the tingling nearness of his body and her constant struggle to cope with the artfulness of his mind. Time spent with him was rousing but dangerous, and she should not yearn for it to be repeated—which didn't protect her from a peculiar tension when callers were expected at Mrs. Laidlaw's, or from a strange stab of disappointment when she and her mother returned home each day and found that no card had been left by Sir Gideon Landor, Bart.

"I fancy Sir Gideon thinks it beneath him to pay a visit to Mrs. Laidlaw's," her mother said one day. "Even to this beautiful house, at the glorious end of town."

"Oh. Now you mention it, I suppose it's just like Landor's pride to think so. If he were *really* grand, it wouldn't matter to him."

"He's quite grand enough. His father is an earl and his mother a countess."

"So he will be an earl when he inherits. And one will be obliged to call him Lord Landor?"

"He will be the Earl of Tracey. We shall address him as 'Lord Tracey.' If we are ever permitted to speak to him again."

"Then why—?" Delphine began, but her mother interrupted her with a helpless laugh.

"No! Don't expect me to explain why he is a baronet as well. It comes to him by some sort of courtesy. These English titles make my head spin."

Not long after this exchange, Delphine received an invitation to accompany Georgiana Howland and the Duke of Combrewood to Vauxhall Gardens, and her mother gave her a little advice before the Combrewood carriage came round to fetch her from Berkeley Square. "There are all manner of personages on parade. If you see anything terribly vulgar, and I daresay you will, simply pass by without comment."

Delphine said mischievously, "What if I sweep past some *grand seigneur* by mistake?"

Julie Dalgleish smiled. "You'll use your own judgment. I'm not saying you should set up as Puritan, *chérie*. We'll leave that to dear Mrs. Laidlaw." When Delphine looked at her in surprise, she murmured, "You've noticed how severe she can be when she talks of men. I'm sure Mr. Laidlaw was kept on a *very* tight leash!"

As it happened, when Delphine went wandering amongst the throngs at Vauxhall, nothing could have been further from her mind than trying to sort out the blessed from the damned. It was picturesque, with the lights creating a faerie effect in the trees, and Delphine, glancing into shadowed paths, saw people appear and disappear as if by magic: a masked gentleman with a lady on each arm walking past a green archway and back into the shrubbery in a flash; a young girl, searching for a friend, who popped her pretty head over a hedgerow for a second and then ducked out of sight. Wearing a mask announced no nefarious purposes, either; if the devil were lurking tonight in Vauxhall Gardens, he had probably come in a much more subtle disguise.

They sat down in one of the summerhouses for a while, to listen to some music provided by a chamber orchestra, and then set off down another alleyway, where a few minutes later Lord Ferron came into sight, walking toward them with a young woman on his arm. There was a shimmering impression of a slim form in a yellow dress, and a pale face framed by feathers and sequins, then the figure was gone. On a signal from Ferron that Delphine didn't detect, the young woman darted through a gap in the hedgerow and departed the stage—dismissed, like a glove puppet clapped into its box by the master puppeteer.

Having dealt with this encumbrance, Ferron came toward them at a leisurely pace, a slight smile on his full mouth. Then someone caught up with their group from behind and hailed them. Turning, Delphine realized he was the Duc de Limours, and when the greetings were over, she spied Ferron step off the path and disappear. So she devoted her attention to the duke. A thin, gray-haired gentleman of about sixty, with perfect manners and considerable address, he was the leader of French émigré society in London. Delphine had met him just once at a dinner, and at the table they had fallen straight into the habits of Paris conversation, expressing all sorts of opinions with little sincerity and not a little wit, in order to test each other out and make the others smile. By mutual consent they had never gotten onto weighty topics, but she had been eager to meet him again after someone mentioned that he was thinking of buying land on Mauritius. They walked behind the others, while the duke questioned her about how she liked London.

"Tolerably. I came here with a purpose but I've been diverted by an astonishing number of entertainments." He didn't ask her about this purpose, so she continued, "Your situation on coming here was so dreadfully different. You have been in England how long?"

"Since 1793. We left before the execution of the king, and we had some hopes of our land remaining intact. Not so, I'm afraid. Most of our possessions were confiscated by the republic, and when Bonaparte became first consul he sequestered the rest."

He was watching her reaction, but she felt for him and saw no reason to conceal it. "What you must have lost, under both regimes!"

"Indeed. Fortunately we brought a good deal here with us."

She considered for a moment. "Under the emperor, France is a rather altered place. He has much more tolerant relations with the church, and have you heard how eagerly he gathers the aristocracy around him?"

There was an ironical smile on his thin lips. "The old aristocracy, or the new?" He shook his head. "I'm fascinated, of course, by what you say. But as for considering a return . . . at the moment, I'm as likely to go back to France as Lucien Bonaparte. He is most enlightening on the subject!"

Delphine was startled. "Do you know him?"

"I do." Lowering his voice, he said, "Lucien Bonaparte is one of the most delightful hosts in England—and who would have thought I'd ever say such a thing of a member of *his* family! If your principles permit, mademoiselle, I would advise you never to refuse an invitation to Thorngrove. He lives just beyond Worcester and the roads are quite fair thus far. Next time I attend, I should be happy to convey you and your mother."

She felt tremendous excitement at this opportunity, but it seemed prudent to hide it. "You are very good. My principles? Ambiguous, I have to confess. I've been informed that the emperor can do nothing for me in Mauritius and I must rally what support I can find in London." After a pause, during which she could feel that she had roused the duke's curiosity, she said mournfully, "In the end, it's a matter of trust, is it not?"

"What do you mean?"

"In your case, it's a matter of trust whether you choose to live in England or France. It all depends which government you place the most faith in."

"And what is your case, mademoiselle?"

She explained about Saint-Amour, and he listened with great attention. When she had finished, he raised his expertly plucked eyebrows and said, "I beg your pardon, but it strikes me that you may stand to gain much more from England than from France in the long run."

She gave him a doubtful look and said, "And you, monseigneur?"

"I too. I've had eighteen years to think about that question, and I've finally reached the point where I'm ready to invest in our future here. I intend to acquire some property, possibly on Mauritius now that it's English. I should be very much interested to hear about the plantations on your island. What they yield and how they are run. Rumor tells me that, for a lady, you are quite splendidly informed on such things."

"I should be glad—" she began as they rounded a corner, and all at once Lord Ferron was upon them.

One look at his tight smile and she was convinced that this was deliberate. He had gotten rid of his inconvenient companion in order to join them, but the duke had intervened, and for some reason this had not been welcome. At last Ferron had grown tired of hanging about waiting for the duke to take his leave and decided to intercept them anyway.

The betrothed couple seemed pleased to see him, and the introduction was made. Ferron said it was most fortuitous for him to happen upon Miss Dalgleish in the gardens, when he had heard so much about her elsewhere.

"But—" Georgiana Howland said, then at a glance from Combrewood didn't finish. Delphine guessed this to mean that she or her fiancé had told Ferron where they would be that evening, and with whom.

Ferron and the French duke were known to each other, but Delphine could see no liking between them; Limours adopted a haughty air and Ferron was very cool in response. It surprised Delphine a little, for the duke's title was superior to Ferron's, for all he was French, and she was ready to bet that Ferron put a high value on rank—but he made no effort to be agreeable. In fact the greetings all round were without warmth. Watching the three British aristocrats, Delphine saw none of the acid scrutiny, the maneuvering for wit, that characterized French encounters of a similar kind. The men's comments were bland and the thrusts were veiled, while Georgiana Howland soon looked bored.

It wasn't long before the Duc de Limours made his excuses and withdrew, taking an elaborate leave of Delphine and ending,

"I very much look forward to our next discussion about Ile de France, Mademoiselle D'Alglice."

"I too. It always delights me to speak of home."

He gave her a keen look before he turned away, and she wondered about him as his tall figure disappeared down the path. He had as good as advised her to look to England in the future and forget France. He had certainly given her to understand that he was adopting this policy for himself. He was prepared to be her ally, it seemed—but the alliance depended upon her switching loyalties for life.

"You look pensive, Miss Dalgleish," Ferron said as he offered her his arm. "The duke said nothing to concern you, I hope?"

She changed her focus. "He did rather. Last time we spoke, the other night at a dinner, he told me that faro is played in some of the best houses in London. I was just about to ask him—how could that be?"

"Faro is popular in some circles. Do you have an objection?"

"But of course. Everyone knows that the advantage always falls to the banker over time. Setting up a faro table in one's house is like announcing one is happy to fleece one's friends."

"But what if one's friends are happy to take up the challenge? There is many a house where I should be very glad to break the bank."

"I'm certain you couldn't be so wicked."

"But we've only just met. Can you be sure of my character in such a short time?" He sighed humorously. "I might have wished to be more mysterious."

"Might you? That is not how I see you."

"Clearly not!" he said with mock despair. Then, "Dare I ask how you *do* see me, mademoiselle?"

"Oh, dear, you have called my bluff, for I know absolutely nothing about you! I must find what clues I can, and read something; I'm afraid it will have to be your eyes, if you permit."

He stopped, entering the game at once. "Not my hand?" He made as if to take his arm away and present her with his palm, but she held on to his sleeve.

"No, pray walk on and do not speak. Concentration is required." She was making all this up from one moment to the next, but to her surprise—and trepidation—he seemed quite ready to go along with her nonsense. There was amusement in his brown, thick-lashed eyes. After solemn contemplation, she said, "I see you in a carriage pulled by four white horses—"

"Gray," he said.

"No, white!"

He gave a low laugh. "Forgive me; I mean the *term* is 'gray.' You have the color quite correct."

"Silence, s'il vous plaît!" He obeyed. This was really a little on the dangerous side; she had never flirted in quite this fashion before. But she felt that he was a man to whom the unexpected would always be intriguing. "I see a device on the door of the carriage—a deer? No . . ." She pretended to search for the word, then said, "Husband of the deer!"

He gave his low laugh once more. " 'Stag.' The male of the species is called a stag."

"Of course; how could I forget? My father was Scots, you know."

He was not to be deflected. "Well, you have the horses and carriage in hand, mademoiselle, but don't you think my character sketch is a little vague?"

"Oh, no, one can tell an immensity about a gentleman from the vehicle he drives about in."

"You don't say? I must take a look at mine some time, if it's so revealing. I must confess I should hardly recognize it in the street."

She could tell this was a lie. He dressed and spoke with care; she was quite sure he would lavish the same attention on his equipage. "I hereby declare it has yellow wheels."

He grinned. "If you insist. Next time we meet I'll let you know whether you're right."

It was time for another change of subject. "My mother and I are debating whether to set up a carriage of our own. It's a matter of great moment. For it all depends on how long we stay in London."

"Your friends must hope," he said suavely, "that it will be for a very long time."

She sank her voice. "I'm not sure that we have any friends. A host of kind acquaintance, of course, but England is no friend to France, and only a fool could ignore such a truth."

"Only a boor would remind you of it. And the real enemy is Bonaparte. In your time here, you'll have heard as many French voices crying out against him as English, I'll be bound?"

"That's true."

"Then take heart. The French are valued amongst us." He grinned at her. "Only think, what should we do for fashion, wit and good taste without you?"

"That is very kind, my lord. I own I *am* amazed at how ready the ladies of London are to follow Paris styles. Though there are some that I hope never reach you. When I was there last I sat in a loge at the theater with a duchess who wore an entire pheasant in her turban. I missed half the performance because of the tail feathers."

He laughed, then said, "And when were you last in Paris?"

"A month or two ago."

"So was I! I went to France as part of a delegation from the British government to His Imperial Majesty." He continued thoughtfully, "We must have just missed each other, on many occasions. What a pity I didn't make your acquaintance there. It was a difficult mission—meeting you would have very much lightened the load."

"Ah. You do character sketches too, then. How do you see me: as a balloon? A bubble?"

He looked a little disconcerted. He was one of those men who didn't listen to their own compliments—he considered it enough to make them at all. But he recovered, and smiled. "Something like . . . a benevolent sprite. I'm sure you can work magic, mademoiselle, and all unconsciously too."

A mindless sprite? "What were your difficulties? Was the emperor very hard to deal with?"

He frowned. "We were seeking an exchange of prisoners. It should have been a decent, straightforward business, but the whole thing bogged down in petty arguments. We came home without a settlement. But my colleagues in the Foreign Office will probably sort it out in a month or two. No thanks to French bureaucracy." Then he seemed to recollect to whom he was speaking and went on, "I confess, Miss Dalgleish, I'm probably rather too demanding a fellow to take care of such an affair. When something's for the good of my countrymen, I like to get it done. At once."

He was a fine figure of aristocratic impatience as he said it too. Delphine, looking at him sidelong, had to admit that Lord Ferron was impressive, for he had the manner that went with power, ease and decision. As for his company, he enjoyed lively conversation, and she had some hopes of his liking her. He could be challenged too—but not too far. The image of a bubble came to her mind again and the corners of her lips twitched. By far her best ploy was to bounce along beside him, flimsy, iridescent and as unthreatening as a child's plaything.

Just then a line of revellers crossed in front of them—all women, dressed in bright, elaborate gowns that must be intended for some sort of charade, and with headdresses that were a riot of colored feathers. Delphine exclaimed, "Oh, how pretty. And there is a pheasant!"

The figure turned, and to Delphine's embarrassment she realized it was a man.

"*Husband* of the pheasant, I think," Lord Ferron murmured in her ear, and Delphine joined him in helpless laughter.

The feathered crowd moved out of their way, and it was at this hilarious point in the evening that Delphine looked ahead and saw Sir Gideon Landor walking toward her.

Gideon had come to Vauxhall with a group of friends from the club, but he had left them at one of the gazebos drinking champagne and waiting for some fireworks that were supposed to happen on the river.

It jolted him to see Delphine Dalgleish—avoiding her so assiduously had given him a false sense of his own imperviousness. She had the knack of appearing to belong wherever she was, which must have had something to do with her natural grace, or her sparkling eyes. She was vividly present, as though no part of her mind were off dreaming of other places or other times. She was engaged, body and spirit, with this fleeting moment, totally at home in this setting of shadows and glimmering lights, as though she had just arrived on earth, quivering and complete.

It took him a moment to realize who the dark figure was beside her. Lord Ferron. They were laughing together like old friends; she had made pretty considerable inroads into society, then, since he last saw her! He recognized that complacent look on Ferron's face too.

She looked down as she drew nearer. He had the unpleasant sensation that she was about to pass him by, clinging for protection to Ferron's arm. God knew what her feelings were about him, but his neglect of her must have had some result, and he could scarcely blame her if she ignored him in return.

But when he came abreast of them, she raised her head and said in her low, appealing voice, "I declare—Sir Gideon!" Gideon stopped, Ferron turned his head and they met. Mademoiselle Dalgleish glowed with animation: "What a quantity of meetings tonight! We are here with Miss Georgiana Howland. Did you see her as you came on?"

Ferron said, nodding toward a pergola that led away toward the riverbank, "They ducked off in that direction. Best way to avoid the crowd."

Gideon said, "And how did you come to the gardens, Mademoiselle Dalgleish? I remember you once debated the approach— by water or by land."

"Oh, by land, monsieur. Was that excessively timid of me?"

"I think you'll find, in summer the river offers by far the better prospect. But I'm biased, perhaps."

Ferron said, "Hardly worth discussing at this time of year. Anyone out boating in this season needs their wits examined."

Ferron on the offensive always sounded pompous. Gideon examined Mademoiselle Dalgleish to see whether she thought the same.

She smiled at them both. "I believe fireworks are rumored. Shall we stroll down and be surprised?"

Gideon nodded and gestured for them to precede him, and as they turned in under the pergola he caught up with her and walked on one side while Ferron occupied the other. She had let go his lordship's arm, which Gideon tried not to find encouraging. He could see that Ferron resented his intrusion, but Gideon was by no means sure what she felt.

"I've just discovered," she said, "that Lord Ferron and I were in Paris recently at the same time, though we never met."

"How is that?"

"British delegation," Ferron said. "Negotiating an exchange of prisoners of war." He glanced at Gideon. "Might have done you an indirect favor for all I know. When did you get back?"

"Well before you," Gideon said dryly. Meanwhile, he could not help recalling the intense encounter with Mademoiselle Dalgleish in the rue Saint-Honoré. He said across her head, "You were in Paris when?"

"February," Ferron said.

She looked up. "Ah, then we could not have met. My mother and I arrived there in March."

As they walked on toward the river, Gideon thought what a strange situation she was in, accompanied on one side by a noble representative of His Majesty's Foreign Office, and on the other by a secret agent employed by the Aliens branch. She must be fully aware of it—but what did she think? If she were comparing him with Ferron, he had a notion that he must be the one to lose out. Lord Ferron occupied a position of responsibility and privilege without shame. He, on the other hand, had willingly chosen a course that relied on secrecy and subterfuge.

It almost silenced him. But not quite. For one thing, he had always thought Ferron unreliable. His lordship wasn't likely to impress Mademoiselle Dalgleish for long; she was too perceptive. "I trust your mother is well, mademoiselle?"

"Yes, thank you."

"Please convey my compliments to her. And tell her I should be glad to call on you when convenient. I've given some thought to your situation at Saint-Amour; perhaps we could discuss it further."

She looked up at him. "Oh. I thought you had quite forgot!"

"I hope not, mademoiselle."

"My mother is at home between two and four on Thursdays. Do feel free to call." She went on in a mischievous tone, "Maman will be *so* gratified. She was beginning to think you might find Berkeley Square not quite the thing to visit."

"Surely not," he said. "Why? I'm in Curzon Street myself, just around the corner."

So close, yet you haven't called. Gideon caught Ferron's subtle smile out of the corner of his eye, and cursed inwardly. If they were in a competition to be agreeable to Mademoiselle Dalgleish, Ferron was winning hands down.

The lady talked nonsense all the way to the riverbank, most of her remarks being capped by Ferron in his careless way. When they got there, they joined a large crowd. Gideon exchanged a few words with Georgiana and Combrewood, who were standing a few paces off, but then took up his place by Mademoiselle Dalgleish again, determined to handle things better than he had so far. There was no reason to let this slip of a young woman cause him discomfort. "Bonaparte is fond of fireworks too, I believe. You must have been in Paris for the celebrations when his son was born?"

"I was. They were spectacular. As a matter of fact, I found his joy very touching."

"He has cut all his siblings out of the line of succession, has he not? The child is his only heir."

"Yes." She pursed her lips a little, then said ironically, "The emperor has a very selective policy with his family. It's quite hard to keep up with who is in and who is out."

"Mademoiselle, this is the first time I've ever heard you say anything that smacks of the slightest criticism."

Ferron interrupted, "I fancy Miss Dalgleish is referring to the treatment of the emperor's brother, Lucien Bonaparte. He waxes pretty lyrical on that subject himself, I can tell you."

"You know him?" she exclaimed.

"We're neighbors. My seat is in Worcestershire."

"I've never met him. What is he like?"

"Dashed pleasing company, as a matter of fact. He's frantically confused in his politics; don't think he has an idea where he stands. But that doesn't matter now, of course. He keeps a fine establishment and his art collection is a treat to see. If you like French and Italian painting, he's your man."

At that moment the fireworks began, catching Mademoiselle Dalgleish by surprise. She jumped and clutched Gideon's arm with both hands, sending a shiver of response through him, but she quickly took her fingers away and pressed them to her lips.

"Oh, how silly of me," she said with a muffled laugh, as showers of golden sparks leaped out over the dark water. "Why are they *always* so much louder than I expect?"

Ferron reached over and placed her hand on his arm. "Would you care to stand a little farther away? We can go up there on the knoll."

"Thank you, no, it's all right." She withdrew her hand; Gideon could see she was annoyed with herself. They watched the display for a while, then in a lull she said, "For a general's daughter, I'm a sad case. You gentlemen are quite at home with your guns, but somehow I've never become accustomed to explosions."

Gideon was perturbed. "You mean you traveled with your father on campaign?"

She shuddered. "Oh, no." She wasn't looking at him. "The closest I've ever come to a conflict, Sir Gideon, was when the British army marched down from our mountains and into Port Napoleon."

He could imagine it. The troops that had landed in the south of Mauritius must have gone by Saint-Amour—they might even have tramped through it. Glancing at her averted face, he dared not ask. She had no right to try to make him feel guilty over that affair! He said, "Thank goodness you've never been in the midst of a battle. It's not a distinction anyone craves."

"Oh, really?" Ferron said. "Isn't that the only way you military fellows can get on?"

Gideon flashed back, "It depends whether you see warfare as a career or as a way of serving your country."

She gave Gideon a satirical look at this, which he could not

read. Did she consider him ruthlessly ambitious? He realized with
a shock that so far he had given her every reason to think so.

She said, "Pray, what was the worst battle of your experience,
Sir Gideon?"

He grimaced; it was impossible to believe that this was a serious question. The answer crashed into his consciousness, however, and he gave it, even knowing that his two listeners were
quite indifferent. "The Battle of the Nile."

She flinched, but she had asked, after all. It was one of
France's most devastating defeats, in which Lord Nelson smashed
the French fleet and ruined forever Napoleon's dream of pushing through the Levant to India.

She said in thin voice, "Oh. Why?"

It came painfully back: the massive explosion, the obscene
bloom of flames over the night-drowned harbor, as the French
L'Orient was ripped apart and blew herself and hundreds of
enemy officers and men into oblivion. He remembered the heat
on his face, the impact that hammered deep into his brain.

Out on the Thames, another rocket slammed into the air from
its raft midstream, and he watched as it arced and shattered,
showering silver stars toward a thousand upturned faces. "Because I saw our power to destroy. Once seen, never forgotten."

"I've heard worse things of Trafalgar," Ferron said. "We lost
Nelson there, after all. I imagine that occasion might have meant
something, had you been present."

"I was," Gideon said involuntarily. He had not meant to set
Ferron right—why should he care whether the man knew? "Pray
forgive us, Mademoiselle Dalgleish. You cannot wish to hear this
kind of talk."

"I must own," she said, her voice rather brittle, "there are
times when I regret that our old association with Bonaparte is so
well known in London. It does make people feel awkward. And
you cannot imagine," she said more brightly, favoring them both
with a stunning smile, "how *very* far that is from my wishes. Lord
Ferron has been kind enough to tell me," she remarked to
Gideon, "that we French should consider ourselves an *addition* to
society. We shall strive to deserve such encouragement."

Ferron smiled. "Mademoiselle, you are an ornament to fine company. And have been since the day you arrived."

Gideon, who was not to be drawn into this flattery, looked on in silence. What did she mean by mentioning her association with Bonaparte as "old"? Was this a clue that she considered it well and truly over? Had the Bonapartist in her begun to give way before the vision of a new future under British rule?

There was the cousin, though, back in Paris, with whom she no doubt found means to correspond. Armand de Belfort had clearly done well for himself on his return to France; his skills and trustworthiness must be very highly regarded if he had found a post in Bonaparte's Bureau of Codes. Mademoiselle Dalgleish's links to the top in France were nowhere near as tenuous as she would like people to think. "And how was Monsieur de Belfort when you left Paris?"

She looked startled but she gave him an answer, which was too low for Ferron to hear, for just then a phalanx of roman candles erupted along the bank, raising a great gasp from the crowd. "I'm sure you know perfectly well."

"How should I?"

She shot him an accusatory look very similar to the one she'd given him in the rue Saint-Honoré in March. Great God, she had found him out as a spy, but she could hardly believe one foray into Paris would make him omniscient! He said, "I know precisely nothing about your cousin, mademoiselle. The last time I saw him—and I pray it *was* the last, for both our sakes—was in the Maison Despeaux. I asked out of courtesy. If you don't care to discuss him, I can well bear the deprivation."

On the other side, Ferron gave a sarcastic chuckle. "Especially since you're in possession of his yacht!"

"The navy has it," Gideon said coldly.

Not surprisingly there was a pause after this, filled with the final, magnificent bursts of fireworks. Mademoiselle Dalgleish, banishing her nervousness, looked skyward in delight, and Gideon was struck by the wonder on her face. She was an extraordinary young woman. She still had the bubbly eagerness of spirit that she must have had as a child, but she also had a

woman's powers of seduction, all the more effective because they
were natural and spontaneous. Her gaiety brought genuine
smiles, and when the mood changed and she flashed him a different kind of look, he felt the force of it, because she was not
afraid to reveal her feelings.

She was fascinating without being false, and candid without
ever being discourteous. Ferron was wrong—Delphine Dalgleish
was no mere ornament; she was a splendid prize. One that he
could never claim.

The thrilling display drew to a close, then the three of them
joined Georgiana Howland's party and trailed up the slope
toward supper tables spread in a summerhouse that Combrewood had hired.

Delphine was perplexed about Landor. He had responded to
her flirtation with him at Lady Melbourne's ball, but his manners
tonight were more controlled. He thought nothing of Ferron,
though his pride never let him step into rudeness. He was self-
sufficient in a way that she occasionally found intimidating. She
persisted in trying to entertain him, however, because being playful with him gave her the opportunity to be so with Lord Ferron,
and that, after all, was the great object. Ferron had even talked
about his visit to Paris, and with great readiness. If she could persuade him that she was leaning toward all things English, perhaps
it might not be so very long before she could coax the full story
out of him about his attempt to buy Napoleon's code. This charade might soon be over, weeks before the emperor could have
hoped, and before she embroiled herself at all in Ferron's
affections.

The thought made her behave very cheerfully with his lordship when they sat down to supper. It was informal, the gentlemen sitting amongst the ladies rather than opposite at the long
table, and she spent the whole meal murmuring half-thought
replies to the attentive Ferron. Sir Gideon was farther down the
board but facing her, seated next to Georgiana Howland. She
could feel him often observing her. He looked away at once if
she happened to glance up, but the surveillance was there, and
his look seemed one of disapprobation. She was Bonapartist, to

be sure—but he was on the same side! And sly, treacherous and underhand into the bargain. How dared he lack decent respect for Lord Ferron when that gentleman was a loyal English diplomat? A rather ill-advised one, if Napoleon was right about his activities behind the scenes in Paris, but true in his allegiances. The contemptuous Sir Gideon Landor, however, was a double agent. *Bon dieu,* he should be grateful to her that she kept his secrets safe!

The close of the evening brought no change in his demeanor. He softened enough to make Georgiana Howland smile and laugh—for he could be agreeable enough to ladies when he wanted—but he was distant with Delphine.

On Thursday, she was faced with the choice of staying in for his visit (supposing he lived up to his word) or avoiding him. She imagined how he would appear—his tall form looming into the salon, his green gaze dousing her spirits like a stinging splash of seawater, his handsome mouth set in severe lines.

So it was that, when Sir Gideon Landor was admitted to Mrs. Laidlaw's in Berkeley Square that afternoon, he found only la Générale at home.

Julie Dalgleish rather relished spending time with the baronet and was sorry that Delphine's dislike of him had made her leave the house. It was clear to Julie's expert eye that Delphine was physically attracted to Landor—a conflict of feelings over which she had no control. For her part, Julie approved of him. The awful business of the yacht notwithstanding, from the first night they met she had found him straightforward, upright . . . and undeniably handsome. Landor was a gentleman, in the best sense of the word. The questions he asked about the problems at Saint-Amour were telling without being intrusive, and he listened to her replies with sympathetic attention. He was someone to whom any woman could instinctively turn for help. Perhaps that was what so confused Delphine, for she had never learned to see him as anything but the enemy.

At one point he said, "I'm afraid my knowledge of military catering stops at how pursers go about their duty in the navy. But the principle seems to be the same everywhere—they try to beat suppliers down to the lowest price. Suppliers do have a choice, though: not to sell. I had a good talk to someone at the navy office in Somerset House the other day, and I can tell you that no garrison in peacetime has the right to force any trader or farmer to sell at prices fixed by the military."

"I think we know that," Julie sighed. "Our problem is convincing Captain Arkwright."

"I have a suggestion, madame. On our family properties in Wiltshire, a proportion of the harvest is sold each year to merchants in Salisbury. Those merchants try to do the same as the navy pursers—drive prices down. But they're prevented from hammering them too flat, because my father and the landowners in the area form a loose association. There's competition amongst them of course, and often it's pretty fierce, but they draw a line on price. Our stewards get together each summer and decide on a figure below which they pledge never to sell. Now, it's my guess there must be an arrangement of the sort amongst plantation owners on Mauritius. Are you aware of it?"

Julie shook her head. "Oh, dear. If there is, Armand never mentioned it. But he took so little trouble to . . . I shall have to ask my daughter."

He looked skeptical. "Mademoiselle Dalgleish?"

"Saint-Amour is hers, monsieur. She has run the estate ever since my husband, the general, passed away."

"I don't quite follow. Monsieur de Belfort gave me to understand that the estate was his, by some form of entailment."

"Oh, no. Not at all. In the will, Armand was made executor and offered a large stipend if he agreed to come to Mauritius and act as steward until Delphine's majority. Which he did. I was left a very generous annuity. But Saint-Amour went to my daughter, whole and entire. And will pass direct to her children, there being no other claimants on the Dalgleish or the Belfort sides." She smiled serenely and examined his face. She could see he was surprised by this news of Delphine's inheritance, but his firm features gave nothing else away.

He said, "All that considered, I should say Farquhar will be obliged to accept your daughter's signature on the oath of allegiance. If the same situation pertained in England, no one would have any doubt; one of my aunts is a countess in her own right, and she signs everything relating to her property. The governor must be made to understand that Monsieur de Belfort stands quite outside the equation and Mademoiselle Dalgleish has full powers. Would you like me to investigate legal opinion on that for you?"

"You think it would help?"

"Most probably. A stiffly worded letter to Farquhar should do the trick. You should wait for his reply before returning to Saint-Amour, whereupon Farquhar will have no choice but to remove Arkwright from his position. Your daughter will then be able to employ her own steward, someone who knows how to get on with the other plantation owners and protect her interests in trade."

"You make it sound so clear!" Julie breathed. "Thank you. You are the first person to give us such encouraging advice. It's refreshing to receive a gentleman's view on our problems."

He smiled slightly, unwilling to be thanked. "I think a good first step would be to get the legal advice. I shall make sure to find you a name." He rose. "Is there any other service I may offer you, before I go?"

She got to her feet. "You have done a great deal already."

His lips twitched. "Not all of it for your convenience!"

She held out her hand. "Oh, monsieur, on that subject I'm ready to forgive and forget."

He took her fingers lightly and kissed her hand. "And your daughter?"

Julie gave a little laugh. "Above all, my daughter needs friends, and I'm not sure that she realizes quite how much."

"Please tell Mademoiselle Dalgleish that I regret missing her today. And do let her know that there is a regatta at Richmond tomorrow that she and her friends may like to see. I know she takes a great interest in boating."

"Does she?" Julie said, then added, "Are you attending, sir?"

"No, I shall be at Greenwich."

After he had gone, Julie sat down and wondered whether there might be a little game of attraction and avoidance going on. But which player felt the stronger force of it was very hard to make out.

Thorngrove

It was the glorious month of July, and Delphine had fallen in love. Despite being accustomed all her life to the spectacular luxuriance of Mauritius and the verdant plateau around Paris, she had never seen anything as seductive as the English country-side. It was deliciously unexpected: the rolling green hills capped by well-tended coppices, the streams rushing through the valleys between, crossed by tiny, narrow stone bridges so pretty that she shared none of the Duc de Limours's concern about the risk to the lacquer on his carriage doors if they scraped against the masonry. Ever since the travelers had left the neat and prosperous city of Worcester, the sky had been cobalt blue and the only clouds very high and very white, drifting above the horizon to the west as though trying to decide whether to mount a reconnaissance there or put about and sail away, across Herefordshire, North Wales and the Irish Sea.

The trees were in their darkest and greenest leaf, the oaks set like magnificent crowns above the woods, the poplars in shimmering columns beside the canals and the horse chestnuts so rich in shade that in the village of Claines a single tree sheltered the whole square under its canopy. Beyond, in the clockfaces of fields that each held a village at its fulcrum, wheat and rye ripened in giant segments of pale gold and amber.

The duke traveled in style and comfort, and to Delphine this excursion in high summer was an opportunity to leave London, just like the rest of good society, and enjoy a long sojourn in the countryside. The invitation to make up a house party at Lucien Bonaparte's Worcestershire mansion was an open one, and the duke had told them he rarely stayed there less than a month, for the hospitality was liberal and the company refined. But Julie Dalgleish had declared she liked Mrs. Laidlaw's card evenings too much to stir from the city.

"I'm sorry Madame Dalgleish wasn't able to accompany us," the duke said in French as they clattered out of an inn yard on the last afternoon of their journey. "She's not concealing some ill health, I hope?"

As he spoke, his sister, the dowager Comtesse D'Auvennois, leaned a little forward and looked at Delphine inquiringly. The duke, a widower, lived and traveled with his sister, who was some years older than he and so deaf that no one, including the duke, troubled to try drawing her into the conversation. But she took part in her own way, often mimicking her brother's gestures, with a kind smile that made her pleasant if comical company.

Delphine shook her head. "She is quite well, thank you. Mrs. Laidlaw's friends like to stay in town, even during the hot months, and they carry on their entertainments just the same as usual. Mrs. Laidlaw allows quite high stakes at her tables. I sometimes wonder if Maman is growing rather too fond of gambling!"

He smiled. "You don't think she may have a private objection to frequenting Thorngrove?"

He was a shrewd old man. The same idea had occurred to Delphine, but her mother had left it unvoiced so that Delphine should not be made to feel guilty about visiting Napoleon's disgraced brother. "She hasn't the curiosity about England that I have. I think Maman may be more homesick for Mauritius than I, but reluctant to admit it."

She tried to gauge the duke's reaction to this. He intrigued her; eighteen years in the country but still showing no obvious commitment to it. He had neither remarried nor purchased land, and he was most at ease in French circles, though he was a respected figure in English high society. Did the Duc de Limours ever feel nostalgic about his homeland? If so, and if he could convince Napoleon that his allegiances had changed, he might well be able to return. The emperor saw advantages in wooing the old aristocracy and might be persuaded to restore some of the duke's privileges, as a reward for support from one of France's oldest

families. Instead, Limours was still here, and what's more he frat-
ernized regularly with the "traitor," Lucien Bonaparte.

He said, "How are your affairs going forward? Have you heard
yet about Saint-Amour?"

"No, it's too soon. We sent the letter in May."

To her astonishment, Sir Gideon Landor had been of tremendous help in the battle against Farquhar. After consulting with
her mother he had moved quickly to get them expert legal advice, and then prevailed upon one of the top lawyers in the Admiralty to act for them. Correspondence had been initiated with
Mauritius at a high level, and without any hitches at the Foreign
Office. Julie was deeply grateful, while Delphine suspected that
Landor's clandestine influence was being exerted in their favor,
and marveled again at his talent for intrigue.

She and Landor encountered each other seldom, despite the
fact that he had lately been spending quite a lot of time in French
émigré society and was as familiar with the Duc de Limours as
she. On the rare occasions when they did meet, she was polite
and pleasant, in recognition of his efforts regarding Saint-Amour,
and he returned the courtesy, presumably in gratitude for her ret-
icence about what he was really up to in London. He must be in
league with the covert Bonapartists. And for all she knew, the
chief of them was sitting opposite her now, bowling along in his
own coach, on the way to check out Napoleon's controversial
brother.

She had thought of asking the Duc de Limours outright
whether he was an ally in the emperor's cause. But it would confirm her own Bonapartist sympathies while giving her no guarantee of unearthing his. He had been encouraging pro-English
sentiments in her ever since they met, and his cover as a royalist,
if it were a cover, was very well established. She was frightened to
make such an attempt before performing her mission. She
wanted no complications at Thorngrove. Once she had reached
there and handed the emperor's letter to Lucien Bonaparte, a
weight would fall from her shoulders and she could concentrate
properly on her other mission—dealing with Lord Ferron.

There, at any rate, she could claim some success. By chance or by contrivance on Ferron's part, they happened to see a lot of each other, and on all occasions he was admiring and partial. He might not yet be in marrying or even in very confidential mode, but he had issued an invitation to the Dalgleishes to visit his Worcestershire seat in September. There, in his old family home, Delphine intended to lay bare the secrets of Ferron's diplomatic life. Without, she trusted, lifting a single veil on her own.

Gideon was at his club, seated in a smoking room drinking coffee. He had a newspaper open but he wasn't reading; he was wondering how Ellis was getting on in a tricky expedition to the coast.

Gideon had been pursuing the Bonapartist connection in two ways: keeping up his own surveillance of the French aristocrats in London, and putting Ellis in command of a team to follow up on couriers used to convey information to the Channel coast. It stood to reason he would eventually detect whose servants were employed for this purpose, what route they took to the sea and how they got over to France. Tonight Ellis and a bit of hired help were tracking a promising fellow down into Kent.

Gideon was inclined to think that the head of Bonapartist espionage in London was the Duc de Limours. But there were a few things against this theory. For one, it seemed too bloody obvious. Then again, these people were amateurs; the obvious, the careless and the plain idiotic were their stock in trade. There were hotheaded royalists all over France doing just the same sort of thing in reverse, launching their pitiful schemes like so many leaky boats, and going to the bottom in consequence. The money the Aliens Office spent on these poor fools must be colossal compared with what Napoleon spared to his faithful in London, who probably collected military information out of pure zeal for the emperor.

These days Gideon felt unbearably restive, trapped amongst a mob of cloth-headed conspirators for whom he could feel no respect. At sea, it was different. British naval intelligence was the best in the world and it served England nobly. His yearning to sail the new frigate away down the Thames grew stronger every week. Meanwhile, his investigation into the Duc de Limours perturbed him; he was nervous about what he would find. One of his reasons for suspecting the duke was that gentleman's close association with Mademoiselle Dalgleish, whose Bonapartist convictions Gideon knew better than anyone else in London. If Gideon found out that the duke was involved in clandestine exchanges of information with Paris, he might also uncover her activities. And he hated the idea.

He would much rather the lady's newfound ease and enjoyment in London be genuine. He would very much prefer to see her relish the comforts of a secure income from Mauritius and the favored social position she now occupied in London. She had found her niche, if she would but admit it. By contrast, she had everything to lose by hitching her star to Boney's.

All at once he heard her name. Three men, youngish by the sound of their voices, had been drinking at a table not far behind him. One of them, the fellow who tended to hold the floor, had just come out with a nickname: "la duchesse," used of Delphine Dalgleish lately because of her close friendship with Limours.

"She might be doochess in earnest soon, Elliott. You'll have to move smartly, old friend. The ancient duke is besotted, so they tell me."

Elliott, whose voice Gideon recognized, protested. "Oh, I say. She may have her pick of London. That's a French friendship, nothing more."

"Reckon you could make an Englishwoman of her, then, Elliott?" a third voice chimed in. "Shown you the right favors, has she?"

The ringleader called the discussion to order. "No, it'll be an English county seat or nothing for the *delectable* Delphine."

"Steady on, Formby," Elliott said.

"I didn't make it up! She earned that one on Mauritius, dallying with a British naval officer—what's his name—Flinders! He was married, though."

"Lord Ferron ain't," the third voice said thoughtfully.

"So you think she has her sights on Ferron?" said Formby. "Hellish tough nut to crack, that one. On the other hand, she's definitely promising favors in that direction. What kind of bet do

I have on Lord Ferron?" Gideon actually heard a rustle of paper, as though the young bastard were getting out a notebook to write it down.

Elliott said in a loud, tipsy voice, "You may count me out. Honor of a lady at stake. The most beautiful lady I ever met."

The third voice said, "I think *delectable* was the word, Elliott. Put me down for fifty."

Formby said, "I'm offering odds of two to one. You still on?"

"Do we have any other runners?" A pause, a clink of glasses and a few sniggers. "Wait a minute! There's another party in tip-top form, hails from the navy. You know: Sir Gideon Landor. Why don't we bring him in?"

Formby said, "Careful; keep it down. He's a member."

It was then that a gentleman walked around the chair into their midst. Formby looked up. And up. And recognized Landor. The baronet turned toward him, and cold green eyes pierced his. Formby had never been a midshipman, but he suddenly had a chilling idea what it must be like to be one, in deep trouble.

Landor was not smiling. This was possibly a hopeful sign. A polite smile would have announced destruction; for the moment this was qualified disaster. Formby slipped the bit of paper into his pocket.

Landor ignored the others, which Formby thought unfair, and said quietly, "Take an interest in Mauritius, do you?"

There was no choice but to answer. "Of sorts, yes. Passing interest."

"You may know that on the island there's a curious geographical phenomenon known as the Cul. A thousand-foot drop into a narrow chasm. Heard of it?"

"No," Formby stammered. "Not as such."

"On Mauritius, when any man is heard talking errant nonsense, he is taken up to the top of the Cul and pushed off. To encourage the others, you understand. I wonder, do you think I should have someone seek out a handy spot in England that would serve the same purpose?"

"With all due respect, Sir Gideon, I don't think that's necessary."

"No?"

The smile did appear at that point, and Formby gulped. "Quite unnecessary. You have my word."

"Thank you."

For some time after the baronet had strolled off into the gaming room there wasn't a word around the drinking table. Then the three friends leaned forward and grabbed their wineglasses. After another pause, Formby said in a resentful murmur, "Bloody hell; I don't suppose there's any such thing as a bloody Cul on Mauritius."

Elliott's mouth thinned into a half smile. "There ain't, that I know of. He made it up. He's an inventive bugger, Landor."

Formby looked across the table. "Anyone know what 'cul' means?"

"Arse."

Formby laughed very low in what he hoped was a careless manner. "Pity I've closed the book. I tell you what; I'd raise the odds on Landor."

Supper at Thorngrove was as leisurely as the daytime activities. Everyone at the table was French and so were the wines, while the superb meals combined the artistry of a Paris chef with the fresh flavors plucked from Thorngrove's kitchen garden or fished from the Severn River, which ran nearby. Delphine liked the company, the priceless paintings on the walls, the jovial ambience and most of all the conversation.

With Lucien Bonaparte and his wife, there was no shyness about ideas or events, and the host's rift with his brother was freely discussed. Lucien, to Delphine's eye, shared some of his brother's passionate intelligence, while his high brow and determined chin reflected the light in a different way—he was the firmest republican in the Bonaparte family, and when Napoleon had begun to dismantle the republic he had been the first to stand up to him. Alexandrine, once Lucien's mistress and now his wife, shared his exile and captivity with a courage that expressed itself in her handsomely molded features and lustrous eyes.

Delphine found that the children were rather fun as well.

There was a domestic harmony at Thorngrove that informed the whole gathering, so that tossing horseshoes on the lawn or debating the pope's next move in central Italy provided equal stimulation. Thorngrove felt like a haven, not a prison. The Bonapartes could not leave the estate, but they had surprising freedom concerning the people they invited to it.

Delphine thought about this at the end of the evening, when the older members of the party had trailed away to the bedchambers upstairs and a few people lingered below, talking in pairs or leaning as she did against the embrasure of a window, fanning herself and looking up at the stars. It was like a French summer evening, such as she had never dreamed of experiencing in England. She felt exhilarated—and at home.

Lucien Bonaparte came to stand on the other side of the window, leaning one shoulder against the wall. He didn't speak for a moment and neither did she. The only movement was the regular beat of her pierced tortoiseshell fan, and the light from nearby candles caught the spangles on it so that they winked like tiny stars.

Finally she said, "I've been thinking of how tolerant my hosts are. Here I am in a party that includes émigrés from the republic, royalists of every persuasion, children of empire, republican theorists—and you even invite the English sometimes! If I were you, with such a quarrelsome crowd I'm afraid I should fall back on telling everyone what to think." She slid the fan shut and held it against her chin, studying him.

He gave a short laugh. "It's our pleasure to hear people talk, mademoiselle, especially when our guests are as charming as you. Fate has set me adrift for a time and I'm cut off from the world. To live as I would wish to live, I must ask the world to come to me. If it didn't come in all its variety, I should be losing a very precious gift." He moved closer, to look out at the terraced lawn. "The Duc de Limours tells me that you were received by my brother at the Tuileries in March."

It was said mildly, but she started. She had not told the Duc de Limours about her visits. She had not told anyone in London that she had seen Napoleon in person. So how had the duke found out? But she must answer. "I was."

"May I ask how he seemed? In health, in spirits?"

"I—" She owed it to her host to cause the least pain. "I was in the Tuileries at the birth of the King of Rome. Would you like me to tell you about it?"

"Certainly; I'd be grateful."

She told the story simply, and as it unfolded she saw how it touched him, for it was about family, about his older brother's first child. Lucien and Alexandrine already had children when the long-awaited son was born to Napoleon. And she was describing Napoleon to Lucien not as the tyrant of Europe or the destroyer of the French republic, but in his first minutes as a father.

He listened with his lips pressed together, and when she ceased she thought he looked sad, but he said only, "Our mother wouldn't go to Paris for the birth; she stayed in Italy. She takes my side in our dispute." He shook his head. "I think she should have gone."

A languid stream of air stirred the drapes at Delphine's elbow and sent a drift of perfume into the room. She glanced around and saw that everyone had retired but the hostess, who was watching the servants clear tabletops at the other end of the room. "Monsieur le comte, the emperor has written to you. He gave me a sealed letter and asked me to bring it to England. No one else knows that I have it. It's here, in my reticule. May I give it to you?"

He stared at her and his dark eyes grew somber. A quiver of the lips told her what he might look like when he was angry. Much like Napoleon, in fact. "And what is it? A diatribe?"

"I have no idea. But when he was persuading me to bring it, he took pains to tell me that it held no . . ."

"Threats? Demands?" But something in her expression mollified him. "Thank you, mademoiselle. I thank you *now*, in case the words fail me when I've read it. You may hand it to me."

She slipped the loop of her fan over her wrist, opened the reticule and took out the small, folded piece of paper.

"Come," he said, and led her to the nearby table and candles. She let him hand her into a chair, then looked up as he paused on the other side of the table. He said, "You will do me the favor of waiting until I've read it. By way of response, you will convey my reaction to the emperor."

"I'm not authorized to take a reply! I'm not even sure that I shall ever see him again."

He looked over her head, toward his wife, who was still at the end of the room but must have turned to observe them. He gave a quick shake of the head in her direction, then sat down at the table. Fixing Delphine with a direct gaze, he said, "If this contains any insults to my wife, I shall give it back to you at the first word."

"If I had the slightest suspicion of that, I wouldn't have brought it into your house."

He broke the seal and opened out the letter. The candlelight showed Napoleon's handwriting in reverse to Delphine through the paper but she could not decypher it. She could tell, however, that the letter consisted of a dozen lines, no more. Was it so short because Napoleon had scratched it in a rage, to make some telling point? Or had he been sincere when he implied he had written it in a burst of emotion? She could not tell from Lucien's face. He read it at least three times before he looked up. His expression was still dark and resentful, but there was a deeper sadness in his eyes. He looked beyond Delphine again and beckoned with the same hand, fingers curved downward. Delphine heard Alexandrine coming forward as he murmured, "He writes well, when his heart is in it."

Alexandrine came to the table and took Lucien's hand, then stood beside him so that their interlaced fingers lay on his shoulder and they leaned toward each other, like two figures in a classical painting. As she looked at them, Delphine wondered again how Napoleon could ever have stooped to trying to divide them.

Lucien raised his face to his wife. "Mademoiselle Dalgleish has done us a service. Here is a letter from my brother. You may read it."

Alexandrine smiled down. "Thank you. I shall do so tomorrow. Today has been perfect; such happiness needs no addition."

Saint-Amour

⁓

The Duc de Limours and his sister intended to stay a fortnight, and Delphine was very happy to stay on with them and relax into the well-managed life of Thorngrove. She would not question Limours under the Bonapartes' roof—she could sound him out on the trip home. Delphine suspected that one of the benefits he brought to the Bonapartes of Thorngrove was information. On whose behalf, she intended to find out.

Meanwhile the weather continued warm and she enjoyed spending time outside. Lucien Bonaparte's four eldest children, by his first wife, who had died in 1800, were too dignified for boisterous pursuits, but the youngest children liked to join Delphine at the ornamental pond in the kitchen garden; the Bonapartes were having a summerhouse built in the grounds and the children claimed pieces of wood to make yachts.

One afternoon Delphine was sitting on the rim of the pond holding a yacht that belonged to the littlest boy, Paul, who was three. "It turns *over*," he said and stamped his feet.

"The sail is wet. Perhaps that makes it top-heavy."

"It doesn't *move*."

A shadow fell across the pond and a deep voice said, "Let me see what I can do, if mademoiselle will permit. She knows I'm a sailor."

Delphine dropped the yacht with a splash and looked up into the sun. Two yards away, his face in shade so that she guessed rather than saw his cold but composed expression, was Sir Gideon Landor.

"Mademoiselle D'Alglice," he continued in French, "I apologize; I didn't mean to startle you."

"Don't give it a thought. I should be used to it by now!"

As always, looking into her wide blue eyes gave Gideon a shock—it was as though she were attracted to him, but he frightened her. Then she rose lithely to her feet. He was sorry; he had admired the picture as he walked across the garden and sunlight rippling off the pond dappled her dress and danced across her fair skin. She was more beautiful every time he saw her.

She was also annoyed with him, though she managed a correct curtsy and a scintillating smile. "And what gives us the pleasure of your company, Sir Gideon?"

There was a hidden accusation: that he was here to spy. Before he could reply, however, Alexandrine Bonaparte stepped into the garden. "I'm so sorry; I was held up by . . ." She looked from one to the other. "You've met?"

"Mademoiselle Dalgleish and I are very well acquainted. I was about to explain the nature of your kind invitation." He turned back to the demoiselle. "I've just hired an architect to build me a summerhouse at Landor, but I've seen none of his work. He told me there was one of his buildings completing at Thorngrove, and suggested I write asking if I could call."

"And we wrote back," the hostess said, "to say that there's nothing my husband likes better than showing off about architecture. Sir Gideon, I hope you'll stay more than a day. You have already met the Duc de Limours, he tells me. We have provided friends for you without knowing it!"

"I'm more grateful than I can say." He caught Mademoiselle Dalgleish's eye. "I had no idea you were here. Or Limours." An unpleasant phrase ran through his head at the name: *the ancient duke is besotted.*

She gave him a satirical stare, then bent to pick the boat out of the water. "Children," she said, "this gentleman is Sir Gideon Landor." She introduced Charles, Letitia, Johanna and Paul, and they greeted him without enthusiasm—he had interrupted their game. She meanwhile stood holding the boat, drops from the sail sparkling on her dress.

"May I inspect the vessel, mademoiselle?"

The children's curiosity revived as she stepped around the

pool and released the thing into his hands. She was wearing a floral scent that blended with those from the sun-drenched garden, but it still penetrated him.

The smallest boy came to her side and slipped his wet hand into hers. "It tips *over.*"

Gideon balanced it at eye level. "It's top-heavy. It's made well enough, though. I wouldn't touch a thing except to give it a keel."

"What's a keel, milor'?"

"I think the best way to explain that is to make one." He bent down and gave the boat back to the child, who had to let go Mademoiselle Dalgleish's fingers. Gideon had the silliest impulse to snatch her hand himself. But he straightened and glanced around the garden. "Is there anything useful lying about?"

Alexandrine Bonaparte said, "May I suggest you try the summerhouse? Mademoiselle Dalgleish, perhaps you would be so obliging as to show Sir Gideon. I have matters indoors . . ."

"I don't want to impose on Mademoiselle Dalgleish," he said coolly. But the children looked at her with open eagerness and she agreed. Alexandrine Bonaparte went back inside and the four youngsters set out skipping and bobbing in front to show them the way.

They didn't speak as they began walking over the lawns toward the summerhouse, whose roof he could see beyond a shrubbery on higher ground. He was not quite sure why she was silent, but there was every reason on his part. It irritated him that she should suspect him of spying here, because it was only a half-truth, as the summerhouse business had genuinely come up by chance. He had been surprised when his architect mentioned the construction going on at Thorngrove, but he'd realized at once that a visit might provide another piece in the picture he was forming of the French in England. And he'd heard nothing about Mademoiselle Dalgleish being here. With or without the Duc de Limours.

What was she doing? Dared he hope that the visit to Thorngrove showed a swerve away from Napoleon? Her patriotic cousin in Paris, not to mention the emperor himself, would be furious if they heard about this visit. "I'm very surprised to meet you here."

He added lightly in English, "I imagine that, for you, this might seem like stepping into the enemy camp."

She gave a rueful laugh. "Oh, Sir Gideon, how little you understand the complexities of French politics!"

He smiled. "That may well be." It was impossible not to say: "Perhaps you think I'm here for instruction?"

She stiffened. "I try not to think about your motives at all."

So she wasn't going to tell Lucien Bonaparte that he was an agent for England? It stirred and perplexed him, as it had in Paris, to find her willing to protect his secret. He glanced ahead and made sure the children were out of earshot. "You're not tempted to betray me to our gentle hosts?"

"No, I shall leave that to you." She looked up and gave a quick, silvery laugh. "You have strayed into an exceptionally clever household, monsieur. You must find your own way amongst them if you can."

To the tune of piping voices, they emerged from the shrubbery onto the grass in front of the summerhouse, whereupon she took her hand from his arm and occupied herself with little Johanna, who had found some wood shavings and was clamoring to float them on the pond.

Again Delphine Dalgleish was protecting him. Again she was not saying why. In Paris, he'd been almost sure that it was because she shrank from seeing him killed. Which meant she at least saw him as a man, not just as a creature of war. How did she see him now? Could that instinctive sympathy carry her any further—toward friendship or regard?

He watched her, full of a new, profound temptation. Every complexity that he had argued over in his mind suddenly fell away, and he was looking at a radiant truth. He was in love with her. Patriotism made them enemies—but what if it was patriotism alone? He felt the most powerful urge to share his truth with her, as though it were strong enough to change both their lives. He was in love with her, and he *had* to do something about it.

Then she looked up, and the gentle smile she had bestowed on the child faded. They moved on to the summerhouse.

The building was large and handsome and the workmen reassured him on all points—the building would shed water in a rational way, and three of the eight sides would be fitted with glass to give shelter against the prevailing wind.

Mademoiselle Dalgleish agreed to step onto the new floor to give her opinion about the inside of the roof, which had exposed beams decorated by fretted moldings. "Very pleasing. It's sad, though, to be discussing rain and wind in a summerhouse," she said, with a quizzical expression on her upturned face. One strand of straw-colored hair had fallen out of the complicated arrangement at the back and was kissing her neck. She had worn no bonnet to come outside and play with the children. What a honey of a child she must have been herself.

"English weather, mademoiselle. I can make no excuses for it." A memory flooded into him as he looked down at her: the gazebo on Saint-Amour, as she leaned against the railing while the breeze from the tropic ocean stirred her hair.

She walked back to the top of the shallow steps, brushing her hands together so that specks of sawdust drifted down. She said over her shoulder, "When is yours to be completed?"

"Not this season. But I'm promised it for early next year. I hope you'll approve of it."

"I?" He saw a hint of pink on one smooth cheek.

"That is . . . I'm thinking of having a house party at Landor when it's done. Provided I'm in England, of course. I should be honored if you and your mother would consent to come down. You might stay with my parents at Buff House; it's more comfortable than Landor, which I've neglected, I'm ashamed to say. It needs . . ." He had been about to repeat his father's favorite phrase about its needing a lady's touch. "I beg your pardon; I've not asked—is Madame Dalgleish here with you?"

"No." She descended the steps. "I traveled with the Duc de Limours." She allowed this to sink in, then concluded, "And his sister, the Comtesse D'Auvennois."

"My word; she travels, does she? I'd never have guessed."

She pressed her lips together in a thin smile, squinted at him as the countess was wont to do and nodded her head with comical rapidity.

He gave a burst of laughter. Then he joined her amongst the wood, shavings and two-inch nails, and made keels for the youngsters' boats.

Delphine felt unsettled by the addition of Landor to the party at Thorngrove. The French were all used to one another by now, and the presence of an Englishman would take the flavor out of the hours they spent together. But to her relief she found she was not to be pitied for having such a man amongst her acquaintance. His French was perfect, which gratified the company. She tried to forget how many nefarious opportunities he had to practice it, and listened to him with a pleasure she had not expected to feel. At table he even made people laugh in a very Parisian way, adding a spark of satire when the subject was solemn, and misleading them with gravity when he introduced something funny.

He didn't presume on the odd and fraught relationship he had with her. In fact he hardly addressed her at all, though she often caught his covert glance. She was especially aware of it late in the evening, when they were all lounging about in the larger salon drinking coffee and listening to crickets shrilling in the flowerbeds under the windows. The Duc de Limours addressed a whimsical question to the air. "Have you noticed how, when everything combines to seduce the senses, even the words that we pronounce add to the enchantment? Consider," he said to Lucien Bonaparte; "what other name could one give to your unique French haven, isolated in English farmland? *Thorngrove.* It sounds like the castle of the Sleeping Beauty." He turned to Delphine. "And before I buy my own haven on Ile de France, mademoiselle, I must know—what is the origin of that beautiful name, Saint-Amour?"

She smiled. "It's a simple old story, monseigneur. Will it go with your coffee?"

"You must tell us, mademoiselle. As a simple old man, I shall not be denied."

The rest disposed themselves to listen. Delphine didn't look at Landor, but she felt the power of his attention like heat on the side of her face. She propped her cheek against her hand and began. "When my father purchased our plantation on Ile de France, he discussed with my mother how they would name it. She knew exactly." There was a murmur of anticipation. "Long ago, for the Belfort family goes back many centuries, there was a crusader and his lady. My ancestor Raymond—for it's his story that I tell—lived in a castle in Burgundy, but his vision drew him into a wider world. The great of the realm were mounting a crusade, and Raymond gathered his knights around him and prepared to depart.

"But the countess came to him and said, 'My lord, I've had a dream. In the dream you gave me a rose before you left for the Holy Land. I took the rose and put it on the windowsill, then I bade you good-bye and you rode out of sight over the hill. Every day I sprinkled water on the rose, and every morning when I awoke its petals were as fresh as the morning dew. But a storm came, and though the windows were barred and the doors locked, when I awoke next morning the rose was gone. My husband, my love, do not go on this journey.'"

"What was her name?" Alexandrine said into the tiny silence.

"Clorinda. Raymond comforted Clorinda, and the crusaders departed for the Holy Land. Before he left, he had a gardener pluck a perfect rose, and he had the rose dipped in gold. He gave it to Clorinda and said, 'Before this rose fades or disappears, I will return to you.'"

Delphine took a breath and a sip of coffee. The air was very still and the crickets had stopped singing.

"When Clorinda held the gold rose in her hands she was afraid, for she feared that, in his deep love for her, Raymond was trying to deny the dream. She took the rose to the watchtower high on a hill near the castle. 'Here,' she said, 'I will keep watch until my lord comes home.' She created a shrine in the bedchamber at the top of the tower, and she laid the rose before a statue of the Virgin, and there she stayed, waited on by her ladies and stewards, but never leaving the tower. 'This place,' she said, 'I call Saint-Amour, sacred love, for all true love is sacred.'

"Nine months passed without news from the Holy Land. Every

morning when Clorinda awoke, she went to the shrine and said a prayer, and scattered water on the rose, which never withered. And on the nineteenth day of the ninth month, she gave birth to her first child, and called him Raymond, after her lord. Another year passed, while she cared for her child in the tower. And finally the crusaders returned. They came with banners and treasure and wondrous tales. And they brought the body of Raymond. On the nineteenth day of the ninth month, a Mameluke arrow had pierced his heart, and he died before the walls of Mansurah."

There was a sigh in the room, and the crickets began their song again under the window. "Clorinda ran to the doors and windows of the tower, and one by one she flung them open. She went to the shrine and took up the gold rose, and holding her child in one arm she raised the other and flung the rose up into the sky from the highest window. It turned end over end in the sunlight and vanished. People have searched for it to this day, but the search will never end, for it did not fall to earth."

Delphine shifted in her chair and arranged her hands in her lap. Every face was turned to her. Never having recounted the story before, she was not sure how to end it. Then her eyes met Landor's. His face had a radiance and openness that she had never seen before. It was as though all their antagonisms were swept away into another world and they occupied a new one that only they could enter, of innocence and joy.

Delphine said softly, "Clorinda descended from the tower and raised her son to manhood. He spent his life on his ancestral lands, and in all his long years the tower of Saint-Amour was dear to him, and the shrine in the highest room was maintained. But no one lived there again."

"Does the tower still stand?" asked Lucien Bonaparte.

"It's fallen down, but roses grow in the ruins. My mother loved it, and my father loved the story. That's why our home is called Saint-Amour."

When Gideon went up to his chamber that night, he opened the casement wide and let the moonlight and warm night air flow into the room. He lay naked with his head flung back on the feather bolster, and the looped bed curtains moved rhythmically on either side like the wings of some great, powerful bird. He soared. He did not sleep.

Next morning, Delphine had a feeling that she would find herself encountering Landor at every turn, but in fact she was free of him for hours. All the Bonaparte boys had begged to go fishing in the Severn, so three of the gentlemen took them out very early. Lucien Bonaparte, unable to go beyond the bounds of Thorngrove, was grateful that they should give his children this treat. Sir Gideon Landor led the party. Later, while Delphine was helping to plan a knot garden behind the house with Alexandrine, a group was organized to bring back some melons and other produce from the village market, and because the eldest Bonaparte girls insisted there was no rustic fun in it unless they carried their purchases home themselves, a couple of gentlemen were required. Landor was one of them.

She saw him at dinner, however, which the Bonapartes tended to eat early, and call luncheon. And after luncheon they went for a walk to the copse on the very edge of the estate. A number of people wanted to go, but in the end Delphine found that only she and Landor had the energy.

"May I suggest you wear a sunbonnet, Mademoiselle Dalgleish?" he said in English, as they paused between the glass doors that led out onto the terrace.

"If I climb the stairs to get it, I shall expend all my forces."

"Your maid will bring it down. Let me call someone."

"No, thank you! Molly is very good, but she often brings the lace cap when I need the satin poke, or the satin poke when I request the straw hat." She gave a flourish with her left hand. "Behold, the parasol. The indispensable tropical accoutrement. If anyone had told me I should deploy it in Worcestershire, I should never have believed them."

So they set off in silence. She wished she could do something about that, but they crossed the lawn and made their way toward the small copse without a word. Eventually she hazarded a remark. "The Bonapartes are living in a cultivated, tenderly enclosed world. But for all their marvelous efforts, it bears little resemblance to the real one."

"I fear so." After a while, "The heat is not oppressive for you?"

"No! You forget Saint-Amour."

There was another long silence. Now she felt as though she had stepped over some invisible boundary. Yet all they were doing was strolling at a sedate pace toward an attractive collection of ash trees, with hazel providing a filmy screen between the massive trunks. "What a lovely prospect," she heard herself say. "I spoke to the gardener today. He seems very knowledgeable." Then the shade flooded in around them. Instead of withdrawing her arm she curved one wrist over his to close the parasol, and swung it gently beside her as they proceeded on, the tip rustling through weeds at the side of the path. "Oh, dear," she said. "Nettles. We must be careful not to step off the path."

He didn't reply. He probably had very little interest in nettles. Indeed, she had not the faintest idea why she had mentioned them. To try entertaining a man who was both cool *and* clever was an impossible task. She must learn to hold her tongue in a proper English manner.

Nonetheless, after a few moments, she said, "How warm it is. I've been taught to think of England as damp all year round. I'm glad this lovely summer is proving me wrong."

They came upon a bench beside the path, and he said, "Perhaps you'd like to rest from the heat a while?" He handed her onto the bench and remained standing in front of her.

She looked up.

"I can't go on," he said. "You overwhelm me. I must tell you— I love you. And I beg you to marry me."

The astonishment was so shattering that she gasped and shrank back.

He said quickly. "Please—hear me before you answer. I should have spoken first to your mother, but something she said of late gave me a chance to hope . . ." Gazing at him in complete disarray, she could not help seeing nonetheless how this outburst of feeling enhanced him. He had never looked so handsome. Or so intimidating. He went on, "I haven't even mentioned this to my family. But when they know you, they must come to love you almost as I do."

"You astonish me, monsieur!"

"I'm sorry. And I know. I know the obstacle." He turned aside and took two paces away, then back. His voice, though full of emotion, was firm, and a fire seemed to light his eyes from within. "I've thought about nothing else for days. And I've decided that no sacrifice is too great for your sake. I cannot ask you to do me the honor of accepting me and meanwhile continue to make war on your countrymen. Against my dearest wishes, I shall request an honorable discharge from the navy. And also," he said with earnest meaning, "from any other service for my country. Frankly, I have no idea what the future holds for me. I've stripped it of every purpose and every passion except one. To devote myself to your happiness, mademoiselle. Pray tell me that I may do so."

He said it with the utmost ardor. *To her*. What did he *think*? That she would blithely set aside everything that lay between them? Held at bay by the flame in his eyes, she battled for words. "I believe I must thank you, sir. For your . . . for your offer. But I'm afraid you presume too far. I must hope that when you give this a few *more* days' thought, you'll be relieved not to make the great sacrifice you propose on my behalf."

There was an appalling silence, and she saw him turn pale. It hit him so hard that he took a step back. But after a short struggle he said in a deep, baffled voice, "I have no right to be *surprised* that you refuse me, mademoiselle. But sarcasm . . . hatred . . . these, I have to say, I did not expect."

A blush began at Delphine's neck and flooded over her cheeks, and she felt a surge of nausea and fright. It was the worst moment of her life. Angry though she was, if she could have gotten to her feet she would have run away.

He began to turn from her, then brought himself back, a look of desperate determination on his face. "It's not customary for a rejected suitor to ask the lady to explain. But our situation has never been normal. You are very adept at expressing yourself. May I beg you to do so now? For my own good, tell me why"—and here, despite his control, she heard a tremor in his voice—"there is no reason for me to hope."

Her eyes felt hot. "You have never had reason, monsieur."

He was so mortified that he bit his lower lip. But he countered, "Because we are enemies by conviction? Believe me, I would never have tried to change your principles; they are sacred to me. What I hoped to change was our life hereafter. I must ask your forgiveness for an idea that clearly causes you the deepest insult. I've been carried away by my feelings, without knowing yours." He colored, and after a fractional pause burst out, "But at least tell me this. Paris. The rue Saint-Honoré. You might have raised the alarm, or betrayed me to your cousin. But you did neither. Forgive me, but can you at least explain that?"

She went cold. "I did neither, because I knew just what you were. I feel nothing but abhorrence for what you do. I've been prepared to protect you for the sake of France. But for no other reason."

"For *France?*"

"I've known what you are since the night we met. After you'd gone, Armand told me you were a double agent for Bonaparte." She lifted her chin. "Did you imagine that could possibly arouse my admiration? To know that you have spent years selling your country's secrets to mine whilst you strut around London as an impostor? Do you think it pleases me to know that by my silence I'm sheltering a man without humanity or honor?"

"Hell," he ground out, and she flinched. He was so alight with fury he could scarcely speak. "The foul, unspeakable—" He mastered his voice with difficulty. "Your cousin is a damnable liar. He helped me escape, then set the legionnaires on me. They would have killed me if an officer hadn't dragged them off. He was protecting *his* base actions, mademoiselle, when he told you I was a double agent." He shuddered. "The very idea is sickening." He approached and said with contained menace, "Will you look me in the face and repeat that monstrous calumny, if you can?"

She was goaded to her feet. She caught his burning gaze so accurately that it penetrated to her heart. He had no need to say any more. She shrank back: he was telling the truth. And Armand was a liar—a selfish, cunning liar whom she had allowed to deceive her. The man before her was not a double-dealing traitor for France; he was an English patriot. And despite the battle lines that had always been drawn between them, he had just asked her to marry him, trusting that she believed in his integrity.

"*Mon dieu*," she whispered. "This is terrible. Forgive me. He has wronged you to the last degree. And I've been grossly taken in."

"Oh, God." He stepped aside and put one hand across his face. His lips drew back from his teeth. "I've been blind." For a long moment he stood motionless, and when he took his fingers away she was horrified to see tears in his eyes. "I beg you to excuse me, mademoiselle, for the offense I've given to your feelings today." He made her a curt bow. "And rest assured you'll hear no more of mine." He turned and strode away.

Exposures

Delphine's knees buckled and she found herself sitting on the bench again. Her eyes clamped shut and she could hear his boots thud across the leaves as he walked away through the trees. Against every reason she could conjure up, he loved her. He loved her, and she had dealt him the worst blow a man could suffer—she had rejected him and abused him as well. No matter that he had no right to imagine he could succeed; he had made a mistake—but *diable*, she had made a much, much more terrible one!

She began to cry, in helpless sobs that she tried to muffle with her hands. It was like being attacked, with no one to turn to for help. Yet it was she who had attacked *him*. And his reaction was unbearable to think of. "Oh," she said aloud, "what have I done?" The sound of her own voice frightened her. She drew out a handkerchief and buried her face in the soft linen, taking shallow breaths.

She tried to retrace the path back to her first error, to understand how she had come to be so unjust, so set against Landor. But it was too painful to take in. All she knew was that one lie from a whole year ago had caused her misconceptions about him. She hung her head, her fingers twisting the handkerchief in her lap. A phrase came back about her mother: *one thing she said gave me reason to hope.* Had her mother been matchmaking behind her back? In other circumstances this would have made her very angry. As it was, she just cried the more.

She couldn't blame her mother for this. The main thing was abominably clear: Landor had never known how she despised what he did. Delphine gave a long, shaky sigh. It was like his arrogance not to notice, but was he at fault? As far as he was concerned, she knew he was a spy for England, yet she, a Bonapartist, had never betrayed him to a soul. He didn't have to be a conceited monster to wonder whether some kind of hidden sympathy spared his life. It had puzzled and intrigued him, and drawn him to her. And, eventually, allowed him to hope.

And her manners in general—where were her excuses for them? Faced with his self-sufficiency, she had teased and challenged him, but she had never valued him enough to find out his real opinions and feelings. Oh, if she had taken the least trouble in that direction, what discoveries she might have made! Now he would see her as shallow, thoughtless and cruel.

She stayed for a long time in the wood. When she thought her tears were over she walked back, terrified at coming upon someone. But the long, hot afternoon had relapsed into stillness and the grounds of Thorngrove were empty.

She felt hollow and guilty. She wanted to run home, but she was by no means sure where "home" might be. The very name of Saint-Amour caused misery. Landor had been lost in her story the night before—how could she have failed to see what that tale of woman's constancy was doing to his emotions? And he had been generous in offering his home to her, setting aside whatever his parents or society might think of the differences between them. Yet she was the Bonapartist daughter of a revolutionary general. *She* would never be ashamed of her pedigree, but there wasn't a marriageable girl in England who envied it. He might have married Georgiana Howland; now, there was a match that had everything to recommend it. Including the fact that the lady was in love with him—for Delphine wasn't blind in that regard, though she suspected he might well be.

Blind. The worst of accusations.

She reached the kitchen garden and looked at it through a blur of desolation. At the pool, she folded the parasol, bent over and splashed water over her face, then raised her closed eyes to the sun. None of the windows of Thorngrove gave a view into this part of the grounds; she had a brief respite to recover before the others stirred after the siesta.

All at once she spied servants emerging from the back of the house, so she walked in the vegetable garden along gravel paths and cowered behind tall rows of peas and climbing beans. It was impossible to face anyone in this state, even a scullery maid. When she finally went inside, she almost ran into her own maid, Molly, who had been dashing about trying to find her. It appeared that Sir Gideon Landor was about to depart, as scheduled, but had expressed a desire to bid her farewell. Trapped, Delphine walked with false calm into the reception hall where he stood with their hosts. He had evidently just said good-bye to them and to the Duc de Limours, who hung back to observe.

Landor looked as collected and cool as she had ever seen him, but this time she was undeceived by his demeanor; the force that he exerted to maintain it seemed to meet her like an electric field as she walked toward him. He said, "Mademoiselle Dalgleish. I could not go without saying good-bye."

She nodded without meeting his eye. "I bid you a safe journey, monsieur."

"Thank you. You return to London when?"

She glanced toward the Duc de Limours. "It's not yet decided."

Landor's eyes were narrowed as though the very sight of her hurt him. "Good-bye, mademoiselle. Please convey my best regards to your mother. And may I wish you every . . ." She did not hear the rest; his last words were muffled when he made his bow and walked outside to the waiting carriage.

Delphine pleaded exhaustion after lingering outdoors in the heat, excused herself from the rest of the evening and declined supper; all she wanted, she said, was rest and an early night. Brushing away the Bonapartes' concern, she walked straight up the stairs to her chamber.

Gideon was in the morning room at Curzon Street, seated by the window, listening to Ellis's report on the pursuit of the suspected courier, which had ended at the Channel coast. Able Seaman Ellis could not contain his triumph. "We stopped him at Dover, sir— and turned up trumps! He had a dispatch from the duke, in French, pushed into the lining of his jacket." Faced by a total lack of reaction, Ellis emphasized, "So now we know, sir. You were right: the duke is the man."

"No more than I suspected. Tell me what happened."

Ellis cooled down and gave a succinct account. He and his assistant had set upon the man in a seaside alleyway after dark, half stripped him and plundered his belongings. Ellis, leaving his partner to keep their winded victim subdued, had gone swiftly to his own lodgings and examined everything. He had found the duke's dispatch, read it with care then slid it back into the jacket. Keeping the man's few valuables, he had gone back into the street, flung the jacket and empty pack at him and taken off into the night. "He thought us a pair of footpads, sir, no more. Next morning we watched him board a fishing boat, as unsuspecting as you please, if a bit the worse for wear, like. So we know the ringleader, the courier and the whole route."

"I told you to keep hold of him if there was anything important in the dispatch. I take it there wasn't?"

"Not as I could see."

"It was addressed to whom?"

"No name, sir. It was a page of news, set out very dry, like a report. No address and no signature."

"And it wasn't in code?"

"No, thank God; I could make it out fine. I have a note of all the points." He presented Gideon with a sheet of paper. "You'll forgive the hand. I'm no artist with a pen."

Gideon read it while Ellis stood looking on with undisguised pride. It contained a list of information obtained from various French people in London who were identified only by their initials. A Monsieur V had lately been taken on a tour of the docks at Greenwich and shown over a warship, whose armaments were itemized. A Madame L had met a militia commander who complained about a hundred of his troops being drafted into the regulars from Colchester, destination Portugal.

Gideon looked up. "This is excellent. You're sure you remembered the Frenchies' initials correctly?"

Ellis beamed. "I've been accused of having a memory like a brassbound chest, sir."

"Very good," said Gideon and read on. This was a single installment of what must be a regular report that the duke sent to intelligence in Paris. Ellis had done well to let the courier go; now that they knew the whole business, they could keep watch until they suspected there was something major to intercept, whereupon they could pounce and expose the network in one fell swoop. Then Gideon came to the last paragraph. *Mademoiselle D est sur le point de faire sa visite chez LB à T. Ferai contact là-bas.*

Mademoiselle Dalgleish is about to make her visit to Lucien Bonaparte at Thorngrove. I'll make contact there.

He got to his feet and walked to the window, and with his back to Ellis stared unseeing down at the street. She had had a purpose for that long journey into Worcestershire. A purpose that was completely opaque to him, like everything about her, but as clear as day to the Duc de Limours. He felt sick. Limours was about to recruit her into his network; no, had already done so. The divide between her and himself was a chasm never to be crossed.

He said to Ellis over his shoulder. "Thank you. You may go." There was no movement, so eventually he turned. "You've done very fine work. Could you use a spot of leave? Three days, starting now."

Ellis's face relaxed. "Thank you, sir, that's most welcome." Then he gave Gideon a curious look. "However . . ." He hesitated. "That is, the valet you took north has left a few things that I don't consider . . . pardon me, but they're not quite shipshape, and—"

"Just get out, would you?"

Ellis's eyes widened, but he gave a correct naval salute into which he managed to throw more than a hint of reproach.

Watching him walk stiffly to the door, Gideon said all at once, "Dammit. Halt." Ellis turned, hurt and wary. "There's something you need to know. In a very short time, what I'm doing in London will be exposed. The Duc de Limours will be the first to find out. That makes me useless to all intents and purposes, and it makes what you do all the more vital. Warn the men, keep your mouth shut and your head down, and await orders."

Dismay spread across Ellis's blunt features. "My oath, sir, what's happened?"

"I've ceased to be of any value to the secret service here. I'm going to recommend that part of my allowance be paid hence-forth to you. I don't know if they'll wear that, but you deserve it."

"Thank you, sir. You don't want me to remain here a while? I . . ." But faced with Gideon's stare, he turned very slowly and went out, shutting the door behind him.

Gideon dropped into the nearest chair and put his head in his hands. It was worse than ever, like a hammer blow on a bruise that seemed to extend from his heart to his ribs and down into his stomach. Just seeing the first letter of her name was painful, but it was torture to have it confirmed that she was completely his enemy. She was in London for Bonaparte, and that pure, obses-sive loyalty of hers had never wavered. She had kept quiet about him because she thought he was working for the same side, but treachery was abhorrent to her. He groaned as he remembered her words: *Do you think it pleases me to know that I'm sheltering a man without humanity or honor?* She had felt nothing but contempt for him from the very first night they met. He pressed the heels of his hands against his eyes as he remembered the horror on her face. She had met his presumption with the sarcasm it deserved. She knew the real state of affairs now, but it would make no difference to her—she might no longer despise him as a traitor to his coun-try, but her dislike was firmly grounded, and his behavior at Thorngrove had only deepened it.

He had never stood a chance with her. He had spoken and been refused—whereupon any reasonable man would have sub-mitted with dignity. Yet he had gone on, oblivious, until they were face to face in appalling opposition, until he had given way to anger, and blasphemed, and abused her cousin. He had never spoken to a woman like that in his life. He had lost control; she had not. She had even apologized for believing Armand de Belfort's lies.

She would tell the Duc de Limours that he was in the secret service. He couldn't do anything to prevent that. She would no doubt inform her cousin that he had been spying in Paris in March. Belfort could go to hell. She would recount his proposal to her mother and they would both be indignant over his effron-tery. Let them. It could scarcely make things worse.

He must get back onto full pay and onto a ship, and to sea as soon as possible—but it was a mechanical thought, offering no pleasure or excitement. His life was a featureless plateau, broken by just one narrow valley in which he turned around and around like a trapped animal.

He had never been touched by love, and truth to tell had never thought he would be. Now that he was stricken by it, he knew that it would last his lifetime. He was in love forever, with a woman who loathed him.

Her winning manners with him had meant nothing. She was like that with everyone—in fact, she was probably *more* like that with every gentleman on earth but him. The nicknames confirmed it, if only he'd deployed a shred of common sense when he heard them. "The idol of the island." "La duchesse." "The delectable Delphine." He ground his teeth over the last. He'd been right on target that evening in the prison when she'd talked about Captain Matthew Flinders.

He ran both hands through his hair. Any sense he'd possessed had been swept away that very night, when he tied her hands to the gazebo railing and her nearness hit him like a tidal wave. Was he nothing but a brute after all? Was that how she saw him—as a brute who also had a cold and calculating mind? No wonder there had been that swift impulse of attraction and repulsion that she could not hide, every time they met. She felt a sexual response to him—but she was frightened of it. Because she was frightened of *him.*

His throat ached. He pressed one hand over his mouth and willed himself to endure this without further tears. He would do better to be angry, and vent that anger in some physical pursuit instead of lingering around in his empty house. The trouble was, the person who caused him the most fury was himself.

On the road back from Thorngrove to London in the carriage, the Duc de Limours broached the subject of Napoleon's letter to Lucien Bonaparte. Delphine was not surprised. She simply asked what made him think she had delivered any such thing.

"The exchange was observed. One has servants, mademoi-

selle." He smiled, and so did the Comtesse D'Auvennois, but
there was unease in the old lady's eyes. Delphine didn't reply, so
he continued, "May I know what it said?"

She looked out at the flat countryside. "Our host didn't tell
you?"

"He said not a word about it. Sometimes he suspects me of
working for his brother. Which I do, I hasten to add." He made
her a little bow. "You'll permit me to explain everything in a moment. But first, what was in the letter?"

"I have no idea. I only know that it was personal, not political."

There was another pause, and she could tell that the duke was
rather puzzled. Did he expect her to fall on his neck now that
he'd owned up to controlling Bonapartist intelligence in France?
He was welcome to it; let him deal with his conspiracies to his
heart's content.

Eventually he said, "I rejoice in this opportunity to be open
with you, mademoiselle. You were told that at the right time you
would be contacted by someone who would arrange for a report
to go back to France. I am that gentleman." She turned unen-
thusiastic eyes on his long, lean face. "As for me, I decided that I
would wait until your first mission was accomplished before I
made my identity known to you. It afforded me the pleasure of
watching you in action. Mademoiselle, let me say that you have
exceptional talent for this work. I had no idea what your first mission was—I could only guess that it had something to do with Lucien Bonaparte. I admire your adroitness. And I put the highest
estimate on its value to the emperor and to France."

"Thank you."

Somewhat let down by such a response, the duke was quiet for
a while. But he could not help persisting. "It will be my privilege
to help in whatever way I can with your next endeavor. Again I
have no instructions. But I shall be only too happy to take them
from *you*."

His flattery grew too much. He was a courteous old gentleman
and she was almost certain he would never overstep the mark, but
still she was sorry she had agreed to travel with him. She wished
she had never met him, and most of all she wished she had never

sought out Lucien Bonaparte or seen Thorngrove. "Please for-give me, monseigneur, but I'm not in the frame of mind to con-tinue this discussion."

His face fell. "Of course; how insensitive of me. I must admit you do seem . . . a little out of spirits. The heat, and your long walk yesterday . . . I hope you are not unwell?" He glanced at his sister, then leaned forward. "Would you like us to stop the car-riage for a while?"

"No!" Delphine cried, and he sat back. "Thank you, but all I want is to get home." To her horror, tears rolled down her cheeks.

The Comtesse D'Auvennois, with a glare at her brother, bent forward and closed her finely veined little hands over one of Del-phine's. Which made her cry in earnest, for many miserable miles.

When Gideon calculated that Delphine Dalgleish had been back in London for a fortnight, he paid a call at Berkeley Square. Leav-ing it any later would have looked like cowardice. He had walked away from her in towering resentment, which was not the behav-ior of a gentleman. It was true that he had bade her farewell be-fore leaving Thorngrove, but he had made a poor fist of that too.

When he was admitted he found that both Mrs. Laidlaw and Madame Dalgleish were at home and the demoiselle was nowhere to be seen, which was the exact opposite of what he had intended. It was an awkward occasion. Mrs. Laidlaw gave him a look when he walked into the drawing room that was charged with her fa-mous Scots sagacity, and he felt like a very large insect displayed in a small, carefully chosen collection. La Générale on the other hand hardly focused on him at all. As they talked he thought she looked downcast, and his heart beat like a hammer as he specu-lated why.

Eventually she apologized in her gentle way. "You'll excuse me for being preoccupied. My daughter and I paid a visit this morn-ing to an old acquaintance in Nassau Street—Captain Matthew Flinders. You said once that you knew of him?"

He replied coldly, "Indeed."

"Such a gifted man. He works so hard on his book, and he and his wife live so modestly you cannot imagine—Delphine and I could scarcely turn around in their parlor!"

Gideon was quite sure he didn't want to hear about Flinders, but he said, "He's writing up his circumnavigation of Terra Australis, I hear. Under the patronage of Sir Joseph Banks."

"Indeed, but living here is ruinous for him. He is on half pay, and has an annuity from his family, but his income nowhere near covers his expenses. And Sir Joseph Banks is no help at all. Captain Flinders applied to the Admiralty for an allowance as a marine surveyor, but this very morning he received a letter rejecting the appointment." She shook her head tragically. "And you should see his maps! Works of art, my dear monsieur."

Gideon, who would rather wring the man's neck, could summon no sympathy, but said, "His friends must hope that when the book is published it will sell handsomely enough to pay off his debts."

La Générale gave a melancholy smile. "We always hear such sound thoughts from you. But I've just been writing to those very friends, on Mauritius, and his troubles *will* creep into my letters, however I try to keep them out. Delphine will be especially distressed. She is so fond of him."

Quelling the impulse to rise from his chair and make another undignified departure, Gideon said shortly, "I beg your pardon?"

"Oh, I had quite forgot. Of course you never met them; they are the D'Arifat family of Wilhelms Plains. Delphine is the eldest daughter—married now and on her husband's property. Captain Flinders stayed on their plantation for years. They taught him French, you know. They correspond like members of the same family."

Gideon felt blood rise to his cheeks under the fascinated gaze of Mrs. Laidlaw. So "the delectable Delphine" was another young woman entirely—but he had no chance to decide how he felt about that. He said to Mrs. Laidlaw, "How is Mademoiselle Dalgleish? Is she at home?"

"She is upstairs. I was just going up myself. I shall inform Miss Dalgleish that you're here." She rose and went out.

Gideon talked on inconsequentially with la Générale, unable

to guess whether she knew of his proposal, and telling himself
how to keep his countenance if Mademoiselle Dalgleish walked
into the room. By the time she did, he probably looked as stiff as
a marine on parade. She entered with the graceful manner he
was used to, curtsied and murmured a greeting, but she could not
quite meet his eye. Instead of choosing the sofa by her mother
she took a chair by the window. He sat down opposite and found
that with the daylight behind her he had difficulty reading her expression. He felt totally lost. Dredging up words was like hauling
something up from a dark well. "Did you have a pleasant journey
from Worcestershire, mademoiselle?"

"Yes, thank you—the roads are tolerable, don't you find?"

"Except around Evesham."

"Except around Evesham; you're quite correct."

"And you left our hosts well?"

"Indeed. And the children thriving." There was a pause, then,
with a kingfisher glance at his face, "The flotilla has been kept
very trim, you'll be glad to hear."

"The flotilla?" la Générale put in.

"Sir Gideon was so good as to help the children with their sailing boats. And take the boys fishing."

La Générale smiled at him. "How nice of you. I'm sure that's
not why you went all the way to Worcestershire!"

No, madame, it was not. But somehow he could not mention the
summerhouse. That whole innocent afternoon and evening he
had spent in Delphine Dalgleish's company was the one sweet
and unadulterated memory he had of her. He was grateful to her
for bringing it up. Was this a clue that she didn't despise him
completely?

Delphine meanwhile was observing him in dismay. He looked
so different; it seemed that even to open his mouth was an effort.
She wished he had not come, but she had to admire him for it.
There was a line between his eyebrows that she had noticed on
the night when he left her in the gazebo on Saint-Amour—when
he had bowed to her, and she had suddenly seen how much he
suffered from the pain of his injuries.

She had not confided in her mother about his proposal. She

yearned to do so, for it was a dreadful burden to bear alone, but she had already hurt him enough. She searched for a way to let him know that this secret, at least, was safe. If only they could be alone, but the thought made her tremble. "Thorngrove is unique. Looking back, in some ways it quite defies description." Oh, heaven, let her find the right words! "There are many things—purely personal things—that I've not discussed with anyone since . . . and that I shall not discuss."

"*Chérie*," la Générale interrupted with a laugh, "what are you saying? You have given us the most glowing pictures: of your hosts, the paintings, the gardens—I feel as though I've seen them all, and without stirring a yard from Berkeley Square."

"But I didn't mention the hazel copse, Maman," Delphine said in desperation, her cheeks on fire and her gaze directed to the Persian rug in the middle of the floor.

"The copse?" Her mother turned to Gideon. "Was there something very special about it?"

Gideon took a deep breath and tried to assemble some sort of reply. He had been thrown a lifeline, but he hardly knew how to thank her. He waited until she raised her eyes. When she did, there was sympathy in their blue depths. He had no right to expect her not to pass on the information that he was a spy for England, but she had used the word *personal*. It was of his proposal alone that she spoke, with a softness that broke his heart all over again. He said, "There was at one time much to be said about the copse, but I hope that Mademoiselle Dalgleish will agree—it's best forgotten, if not forgiven."

She was still blushing, but her gaze was steady. "Both, sir, if that is your wish."

"You are charitable, mademoiselle."

"Well," la Générale said with a laugh, "if this is a riddle game from Thorngrove, I must say I'm glad I wasn't there. My daughter told me how amusing it was, monsieur, but I should never have had the faintest idea what anyone was talking about."

Gideon rose. "I'm afraid I must be going."

"So soon?" La Générale rose, startled.

He had stayed the regulation fifteen minutes and it was beyond him to manage more. But he had achieved something: it would now be possible to meet Delphine Dalgleish in public and be as polite, if not as talkative, as before. Politically they were enemies, but they had both pledged to consign to oblivion the misguided offer he had made in the copse at Thorngrove.

He said to both, "I'm very glad to have found you at home. Thank you."

Mademoiselle Dalgleish tugged the bell pull and a servant came and opened the door.

He bowed, and Madame Dalgleish said, "It was such a pleasure to see you." Mademoiselle Dalgleish curtsied and said nothing.

Gideon was shown downstairs and out the front door, and walked away beneath the trees of Berkeley Square in the direction of Curzon Street. It was one thing to promise to forget. It was another to accomplish it.

Lord Ferron

~~~

Delphine was dancing with Lord Ferron in the elegant town house of the Duc de Limours. His lordship was dominating her company and she let him, for it protected her from the duke, who seemed to be looking for the chance to catch a word in private. Meanwhile, she had to keep her wits about her when handling Ferron. Since the first moment they met, she had held him intrigued without giving him hope of conquering her. But he was used to conquering: he was a rogue where females were concerned, and he didn't mind that she knew it. Although he was irreproachably polite, she felt a heightened awareness between them that they both concealed beneath practiced banter. Everyone knew by now that Lord Ferron was pursuing Mademoiselle Dalgleish, but no one, including Delphine, could be sure of his intentions. As for herself, the flirtation created no link to her inner feelings. Something stood in the way of attraction when she was with Ferron, and she was glad of it.

They were in a reel, and waiting at the far end of the row, when Lord Ferron said, "This is my first invitation from the duke. In fact his is the only French house I've ever stepped into in London. I don't remember anything like it in Paris. Tell me, do they dance like this of an evening?"

She laughed. "Never. In Paris, one asks people for supper or conversation. There is no dancing, unless one gives a real ball. The idea of dancing like this, after supper, with ten couples in a drawing room . . . it's impossible!"

The movement reached their end and they skipped up the center, Ferron's hand lightly clasping her gloved fingers. "In that case, do you think our host may be taking on English ways at last?"

"I couldn't say." She half turned and took her place opposite him. "Your guess is as good as mine."

He shrugged. "We hardly speak to each other. I was at a loss to know why I received tonight's invitation. But then I realized," he said somewhat lower, his voice almost drowned by the pianoforte, "I've been discovered."

"What do you mean, milord?"

"I have a confession. I haven't dared make it to you until now, but the truth is, I've never been fond of the French. A failing, I daresay. But lately I've undergone a conversion, and the duke may have noticed." They prepared to move off again, hand in hand as before, and as they bent to go under the raised arms of another couple, he said in her ear, "Now that I'm converted, will it offend if I tell you why?"

She thought a little teasing might be in order. "I imagine you succumbed to the charm of Thorngrove, my lord."

There was an instant spark in his glance. "Thorngrove! That was neighborly curiosity, no more. No. The charm that works this dangerous magic lies elsewhere."

The suave tone, the flattering gaze were intended to disarm her, but she felt a stab of anger at what he implied—that she was the only French person he could stand. She thought of Landor, even more her enemy than Ferron, who had nonetheless been effortlessly agreeable at Thorngrove. Landor fought against her countrymen, but he didn't hate them.

She looked at Ferron under her lashes. "Dangerous? When was charm ever dangerous? Hyde Park and the Walk enchant me, but I feel in no danger when I stroll there on a fine day."

The dance was over, and with a bow he gave her his hand and they walked to the side of the room. They had met in the park only last week, when she and her mother were on foot and he had pulled his horse to a halt and bent down from the saddle to speak to them. "Ah, mademoiselle, I can't expect you to understand what it does to a gentleman to catch sight of a splendid bird of paradise amongst the little English doves. I'm in as much danger as I ever was in my life, whenever you are before me."

She laughed, took her hand from his and opened her fan. "I assure you, milord, I mean not the slightest harm."

"Really? Then may I hope that your mother has accepted my invitation for September? I long to have the honor of receiving you both at Paget."

He had asked them to a hunting party at his country estate during the first week of the partridge season. It had sounded like a gentlemen's gathering, but now he looked all keenness. "We have not fully discussed it."

"May I send tomorrow for your answer? There will be everything for your comfort and I'm happy to say a number of ladies are staying. Do you hunt?"

"Sometimes." She plied the fan thoughtfully. "But I don't shoot." He laughed, and she kept up the joke. "My aim is atrocious."

His smile broadened and he said with glistening eyes, "On the contrary, mademoiselle, it's mighty accurate."

He monopolized her for the rest of the evening, but at one stage she went alone into the corner to accept a glass of punch from the Comtesse D'Auvennois, who presided over the punch-bowl. As Delphine turned back to the room, the duke appeared at her elbow. Delphine took a sip as she watched the dancers. "You have given us a lovely evening, monseigneur."

"I'm gratified," he said. "Particularly by the presence of Lord Ferron; I suppose you know he's always been unobtainable. Of course I have no illusions about why he breaks his own rule tonight." He gave her a glance of deep meaning, which she chose to ignore, especially since there was a hint of jealousy in it. He didn't like Ferron, yet of course he was pleased to be rubbing shoulders with him at last. Napoleon's interests came foremost in the duke's mind at all times—for they were essential to his own ambitions in France. But there was jealousy in his next remark too. "His lordship cuts a fine figure. Always has, despite the fluctuations in his fortune. But he's at a low ebb just now; his gambling debts are crushing. Someone mentioned it to his face at one of the clubs the other night and everyone thought he'd call the other fellow out. But he was in his cups, and he just laughed and said he's got the remedy up his sleeve. It's called 'a capital marriage.' "

If this was a warning, it was the height of impudence. Delphine said with a vagueness borrowed from her mother, "If I cared at all about Lord Ferron, such a story might interest me, but in the event . . ."

There was a pause; then to her indignation he returned along the same track. "Ah, yes. After Thorngrove, of course I realized to my sorrow that you too know what doomed affection is like. Well may they talk about the perfidious sons of Albion! I must entreat you, mademoiselle, never to consider union with an Englishman. You are too precious a jewel for such a dull setting."

Delphine began to tremble. He was referring to her tears in the carriage—and he interpreted them as blighted love! What, she was supposed to have been spurned by Landor and determined to fling herself at Ferron? She put her glass on the table. "Monseigneur. When I want your advice, I shall ask for it. When I need a courier to take my final message to the emperor, I shall call on you. Beyond that, no contact is required. In all other matters, whatever you do, pray forget to include me."

She walked off, giving him no chance to protest, and took her leave of the other guests. Her inner fury lasted during the brief leave-taking from a startled Lord Ferron, and all the way back to Berkeley Square. She would write a letter to the Comtesse D'Auvennois apologizing for her rudeness. Beyond that she had no regrets; she was too angry. She was in a hateful situation in London, and she hated herself for ever having consented to it. If only she could go—sail away to Mauritius and leave the intrigues and shattered illusions behind her. She sat on her bed and rubbed her eyes. Would a letter ever come from Farquhar? If she knew Saint-Amour was hers, she would return to the island now, without completing the emperor's second task. Now she knew about the life of espionage, because she knew the Duc de Limours—and it was like being trapped in a sticky web.

She took her hands down and put them beside her on the coverlet, rocking forward on her palms. She *mustn't* give way to despair. In a week or two, she might be able to rip this imprisoning fabric apart and leave it in tatters behind her. She would accept the invitation from Lord Ferron and see what she could achieve in the few days on his estate. She had made a promise to the emperor—she would do her best to fulfill it, then free herself of every obligation to the Bonapartists in England.

She was not made to be a spy. She was not made to enjoy the lies, the subterfuges, the false loyalties, the devious mining for information that formed the triumphs of the Duc de Limours's self-seeking career. Look where conniving and concealment had led her—if she had come to London without ulterior motives, and without bizarre suspicions about everyone else's, she could never have made that dreadful mistake over Landor. He might have proposed, and she might have refused, but however painful the exchange, he would have at least known that she esteemed him. For she did, now that she recognized his true nature. He was an admirable man. He stood as far from the self-indulgent Lord Ferron and the malicious Duc de Limours as a snow-covered mountain peak towering above sodden marshland. He was beyond her reach. Which was nobody's fault but her own.

Gideon was on a visit to Landor. Without enthusiasm, he inspected the foundations of the new summerhouse, walked through the empty mansion with the housekeeper and let the steward tell him how well the orchards were bearing. Then he rode over to Buff House to spend a last night with his parents. It was by way of farewell, since his frigate was fitted out and would be launched in mid-September.

"What have they called her?" Lord Tracey asked over supper.

"Aphrodite."

"Really? Isn't that the name of the yacht you sailed back from Mauritius?"

"I'm afraid so. Some navy clerk's idea of a joke, I suspect."

The countess raised her eyebrows. "Can they do that?"

"They can do what they like. Including forcing me to kick my heels for nine months."

She considered him from across the table, her hazel eyes glinting at him through the whorls of a silver candelabra. "But you
don't seem quite so keen to be off and away. Not like last time."

"It's all the same to me; London or Lisbon I can take or leave."
He caught her concern and added, "Don't fret, Mother, I may
even be back by Christmas. I'm escorting a convoy to Portugal.
Routine stuff—we control the sea route and the French have gotten nowhere near it in months. The blockade is like cast iron."

The earl shook his head. "You'll miss the cub hunting! Dashed
shame."

"Not all of it. I'm going shooting in Worcestershire for a few
days before I leave."

His parents each adopted a blank expression, which meant
they were trying to hide disappointment that he should waste his
last days in England at someone else's country retreat when he
might have spent them at Buff House. When his mother withdrew
so that his father could smoke a pipe, Gideon determined to say
something.

His father got in first, fixing him through wreaths of smoke.
"Your mother worries, you know."

"I'm aware of that. I've something to tell you, sir, and I know
it won't go beyond these walls. I've asked for leave from the secret
service. It's been granted, but there are a couple of items to wrap
up before they'll let me go back on active duty, and one of them
takes me away from London for a few days. After that, I can assure
you, if they want any further action out of me, it has to be in
uniform."

The heel of the pipe hit the table with a thud as the earl's
hand came to rest beside his brandy glass. "Bloody good news!"
he spluttered. "*Bloody* good news. Thought you were looking a bit
under the weather. Been debating it with yourself? Well, let it
trouble you no more. Best decision you ever made." Beaming, he
shook Gideon's hand across the table, scattering dots of ash
across the board. "Now, put paid to that cognac, and we'll go in
and join your mother."

The rest of the evening passed in good cheer on his parents'
side. It was odd: he was about to go to war again, but they could

accept this with greater fortitude than the idea of his spying for England. On his side, he wouldn't feel any sense of release until the *Aphrodite* sailed, and it riled him that the secret service wouldn't let him leave until he took care of two last tasks. One was to mastermind the destruction of the Duc de Limours and his network. The other was to deal with Lord Ferron.

Able Seaman Ellis's surveillance of Limours and his couriers had been relentless, and a strike at any time was guaranteed to lead to the arrest of the duke and most of his informants. But Gideon was haunted by the fear of exposing Delphine Dalgleish. He must close the trap on Limours soon—and he could not warn her beforehand without risking the success of the raid. So he delayed, day after day, and woke up each morning with no solution to the dilemma.

The Ferron business, on the other hand, was plain infuriating. Apparently, when his lordship had gone with the February delegation to Paris, he had tried to bribe a Ministry of Marine and War official to hand over a portion of Bonaparte's great code. He had failed, but lately he was claiming success. Late at night after a supper party at his county seat, Ferron had been drinking deep and regaling a friend with his exploits on England's behalf. Taking this gentleman into the library, he unlocked a desk and produced a piece of paper that he claimed to represent Bonaparte's *grand chiffre*. Impressed but alarmed, the friend later spoke to someone in the secret service. The Aliens Office was horrified: Ferron must be tackled, the paper removed and the affair hushed up—everything must be done to ensure that the French got no wind of England's possessing part of the code. The only hitch was that Ferron held a high position in the Foreign Office and had powerful cronies. Taking his lordship to task on the basis of drunken gossip could have embarrassing consequences. Not only that—his claim had to be a lie. Ferron like others had at one stage been given access to the unfinished sheet of the *grand chiffre* that Gideon had brought back from France. It was obvious that Ferron must have had it written it out and then kept the copy as a trophy. In consequence, the surest way to teach his lordship a lesson, without risk to national security, was for someone to lay hands on the paper, identify it and remove it from Ferron's possession in such a way that his lordship would never mention it again.

To his disgust, Gideon had been chosen to manage the affair. Since he was the best person to make a judgment about the document, he could scarcely refuse. But the thing was distasteful. For a start, the thought of Ferron claiming credit for something he had achieved himself was galling—but he would rather someone else gave the gentleman the lie. More especially . . . well, there was Delphine Dalgleish. He had heard the rumors about her and Ferron. If he investigated his lordship, there was every chance of running into Mademoiselle Dalgleish. And he would give a great deal not to face such an encounter.

He was forced to act, though, for he wanted to be gone from England at the earliest opportunity. Ferron was holding a shooting party at his county seat in the first week of September and Gideon had obtained an invitation. It was easy. Ferron was badly in debt of late and this increased rather than diminished his reliance on gambling, so he would bet on almost anything. In the club one night, Gideon had started a debate about sporting guns, giving a few tantalizing details about a new shotgun that had just been delivered to him by Earl Tracey's gunsmith. By the end of the evening, Ferron and his friends had arranged for a match between Gideon and their finest shot, to take place one afternoon during the hunting party and to be adjudicated by one of the local squires. The bets were high, and much amusement was expected from the contest. Resigned, all Gideon could hope was that Delphine Dalgleish had not been invited. As for locating Ferron's so-called portion of the grand code, Gideon would just have to play that by ear when he arrived in Worcestershire.

It was no wonder he often fell silent while he and his parents were sitting in the great salon with their coffee, but it wasn't until after his father had retired to bed that he realized just how much his face betrayed to his mother. She came to sit beside him on the sofa and said, "My dear, you may tell me what's wrong."

He summoned a smile. "Nothing that a little escape to Portugal won't fix."

"It's not navy business, though, is it?" When he didn't reply, she said thoughtfully, "You know Georgiana Howland is married?"

He gave a short laugh. "No need to seek in that direction, Mother. I'm happy for her, and Combrewood's a very good man."

She raised her beautifully shaped eyebrows. "So . . . ?"

He said, "You know at the beginning of the year you said I might marry where I pleased? I'm afraid that's scarcely the case. I learned the lesson from a lady, in no uncertain terms." His mother looked as hurt as if she'd been spurned herself. She also had a right to be offended that he had not discussed the lady beforehand with her and his father. He explained, "It was an impulse. Which I instantly regretted."

She put a hand on his arm. "Oh, Gideon."

Her warm touch was a comfort, and a threat to his composure. He put one hand over hers and looked down. She had tapering artist's fingers, and to keep them free for her painting and other hobbies she wore few rings. The largest, an heirloom ruby, glowed up at him like a rosebud in the midst of flames.

Finally she said, "You do realize that with a lady of independent spirit, it's possible to give her too little time?"

He met her eyes with wonder. "How did you know?"

"How can I guess her character? I can't. I only know that if you love her, she is someone out of the ordinary."

"Madame, if I had given her until next Christmas to decide, the answer would have been the same."

"This is so hard to imagine. You don't see any hope? Any hope at all?"

He shook his head. Then he gave her a sardonic smile and said, "There's one benefit—I'm cured of trying to choose for myself. You and Father have free rein in that department. Do your damnedest, and I promise to marry the lady, whoever she may be."

Her eyes clouded and she took her hand away. "How long do we have? Until this Christmas or the next?"

"As long as you like!" Then he bent forward and kissed her cheek. "Oh, Mother, I don't care. I wish I did. Let's talk about this when I get back."

Paget

Lord Ferron's county seat in Worcestershire lay some miles beyond Callow Hill, near the border with Shropshire. The grounds consisted of a very wide wooded valley through which ran a stream that was diverted at various points into a serpentine lake, a haven for water fowl surrounded by birch and willow, and a cascade and grotto amongst a monumental pile of rocks half a mile or so from the house, beyond which the home farm began. The gentlemen walked that way every day at dawn to shoot in the fields and marshes, while the ladies confined their exploring to the shrubberies and flowerbeds around the mansion, where roses grew on terraces, and deep drifts of delphiniums, daisies and tall cottage plants softened the gray stone of the walled gardens with the last of their summer abundance.

The local hunt gathered one morning to hunt fox cubs and teach the new hounds—the entries—the ways of the pack. Delphine joined in, mounted on a strong, supple mare from Ferron's stables. They ventured a long way, across several properties, but made no kills, very much to her relief. When they were returning in the early afternoon, Ferron, who had stayed close to her during the exercise, invited her to rein in on the top of a knoll and let the others precede them. He wanted her to see the view, and she had to admit it was charming: the brown-and-white hounds spilling down into dense woods below, and farther on a green swell of pasture edged by a white track that twisted up the far slopes toward Paget, the splendid house crowning the hill with its crenelated roofs set in a crescent of plane trees.

"I don't wonder you like to be here at this time of the year. It's magnificent."

"No more so than today." Her mare fidgeted, and he leaned over to place a hand on the rein. "Seeing it through your eyes, mademoiselle, is the rarest of pleasures."

"I never thought I should learn to love the English country-side." As she said it, she remembered the lift of the heart that she had felt on her journey out of London in July, and the first care-free days at Thorngrove. In that precious interval she had tasted a sweetness she could never recapture.

"Dare I hope that you have?"

She looked up at him, lost for the moment. "Have what?"

He pressed his lips together, then resumed in a lighter tone, "Dare I hope that you have learned to admire our landscapes— and even, perhaps, our landscaping?"

"I have. I like what nature has provided, and I'm enchanted by what man has done with it."

He released the mare's rein and his big hunter took a gliding step away. The afternoon light gleamed on the russet hair curling out from under his hat brim and glinted in his intent, black-lashed eyes. Seated on the powerful horse, attired as immacu-lately as if he were just leaving for the hunt instead of returning after a hard morning's ride, he might easily have posed like this for his portrait. Lord Ferron of Paget, master of all he surveyed. "I have a particular reason for wishing your approval of this scene, Miss Dalgleish. Can you imagine what it is?"

She was suddenly nervous. "You are afraid I'll make compar-isons with my home on Mauritius. But I wouldn't do that. The two places are too distinct. Each has its beauty."

He gave a slow smile. "As long as you tell me that beauty may continue to reside at Paget, I shall have nothing more to wish for."

It was unmistakably pointed. All she could think to do in re-turn was to smile and set the mare in motion. He didn't press her. They rode the last three miles or so talking the same amount of nonsense they usually exchanged.

When they arrived at Paget the riders and hounds were milling about on the gravel sweep before the portico, and at the same time a shooting party was coming in over the lawn from the other direction. Looking at the gentlemen as she approached, Delphine drew in a soundless breath of surprise, for amongst them was Sir Gideon Landor. Meanwhile Ferron, leaping from his hunter and giving the reins to a groom, devoted himself to handing her down safely in the midst of the hubbub.

His lordship succeeded in making them the focus of a scene very much like an English equestrian painting, and Stubbs would have excelled with it: *The Return from the Hunt.* But Delphine made a poor effort of getting off the mare. She teetered, slid, was rescued and found herself laughing and blushing, her feathered toque over one eye and her waist firmly clasped in Lord Ferron's arms.

Twisting free, she turned away to retrieve her countenance and straighten her clothing, and met the pale green, inquisitorial eyes of Sir Gideon Landor. He had seen the whole tableau as he approached, and she could tell at a glance what he thought of it. He didn't greet her at once. He had no need to remove his hat, which he was tapping against his thigh, and the other hand was hooked into the strap of a long, double-barreled gun slung across his shoulder. He simply stood there, poised as though she had just said something disagreeable and he were waiting for an apology.

Lord Ferron spoke from behind her in hearty accents. "Landor! When did you turn up?"

"Around ten. Good afternoon, Mademoiselle Dalgleish." He bowed at last, and she gave a curtsy.

"Is that the gun?" Ferron said, coming to her side.

"It is." Landor unslung it from his shoulder and put it into Ferron's outstretched hand. "You'll discover its merits soon enough."

"Why, how many birds did you bag today?" Before Landor could reply, Ferron turned to Delphine and said, "Landor's here to win a wager. His weapon against Viscount Gascoigne's. If you're disposed to bet, it will be my pleasure to offer you handsome odds."

Landor addressed Delphine. "Is your mother here, mademoiselle?" She was struck by the contrast between his expression and his words; his face had a frigid politeness, but his voice, deeper and somehow more stirring than Ferron's, had a natural energy in it that even this uneasy situation could not diminish.

"She is, thank you."

"Then I look forward to seeing her later on. Excuse me." He dipped his head to her, nodded to Ferron and strode off, leaving him holding the shotgun. He was followed by two beaters carrying a collection of game and bags.

"Brusque," Ferron said condescendingly. "Good breeding, a fine shot, but brusque. How do you find him?"

He examined her face as he waited for an answer. She wondered if he wished to know whether he should be jealous. Had he heard anything? Heaven grant that no one besides the Duc de Limours connected her feelings in any way with Landor. "He can sometimes be very amusing. It rather depends on the company."

"Then I'll expect to be amused tonight. For in all modesty, Miss Dalgleish, you'll find I've assembled a capital crowd."

Gideon was furious with himself. He'd known she might be here and yet he was totally unprepared—for her glowing beauty, her laughing ease with Ferron and her embarrassment when she caught sight of him. They could never talk normally again after his catastrophic proposal. He was doomed to look resentful and she a coquette—and she was doing a damned good job of that today. He had not missed the play of hands and glances as Ferron helped her down from the horse. Nor had anyone else, he noticed. It was a blatant display of proprietorship on Ferron's part, and she lent herself to it.

When he'd changed and walked downstairs again he caught sight of la Générale in the music room, sitting in a corner listening to one of the young ladies practicing on the piano. As he passed the door she looked up and gave a surprised smile of welcome. He walked in and greeted her, then joined her on the sofa as the lady at the piano continued to play.

While la Générale chatted, he speculated about her plans. She had given him mild encouragement not too long ago—and look where that had led. The marital prospect was much more likely to be Lord Ferron. But in the end, did she really want her daughter to marry an Englishman?

"Have you heard from Governor Farquhar at all?"

"No," she said, then brightened. "But Madame D'Arifat saw him not long ago; she's positive he'll write to us soon. And they say Captain Arkwright is about to come to England! He's been granted leave."

"What about the plantation?"

"We don't know the details yet. But a change like that . . . well, I think it would require our return. Or we'd have to appoint a steward. Either way, my daughter may soon be able to take Saint-Amour back in hand. The relief! You've no idea."

"I hope so, for your sake." He watched her face as he said, "And what is your preference? To return to Mauritius, or stay in England?"

He saw a sudden sadness in her eyes. "Ah, you are forgetting the third alternative—France. And do you know, I really can't tell you? I want the best for my daughter, but these days she seems quite unsure about what she wants." She adjusted her Indian silk shawl over her forearms. "She has a very determined character, monsieur, as I'm sure you've noticed. I'm not used to her being indecisive. It worries me."

He could not tell whether there were any special clues for him embedded in this little confession. He wasn't going to contradict her about Mademoiselle Dalgleish's strength of will! "I must bow to your judgment, madame. I can't claim to be in Mademoiselle Dalgleish's confidence."

La Générale said gently, "But we value your friendship. If she were to turn to you for advice, what would you say to her?"

"I?" It was a bitter conversation to him, made all the more so by the trusting sincerity of la Générale's question. "If I thought she would listen to me, I would advise that she first resolve the issue of Saint-Amour. She loves it; it's her true home. I thought— I think—she might be able to find happiness elsewhere, but only if Saint-Amour were secure and unspoiled."

La Générale sighed. "You're right, monsieur, as usual."

Gideon, who was more used to being egregiously wrong,

changed the subject. "I see nothing of the Duc de Limours these days. How is he?"

"We don't see him either. My daughter has fallen out with him. A pity—he and his sister are such pleasant old people."

His heart lurched. Could this mean she'd broken with the Bonapartists? "What caused the rift?"

She looked unhappy. "I've been told it was too insignificant to discuss. So I have no idea. But the connection seems to be over."

This was it: now was the time to strike Limours. Now, while Delphine Dalgleish's name was not linked to the duke's. What evidence was there against her? Possibly only the paper he still held, which contained the reference: *Mademoiselle D is about to make her visit to LB at T.* When he handed it over with the rest of the documents condemning Limours, could anyone decypher that phrase without his help?

He rose. "I shall leave you to enjoy the music, madame. I look forward to seeing you at dinner."

Delphine found the dinner and supper intolerable. She saw Landor at both meals, but not once during the hours between. Many of the gentlemen had separate pursuits—billiards, riding, fishing—and Landor was presumably one of them. Meanwhile, the shooting match was scheduled for the following morning, after the game shooting proper, on a lawn near the Greek folly at the head of the serpentine lake, and everyone expected Landor to win. The ladies had all placed their bets on his side; only Delphine had declined to wager, and Ferron, perhaps rather pleased with this, had not tried to persuade her otherwise.

The meals were lively and Landor participated—not with as much brilliance as he had displayed at Thorngrove, but with enough address to keep his part of the table animated. She was galled by being a witness to this while not being able to contribute, for he was at a distance and she could not make out what he was saying through Lord Ferron's constant attentions. At supper she was seated on the host's left, which was already conspicuous enough. Darting her eye around the table, convinced that in the English scheme of things there was bound to be a lady of higher rank, she could see no one who strictly speaking should take precedence. His lordship had chosen his female guests with cunning flair. Her mother was the only lady who had claim to a higher place, and she was lying down with a headache. There was no denying the position where favoritism had placed Delphine, and as she looked down the board she caught a glance from Landor that looked like frosty disdain. Which made it a point of pride for her to aim a great deal of liveliness in Ferron's direction.

Gideon meanwhile was running out of patience and time. He cursed himself for being in this diabolical situation, forced to watch Delphine Dalgleish's public partiality for Ferron and his lordship's for her. He tried to keep the people around him entertained, to drown out the sound of her musical laughter from the head of the table. In a spirit of malice he chose the subject of his incarceration on Mauritius. He gave acid descriptions of the evenings when the British inmates at the Maison Despeaux were treated more like guests than prisoners, and he satirized the ridiculous side of Decaën's stiff-necked autocracy. He was tempted also to give a witty version of his escape and the theft of the yacht, and one or two people in the know were obviously hoping he would stray onto that adventure. The thought trembled in the air, electrifying his section of the table.

And all the while he longed to go—straight back to London. His object at the moment should be Limours, not Ferron. He caught himself drinking too much wine and made himself slow down. He would have to take care of the Ferron issue tonight. Later, when everyone was asleep, he would try the desk in the library. He still had the keys that had delivered the whole code into his hands in Paris—God grant that they would uncover one cursed sheet of it in the next few hours. If he had no luck, he would drag his lordship out of bed and confront him. Gideon's tolerance had run out the moment he came back from the morning's shooting and looked into that bloated, complacent face. And he wouldn't be hanging around for tomorrow's contest! Let Ferron fight his own matches.

Delphine Dalgleish was safely here in the country, which made it imperative that within the next few days Gideon unleash the troops on Limours and his cohorts in London. What happened after that would be out of his hands. There had never been such a roundup of spies in England, so he was unsure what verdicts would fall upon the conspirators when they came before the courts. If significant documents were found in Limours's possession, he might hang for espionage. If not, he faced life imprisonment, probably on one of the hulks in the Thames where England kept her political prisoners and her military captives of low rank. No Garden Prisons for them! The rest faced jail, or deportation to France with their families and confiscation of everything they held in England.

It was Gideon who would sweep these people from English life, but the idea caused him no triumph. He felt revulsion, increased by a haunting dilemma about whether Mademoiselle Dalgleish could escape the net. But he had to get beyond that. The time had come.

Delphine wondered how had she gotten into the state where one boring meal in the midlands tore her apart in this fashion. She was being pursued by a nobleman whom she scarcely even liked, and her whole attention was captivated by the very man who most deserved to be called her enemy. Landor was the only man at this table who had really experienced the conflict that opposed her country to his; he had fought the French in an arena that no one in this dining room had ever been forced to enter. Through a singular error, he had overlooked that truth for one dreamlike interval, and proposed that they forget the barriers that divided them and leap over into a new existence. And she had turned away, horrified by the idea that any understanding might exist between them.

She could not help watching him as he spoke to the people around him. There were nuances in his expression that to her observant eye seemed beyond the capacity of tonight's company to pick up. He looked lonely in the way that people sometimes are when their deepest preoccupations stand at a tragic remove from the company they have fallen amongst. It was strange, but of all the people in the room that night she was best equipped to speak to him on an intimate basis. But the gates were closed between them.

She kept noticing things about him that had always been there, and that she had registered despite all her former enmity. The way he ran a hand back through his hair, after which one fair lock always escaped from discipline and fell forward above his right eye. The contrast between the brightness of his hair and the dark, exclamatory eyebrows. The submarine surge of irony in his green eyes when someone next to him made a foolish comment. The way he waited, his well-shaped mouth curving, unhurried and amused, for the right moment to retaliate. His self-sufficiency had always scandalized her. For the first time—and much too late—she saw how far it lay from self-indulgence.

Later, over coffee, she sat in a corner, waiting for the gentlemen to walk through into the gallery and join the ladies, and surrounded by French and Italian paintings, in a stately home owned by an English lord who hated every one of her countrymen apart, presumably, from the most successful artists. To her surprise Landor was the first to walk in for coffee. Cup and saucer in hand, he looked around, and for reasons of his own ignored the eager looks flung at him from each side of the long room and headed for her corner.

She drew in the embroidered panel of her cream sarsenet gown across the sofa, but after greeting her he sat opposite in a chair and flicked a glance upward. "Do you know the painter there above you?

"Ingres? Not personally. But I admire his work. Why?"

"No special reason. I know very little of French painting. I thought you might enlighten me."

She didn't turn toward the picture, which as far as she could remember featured an oriental lady displayed on a sofa. Or a French noblewoman draped across an ottoman. "I'm more familiar with Ingres's portraits of the emperor and his family. I believe he has the idea of painting Lucien Bonaparte and his children one day."

"That seems unlikely in the near future." He crossed his long legs and raised the coffee cup to his lips.

"Who knows?" she said. "If they are ever allowed to leave England, I should be surprised to see them go anywhere but France."

He lowered the cup. "You don't see them petitioning to move on to America?"

She shook her head. "The emperor pushed them to the limit. He has a habit of doing that; he presents people with an idea of France—and if it's too extreme they find themselves rejecting France and him at the same time. Then, after a dismal period, they return and tackle him again, for the love of the country they turned their back on. If your armies are successful, Lucien Bonaparte will go home one day, and everyone will take up the old arguments from where they left off."

He followed her reckless lead. "And you, mademoiselle? When will you return?"

"I have no idea. The France that my mother and father knew is long gone. I see my motherland through Mauritian eyes, and the longer I live away from it the more distorted that view becomes. I wish I could go home. But I'm not sure where home is."

"You feel nothing for Scotland, your father's birthplace?"

"No, how can I? Mrs. Laidlaw and I have discussed it—Edinburgh especially. But I can't build a country out of her memories."

"Your father told you nothing about Scotland?" He looked troubled, as though pitying her for such a deprivation. This was one of the frankest conversations they had ever had. Was he entering into it because he thought it might be the last? Did he imagine Ferron was about to thrust himself between them for good?

"No. But he did tell me what it was like to abandon Scotland and join France, with only his ideals to sustain him. He was not young when he threw in his lot with the Convention. Nowhere near as young as Napoleon Bonaparte when they managed to win the siege of Toulon together. But he was committed, and remained so all his life."

He put down the coffee cup and saucer on a spindle-legged table at his side. "Did he die in action?"

"No. He was at Saint-Amour, under my mother's care. It was a kidney complaint. There was nothing anyone could do." She was brushing her right hand down one panel of her gown. "It has given me a horror of waiting for disaster. I tend to react strongly instead. Sometimes without thinking overmuch." She saw a thread of color appear along his high cheekbones: oh, God, was he recalling how she had turned him down?

He said, "How long do you and your mother stay here?"

"We've said a week."

He nodded, as though he found the answer satisfactory. "Then I shall be back in London before you." He paused a moment and the green of his eyes grew veiled, like the sea on a misty day. "I sail from Greenwich very soon."

It felt sharp and unexpected, even though she had known that he must return to duty at some point. "How long will you be away?"

"Some months."

"And where do you go?

A cryptic smile. "That's unconfirmed, as yet."

"Oh, of course you can't tell me. But I meant—if you go back to the fleet in the Indian Ocean, you'll see Ile de France again before I do."

"I do not go so far." There was the sound of male voices approaching and he rose at once from the chair. "I'm glad I've had the chance to bid you farewell."

She rose too and exclaimed, "But you don't mean *now!*" She was filled with the ridiculous apprehension that he was about to walk out of the house this instant, never to be seen again. "Surely . . . you haven't forgotten the contest tomorrow?"

"No, but I wouldn't count on my presence, Mademoiselle Dalgleish."

She looked at him in astonishment. "Monsieur, you must be bamboozling me. It's not like you to walk away from a confrontation!"

The gentlemen walked into the room behind him and Delphine saw Ferron at once look her way. Landor said with a sardonic smile, "Do I take it you've wagered deeply?"

"I've done no such thing! I can't believe we're talking about bets when you've just told me you are leaving the country."

He spoke very low. "Please don't mention this to anyone. I should have liked to say something to your mother too, but since she's unwell . . ." There was movement behind him; their tête-à-tête was over. "Allow me to wish you both every blessing. Good night, Mademoiselle Dalgleish."

She extended her hand, and he took it, bowed over it, then raised it fleetingly to his lips. Her fingers burned. She withdrew them, feeling hollow and dazed. "I don't understand. This seems so wrong."

"Until we meet again." Without another word to anyone he walked out of the gallery.

Upstairs, Gideon gave Ellis his instructions. He could see they were not too welcome; Ellis must have set his sights on one of the women servants. The speed at which the man worked was impressive. "You can pack first. Then roam about, keep your eyes open and come and report to me as soon as everyone's in their chambers. Everyone, you understand?"

The rejoinder was stiff. "Very good, sir. Will there be anything else?"

"You can cheer up, for God's sake. The reason we're going back to London is to tighten the noose around the Duc de Limours. A noose of your own making, Ellis. Tonight's piece of work is a bagatelle compared to that."

Delphine stayed on in the gallery, fielding Lord Ferron's conversation while she puzzled about Landor. What did he mean by striding across the room to accost her, then making that abrupt farewell? After coffee everyone trooped off to the music room, and during the performances she went back over Landor's every word. He was jealous of Ferron, no doubt, though he managed to look almost as superior and invulnerable as ever. Distaste for her flirtation with his lordship might have made him decide to leave Paget after just one day, but she wasn't accustomed to seeing him run before an opponent. No, there was something else going on.

He had looked almost *relieved* when she said she wasn't going back to London for a week. Why should that be? What was he planning that made her absence desirable? A chill settled around her heart at a sudden idea—maybe he was about to offer for someone else. As autumn began, families were drifting back to town; had one of the mamas of last season sealed her daughter's prospects with him after all? Delphine had no right to object to this—but how would she bear such a consequence of her hasty words at Thorngrove? He was a man of action. He might well have taken a decision about his future in a rash moment after she turned him down.

Finally she excused herself, pleading worry about her mother. Lord Ferron let her go, with many expressions of concern, and she went upstairs in haste, desperate to be alone. Her mother was asleep, so she went to her room, ordered some chocolate and sat fully dressed on the bed.

It was diabolical of Landor to come to Paget. She could not feel easy or derive the slightest enjoyment from the occasion while he was by. Every time she spoke to Ferron she felt false. Every time she spoke to Landor she felt accused—yet nothing in his eyes condemned her; in fact, she admired his control. But whatever he did or said, he made her feel as though she were lending herself to some horrible charade. She must put a stop to it, tonight. The chances of inveigling her way into Ferron's confidence were high, but she hadn't the stomach to continue. She must leave her room tonight when everyone had gone to bed, and see what could be discovered amongst his papers. She had found out where most of them were, and a deft search would show her what she wanted to know. The emperor had let her see a simulated page of the code—if Ferron possessed anything like it, she would recognize it at once. She must have done with this mission, before it destroyed her self-respect. She was here for one purpose. It was time to accomplish it.

The wait was agonizing. She was in one of the principal rooms and thus close to the heart of the great house rather than relegated to one of the wings like the less favored. Every now and then she heard someone on the staircase coming up to bed, but there were voices below from time to time, and she guessed that some of the gentlemen had lured one another into a few more hours of billiards, brandy and cigars. She dismissed her maid, Molly, and after a failed attempt to concentrate on a book, she extinguished the candles, except for one in a small candlestick that she shielded with the unread tome.

Finally she heard another group of men come up to her floor, with Ferron amongst them. This must mean the servants would be scooping up the debris before they made their own less clamorous way to bed. Half an hour should do it.

When she emerged, it was with a feeling of dread. As she went down the stairs in her slippers, she had the impression of being watched by the dark family portraits on each side, as though she were running the gauntlet of a score of stern, judgmental Englishmen. She held her candle low and listened to the great house settling around her. Apart from the ancestors, no one was watching her stealthy progress.

She reached the library with a silly, wild relief, closed the door behind her and placed the little candlestick on the central table. It was a vast, square room that she had admired when Lord Ferron gave her a tour in the afternoon. It had a large fireplace, unlit in this season, and the walls were lined with books, except for a few floor-to-ceiling panels hung with trophies or paintings. Against one panel, opposite the door, was a handsome desk with pigeonholes above and compartments below.

It must be a quiet and pleasant place to work. There was a thick carpet under the table and the door was padded. Delphine stood in the silence, breathing shallowly. If someone came in, she could claim that she couldn't get to sleep without something to read. A feeble excuse, perhaps—and useless if she were found elbow-deep in Ferron's private papers. But she had come this far; she would carry out her promise.

She put the candle on the left corner of the desk and began with the pigeonholes on that side. The results were encouraging; these were not his lordship's billet doux, but recent correspondence to do with the estates. She worked fast. She had no need to read anything, for a glance at each was enough. The section of the code that she had seen was very distinctive: a squared, regular grid filled in with neat writing. If she found such a page, she could not mistake it.

There were some central drawers above the desktop, which she opened once she had gone through the pigeonholes, having returned every document with care so that nothing would look disturbed. The drawers yielded piles of papers folded and dated on the outside—copies of accounts. She was engrossed, swiftly scanning then stacking them in the right order. It was much easier than she had expected. At this rate, she would be through the whole desk in less than half an hour.

If it had been any other room than a library, she might have been more attentive to what went on around her. If there had not been that cushioning of books, that protective hush that a fine reading room affords, she wouldn't have allowed herself to be so absorbed by what she found there.

She had no idea there was anyone on the same floor, let alone in the same room, until she heard a footfall behind her and whirled, choking with terror, to be transfixed by the pitiless gaze of Sir Gideon Landor.

The Arrangement

⌒

She screamed. But it happened in her head. In reality, her voice failed her. She gasped instead, the intake of breath muffled by her hands as she pressed them to her mouth and shrank back against the desk in a frantic movement that made the candle flame flutter.

Landor, his broad shoulders and the strong planes of his face fitfully touched by the light, loomed out of the shadows. "Silence," he hissed, "silence, for Christ's sake."

Her ears rang as though he had dealt her a blow. Tears of panic sprang from her eyes and ran down over the fingers pressed to her cheeks. She would have fallen if the edge of the desktop had not given her some support. *Caught.* She was caught out, guilty of spying on her host. Even in her terror, there was a stab of pain that it should be Landor who had come to frighten her with his wintry gaze.

They stood looking at each other for a second, which to Delphine stretched to an intolerable length. She struggled to breathe. Then suddenly, from across the room, she heard a sound outside the library door. She gave a helpless, inward sob and her eyes widened.

Landor's head turned and he threw a quick glance over his shoulder. Meanwhile Delphine lowered her hands and felt the tears go cold on her cheeks. Landor had discovered her rifling through Ferron's papers. Behind her, the desktop lay stacked with documents and the drawers were open. She was brutally exposed, and now came retribution—for over Landor's shoulder she saw the door move, and she knew that Lord Ferron was about to fling it wide and walk into the room.

Landor turned back to her. There was a spark in the green eyes like a rogue fire in a summer field, then he stepped forward and kissed her. Both hands went about her waist, riveting her body to his. His lips were firm and warm, and they delivered an impact that filled her mind with white flame. She had not an instant to protest or even form a thought. She was engulfed, overwhelmed, and at the same time a fiery energy coursed through her, dissolving her terror of Landor. She was afraid of Ferron, but not of this man. What was more, she found herself responding. It was impossible not to raise her arms and slide them around his neck, seeking this chance of shelter and release. It was irresistible to bury her fingers in his hair and draw his head down, deepening the kiss and causing him to utter a wordless sound in the back of his throat that found an echo in hers.

Her lips explored, questioning in a new language whose existence she had never guessed. She forgot where she was. The world shrank to a golden pool of candlelight where she floated against him, her mouth opening while with lips and tongue he spoke to her in a way that she recognized, even though she had never in her life held a man like this. She knew desire and felt instantly drunk with it. Until now, everything they had said to each other had seemed wrong. All at once, in this dazzling moment, what they did felt miraculously right.

Through half-closed eyes she saw that his were tight shut. His breath quickened and his skin grew hot against her face. But he released her mouth and drew back, and his eyes opened, glittering with an unspoken demand. She clung to him, trying to gather her senses. This was scandalous; danger screamed at her from every side, but her whole body yearned for the intoxicating moment to continue.

He whispered, "Don't say a word," then he tightened his right arm around her waist and turned with her so that they stood facing Ferron. Landor pressed her to him and her left arm was hooked over his shoulder. To keep her balance she gripped the edge of the desk with the other hand, a few inches from the candle flame. Before she could bear to look at Ferron's face she closed her eyes and breathed in Landor—the fresh linen of his evening shirt, a hint of the soap he used on his smooth skin. On her fingers, later, she would carry the scent of his sun-bleached hair. And at the same time her mind began to work. Whereupon she realized that in the intimate posture he had chosen, they obscured the havoc she had wrought on the desk. Ferron could not see that she had been going through his papers. He had not yet found her guilty of spying. Instead he had found her embracing Landor.

She opened her eyes and saw Ferron's face. Jealousy and anger distorted it so radically that he looked ill. He was staring at Landor with fury, his expression illuminated by the candle he held. He must have somehow heard Landor descending the stairs, grabbed a light and followed him. But whatever his lordship had expected to find, it was certainly not this scene.

Landor spoke, his voice deep and serious, reverberating through Delphine's ribcage. "I apologize, Ferron. You were not meant to witness this." Ferron took a step forward, his lips drawn back from his teeth in a grimace of outrage. Delphine trembled—this meant a duel. No gentleman could allow another to force himself upon a lady staying under his roof. Landor continued with the same firmness, "I'm sorry you've found out in such a way. But I must tell you: Mademoiselle Dalgleish and I are engaged."

Ferron stopped as though he had been punched in the chest. He looked at Delphine, and she quailed before the ugly contempt in his eyes. He was so stunned, he could not tell whether Landor was telling the truth or not. He needed her to confirm a monstrous fact—that she had been dallying with him by day but she was prepared to carry on like this with Landor by night.

Her throat closed. She could not have spoken if she'd wanted to. For concealed behind her lay the far more damning evidence that she was a spy in his house.

Ferron held her gaze. "Is this true?"

Landor's arm tightened around her and he said with finality, "Yes. In future you may address such questions to me."

Ferron stepped back. His black eyes smoldered like dying coals as he ground out, "I want you gone. I want you both gone tomorrow!"

Landor said, "As you wish. Good night, my lord."

Ferron gave an exclamation that sounded like the beginning of an insult, then turned on his heel and marched to the door. He wrenched it open, and without looking back he stepped into the hallway and was gone.

The door closed on its finely oiled hinges, and Gideon withdrew his arm gradually from around Delphine Dalgleish's waist. She was looking straight ahead, disbelief on her face, as the door finally shut with a sigh and they were alone again. When he moved away and turned to face her, she looked so overwrought that he feared she might fall. "Sit down," he said, yanking the chair forward so that it was angled toward him.

With a shudder, her voice returned. "What have you *done*?"

"Sit down. And listen."

She sank into the chair. She still looked as pliant and warm and divine as when he'd kissed her, but she was about to defy him, nonetheless. He was brutal. "Do you know the penalties for espionage in Britain?"

She paled. "What makes you think—?"

"Oh, spare me, for God's sake." He controlled his voice. "I've just saved you from death by hanging. If you had escaped that, it would have been life imprisonment in unspeakable conditions. Or deportation to France, with the loss of all your English possessions. Including Saint-Amour." That hit her. Her mouth opened and she looked at him in horror. He ran one hand through his hair. "Are you crazy? Have you given this no thought at all? You risked your life tonight. If Ferron had come in before I did, nothing could have saved you. He's no idiot; he'd have known exactly what you were doing." She was shaking. "But he might not have been able to guess what you were searching for. Which was . . . ?"

She sat back. "You've just accused me of spying. Do you expect me to tell you?"

"You have no choice." He watched the admission fill her eyes: her life had been in his hands from the moment he came into the room. It still was. He said, "You were looking for a document. I have a right to know what it was. That, at least, you will tell me."

She thought for a moment, her hands clamped together in her lap so tightly that he wanted to lean forward and take them in his own and part her fingers. Then with a bitter clarity she said, "When Lord Ferron was in Paris, he tried to buy the emperor's grand code for Spain." Her words slammed into Gideon and he looked away from her, hiding his intense surprise. She went on, "He asked me to find out whether Ferron had any pages of the code in his possession."

He rounded on her. "*He* being Bonaparte."

"Yes."

He must divert her away from the code, until he could handle everything that this meant. "And? What else brought you to England?"

"I delivered one letter."

"Also from Bonaparte, I gather. To whom?"

She sat erect again, smoothing the embroidered gown. "You've cornered me about my own secrets, monsieur. But I will not betray anyone else's."

He riposted, "Do you really think they'd show the same fidelity to you?" He was so close to naming the Duc de Limours that he had to bite his tongue. She had no idea that Limours was exposed. At the risk of his country's security, he was trying to shield the woman he loved from arrest—he could not compromise it further by letting her warn Limours. He half turned away and waited for her to answer.

Her voice was very quiet. "I believe they would. And I've told you the truth. This was my last act for the emperor in England. I've failed—I have no idea whether Ferron holds the code."

A great throb of relief made him turn back to her. "He doesn't." She started and gave him a penetrating look—pray God she never guessed that it was the code itself that had taken him to Paris, but there was no reason why she should make the connection. "Ferron does not have it. He tried to buy it, but he didn't succeed. You have that on my word of honor."

It was painful to see her consternation, and even more painful to see how she struggled with the notion of taking his word.

He pressed the point. "Your mission is over, mademoiselle. Do me the honor of believing me." His voice fell. "I shan't speculate about the understanding between you and his lordship. But you must have noticed one thing—he exaggerates his power and his achievements. He may have boasted about having the code. If so, I can assure you, on everything that's sacred—he didn't obtain it."

She lowered her head and looked at her hands. He could not tell whether she believed him. She might be about to cry, to curse him, to run from the room—he had no clue. It was all he could do not to fling himself down before her and take her in his arms again. Then she raised her head, her blue eyes as candid as a summer sky. "I never wanted any of this. I did my duty."

"Then I beg you, accept that it's over."

"Very well." She pressed her fingers briefly to her eyelids and said, "You will now explain what in heaven's name we do next."

"You mean what I said to Lord Ferron? The engagement?" She lowered her hands and nodded. He said in hard voice. "It was necessary."

"But what do I do now?"

It had gone from *we* to *I*. That quickly. "Why do you ask? You'd sooner run after Ferron and deny it?" He stepped aside and gestured to the door. "Consult your own wishes, mademoiselle. You do realize he would call me out? But go ahead if you like: I've no objection to killing him."

She shivered but stayed put. She said, *"How could you do this?"*

Had she really been after Ferron? If so, her regrets must be tenfold. But she must also understand there was no going back. "I already know just how unpalatable you find the idea of betrothal to me." Before she could demur at this sarcastic opening he went on, "But be assured there is a simple release at hand. To convince Lord Ferron, we must convince the world—but we don't have to be side by side to do it. You haven't forgotten that I'm about to go to sea? I expect to be back by Christmas or the new year: you may jilt me then, and regain your liberty. A small price to pay, I suggest, for your life."

She took it all in like an unpleasant draught of medicine. "Four months?"

"More or less. During which time everyone will assume that our families are working out the marriage settlement."

"*Ah, mon dieu. Ma mère.*"

"Indeed. And my parents. They must all be told the truth. We owe it to them." She gasped and he went on, "I insist. Mine will abominate the lie but I can guarantee they'll maintain it. I pay your mother the tribute of believing the same of her. No one else must know."

"*Oh.* This is so terrible."

"Come, it's in name only. You won't have to see me for months. And as soon as I return you can break it off. I leave tonight."

She looked bewildered. "So you did mean that, earlier? Then what were you *doing* tonight? Why did you come in here?"

"I happened to be in the hall when you came out of your room. I followed you."

"You crept after me!"

"Yes. I was curious to know where you might be going at that hour."

"But that's dreadful."

"No more so than what you were doing when I entered this room." He had to hope she wouldn't suspect that he had come to the library on the same errand as she. In fact, he must hope that she thought him jealous; that he had followed her to see whether she was keeping some midnight rendezvous with Ferron. "I think you should go."

She rose, only inches away. The kiss burned in his mind. She had responded; her body had clung to his, against her will and judgment. He had saved her with that hot, impetuous embrace. If it meant as much to her as it did to him, she would remember it for the rest of her life. But looking into her sky blue eyes, he could see only clouds of confusion.

He said, "When you leave tomorrow, don't go to London. Pay a visit to the Bonapartes at Thorngrove. Stay a few days at least, just in case: it's the best cover you could have."

"Do you really think—?"

"Promise me. Promise me to do so." He took her hand; he couldn't help it. "Do we have an agreement, mademoiselle?"

It cost her a lot. It caused him a sharp access of pain to see how heavy a burden she thought it, but she twisted her hand and gripped his fingers. "You have my word."

He released her and bowed. "I shall write. Solely to give credence to the arrangement, no more; have no fear."

"Thank you."

He went to the central table and took up a single candlestick. Then he lit the candle from the one she had on the desk, and handed hers over. Their fingers did not touch.

Without looking at him, she moved off, and then, halfway across the room, she paused and turned back toward him. Her low voice, normally so fluid and playful, sounded as solemn as a church bell. "Thank you," she said again, and left the room.

Gideon collapsed into the chair she had vacated and leaned one elbow on the armrest, his clenched fist pressed to his lips. There was a harsh sensation in the back of his throat, like the taste of blood. She was safe. He had to believe that. Ferron, humiliated and uncomprehending, would give la Générale's indisposition as a reason for her departure and then never mention the Dalgleishes again. And woe betide anyone else who did so in his lordship's presence.

His tired brain shrank before what he had done. He had acted for her, in desperate necessity, and he must face the consequences. Meanwhile, the chaos she had created on the desk was on full display. Eventually he stacked the papers and returned them to the upper drawers. Then he pulled out his bundle of cabinetmakers' keys and tried the locked compartments below the desktop.

As in Paris, they finally yielded. This was the inner sanctum: here were the love letters from women—or begging letters from courtesans, whichever way one cared to read them. Here was a lengthy trail of dealings with moneylenders in Greek Street. He worked fast and came to the last piece of paper on the last shelf;

the very evidence that Delphine Dalgleish had been searching for. He pulled it out and held it under the candle flame. He recognized the ruled grid, the very same list of words and parts of words that he had recorded in the bureau in Paris. It was so meticulously copied that at first glance it might have been the same sheet. But the writing, though modeled on his, was not in his hand. And there was a minor spelling error in one line. Someone with an imperfect knowledge of French had made that tiny mistake when they forged the copy for Ferron.

651 mieu

One missing "x" made the difference between the genuine code and a party trick.

He flattened it against the desktop and looked at it. This was what she had risked her life for. And if she had discovered it, she could not have known that it was meaningless—a mere facsimile of a copy. She would have believed that Ferron had bought the code; that the English had the whole of Napoleon's *grand chiffre* in their possession. Whereas all England had was the unfinished sheet that Gideon himself had extracted from Paris.

He crushed the paper in his fist. He wasn't going to leave Ferron with this, but its absence would be noticed, and he could not risk Ferron suspecting that Delphine Dalgleish had been in the library for anything other than a nighttime rendezvous. He thrust the other papers back and locked the compartment, then went from the library and up the stairs with the candlestick in his hand, the tall flame quivering with his progress. He knew Ferron's room. When he reached it he simply pushed open the door and walked in.

His lordship was in bed but not asleep: the dark head came up instantly from the pillow and a hoarse voice reached Gideon from across the room: "Damn you, sir, what the hell are you playing at?" He flung back the covers and was half out of bed when Gideon got to him and thrust out paper and light.

"This." Ferron's gaze fell on the code and he gave a sharp intake of breath. "Yes," Gideon said, then turned on his heel and went to the washing table by the wall. He dumped the candlestick in the ewer and held the sheet of code over the flame. As the paper curled and ignited in his fingers, he said, "You never saw it. It never existed. And you will never speak of it again."

"Who gives you the bloody right to go through my affairs!"

"I think you can guess. That's why I'm at Paget. I waited until I was alone in the library and then opened the desk. I presume there's nothing more I should be looking for?" He dropped the last scrap of paper into the ewer.

"No!" Ferron was standing, advancing. "Then what the devil was *she* doing there?" Without waiting for an answer he said in an ugly tone, "You're no more engaged than I am, are you? And she's nothing but a—"

"Watch what you say," Gideon snapped. The man was dying to fight him, but that was no part of tonight's aim. "She deserves every respect. We are engaged; you have my word." Baffled, Ferron bit his lip and clenched his fists. Gideon could almost feel sorry for him. "I'm in love with her," he said painfully. "Are you?"

Ferron's eyes probed his, dark and threatening. But Gideon's honesty, or some vestige of his own, made him answer. *"No."* He collected himself and sneered, "Is that all? Am I about to see your fucking back?"

Gideon left the candle where it was, stepped back and bowed slightly. "Excuse me," he said as though he were leaving a drawing room, and walked out.

At her toilette the next morning, Delphine heard the story of Landor's departure from her maid. Molly, agog, had heard it from one of the valets, who had been tipped off by one of his lordship's grooms, who had been roused by Ellis in the early hours and ordered to help Sir Gideon's coachman put the horses to. Molly sounded as aggrieved as Ellis must have: "He says it's become the way with Sir Gideon lately, miss, and a fearful inconvenience it is. Ellis says they always leave at the very same time—always at blighted midnight!"

Delphine, watching in the glass as Molly fixed her hair, murmured something, trying to work out what she felt about Landor being gone. Did Molly have a penchant for his valet? "Is Ellis the fellow Sir Gideon had at Thorngrove?"

"Oh, no, that one didn't know half his duties, Ellis said. He was dismissed within the month."

"I presume the grooms were given something for their trouble this morning?"

"Oh, yes, miss. Ellis says Sir Gideon is nothing if not liberal."

"Speaking of which, you'll inform Lord Ferron's housekeeper that we leave today." Molly paused with a comb in the air, her round, pretty face all astonishment. "If my mother is well enough to travel, that is. Could you finish, please? I want to go and see her."

Too amazed to speak, Molly did as she was told, and after a while Delphine said as calmly as she could manage, "Before we leave, you may hear a rumor around the house. If so, you are not to deny it." She fixed Molly's brown eyes in the glass. "You may be told that Sir Gideon Landor and I are engaged."

The comb dropped. "Goodness! Oh my *goodness!*" Turning crimson, Molly bent to pick it up. "Am I—am I to wish you joy, miss?"

"Thank you." Delphine rose, and Molly put the comb on the dressing table and moved away. "Now you may go and find the housekeeper."

Molly said in bewildered tones, "Shall you be breakfasting downstairs, miss?"

"No, please have something brought up to my mother's room."

"Very good." Molly bobbed a curtsy and withdrew.

Delphine walked to the window and looked down on the gravel sweep and the grassed terraces before the house. He was gone. But every touch from the night before was imprinted on her body. With one passionate kiss, he had saved her from execution. With one swift lie, he had sheltered and protected her. He loved her, but he had walked out of her life, leaving her free.

She had accomplished nearly everything she was in England to do. Only the fate of Saint-Amour hung in the balance, and even its direction, if she regained it, would be owing in part to him and his efforts at the Admiralty. It was love that had prompted him to consult the best of English legal opinion for her sake. It was love that had driven him to compromise his own patriotism last night and conceal hers. He had just shared one of his country's secrets with a woman he had caught in the very act of spying—a woman, moreover, who had rejected him only the month before.

Would his love outlast the reproach he must be inflicting on himself at this moment? She should be hoping that it would not; she should be praying that the months at sea would strip every tender feeling away and leave him as cold and passionless as she had believed him to be from the first. But his kiss lingered, telling another story. She put her fingers on her lips, as though the clue to his emotions lay there, still to be decyphered. Impossible longing filled her again, making her throat ache and her body tremble. It was almost as though with one embrace he had become tangled in the fibers of her being. And at that very moment he had decided to wrench himself away.

This wouldn't do. No power on earth could help her understand him. To regain control at all costs over her own will, she left her chamber and went to knock on the door of the next. The mortifying time had come when she must confess to her mother everything she had been concealing over the last six months.

Betrothed

〜

In the second week of September 1811, there was a series of raids in French houses across London. Troops armed with warrants acted at night, when the Bonapartists were at home, and too swiftly for them to pass on warnings to the others in the network. To the astonishment of society, the Duc de Limours, one of the oldest and most respected of the émigré community, was indicted as the ringleader of a long-standing conspiracy, and a cartload of documents was confiscated from his town house. The investigation to follow was expected to put his guilt beyond doubt.

The ton was back in town, ready for entertainment after a restful month or two in the country, and feelings ran high at gatherings across town. Everyone French in the capital suddenly became questionable, and dramatic sides were taken. Those who were known to have enjoyed the company of the Duc de Limours and his sister for the last eighteen years or more could only fall back on speaking of "witch hunts." Those whose association with the duke had been more casual or more recent, such as Lord Ferron, claimed they'd been suspicious of him all along.

French people returning to the city after the event were subject to speculation. The Dalgleishes, for instance, absent from London on the night of the arrests, were much talked about when they came back. Oddly, though, la Générale's links to Napoleon Bonaparte were her salvation, for the very reason that she had never hidden them. Her daughter mixed in émigré circles in London but la Générale had until now tended to avoid them. And interestingly, she was known to have spent a few days at Thorngrove with her daughter. This suggested a new anti-Napoleonic leaning that caught the imagination of the ton.

And then there was the betrothal! The story that filtered back from Paget was delicious. Now, there, *everyone* had been taken in. Opinion had been categorical that Delphine Dalgleish would end up with Lord Ferron—their long-standing flirtation and his financial circumstances pointed that way. But then came Sir Gideon Landor's lightning coup. No one except a few young men at his club and, it was said, Georgiana, Duchess of Combrewood, had seen even a hint of partiality on either side. It was all thrillingly sudden: he had gone to Paget on the pretext of a shooting contest; he failed to stay on for that, and so lost the wager—and meanwhile, from under his lordship's nose, he won the contest that really mattered. The families were said to be drawing up a settlement in preparation for the wedding in the new year, and no one was going to doubt Mademoiselle Dalgleish's credentials in high society after that news.

Delphine was at Berkeley Square on a misty morning toward the end of September, safe and utterly wretched. The arrest of the Duc de Limours appalled her, all the more so because she realized just how close she had been to sharing his fate. He had not yet come to trial, terrible things had been heard about the prison where he was being held and no one could visit him. His worst enemies considered hanging too good for him, but others thought there should be a plea for leniency on account of his age. The Comtesse D'Auvennois had also been arrested, but she was released within a week after depositions were taken from two of her servants, also in custody, who insisted that the duke had kept her completely apart from his affairs. She had not gone back to the town house, which in any case was now in the hands of the military; she was staying with a family in Henrietta Street, the Austens, Mrs. Austen being a French émigrée with impeccable royalist connections. The old countess had been offered safe conduct back to France, but she could not agree to leave her brother behind. Delphine intended to pay her a visit, but she kept putting it off. Since returning to London she had scarcely left the house, and meanwhile her mother, the one person who might have provided solace, would hardly speak to her.

Delphine and Julie were sitting at the breakfast table reading their correspondence and not looking at each other. Breakfasts were not the cheerful, amusing meals that they had once been, and Mrs. Laidlaw, who didn't enjoy the tension between mother and daughter, now took her meal in bed. A small box had been included amongst Delphine's letters, and she left it until last to open, hoping her mother might be curious enough to start a conversation. When she drew it toward her, she glanced over at la Générale's face. How often had that sweet, serene expression given her strength! And how she had taken it for granted! The memory of her confessions at Paget hit her with redoubled guilt. For at the end of them her mother had burst into tears. She had cried for some time, so swamped in her grief that she would utter nothing but exclamations of reproach. She had left Paget with Delphine at noon, huddled in the corner of the carriage, her eyes turned toward the window, replying in monosyllables to Delphine's anxious inquiries.

Delphine had never realized how devastated her kind and tolerant mother would be by the thought of having been kept in the dark about so many vital things. The emperor's instructions were sacrosanct to Julie and she knew Delphine wasn't supposed to share them, but she was bitterly disappointed that her daughter had not at least confided that she had secrets to keep! Now Delphine could not even discuss the latest disaster, her bizarre engagement, for her mother declared that since her advice was considered worthless she declined to give it.

"I wonder what this is?" Delphine said. "It came by private courier. Did we perhaps leave something behind at Thorngrove?"

Her mother didn't reply. Delphine sighed and removed the last of the brown paper. Under her hand was a handsome little jewelry case padded with red moiré satin, and sealed around it was a single folded sheet of paper. Delphine had a premonition that this was Landor's promised letter. But what could the box contain?

The wax seal was in the form of a classic rose with single petals, simply rendered. She gave a sad smile as she broke the seal. The symbol was probably part of the Tracey coat of arms—indelibly

English. Then she unfolded the letter, seized by dread and excitement. Landor's firm signature was at the bottom.

She felt her mother's gaze on her and said, "It's from Sir
Gideon."

Dear Mademoiselle,
I write from Greenwich, from which I depart within the hour.
Having promised to send you a report before sailing, I can
now tell you that everything has gone forward as we agreed on
my side. On yours, I hope that you and your mother are in
good health, and that our engagement has received the sanc-
tion if not the blessing of Madame Dalgleish. Please convey to
her my deepest gratitude for her forbearance.

On the same subject, my parents think it appropriate to
meet you, and intend making contact with Madame Dalgleish
when they are next in London, which will probably be in November. This does not happen at my suggestion, but I understand their motives and I hope you will be so generous as to
make allowance for them.

The next request, however, is my own. Forgive me, but it
would not stand well with my conscience if the world were
asked to believe that you are betrothed to me without wit-
nessing any token of that betrothal. My scruples are perhaps
at odds with yours on this point. Nonetheless I am hoping
that you will do me the honor of wearing until my return the
enclosed ring, which is always worn by the betrothed of the
heir to the earldom. My mother has very kindly had it cleaned
and packaged for you.

If circumstances were different, I should be putting it on
your finger myself, with emotions that I'm sure you agree
have no place in this letter. As things stand, I can only beg you
to accept it in earnest of my continuing regard and with the
most sincere wishes for your future happiness.

Please convey my compliments to your mother.

Until we meet again,
Your most devoted servant,
Gideon Eric Patrick Landor

Something in Delphine's face ensured that she had all her mother's attention. She handed over the letter, then opened the box. Inside was a large ruby, multifaceted and as vibrant as a flower. Fascinated and afraid, she slipped it onto the ring finger of her left hand. It fitted perfectly; the countess must have slender fingers. Then she took it off as though it burned her, and reached across the table to put it before her mother's place. "Oh, Maman." She sank her head into her hands. "His mother parted with it for me. All I seem to do is hurt people."

La Générale looked up from the letter. "This is very measured and considerate. If he is deeply wounded, he does not show it."

Delphine gave a despondent laugh. "You don't know him as I do!"

After a while, her mother put down the letter and took up the ring. "My word. Extremely handsome. Have you noticed that the old English aristocracy have a tendency to underplay their capital? Lord Ferron's title, on the other hand, is recent. He puts a great deal on show—but if one were to look into the true heirlooms of his line, I suspect he could produce nothing as fine as this piece."

"Maman, tell me frankly; if Lord Ferron had offered for me, would you have encouraged me to say yes?"

"Is there any point in that question, since you do what you like, whatever I say?"

"You know very well that I always listen to you. You are not my conscience, for I hope I have one of my own. You are not my only guide, for I do try to keep my wits about me. You are my mother—and not a person on earth loves me and cares for me as you do." Tears came into their eyes, and Delphine rose and ran around the table into her mother's arms.

After a while Julie Dalgleish, muffled in Delphine's embrace, began to laugh. "Sit down, my child. This won't do; if Mrs. Laidlaw comes in and finds us in floods she'll be strongly tempted to throw us out, and who could blame her for wanting a little peace?" When Delphine was seated next to her and they had both dried their eyes, she patted her daughter's hand and said, "Come, put the ring on. Let's see how it suits you." They inspected it together. The warmth of the ruby spoke to Delphine, suggesting the glow of fire in the winter to come. Or a last rose of summer before frosts descended. "It becomes you, *chérie*. And I think it looks better on you than anything Lord Ferron might bestow."

Delphine gave a little shrug. "Say what you like, Maman, it's not a case of my having one gentleman or the other. It's neither."

"Really? But tell me, if Sir Gideon Landor came to me and asked for your hand again, would you encourage me to give my consent?"

It was too tormenting. Delphine rose to walk about the room, touching her mother's shoulder lightly as she passed by her. "That's impossible. No man would ever propose again after such a refusal. And look where we are now; betrothed in name only. There is no trust or understanding between us. There never can be."

"He saved your life, Delphine."

"If we didn't stand on opposite shores of a divide, he wouldn't have had to! I'm a French patriot. Speaking of which," she said, her fingers brushing over Landor's letter, "I must go and see the Comtesse D'Auvennois. Now that all the duke's couriers have been arrested, she is the only person who can take my answer back to the emperor."

Her mother was startled. "Is this honorable, *chérie*? You are a free woman in this country only because you told Sir Gideon you would cease to be a spy."

"But he must know that my last message *has* to go back to France. He swore to me, with the utmost meaning, that Ferron didn't obtain the code."

"But what if someone else did? You would be misleading the emperor if you insisted that no one in England possesses it. Your message should be specific. Confine it to what you know, and make no other claims."

Delphine sighed. "You're right, Maman. But I must see the countess. The moment she agrees to take my message to Paris, I shall have finished with espionage. Good heavens, was there ever a less competent secret agent than I?"

La Générale considered her ironically. "Don't disparage your talents. You have a gift for discretion that deceived your own mother. With the right opportunities, you might go far."

Delphine put her hand on her mother's shoulder once more. "The only opportunity I'd like in London right now is to fade into the background, like one of those insipid figures on a printed wall. But that's impossible. Do you think there is *any* way we can avoid meeting his parents?"

La Générale smiled and closed her fingers over her daughter's hand. "No. But aren't you curious to see from what stock your splendid fiancé derives? I'm not used to seeing you afraid: I thought you would rather look them in the face."

"If I liked basilisks, Maman, I daresay I might."

La Générale laughed and Delphine, relishing the sound, tried to find courage for the days to come.

Gideon was alone in the stern-gallery of the frigate, having dismissed the lieutenants and midshipmen from the table after supper. It was the first meal at which he had been able to relax, and he hoped his officers had taken note. The ship's company was beginning to come together, but he had had a struggle to improve the standard of the crew and stores aboard the *Aphrodite*. Most of the men had been impressed into the navy and were ignorant of the sea—and they were on a new ship that would require prodigies to get in sailing order. He kept a steady eye on the noncommissioned officers who were to drum the new sailors into shape, but the stores were another matter: badly chosen and even more poorly stowed. He was so furious that he gave the purser a dressing down in full hearing of everyone on the dock, and told him he had three days to heave out the useless victuals and if necessary cut into his own profits to buy edible supplies. Then Gideon spent the extra days getting down to Wiltshire to confront his parents.

He put one elbow on the table and rested his forehead on his hand as Ellis cleared up around him. What a diabolical bloody interview that had been. His father had been incredulous, his mother at a complete loss, on hearing the story and then learning that he was involved in a sham engagement that was to last until he returned, whereupon it would be broken off by the lady.

"She is to *jilt* you?" his mother had said indignantly.

"You wouldn't have her marry me, would you? I've explained: she is French, and Bonapartist, and by rights should be in prison for it."

"Then why you are doing this?" Earl Tracey said.

"If you had the power of life and death over a lady, sir, wouldn't it give you pause? I came upon her that night by accident; until then I had no idea—at least no proof—she was a spy. I protected her on impulse, and I can't bring myself to regret it. She's given her word she's no longer involved in espionage. I believe her. That may not square with your conscience, but it does with mine."

"I'm not saying you should hand her over—I'm only asking why on earth we're to tell the world you're engaged!"

"I said it to satisfy Ferron. It was the only way to stop him discovering what she was up to. Good Lord, do you think I *want* this?" His mother looked at him sharply and he tried to banish the despair from his voice. "I did it to protect her, and I won't go back on my word. As for what you tell the world, it's not as though you get about in it much. You need say little or nothing."

"Really, Gideon," his mother said, "don't expect us to behave beneath our dignity. We'll do what's right as to the announcements, her mother and all the attendant details. And until your fiancée brings this *extraordinary* arrangement to an end, I shall also speak of her with respect. Now kindly sit down and tell me why that respect is due."

"Steady on!" The earl briefly changed sides. "He's had the sense at least to hitch himself to a gentlewoman."

"If you met her—" Gideon said in sudden fury, then controlled his voice. "She is genteel, intelligent, cultivated, and admired wherever she goes. I would challenge anyone to find an imperfection in her. I can tell you she has strong loyalties and the courage to hold to them. She is a very affectionate daughter." It was strange to be describing her, and it hurt to do so in such an analytical way, but he could not help wanting his parents to esteem her as he did. An absurd proceeding! Finally he said, rather low, "She is also very beautiful. In short, she is everything you could have wished in a daughter-in-law. Except that she is French. And she hates me."

He had looked up as he said this, and his mother's expression had changed from perplexity to sad surprise. "Oh, Gideon. Is she the one?" He didn't reply but he had no need to. After a moment she said with a meaningful look at his father, "We'll do the best we can."

Alone in the frigate's gallery now that Ellis had cleared away, Gideon recalled his mother's fearful question. The answer to it was still: *Yes. She is the one.* Absence from England, the demands of his first captaincy, his escort duties with the convoy, made no difference to his obsession. He had not left Delphine behind in London, he had brought her with him. He kept reliving the unbelievable moment, never to be repeated, when she returned his kiss in the library at Paget. He kept trying to penetrate the cloud of confusion in her eyes when she asked, *What do I do now?* He could not stop imagining other outcomes for their insane engagement, but they were all illusory. He had forced into betrothal a woman who had rejected him with anger and loathing only the month before.

The decanter and his glass were still on the table. Able Seaman Ellis, though he'd been told nothing, had no doubt guessed everything, and he seemed less happy at sea than he had been in London, as he'd fallen for Delphine Dalgleish's maid, Molly. Having Ellis about was usually a comfort in hard times, for ever since Gideon had saved his life after the sinking of the *Revenge* in the Indian Ocean, there had been an unspoken bond between them. Gideon had given the French on Mauritius to understand that Ellis was his servant, and thus got him assigned to the Garden Prison instead of a filthy jail somewhere in town. But in doing so he had realized that Ellis's job and his own would be impossible if the man's gratitude occupied the forefront of his mind, so he'd always treated Ellis with a certain brusqueness that exactly suited them both. He was not going to draw him into confidences now.

Gideon poured himself a measure of port and thought about

Ellis's excellent work in the case against Limours. He couldn't see the old man being strung up, in the end. They would whip his arse back to France. And "Mademoiselle D"? Would she ever guess his own hand in that affair? If she did, could it make her opinion of him any worse?

He got up from the table and went to the leadlight windows. The twin curls of the wake were barely visible in the gloom beyond the salt-encrusted panes, and the night sky was indistinguishable from the Atlantic waves that reared behind the ship. He leaned his shoulder against the frame, held the port up to the light and watched the ruby liquor sway in the glass. He thought of his mother's ring, now on Delphine Dalgleish's finger; that is, supposing she consented to wear it. He had said nothing to his ship's officers about the betrothal, but they all knew. This evening he had been afraid that one of the lieutenants was about to venture a toast to that effect, but something in his expression must have put the lad off, for at the last second he said only, "To the ladies."

His sight blurred as he held the glass farther up against the light, and lonely words formed in his mind. He tried to say them aloud. "To the idol . . ." Then his throat closed and he hurled the glass across the gallery so that it burst like a gout of blood across the new timbers.

"You look nervous, my dear," Mrs. Laidlaw said as Delphine pulled on her gloves on a chilly November morning. "I can't think why. The gentleman has an irredeemable passion for you and he must be quite sure his parents will follow suit."

Delphine's heart fell. So the Scotswoman's eye had been just as keen as usual during Landor's visit after the proposal.

"But he has left my daughter to face them on her own," Julie said.

Mrs. Laidlaw riposted, "Ah, just another sign of his confidence in his choice. Come now, you are not about to quarrel over him again? What a house this was, when you first came back from Worcestershire! I used to say to my friends: when the daughter *will* have him, and the mother will *not*, what hope have I of playing the makepeace?"

Delphine knew Mrs. Laidlaw's interpretation of that awful time, but she had not realized that the story had been shared. "With whom did you discuss this?"

Mrs. Laidlaw's eyes twinkled. "With gentlemen whose feelings might need soothing, my dear." But she spared them further railery and let them go, with fond wishes for their success in Curzon Street.

It was a private visit: the earl and countess had made it known they would be at home only to the Dalgleishes at that hour. Julie, on her greatest dignity, would have preferred to receive *them* first, but a meeting at Mrs. Laidlaw's wouldn't have been wise. It felt as though she and Delphine were coming as supplicants to the Traceys, and her French pride revolted against it.

Delphine threw her an admiring glance as they stepped out of the carriage before the Curzon Street house. Contrary to her usual style, Julie wore dark clothing—a navy blue merino dress trimmed with black satin cording and tassels, and a sable pelisse; the whole effect was rather like that of some sleek oriental beast getting ready to show its claws.

Delphine too had dressed with care, in a light blue woollen dress cut on the cross, with a grosgrain pelisse decorated with silver leaves in floss silk. Her bonnet, gloves and ankle boots were also silvery gray and she noticed, far too late, how the ruby ring flared against the sheer fabric of her glove.

She had no time to study the house, seeing only that it was suitably grand before their footman knocked at the great door, which opened at once. Julie swept in, and Delphine followed with crushing reluctance. Her agonies were quite the opposite of her mother's. Julie would be forever grateful to Landor for saving her daughter from arrest, and if she had met him in the hours that followed she would have embraced him in hysterical relief. But she preferred not to dwell on the emotions that drove him to that rescue, whereas Delphine could not forget that Landor was trapped in a mockery of an engagement, when with all his heart he had offered her marriage only weeks before. His parents must know. How else could they countenance what he had done, and what he now expected them to do? They must know that all the love was on his side and all the benefit on hers. It was as much as she could do to step across the threshold of his house.

They were shown upstairs immediately. The interior was as splendid as the outside and at the same time had a comfortable, lived-in look. That must be his doing, for he'd said his parents scarcely ever traveled to London; indeed, their coming this month could well be on her account alone. She felt worse with every step she took, and by the time they reached the double doors into the second-floor drawing room she could scarcely stand. But she stepped between them and she and her mother were announced. Through a haze, Delphine detected two tall figures on the other side of the room. She had to put one hand to the wooden embrasure to support herself until her sight cleared.

If the woman who came toward them saw this sign of feebleness, she showed nothing of it in her face, which had the pale composure of Attic marble. They were given a cool greeting and brought to the fireside end of the vast room, where a fire blazed and the earl stood waiting for them. He bowed, and when his silver head came up it was framed by a massive battle scene that hung over the mantelpiece. His gaze reminded Delphine of the accusing eyes of the ancestors who had watched her creep downstairs at Paget.

The conversation was a torment; Delphine drank tea, and exchanged nothings, and waited in sick suspense during a quarter of an hour, until suddenly it burst upon her—his parents would not mention the engagement. It was enough for the world to know the meeting had taken place; it was beneath them to actually discuss the excuse for it. She looked across at her mother. Had Julie guessed? If she had, it caused her no humiliation, for she was well into a conversation with the countess about watercolor techniques, while the earl looked on from the fireplace.

Free from their scrutiny for a moment, Delphine studied Landor's parents. They were a very handsome couple. He had a pleasing face, and the set of his full lips and the lines at the corners of his eyes suggested that he was an easygoing, genial companion. Today he was reining himself in, and hating it. His wife was a beauty—tall and elegant, with a calm manner that had more of the regal in it than even Julie could summon, and a melodious voice.

They had but one son. If Delphine had not come into their world, their little triangle of people would at this moment be living a different story: Sir Gideon Landor would be introducing to his parents another young woman, whom they could spend their time getting to know and appreciate. Or, had she acted differently, the man she had banished from her life would be at her side, on the very sofa where she sat alone, while he entranced his parents and her mother with a vision of their future together. But she had destroyed that vision.

Delphine put down her dish of tea and bowed her head. Thank goodness no one had asked her view on anything other than the Walk in Hyde Park or the appointments at Vauxhall Gardens, for she had no hope of answering a more complex question. She was on tour in this territory. She had earned no connection with it, and even if she wanted to do so it was too late. To her horror, tears surged into her eyes. What was *happening*? She could only extract a handkerchief from her reticule and pretend to have a case of the autumn sniffles.

Delphine had nowhere near conquered her weakness before the countess abandoned the chair by the fire and came to sit beside her on the sofa, her hazel eyes at once kind and penetrating. "What would you like us to do?"

The shock gave Delphine back her self-control. "I have no right to ask. You've already done a great deal by consenting to see me."

"On the contrary, mademoiselle, all we've done is adopt the role of spectators. One has no power over one's children. One can only wish. And the greatest wish is for their happiness."

The earl said dryly from his stance by the fire, "And much good may it do us, in these circumstances."

Not at all discomposed, Julie Dalgleish said, "I have a suggestion, if you would be so indulgent as to consider it." The others strove for a look of polite inquiry. "I propose that we wait until Sir Gideon's return. No talk of settlement can take place until we know my daughter's position. Captain Arkwright, who administers the estate of Saint-Amour, arrives in London shortly. After we have spoken to him, we shall be much better informed on all subjects of mutual interest."

The earl almost smiled. "I shan't argue with that, by Jove."

Delphine looked from him to her mother. *"Arkwright?"*

La Générale nodded. "In a fortnight or so. I heard it today from the D'Arifats."

In the midst of her annoyance at having this news sprung on her at such a moment, out of the corner of her eye Delphine could see the countess looking at her with ironical understanding. The look reminded her suddenly of Landor's. "I beg you to believe, madame—I would give a great deal for things to be different."

There was an awkward pause. She expected instant, satirical agreement from the woman by her side, but instead her left hand was taken and the countess examined the ruby and smiled. "It becomes you."

"You don't wish for it back?"

The countess released her, with a soft sound that was almost a laugh. "I've told you what I wish. If it's not in your power to grant it, you will let me know. Until then, it pleases me to see you wear the ring." She rose and went to stand by her husband. "We're not here long, but we're invited to a reception at Lady Melbourne's the evening after next. Shall we see you there?"

Julie Dalgleish, alive to the hint, also rose. "A wonderful hostess, is she not? *Chérie*, it's time we were going."

So they left, with almost everything unsaid, and nothing in the least settled. On the short carriage ride home, Delphine sat with her head bent and her hands in her lap. When at last she looked up, her mother was regarding her with a quizzical expression. "Delphine, I hardly recognized you in that house. I've never heard you say less. Shall I tell you what it was like? It was like a trial. As though they were judge and jury—as though they really *were* to be your parents-in-law! And you were afraid that any evidence you gave would damn you."

On top of everything else, this was too much. She lashed out, "And what was the verdict, according to you?"

La Générale shrugged and gave a little laugh. "I think you may be in danger of making them as much in love with you as he is."

The Code Breakers

To Sir Gideon Landor, Bart.
The Navy Office, Lisbon
Portugal

Dearest,

No doubt our letters will cross, but I owe you this. The meeting has taken place. Nothing is resolved, but of course nothing can be without you—we all await your return.

I congratulate you on your connections: Mme D has superior elegance and address; she showed some hauteur, but when she saw we were disinclined to quarrel she was at once civil and agreeable.

I must confess myself surprised by Mlle D. Besides what you told us, I've heard much from London friends about her vivacity and wit. But she met us in low spirits, spoke but little and I fear was unwell—she could scarcely support herself on entering the room. Our behavior could not have caused this response: your father was formal but not unkind, and I was my usual self—and if I have ever cowed anyone I have yet to hear of it! Even in distress she had a charm all her own. I pitied her and longed to hear her speak with more animation, but it was not to be. I had hopes of meeting her again at Lady Melbourne's but the ladies did not attend. Do not be anxious about her health, however—Georgiana Combrewood saw her at the theater the night before Lady Melbourne's rout and she was perfectly well.

Congratulations flow in, but less copiously now we have left town. You will not wish me to repeat them here. I send you my love, and I have leave to say that your father sends his.

He also wants you to know that Starbright has whelped—apparently a great event—and has four puppies in capital shape.

God keep you,

Your affectionate Mother

Gideon, meanwhile, was undertaking his first journey into Portugal. It was a surprise to be riding several hundred miles to British army headquarters in Frenada, on the Beira Plateau near the Spanish border. The convoy had reached Lisbon unchallenged by the French, just as he had predicted, and he had expected to spend but a week or two in port before receiving orders to escort another flotilla home. But his superiors had other ideas; the *Aphrodite* was to stay at anchor while he carried out another duty, requested by none other than the commander in chief of the armed forces in the Peninsula, Sir Arthur Wellesley.

Gideon was summoned to see George Scovell, the man to whom his own hard-won portion of Napoleon's grand code had been sent. Scovell, one of Wellesley's "family," was stationed with the commander in chief in Frenada. He held the rank of major and he had an unparalleled talent for breaking codes, or so Gideon heard from his companion on the journey, Lieutenant Colonel Colquhoun Grant.

Grant, a well-muscled, energetic gentleman with very observant eyes, hitched up the collar of his riding cloak and jerked his chin at the barren hills ahead of them as they rode. "Cold enough for you? Wait until we get the wind off the snow in January—then everyone will be glad we're not on campaign."

Gideon shrugged. He was warm in his naval greatcoat and he had no fancy to kick his heels with the army until the snows of the new year. "I'll be well gone by then. What I've got to tell Major Scovell would hardly entertain him between one glass of wine and the next. By the way, I hope they've better vintages at headquarters than the stuff you've found me on the road so far?"

Grant laughed. "Be assured—nothing but the best for Sir Arthur." He gave Gideon a keen look. "If your information's so paltry, then you might as well tell it me now. Hardinge as good as let on when they sent me to fetch you; you know something about Boney's codes that we don't."

"I doubt it."

Grant made an impatient sound that set his mount dancing a few steps farther along the rutted, sloping road. Ahead was a crag topped by an ancient olive tree with twisted branches that stretched out above the bend in the road like a gnarled hand pointing south, along the line of the hills. Somewhere beyond the crag, out of sight on a great plateau, was Frenada. Behind the two riders, straggling up from a cutting they had left fifteen or so minutes before, was a wagon train of supplies ordered up, like Gideon, from the docks of Lisbon. Gideon glanced over his shoulder, impressed by the commander in chief's organization: Wellesley tried never to take an army beyond his supply line and never to let that line be threatened by the enemy. Hence he held Portugal, and Gideon was uncommonly glad of it. Grant had had nothing to cope with on the long journey up from the coast except securing comfortable quarters each night.

Grant reined his big horse back. "Scovell won't rest until he's had every last syllable out of you. He's a genius with detail. And tenacious! Don't underestimate him. Sir Arthur certainly doesn't."

Gideon probed in his turn: "What will Hardinge have you doing once we reach Frenada?" Sir Henry Hardinge was Wellesley's head of intelligence in the Peninsula, and Gideon guessed that he usually employed Grant on something other than escort duty.

"I don't doubt I'll be slipping back into Spain again. No rest for the wicked. While everyone else is out after foxes on this side of the border, I'll be doing a little hunting of my own on the other."

"With whom? Guerrilla fighters?"

"I go alone mostly. In uniform," adding at Gideon's surprised look, "for it's no part of the plan to have me shot as a spy. I scout the enemy positions and gather information—from *guerrilleros,* as you say, from Spanish guides and from bandits. Occasionally we snatch a prisoner. Don Julian Sanchez brought in a French captain called Regnaud last month and Wellesley wined and dined him like a lord. All bloody civilized and no coercion used, of course, but it's amazing what you can glean at a well-laid table. Regnaud told us more than he thought: the French commanders in Spain are still eyeing each other off and their coordination's suffering in consequence. We've to hope their differences will outlast the winter."

They rounded the bend in the road and Gideon saw the first evidence of the British army encampment: two soldiers on picket duty who must have been watching them for hours from the top of the ridge and who went through the routine challenge. When Grant had dealt with that, they pushed on past a limewashed farmhouse, where soldiers were cleaning weapons and uniforms, sitting on upturned boxes in the pale winter sunlight. Then the baggage train breasted the last slope and the high plateau came into view.

Gideon was looking at long, neat rows of tents decorating the contours of the land, with here and there the hard-drawn lines of gun batteries, the sheds and yards commandeered for cavalry mounts, and in the distance, at last, the orange-tiled roofs and huddled stone buildings of the humble village of Frenada. It was as though a greater-than-human hand had reached down and placed the enormous concentration of men in this foreign land-scape. It was hard to imagine the army in movement; it looked frozen in place by a mysterious spell.

Gideon turned to Grant. "When is he going to take this lot back into Spain?"

Grant gave a cynical smile. "Ah, the London papers are still calling him a laggard, are they?"

"I've no need of newspapers to hear what's going on. He says Ciudad Rodrigo is the key to Spain, but he's just let the French walk right into it. What are his plans, once the fox hunting's over?"

"Who knows? His staff certain as hell don't. They spend all their time watching each other like hawks to see whether he's passed on any ideas, but there's scarcely a word out of him until he's ready to move—and by heaven do they get an earful then! If he has a whim to see you, take due note. Never says much, but it'll be to the point."

"I'll let you know if he gives me any tips," Gideon said dryly, and Grant grinned. Gideon was beginning to like him; it was clear that he had no wish to hang about waiting for scraps from the commander in chief's table. "I have heard Wellesley's cautious."

"To a fault, some say. My view's different, but it's bound to be." They were approaching the village, and Grant received salutes and greetings as they clattered past men and officers. "He sets great store by intelligence. He has to know what the French armies are up to; they outnumber us, dammit. If they all joined up at once we could kiss Portugal good-bye, let alone Spain. He needs to know if they're concentrating their forces, and where. If the French stay scattered over the winter, we've a chance, for then Wellesley can use his favorite tactic—and Boney's, come to that— isolate one army and smash it before the next comes up."

"Meanwhile, you're keeping an eye on the nearest French."

Grant grinned again. "That's it."

Gideon let out a small sound between his teeth. "Good luck. I don't fancy being in your boots."

Gideon's first meeting with George Scovell was in a modest, two-storied stone building in Frenada, the headquarters of the quartermaster general's department to which Scovell belonged. A compact man in his late thirties, wearing the brown cavalry uniform of an officer in the Mounted Guides, he had a prominent nose, large ears, and chubby cheeks decorated by dark red, bushy sideburns. Gideon, sitting alone with him at a chart table, felt as though he were entering into conversation with a fox—and a very alert one at that, for Scovell's most distinguishing feature was his penetrating blue eyes.

Scovell made the usual inquiries, and Gideon answered with inward impatience: he was well fed and rested, and his only interest was in finding out why he'd been asked to come hundreds of miles to this meeting.

In fact his question was anticipated. "Wondering why I'm glad you're here? Not to mention relieved, grateful and envious . . .

You're the only Englishman who's ever set eyes on the grand Paris code. Thank you for coming. We'll trespass on your patience for the shortest time possible, but *in* that time," Scovell continued, his eyes brightening like sunshine over the ocean, "you can do us an enormous service. Simply telling me how you came upon your one piece of paper may help us as much as the thing itself."

"Why?"

"Because we're obsessed here. We eat, drink and dream codes. I puzzle over them in my sleep; the commander in chief scribbles at his breakfast table; the aides-de-camp run through syllables in their heads while they're hounding game across the boulder country. We all have a mania for minutiae; it's like chasing a hundred rabbits down a warren. And *then* we find out that the prey—the very one you've laid hands on—is bigger than we ever imagined. So we're going to run it to earth. We have to."

"I see. I'll do what I can, but I'm sorry all you've got to depend on is my memory. I wish I had the code itself. I'd have gotten away with more, but there was a patrol—"

"Good God, Captain, I know what you achieved, and how, and no man could be more thankful. And I wonder whether you're even aware—" He changed tack abruptly. "The French armies in Spain are always coming up with new codes. As fast as we break them they've invented another; the keys change constantly. They're workmanlike, somewhat similar in construction, succinct—do you know how many numbers a typical code employs?" Gideon shook his head and Scovell forged on, "One hundred and fifty. Now"—he leaned forward eagerly—"I'd like you to think back and tell me the *final* number you saw in the gridlines of the grand code."

Gideon stared at him. Scovell already knew the answer but he wanted it said out loud, by its discoverer. For the first time, the significance of that eerie moment in the dark building in Paris came back to Gideon with full clarity. "Twelve hundred."

"*Twelve hundred,*" Scovell said, with relish and awe.

"Are they still using it?"

"The exact one you recorded? Not lately. And I wish they would. Until they do so again, I don't have enough examples of it to work on—so I'm afraid there's very little hope of cracking it. I made a damned good start with the sheet you got out of Paris, but I've been at a standstill ever since." Scovell shook his head. "I think they must have developed the grand code some time last year. They used it briefly, not long before your mission to Paris, but since then everything we've captured has been back in their local codes—Marmont to Foy, Foy to Joseph Bonaparte and so on. Doesn't mean the big one isn't being used, of course—only that we haven't intercepted anyone carrying it. But I'm expecting a development. You see, in April, Joseph went to see Napoleon in Paris. To complain, I'd say—he's supposed to be conducting the armies in Spain but Napoleon bypasses him and so do his generals. And now that Joseph's back in Madrid, I have a fancy we'll soon find the grand code in use much more.

"Joseph's been sent a new military adviser and Napoleon's recalled one of his best commanders to France. The emperor seems to have plans in northern Europe—huge plans; we know that much—and if he's going on the move again, it stands to reason he has to leave Spain secured behind him. So that's why we'll be seeing a return to the *grand chiffre*, because he'll be using it universally, to all the generals here."

Scovell put his hands on the table, clamped together. "He wants them to fight a combined campaign, to smash us. And once they've gotten *that* message, who's to say they'll wait for the end of winter to carry out instructions? Coney hunting may go by the board within weeks, for all we know." He gave a small smile, his upper lip rising over his top teeth so that he reminded Gideon once more of a keen fox. "You see why I'm glad you're here?" Scovell leaned forward, his forearms on the table. "Now, tell me everything you laid eyes on, from the instant you got into the Ministry of Marine and War."

Now that he understood why, Gideon gave the description with meticulous care. Meanwhile, Scovell took pen, ink and paper and began using them, his eyes regularly flicking up to examine Gideon's face. While the entry to the building was unfolding, Scovell sketched a rough map of the layout, which Gideon realized wasn't so much a record as a prompt. He responded,

closing his eyes on occasions to recall the smallest detail of the
military sanctum that he had invaded.

When he got to the upstairs bureaus, Scovell began to ask quiet
questions. How many rooms? How many desks in each? Equipment? Documents? He was thrilled when he realized Gideon had
memorized the name of each functionary in the offices. His fingers actually quivered as he wrote them down. These gentlemen,
after all, were his equals, his opponents. Theirs were the minds he
matched his skills against, across an occupied continent.

At the name of Belfort he raised his eyes. "Belfort? You're
sure?" Gideon, seeing no need to confess his own connection to
the bastard, just grunted assent. Scovell went on, "I've read the
name somewhere before. *En clair*—uncoded, you understand—in
a French dispatch." He shook his head. "We'll get back to that."
He laid down his pen, as though writing would spoil the satisfaction of the next moment. "Now. Alphonse Dauriac. Tell me every
secret you divined about him. And then read me his code."

This, suddenly, was the hard part. Whatever Gideon had come
away with from Paris was crushingly outweighed by what he had
left behind, untouched and unrecorded. As he spoke, with the utmost precision, his hands felt empty. He looked down at them
clenched before him on the tabletop, and was angry with himself
for having so little to offer the gifted man on the other side of the
table.

But when his voice ran out and he looked up, Scovell's eyes
were alight. "You're frustrated by not getting it all? Don't be.
Think like a code breaker instead. What we have, *however* little it
is, *always* in the end gives us what's missing. It's a question of ma-
nipulating the pieces of the puzzle until a gap takes a certain
shape and, *voilà*, you have the whole picture. And be assured—by
our standards, what you've given us is a very great deal." Suddenly
he switched to French. "Words—this is all a matter of words. I
want you to go back to when you first opened Dauriac's drawer.
There is the code, under your hands. What does it look like?
What can you see?"

Gideon closed his eyes. "A grid, with numbers on the left of
each column, words on the right."

"Beginning with what number?"

"One."

"What's written next to one?"

Gideon shook his head, furious again. "I can't see. I just can't wait to grab the bloody thing!"

"Very well," Scovell said soothingly. "You take the papers out. What do you do with them?"

"Flick through. The decryption code's on top. I want to see if the encryption code's there too. It is! Underneath."

"Starting with?"

"*Abs.* Is that right?" He shook his head.

"Number beside that?"

"Don't know. But further down—*abandon*! I remember, it felt like a warning."

"And next to it?"

"One thousand and thirty-five."

Scovell's pen scratched and his voice floated lightly over the table again. "Next syllable?"

"*Able.*"

"Number?"

"Two." At the sound of the pen, Gideon looked up and cursed. "No, I mean there were two numbers. But I can only remember one of them. Eight hundred and eight."

Scovell bent to the paper again. "Take another look. What do you see?"

They proceeded in this fashion for another few minutes, then Gideon gave a helpless laugh. "Don't push it, or my mind will start playing tricks." He looked across as Scovell smiled wryly and laid the pen across the paper. "If I dream a few more lines tonight, I'll tell you them at breakfast."

"So you dream in French like me, do you?" The other man's good-natured grin widened. "Of course—no wonder your French is so good. Your future wife is an émigrée, I believe?" Gideon didn't reply. After a moment of embarrassment, Scovell beat a retreat. "My apologies. You've had quite enough interrogation for one day. I was referring . . . my own situation is somewhat analogous to yours. My wife is still in England, though I've put in many a plea for her to be allowed to sail to Lisbon. Absence, you know, gets no easier. Especially when other military are given permission to have their wives here. I can't tell you how overjoyed I shall be when one of you fellows brings me my Mary one of these days."

"On the road up here, Major, I was firmly promised a taste of Wellesley's fine wines. Are you ready to fulfill it? If so, and you propose a toast to the ladies, I'll second every syllable."

Winter

⁓

Melbray Arkwright was devastated, confused and profoundly tempted in London, all by Delphine Dalgleish. He arrived in December, on official leave and charged with a letter from Governor Farquhar to the Dalgleishes, which he meant to deliver in person. At a soirée shortly after he landed, however, he heard the news of the demoiselle's engagement, which destroyed his fantasies of seeing her again. He had the papers delivered by an army courier, and it was not until a fortnight later that he came upon the ladies at Almacks, having been persuaded to make up a party there with some of his cousins from Mayfair. Arkwright was well connected and enjoyed hanging about London, so he had realized he must run across the Dalgleishes at some stage, and he expected them to resent his not calling on them. He was perplexed to find Mademoiselle Dalgleish grave and polite but not at all his enemy. And as the evening progressed she began to treat him with a nice blend of wit and flirtation. Her behavior reminded him of an evening at Saint-Amour, when she stopped arguing with him for a blessed few hours and surprised him with some humorous comments about French and English manners. Taken off guard, he had been slow to respond. To lighten things, she had begun to tease him, but he could not switch moods as quickly as she could, or begin to match her liveliness. When he looked back he could not blame her for giving up the attempt. Nor could he help the regret that she had never made another! He was determined to be different tonight, and he was captivated all over again because *she* seemed just the same; the only thing that confused him was that such manners were hardly those of an engaged woman.

At one point he said to her, "I hope you received Governor Farquhar's papers? I wasn't able to deliver them myself, so I—"

"Oh, yes, thank you. He writes a good hand. Don't you think so?"

"I . . . I've never received enough from the governor to give an opinion. Our dealings were usually in person."

"*Were?* Does this mean you're not returning to Mauritius?"

"No! That is, I shall certainly be going back to Port Louis. But in a different capacity, as town major. I'm sorry—I thought the governor would have made that clear in his letter."

Her sapphire eyes sparkled with amusement. She was standing by tall candelabra at one side of the ballroom and the glare of the banked candles was resplendent on her white skin and the pale silk of her gown. "Very little is clear from his letter, I'm afraid— aside from his penmanship. And what messages do *you* bring me from Saint-Amour?"

He'd been wrong—under the insouciance, she still resented him: for taking over the plantation, for having the support of Farquhar and for avoiding her in London. Little did she know that he had arrived with the idea of paying court to her! "Excuse me, such was the surprise of seeing you that I neglected to offer you my felicitations. I'd scarcely set foot in England before I learned of your betrothal. Please accept my wishes for your happiness." The glint in her eyes disappeared and she looked away across the packed room. After an odd pause, he went on, "You must be wishing for news of the estate. All is in train. The village and the workers are much as you saw them last. The Brahmin Chavrymoutou has left us and taken his family to the Camp des Malabars and does well, I hear. Apart from him, all your old friends have stayed put. They came in a delegation to beg me to convey their greetings to you."

She gave a little laugh, and there was a glow as she said, "A bagatelle that the governor took no trouble to tell me of—but you have remembered. Thank you. Nothing could give me greater pleasure; not even if I heard that Saint-Amour's profits had doubled under your supervision." She was teasing him again.

"Some months after you left, mademoiselle, I decided Saint-

Amour should go back to the plantings that the overseers were used to."

Her smile widened. "And I see from the accounts that you've abandoned the idea of using all the land for sugar."

"Not entirely. But the overseers were glad to return to the crops they'd raised before. My relations with them became easier in consequence."

"But the income! I thought you expected wonders from sugar."

"I see that you have read all the plantation records from Governor Farquhar."

"I have, and I'm perplexed. Despite your sad experiments, Saint-Amour is earning very much what it was before the invasion."

"If not more. You will be pleased to learn I've put the terms of trade with the army and navy back in your favor."

"With the governor's encouragement?" she said shrewdly—but her gaze was not unkind.

She was right: Farquhar had decided there was more to be gained by securing the wealth of Mauritian plantations than from grinding prices down for the military. Kept in balance, the fortunes of both were increasing, and land speculators from Britain were attracted to the island. Without any knowledge of growing sugar, Arkwright had given up his experiments and gone back to Saint-Amour's original crops. "My good counsel prevailed. And in my submissions to the governor I made use of information that your overseers were able to give me."

She beamed again. It was ridiculous that she set such store by the stiff-necked Indians on Saint-Amour, but it pleased her when he praised them, and he wasn't about to tell her that his struggle with them had only ended when Farquhar told him that no new imports of slaves from Africa would be permitted, and he would be better off using to the hilt the labor he had.

She was still smiling. "It would be terribly ungrateful of me to regret seeing you in London, when you bring us such good news. Now, who is managing Saint-Amour in your absence?"

"The governor didn't mention him?"

"He gave me a name: Lieutenant Pendleworthy. He didn't give me his credentials."

Arkwright said, "The lieutenant has been my assistant for some time. He has only to follow my instructions for the next few months, and he will maintain productivity." She looked unconvinced, and he played the trump: "Besides, your cousin in effect gave his consent."

"*C'est pas vrai! Armand?* He was . . . he's been back to Mauritius?"

"No, it was settled by correspondence. I suggested the governor write to Monsieur de Belfort, requesting that he return and sign the oath of allegiance. He wrote back, declining. In quite high terms, I believe—Bonaparte was invoked more than once, as though an international incident could somehow be made out of it!"

Delphine looked away briefly to hide her expression. Once again Armand had let her down. He had no doubt *sounded* threatening enough, but while he remained in Paris he could give her no help. Then she turned back and said sweetly, "It's more of an international issue than you seem aware of, sir. Has the governor not shared with you the legal correspondence between London and Mauritius over Saint-Amour?"

Cornered, he said, "Of course. The governor wrote back to France, pointing out that if Monsieur de Belfort denies responsibility for Saint-Amour, its administration must remain in the hands of the military until the two years are up." He pursed his small mouth in a gently ironical smile. "Your cousin has not yet deigned to reply. He seems to have washed his hands of Saint-Amour."

Delphine's voice was flat. "So the governor does what he likes."

Arkwright was not provoked. "For the benefit of all, yes."

"You will excuse my seeing *benefit* in a different light from you. But let us not quarrel, monsieur; we are not in Port Louis. You are on leave for how long?"

"Until the end of February."

"And then you return as town major. You are committed to living on our island, then? Or is this a fillip to your career? A step toward grander service in India, perhaps?"

There was a heightening of color along his cheeks, visible under the high tan he had taken on in the tropics. Had she hurt him by speaking so flippantly of his prospects? Then he should take care not to disparage *her* diplomatic efforts in London!

But after a pause he said, "Are you surprised that I've become fond of Mauritius? As for whether I make my life there . . . that doesn't depend entirely on me. But I must tell you, I should have been very sorry to leave Saint-Amour if it had been for any other place than Port Louis."

She saw, then. It wasn't difficult, given the caressing timbre of his voice and the soft look in his dark-lashed eyes. By taking his hands off Saint-Amour, was he looking for a way to step back into her life again, in another guise? *Bon dieu*, what made these Englishmen think her such easy prey? Then she remembered, with a pang, that one of them had given her a deterrent against any others. She raised her fan and allowed Arkwright a good look at the Landor ruby blazing against her white satin glove. It sobered him at once, and she was able to hold a satisfying conversation with him about the Indians of Saint-Amour.

At Christmas, Julie Dalgleish received a short seasonal message from Countess Tracey. Julie's only comment was, "Fine handwriting. Beautiful control of the pen." Then she gave it to Delphine to read alone.

Delphine sat on the window seat in her bedchamber, her knees drawn up, her stockinged feet on the cushion and her temple against a cold pane, reading the countess's calm account of what was going forward at Landor, and her ironical descriptions of Wiltshire weather. There was but one reference to her son. *Though forewarned, we had hoped that Gideon might be home in time for Christmas. Not so; his last letter from Lisbon tells us he is delayed there longer than expected. He professes himself well, for which we are as ever thankful.*

Gideon. It should not have felt strange to see his Christian name in his mother's message, but it made a curious impact on Delphine. With a fingertip, she traced the first letter. The countess had written the "G" with a flourish to the tail, and the other letters looked darker than the rest, as though she had lingered over her son's name; as though those three syllables expressed the profound tie that bound her forever to one precious person.

Delphine whispered the name, her breath misting the glass at her cheek. This letter, with all its hidden love, shut her out. On his arrival in port, Sir Gideon Landor had written to his mother, not to her. He had sat in a dockside inn, or in his cabin, one lock of hair drifting across his forehead, his fingers drawing the quill vigorously across the paper, thinking of . . . what? Nothing that he could share with Mademoiselle Delphine Dalgleish.

Lisbon. He had not told her where he was going, but his parents and others must have known, or the countess would not mention it so openly.

He professes himself well. Four words that revealed all Landor's iron self-sufficiency, and all the countess's relief and anxiety.

Delphine's eyes burned, and she reformed the letter in its original shape and studied it: so thin, just one folded sheet with a broken red seal on the back—a single English rose, its petals torn across.

He had gone. Now, the very time when she wore his ring and received letters from his family, marked the end of their relations. They were not just separated by distance; if he were in the room with her at this moment, it could not change the fact that intimacy between them was impossible. He had gone and might never come back. She had loathed, feared and resented him, and those feelings had put a permanent bar between them. Whatever happened now, wherever he lived and breathed, he was lost to her.

So why should she care whether he returned, or try to guess what dangerous mission might keep him in Portugal? Why did the chill outside in Berkeley Square make her dread the winter storms in the Bay of Biscay? She shrank from the answer, but it flooded her being. She loved him, against reason and against all their history. One kiss had told her the truth, and her blind resistance since then had been in vain.

She imagined what might have followed at Paget if she had remained in the library with him instead of returning, stunned, to her room. But she could create no dialogues in her head, because no words could explain her tumult of emotions. She remembered his face and the bitterness in his voice as he said, *I know how unpalatable you find the idea of betrothal to me.* What counter was there to that, except a silent one? An approach as swift as his had been, a wild embrace from which he could not escape, a kiss so fierce that it banished all words, all thought, and left space only for the intoxication of touch. To Delphine on that night, such an action would have seemed utterly impossible. Now, looking back, it felt like bliss denied.

She bowed her head and the countess's note fluttered to the floor. In his arms, for one miraculous moment, she had lost herself and found him. She had possessed him, as though he had always been part of her life and would be her future. What a potent illusion it had been, overwhelming her even while Landor turned her to face Ferron. *Don't say a word,* he had whispered, unaware that she was scarcely able to stand, let alone speak. The dream had lasted while she was clamped to his side, his arm around her waist, and it didn't vanish completely until Ferron was gone and Landor withdrew his hand, his warmth and his body, and she swayed on her feet, bereft. And then he forced her to awaken and to recognize that they were still enemies.

She had fallen in love with Landor that night, yet by her own free will she had walked out of the room, with no more good-bye than a murmured, *Thank you.* And she had not seen him since.

She clasped her hands around her shins and pressed her forehead to her knees. Thinking would get her nowhere. All the questions and all the answers were flowing in her veins, tied in knots around her heart. Her body throbbed with need for him, while her skin registered the cold truth: she was alone.

Then Julie Dalgleish walked back in, and Delphine raised her head. Julie crossed the room, absently realigned Delphine's ranks of brushes on the dressing table and sat down on the stool before it, her back to the mirror.

There was nothing for it but diversion. "Maman, we must go home."

"To do what, *chérie?*"

"Reclaim Saint-Amour. I'll sign the oath of allegiance, we'll move in, the lieutenant will move out and we'll have our home back."

"And live happily ever after. What makes you think Farquhar will let you sign? That's the one crucial thing he omitted from his letter."

"He's ready; I know it. We have only to turn up, and he will grant it. It fits his new vision for Mauritius. The only reason he left it out of his letter was to give Arkwright a chance to present it as a gift from *him*. When we arrive, Farquhar will shrug his shoulders and turn over Saint-Amour to me."

Julie clapped her hands softly. "I agree."

As easy as that. Delphine felt desolate, like a child given a new toy already outgrown.

Julie said, "Before we leave our London friends behind, I'd like to be sure that we can trust Farquhar's accounts. If we're to contest them, it must be now."

Delphine slipped her feet into her silk indoor shoes and smoothed her gown. "I believe them to be correct. I have something to compare them to: Chavrymoutou has just sent me a very faithful record with his last letter."

"*What?* You read to me from that letter—and you didn't say a word about the accounts. What else has Chavrymoutou been writing to you, all this time? *Bon dieu*, how can this be?" Julie sprang up and came to stand over Delphine who, trying to rise, was rammed back onto the seat by her mother's hands on her shoulders. "What has happened to you? These secrets! What has turned you into this creature of deceit?" Julie took a step back, and furious tears welled into her eyes. "This is not you! What have you become? Your father wouldn't recognize you. *I* don't recognize you!"

Delphine spread her arms, gripping the cushion at each side of her to prevent herself from retaliating. But her protest rang out. "What can I do? What do you *expect* me to do? I've been surrounded by secrets and intriguers ever since the Garden Prison. Ever since Armand told me Gideon Landor was a double agent. Ever since the emperor taught me to lie. How can I trust *anyone* again?"

Julie gave a cry and fell to her knees. "*Chérie.* Trust yourself. Be yourself. If you hide too much it will eat you away."

"I don't understand."

Julie's eyes sparked behind the tears. "Deceit is cowardly. You must face this fact: everything is a risk. Just because other people run from danger does not mean that you should. There comes a time to fight in the open." The white square of the countess's letter on the polished floor caught her eye. She bent to pick it up, and placed it on Delphine's lap. "Are you in love with Landor?"

Delphine snatched the letter, which buckled in her fingers. There was a long moment, when her brain crashed against the barriers around it like a caged creature. She looked down, and her fingers parted. "Yes."

"Ah." Julie rose smoothly to her feet. "I should prefer to stay in England until Sir Gideon returns. Can you stand that?"

Delphine spoke to her lap. "You think Saint-Amour should wait?"

"I do."

"Very well."

Without another word, Julie withdrew.

Snow came to the Beira Plateau before Gideon left. It fell heavily to the north, on Almeida, where Wellesley had gathered the heavy artillery and siege equipment, and which Gideon saw on a three-day expedition with Scovell, and it blanketed the heights across the border, where he went with Grant, both of them cloaked and in uniform. It was a reconnaissance trip to collect information from agents who worked in and around the French-occupied towns. Gideon had talked Grant into taking him, and Grant had gotten it past Hardinge, and so the two pushed into the countryside to meet up with the peasants who brought messages out along the mountain trails. There was less intelligence than Grant would have liked—he heard that the informant in Salamanca, a Father Curtis, was currently under suspicion from the French and could get nothing out of the city, and there was a similar blank about Ciudad Rodrigo.

But they did meet up with a group of bandits from the north, and Gideon spent one evening around a tiny campfire in a gully beside the Agueda River, watching the men as they passed on to Grant what they had heard about troop movements in their region. None spoke English, but one talked to Gideon in French about a rumor that the northern armies were about to march east to Valencia; then the others voiced some disagreement and the debate moved into Spanish again. Their eyes flashed in their hard faces, the firelight flickered on their naked weapons and the bright sashes at their waists, and behind them was the backdrop of the black night and the icy stream running by between snow-covered banks. For an unreal interval, Gideon felt lost, as though no meaning could be derived from such a scene, but later the leader brought out a piece of paper from the breast of his padded woolen jacket and handed it to Grant. It was a message in code, taken from a French captive belonging to Marmont's army. That at least Gideon grasped, on a surge of excitement. He also understood the rapid gesture that explained what had been done with the captive, and the mirthless smile that accompanied it.

On his last day in Frenada he rejoined Scovell at the quartermaster's table and helped to decypher the message, fascinated by the speed with which Scovell laid bare the key—a fresh one using 120 numbers. When it was done, Scovell pushed the decrypted message across to Gideon. "The commander in chief will welcome this. Have you a mind to take it to him?"

Gideon shook his head. He had glimpsed Wellesley on two occasions, as he rode out of town on a tall hunter along with a covey of aides, and he'd felt no wish to be summoned into the general's presence. "Another time, perhaps." Then he grinned. "Though why I should say that, I don't know. By the time I get back to England I must hope you'll be in Madrid."

"Amen to that." Scovell smiled back. "It's been instructive, having you here. I appreciate it. Anything I can help you with, before you go?"

Gideon took a breath. "You can tell me where you heard the name of Armand de Belfort. You'll recall, you thought it meant something to you?"

"That's right. In a French despatch. I've a copy; I put it in here for you." Scovell rose and went to a drawer in another table, then returned and spread out a sheet of paper. "Here. Just one mention, but clear enough. 'Armand de Belfort returned from England; the duke in funds for the next year.'"

Gideon went cold. "He was in *England?* When? Do we know the date of the dispatch?"

Scovell turned the sheet over. In his neat handwriting it said *October 1811.* "We got it four months ago. No telling when Belfort was there, obviously, but perhaps a month or two before. In August? He was clearly making a payment to someone. You don't happen to know who this duke might be?"

Gideon felt sick. "The Duc de Limours. An émigré and a spy. He was arrested in September, not long before I sailed." He got up, his chair scraping back across the stone flags. August. He'd been down at Landor for part of that month, while Delphine Dalgleish was in London. Had there been a rendezvous between the cousins? Was this yet another dire secret she was keeping from him?

Scovell shot him a concerned look. "Anything amiss?"

"Why should something like that get into a dispatch in Spain? Belfort works from Paris. What connection could there be?"

Scovell pondered for a while. "He could well have been sent down to Madrid after his England mission. On the business of the grand code, perhaps. Why? What's worrying you?"

It was best to hide nothing. "The man is related to my fiancée." There: he had said the word for the first time. He held Scovell's eye. "Mademoiselle Dalgleish is the soul of honor. Belfort is a reptile. I'd trust him with nothing, not even her life. If you hear of him again, I'd be grateful for the information."

"You shall have it." Scovell rose and extended his hand. "Godspeed, and a safe journey."

So Gideon rode down to Lisbon, without Grant for company this time, and with ample leisure to speculate about Armand de Belfort's clandestine visit to England, and to torment himself with what it might mean.

Playacting

⌐⁀

The Duc de Limours was being deported to France. He had been escorted by the military as far as the coast, and the Comtesse D'Auvennois, after faithful months of waiting, was booked to leave on a stagecoach with her maid and join him at Dover. The day before her departure, Delphine went to visit her, unannounced, at Henrietta Street. None of the Austens was home except a country cousin, who received Delphine in the drawing room, sent someone for the countess and begged her to sit down and take some refreshment. "I'm sorry my brother and his wife are not here to receive you. They are traipsing down Bond Street at present. I've not perfected the art of traipsing, so I chose to stay home and keep the countess company."

"How kind of you. Is she very distressed?"

"Do you know her well?" Miss Austen asked, her small hazel eyes observing Delphine intently.

"I saw a great deal of her and the duke for many weeks. I know her as well as most."

"Then it will pain you to hear that I've not seen her smile once since I came to London. On my last visit, she was good cheer itself. There has been a sad change."

Delphine sighed. "It's such a pity that she should have to go through all this for a second time! When she and the duke first came here long ago, they were in flight from terror. And now, when she might have been living out her days here in peace, she's forced to make her home in France again. I don't know whether she will have the heart for it."

"And would you, mademoiselle? Or would you feel the same reluctance to exchange London for Paris?"

Delphine was silent in confusion. Why was the question so hard to answer? She tried to make light of it. "Paris and London have more similarities than you might think. One can make the choice between them on pure bagatelles—the quality of this year's asparagus, or the price of gloves." She paused, then said slowly, "But England . . . I'm fonder of England now than I ever could have imagined." She shrugged. "In any case, when I leave it will be for Mauritius, not France."

Just as she said this, the Comtesse D'Auvennois came into the room. Miss Austen got to her feet at once and helped the old lady onto a sofa while Delphine went to sit by her side. Fear and anxiety seemed to have shrunk the countess—her shoulders sagged, and her lips trembled as she tried to summon a smile of welcome. Her eyes, once so benevolent, showed a deep alarm that made Delphine feel guilty, as though her visit were yet another challenge to be faced.

After they had made their greetings, with the wordless gestures that the countess was used to, she put out one gnarled hand, laid it across Delphine's fingers and patted them slowly.

"I'm so sorry," Delphine mouthed, and the old lady nodded. Then Delphine drew her hand away, opened her reticule, took out a folded piece of paper and handed it to her. She looked across at Miss Austen as the old lady read it. "I hope you'll excuse my communicating with the countess like this. It was the only way I could think of that wouldn't tire her. I'm just giving her my sympathy and conveying my regards to her brother. And I wish her well."

"I'm sure we all do."

"I've asked for the letter back—they will be searched in Dover and Calais and heaven knows what excuses may be found to torment them. I wouldn't have anything of mine be the cause of trouble."

She turned back to watch the countess's face as her eyes reached the bottom of the sheet. There, Delphine had written: *In the goodness of your heart, I beg you to have a message conveyed to . . .* followed by a tiny drawing of a bee. The countess would know this was Bonaparte's personal symbol, but it would convey little to an

English person glancing at the sheet. As it happened, the precaution was needless, for however alert Miss Austen might be, she remained opposite, unable to see the letter. Delphine had continued the request: *Please let him know that F did not obtain the information we feared.* There was no need to mention Delphine's second mission to England—the delivery of Napoleon's letter to Lucien Bonaparte—for the duke already knew of it and would pass it on.

The countess nodded, her eyes fixed on the paper. Delphine, glancing across at Miss Austen, caught a look of intelligence that made her cringe inwardly. She wondered why she should care what the Englishwoman thought of her; then she looked back at the Comtesse D'Auvennois and saw lines of suffering etched in her patient, tired face. It was a moment that Delphine could have avoided. She could have chosen not to complete her duty to the emperor—and not to burden the old lady. The countess had sought refuge in England, only to have it compromised and then destroyed by her brother's intrigues. Perhaps it was cruel to press a final secret on her as she prepared to reenter the country she had fled from in fear of her life eighteen years before.

But the old lady folded the paper carefully and placed it in Delphine's lap. Then she raised her eyes, which all of a sudden crinkled at the corners in her habitual way, and a gleam of purpose arose, transforming her face and spreading to her tremulous mouth. She clasped Delphine's fingers, her lips formed the words and in her threadlike, seldom-used voice she quavered: "I shall tell him."

Whether she meant the duke or the emperor, Delphine had no more idea than Miss Austen. But she saw that the moment had aroused in the countess a strength that had always been there, and that lent her a dignity to be envied and admired. Delphine freed her hands and leaned forward, and they embraced.

January brought snow, blanketing the center of Berkeley Square in white and turning the surfaces around it into a slurry in which horses slipped and stumbled, while coachmen and grooms exchanged vociferous insults, and carriages and cabs skidded nar-

rowly past one another across the thoroughfare. In February the
pavements were swept clean so that they rang under the hooves
of the teams, but the air was no less icy, and Delphine was grateful for the stuffy comfort of Mrs. Laidlaw's house and for the
human warmth that was generated in the crush of the fashionable gatherings to which she and her mother continued to be invited.

One evening, Delphine found herself bowling through the
streets to the theater with Georgiana Combrewood and two of
her friends, a pleasant couple who also lived in Mayfair—all of
them well rugged up, and Georgiana enveloped in a swathe of silver fox fur. "Where is Combrewood?" Delphine said as they made
a slithering turn into the Mall.

"I've no idea. Somewhere beyond Colchester. There's a property out there I've never been to—Combrewood says it's far too
flat to amuse me so he always goes alone. Where's Landor?"

His name jolted Delphine, as it always did. She could never get
used to the absurd pain of her situation—engaged to the man she
loved, but loving a man she could not marry. Georgiana's question, said carelessly but perhaps concealing a certain weight of
feeling, touched her on the raw. For she had no idea where Landor was. She had received not a single message from him since
the note on his departure from Greenwich. "Still at sea. A dreadful phrase, isn't it? It almost makes me wish I'd plighted my troth
to a gentleman in the army. At least I could give a good account
of his whereabouts."

"Whichever," Georgiana said in her slow, amused drawl, "you
have a talent for keeping them at a distance."

The Mayfair couple smiled, taking this as a joke. Delphine,
much less certain, smiled also.

At the theater, entertained by a succession of gentlemen visitors to the Combrewood box, Delphine found that Georgiana's
remark rankled. So she handled males with a certain dexterity—
what of that? And why should Georgiana accuse her of keeping
men at bay, when the rest of society would probably be much
more willing to condemn her for a flirt?

The play was a tragedy, and tragically acted, in Delphine's view.

She could not take the posturing on stage seriously and nor could her companions, so the talk in the box during the first interval was very gay. Delphine, smarting under Georgiana's accusation, was the gayest of all. In the eyes of conservative people, she knew she was not behaving like a betrothed woman, but she had no choice—for in every public arena she was conscious of one inescapable truth: when Sir Gideon Landor came back, she had promised to jilt him. She, a temporary fugitive from France and Mauritius, the child of a Catholic and a revolutionary, a supplicant wholly dependent on English goodwill, had been offered the hand of a British aristocrat, whose station, fortune and looks were matched only by the distinguished wartime service he performed for his country. From society's point of view, if she were in love with Landor she could not have chosen better. And if she were not, and self-interest alone moved her, the verdict was the same: she was brilliantly matched, and a fool if she couldn't see it.

So she must appear to be not in love, and a fool. Otherwise, no one would believe when she threw him over. And if they didn't believe, questions and inquiries would begin. People would start to dig, avid to discover what was hidden beneath the surface of their relationship. She and Landor would be in danger of someone laying bare the series of events that had led to the false betrothal. The idea chilled Delphine to the bone. She could not risk the history of her dealings with Landor being unraveled—their confrontations, his work for England, her spying for France, and the final cloak of deceit that he had drawn around them for her protection. Exposure would put her in the same peril that she had courted when she crept into the library at Paget. And it could destroy his honor forever, if it didn't cost him his life.

Delphine's surest defense, and his, was her own frivolity. Georgiana Combrewood, who was, oddly enough, the closest female friend she had, already thought her heartless. She must appear worse than that—volatile, changeable, tempted by every amusement and amused by the slightest temptation. She must appear to enjoy men's company as much as she had before her engagement to Landor. Everyone knew she had given up Ferron for his sake . . . she must make it easy for people to imagine she might

give up Landor in his turn if her affections—her *foolish* affections—
were gained by another.

Candidates were not wanting. She met them at every turn.
Along with Arkwright and friends like Elliott, there were the fa-
vorites of the new season, marriageable gentlemen who were
drawn to her partly as a diversion from the predatory mamas and
their daughters, partly because she was both French and
betrothed—a kind of double guarantee of harmlessness. She intrigued them and played up to them, using the skills that she had
developed in Paris, where clever self-expression was an art, and
finding that here those skills helped her achieve exactly the
opposite—a resolute concealment of all her natural feelings.

This behavior had become torture to her, but she could see no
end to it until Sir Gideon Landor came home. Which meant that
she should have been looking forward to this event; yet it too was
dreadful. She had no idea how she would cope. The last months
had been horrible; with every day, she was deeper in love with
Landor, and the more discretion she exercised while he was
gone, the more she despaired of hiding her reaction when he
reappeared. Whether the first meeting were in public or in private, she feared for her self-control.

But what would he be like? She could not know how strong his
feelings might be after such an absence, but she could make
some guesses about how well he would contain them. Unlike her,
when it came to love he had some practice in endurance and self-
command. And it was she who had forced him to learn those
skills.

When the play resumed she was wretched, but she stared at
the stage so fixedly that Arkwright, seated beside her after a deft
piece of maneuvering at the end of the interval, gave up trying to
catch her attention. The second interval came, and she determined to rally. She stayed in the front row of the box but turned
to speak to Georgiana and the lady from Mayfair behind her. The
lady's husband came back with friends, who crowded in, bearing
refreshments obtained in the corridors behind, and Arkwright
disappeared to find Delphine something she didn't want or ask
for.

Suddenly, in a burst of laughter, Georgiana started, and her eyes widened as she looked down past Delphine into the stalls. "Landor!"

Delphine twisted around and snatched the bar of the parapet in both hands. She saw him at once. Most of the crowd below were standing, but he was like a beacon in the sea of heads, his tall form very still and his fair head thrown back as he gazed straight at her. It was hard to breathe. She took her hands from the rail and brought them to the base of her throat. That was the sole signal between them. Her face, she knew, showed acute distress; his showed a suspense that turned his cheeks pale. Then he turned and made his way through the crowd to an exit.

"Oh! He's here."

"At any moment," Georgiana said. "Would you like us to . . . ?"

"No!" Delphine sprang to her feet. "Thank you, I shall—" She left shawl, gloves and reticule on the seat, lifted the hem of her gown and made her way through the gentlemen without looking at them as she passed. When she pushed aside the curtain and emerged into the space beyond, the box went quiet behind her. The corridor was hopelessly narrow, as in all the English theaters, and thronged. She shrank back within the alcove formed by the entrance into the Combrewood box and waited, shivering.

He seemed to take a long time. Was he coming upstairs, or had he walked out? He was in evening dress, so he had not come directly from Greenwich. Where had he been before the theater? Had he known she would be here, or was this a whim, a bid for entertainment on his first night back? If he had been watching her for some time, the sight of her lost in laughter amongst a crowd of men might have been enough to send him away. No: he never ran from a confrontation. And just as the thought sped through her mind, he appeared, striding along the corridor toward her. He faltered when he saw her, and had to step aside for two young ladies who looked back at him, whispering, as he walked on. Then everything around him dissolved, and all Delphine could see was the black and white of his form and the brightness of his hair and eyes.

He stopped before her, closer than he had ever been except

when he kissed her. His eyes were burning but he didn't speak. She raised her right hand, and he took it. On impulse, she folded her left hand over the ball of his thumb, so that he took both hands to his lips. He kissed them—the right, then the left—and she closed her eyes. There was a soft shock in the core of her body, and a weakness descended on her, filling her with a strange alarm and delight.

When she opened her eyes again he lowered his hand, releasing her right but retaining the left while he looked down at the ruby on her finger. The color returned to his face and the green eyes glittered.

"You're safe," she said.

"As you see. And you're well?" His gaze overpowered hers. "You look it."

"Thank you. Is this by chance, or did you know I was here?"

"I called at Berkeley Square. Your mother told me."

"When did you arrive?"

"This morning, at Greenwich." He released her hand, glancing irresistibly down once again.

She clasped her right hand over her left and brought both to her midriff, concealing the intense spark of the ruby. "I've worn it every day since you sent it to me." She might as well have said, *I love you.*

"Thank you." His eyes said the same. But he continued, "You're with whom?"

"Georgiana Combrewood and two of her friends."

One dark eyebrow twitched. "Only two?"

As if on cue, Melbray Arkwright appeared at her elbow, bearing tall glasses of barley water. He thrust one of them at her. "Miss Dalgleish."

She took it and nodded. "Sir Gideon, may I introduce Major Melbray Arkwright? Major—Captain Sir Gideon Landor."

Arkwright's consternation was so transparent that she would have felt sorry for him in another world. Her present one, however, contained only the man she loved, and she watched Arkwright try to smile and make a bow, with his glass tipping in his hand, as though he were a being from another sphere.

Landor must have said something to Arkwright, but all she heard were the words addressed to her. "Shall we go in?"

She gaped at him. "You wish to see the play?"

"I should like to join you, if I may."

Arkwright, ignored, muttered an excuse and was about to turn away. Delphine took a sip from her glass, handed it back to him and said, "I'm obliged to you." He blushed deeply and walked off.

Delphine stayed with her back to the box, where merriment had struck up again beyond the curtain. This was so unexpected. Whatever mood Landor had arrived in, she had feared—and desired—that he would want to be alone with her. Continuing this encounter in the glare of the theater seemed far too much to handle. But for some reason he was adamant. He offered her his arm, with a half smile at her confusion, and she turned with him and entered the box.

Silence fell when they emerged into the light, then someone clapped, and there was laughter and a burst of voices congratulating Landor on his return. He bore it well, with a friendly smile on his face that grew warmer as he greeted Georgiana.

The animation continued until their hostess realized that the theater was settling down for the last act. "If we are not to make a *total* spectacle of ourselves, I beg we sit down. Sir Gideon, please take the front with Miss Dalgleish—the audience deserves nothing less. We'll leave you the box, and—"

"Nonsense, we shan't deprive you of your seats. Pray take them, and the rest of you may clear off with my blessing."

One of the gentlemen laughed. "Glad to hear your manners haven't mended any at sea, Landor. Welcome back!"

As he waited for Delphine to sit down, Landor said, "You're shivering—would you like your shawl?"

"No, thank you." She felt anything but cool. "I'll just put it here." She draped it hastily over the rail and sat down with her gloves and reticule in her lap.

He composed himself beside her, not leaning intimately close, but not too far away either, and it seemed to her that there was something proprietorial in his stance. Even while her mind questioned this, her body responded, and she sat in a haze of longing.

The play, as far as she could tell, didn't improve much in the last act, and few in the audience hesitated to make comments to their neighbors. Delphine, swamped by imperious sensations, had no thoughts that could be shared. She was wondering whether Landor was really expecting her to jilt him after this, and she could feel the intense curiosity of Georgiana and her friends behind them as the silence between herself and the man at her side went on and on. Finally she collected herself enough to say, "What are your duties, now you're home?"

"I've navy business to attend to for the next few days. Then I go down to Landor." He glanced at her. "So I shan't be able to see you. But you'll permit me to send a note?"

It was a sharp disappointment. "A note: that's more than you vouchsafed me at sea, sir!"

He held her gaze. "Do you wonder at that?"

All at once she thought of what might have kept him from writing. "Your voyages. Portugal. You didn't run into danger?"

"None to speak of."

"Thank God!"

He looked away. He was moved; she could feel it but didn't dare observe him. She wanted to throw her arms around his neck and bury her face in the crook of his shoulder. She wanted to scream at him. Alone, they would have come to explanations— which might just as easily have driven them apart again—but surely they owed them to each other? Instead, Landor had placed her in the pitiless arena of the theater, where neither of them could be natural.

The silence lengthened again. She could have wept with the effort to maintain it. But she knew her power to hurt him, and heaven now knew his power to hurt her—she wasn't going to utter some ill-judged remark when they would each take the memory of it away with them for days or weeks before he permitted her to see him again.

It was the most lowering play she had ever sat through. There was a quite unseemly burial, with a ghastly harangue over a dead woman's body, and eventually a court scene where everyone mouthed things they didn't mean and drank things they should never have touched.

Then all of a sudden swords came out, and the din and speed of the fight made her grab Landor's wrist where it lay on the armrest between them. This time he caught her hand and didn't let it go. He leaned toward her, his breath on her cheek but his eyes directed to the stage. "I remember, Mademoiselle Dalgleish—you are not made for war."

Her voice trembled. "They're so inept! I'm terrified we'll see someone die in earnest."

"Fear not. The blades are as weak as noodles and there are buttons on the points."

"No, someone said *un*buttoned, I'm sure they did."

"Poetic license."

"You call this man a *poet?*"

He laughed softly, the tremor traveling down his arm and into her fingers. "It's all right; he's nearly done. You don't have to put up with much more."

Then she realized that as long as Landor held her hand, she could endure another century of it. She went still, praying he wouldn't shift away, and concentrated on the play. And was captured, at last. When the hero collapsed to the boards and his strength began to fail, she held on to Landor's fingers as though her own life depended upon it. When he died, a real tear ran down each cheek.

"Don't," Landor said, and unclasped his fingers. "It's all right," he said again as she took a handkerchief from her reticule and dried her face, unable to look up. "It's over."

They were surrounded by applause, relieved laughter and loud voices. It was over indeed.

Downstairs, Landor said to Georgiana, "I came by cab; I've no means to convey Mademoiselle Dalgleish home."

"She will come with us, of course," Georgiana said.

"Then I bid you all good night."

As he bowed, Delphine realized he wasn't even going to wait until the Combrewood carriage came up to the steps. Was he escaping? He looked too calm for that. No, not calm—collected, as though for some important action. Whatever it was, it didn't include her! "Good night, sir."

"You'll hear from me tomorrow. If you permit."

Her voice was like a thread and her response impossibly lame. "Very well."

He bowed again, turned and walked away. She watched him go, careless about who might be watching *her*. In the carriage she was silent and Georgiana and the Mayfair couple were obliged to maintain all the conversation, but when they pulled up at Berkeley Square, and Mrs. Laidlaw's footman came out to let down the steps of the vehicle, Georgiana's voice halted Delphine in her descent. "My dear, I must own, I've misread you these last months."

Delphine glanced over her shoulder. "No more than I wished you to."

The Summerhouse

$\backsim$

Gideon was writing letters in the morning room at Buff House, before a window affording a pleasant view across a close-cropped lawn and through apple and pear trees espaliered on wires. Their latticed branches were bare, but they stretched across a blue patch of sky that held a faint promise of spring. He had breakfasted earlier, but he stayed on to write and keep his parents company. Now his mother had left the table and his father, who was about to walk down the hill to the kennels, paused by Gideon's desk. "Have you written to the Dalgleishes?"

"Not yet."

"Damme, not much point in inviting a whole host of others, if you've not secured the ladies beforehand! What keeps you from putting pen to paper?"

"The phrasing, Father. If you've a mind to assist, you may tell me how to explain myself. So far it goes roughly like this: 'Pray take the advantage of jilting me on a country visit—by the time you get back to London it will be a *fait accompli* and we'll both be spared the worst embarrassment.' If you've any improvement on that, I'll be glad to know it."

The earl stiffened. "You got yourself into this, and I'm hanged if I can be expected to get you out!" He paused, then said in another tone, "Forget the phrasing—what are the lady's wishes?"

Gideon shook his head and concentrated on melting a stick of sealing wax over the candle. He wished his father would push off.

The earl said, "French, Catholic and hand in glove with Boney. From everything we heard, we had her branded as the last woman in England we'd countenance as a daughter-in-law. I don't mind telling you, your mother had her work cut out to persuade me to meet her." He paused again and waited until Gideon had sealed the letter. "And then I *did* meet her. And I have to say: this coil you've gotten yourself into—I understand you. I can't tell you how to deal with it, but I understand you. All I can advise is: before you act, make sure you understand what the lady wants. Because there's no room for mistakes this time."

Gideon's heart jolted. "What do you mean? If it were a genuine betrothal, how would you view it?"

The earl snorted. "How do *you* view it, sir? *I'm* not pledged to the girl!" Then his gruff voice softened. "Very well. French, Catholic . . . no more than one of your ancestors, you know. Marie de what's-her-name; seventeenth century. Her portrait hangs at Landor, the second one as you go up the main staircase."

"I never realized." Gideon hesitated a moment, and his voice fell. "Bonapartist . . ."

"From Mauritius. Which makes all the difference, if you and the demoiselle can agree to think so." The earl turned to go. "For pity's sake, sort it out between you; invite her and her mother here and settle it once and for all."

Gideon drew a fresh sheet of paper toward him and dipped his pen in the ink. When his father had gone, he left the quill propped in the bottle and sat staring at the blank page as the night at the theater came flooding back to him. He remembered the look in her eyes when he reached her, the warmth of her responses, her surprise and then her submission when he asked to join her. He recalled the incredible sweetness of sitting beside her. Of exchanging looks, words, touches, that proclaimed intimacy and affection. Of living one hour as her future husband, acknowledged before the world. It was a homecoming that made all the agony of absence worthwhile. He had claimed all this, and she had not been able to refuse him, but what had it meant to her? He couldn't know until he asked her, and he didn't have the fortitude; the miraculous hour at the theater had been too overpowering for him to relinquish every hope of another. How brutal it would have been, to visit Berkeley Square the next day and learn that she was standing firm to their arrangement!

He had written to her instead, something about the pleasure

of seeing her, of having her company at the theater and of looking forward to writing again once he reached Landor. It was an incoherent letter, from which his feelings must have shot out like errant sparks. And how he feared a reply! Every day when the post was brought into Buff House, he dreaded to find a package addressed to himself, containing a ruby ring accompanied by a formal note. So far, he had not received a word.

But she had the right of choice, and no matter how his soul rebelled, he must give her the opportunity to break the engagement off, with the least social damage. The event must occur out of London, and provide time for the world to more or less forget about it by the time she and he returned there.

His new summerhouse was completed. On its own it would have provided a laughable excuse for a country gathering, especially when the London season was on, but there had been other renovations at Landor that were also finished, which made some sort of focus for inviting guests. He sent invitations to a select group who were unconnected with Mademoiselle Dalgleish. There would be no luminaries such as Georgiana Combrewood: the list included mainly people from the region to whom his family owed consideration—the local squire, the landed neighbors— plus a few of his parents' acquaintance from London. At any other time such a collection would have royally bored him, but he was depending on their lack of distinction. He wanted no footlights to illuminate Mademoiselle Dalgleish's decision, and no highly colored scenes to be conveyed back to the ton. At Buff House and Landor there would be ample chance for them to confer privately; what she did with that was up to her. Which was why the letter was so damnably hard to write. In the end, he sent her an invitation very similar to the one he had issued to everyone else. For he could not bear to watch her walk out of his life, and it hurt him to the quick to give her the means to do so.

Delphine was sitting in Countess Tracey's painting room at Buff House, having her miniature done. It was an agreeable space, lit along one side by conservatory windows that must have been put in for the purposes of her hostess, who was seated at a little table close by, holding a small board taped with paper on her lap, and using a set of colors that took up no more room on the tabletop than a child's tea set.

Delphine and her mother had arrived at Buff House the day before, in time for a supper that catered for ten guests. The remainder had come that morning, and the countess had quite blithely left the gentlemen to entertain them, and laid claim to Delphine. It felt like absconding, to sit in this sunlit room while everyone bustled about elsewhere. But it gave her no respite from the anxiety of how to deal with Landor. Last night, under their courteous greetings, there had been the same intense attraction, the same wordless tumult that she had felt at the theater.

The countess was saying in her musical voice, "This won't take long. I'll ask you to change position in a moment. I'm doing a few watercolors in succession, so I can choose the best pose to prepare for oils."

"How does one paint a miniature? It's a mystery to me."

"Do you mind looking a trifle more toward the window? Thank you. I find it helps if I imagine you as a figure in my doll's house. You haven't seen it; I must show you. It's Tudor, in theory, but when I get carried away I make Stuart furniture for it sometimes."

"*You* make it?"

"Yes, I've a workshop, through there." She pointed with a brush the size of a toothpick, then studied Delphine's face with amusement. "I think I've confessed to all my eccentricities now. The doll's house was my last secret."

Delphine, seeing that the countess rather expected to be teased about this, replied instead, "How rewarding it must be, to create so many beautiful things. I especially like your miniatures."

"Thank you. Is that why you consented to have this done?"

Delphine took a deep breath. "I thought . . . it would give us the chance to talk alone. Though I find it very hard to know what to say."

The countess looked up, a smile sparking in the depths of her hazel eyes. "And now present your right side, if you would. With a slight movement of the torso."

Delphine obeyed, so that she was facing the inner wall, where a large painting at once caught her eye. *"Ciel!"*

"Yes?" said the countess, busy on a fresh sheet. "Oh, dear; have you seen something terribly odd? This is rather like a trophy room. There are all sorts of things that my son prefers me not to show in other parts of the house. You'll notice over there, I made a model of his first ship, which embarrassed him terribly."

"But—a portrait of Napoleon!"

"Oh." The countess laughed. "Well, you see my point. Half our neighbors would have an apoplexy if they found it in the great hall."

"Where did he—*When* did he—?" The countess just went on working, so Delphine continued to examine the portrait, which dominated that wall of the room with its rich colors and dramatic composition. "I seem to recognize the artist. French, of course, and—"

"The signature shows the initials 'EUG,' then the particle 'de' and a cross."

"*Mon dieu!* Eugène Delacroix! Madame, what you have there is priceless."

"Oh, really?" the countess said, and Delphine realized she had known all along. And unless Delphine asked Sir Gideon Landor himself, she wasn't going to learn how—or indeed why!—the portrait had been obtained.

In the afternoon, Gideon was electrified to find himself out riding with Mademoiselle Dalgleish. The arrangement had been made at the dinner table by Earl Tracey, and the lady had lent herself to it without demur. Gideon was touched by seeing his father as the host of crowd; he had a keen enjoyment of life that he conveyed to others, and a passion for his own country that made him long to share it with everyone. Apart from seating Delphine Dalgleish close to him at the head of the table, he had not singled her out; he beamed down the board at all and sundry and kept up a flow of inquiries and information to which people found ready responses. It was the lady herself who had created the opening, by laughing when he was in the middle of a description of the beef herd at present housed in the byres near Tisbury Wood.

"Polled Angus!" She put a napkin to her lips to mask her smile. "I'm sorry, but what a name! It makes me wonder what on *earth* they look like."

The earl gave this bright-eyed consideration. "Polled Angus? As handsome creatures as ever lived. Dashed if I can do justice to 'em, though. I recommend you see them for yourself. Gideon will squire you." He said to his son, "You'll make Penelope available to Miss Dalgleish. Lady's horse, lady's horse, not like your brute, which can do with the exercise, by the by."

So here they were, riding across the valley through ploughed fields, and now and then along public paths where the folk abroad on this crisp day all replied to Gideon's nod and word as they passed. Delphine Dalgleish rode as Gideon had seen her at Paget, with grace. It was almost enough to erase from his mind the image of Ferron's arm around her waist when he'd made her slip as she dismounted. But it was not enough to dispel the tension. When Gideon spoke, his heart hammered in case she replied with something annihilating.

She said at one point, "I think you must be more of an agriculturist than you led me to believe. You know this place so well. You seem close to it, and to the people."

He was amused. "I was born here. It would be something of a surprise if they didn't recognize my face."

"No, I can tell it by the way they greet you. They look you in the eye. If you saw how the workers at Saint-Amour look at Major Arkwright, you'd catch the difference at once."

He'd heard rumors in London that she was encouraging Melbray Arkwright's pursuit, but this sounded like rank disapproval. "I hope he's not still troubling you . . . over Saint-Amour?"

"Thank you, I believe he's been circumvented at last. The estate is safe—my mother and I can return at any time."

He tried to keep his voice as even as hers. "Congratulations. When do you intend doing so?"

She was looking straight ahead as they approached Swallowcliffe Copse. "That depends, monsieur, upon one gentleman alone."

"Whom?" When there was no reply he pressed: "Farquhar?" He said in a lower voice, "Arkwright?" When he looked over she was blushing with what seemed like anger. She escaped by putting the mare to a canter along the ride.

She recovered as they swung along the valley bottom to Tisbury Wood, inquiring about the dwellings they passed, and praising the countryside. He pointed out the signs that spring would be early this year; the frosts had ceased, and crocuses already studded the grass under the trees. She was intrigued by the patterns that masons had achieved with flint in the walls of cottages and in the bridges across the Nadder River, and she liked the weaving of the bare hedgerows, whose stems gleamed like fretwork against the rich, dark soil on either side of the road. She asked when the bluebells would appear, and he had to suppress the extremely stupid remark that her eyes reminded him of their exact color.

At the byres, she dismounted and went inside so as to give a good account of the Polled Angus to the earl, and on the way back he took her to the kennels, knowing this would please his father and hoping there would be new puppies to amuse her. There were, and she dismounted again, bent down and let them climb in and out of her lap without any regard for the dirt on their paws, just brushing her hands quickly together as she stood. At that moment her gaze was caught by something beyond him and he looked over his shoulder. Through a small stand of ash, the manor was visible on the hill behind. He turned back. "Yes, that's Landor. If you're agreeable, we'll all move there tonight— except for my parents, of course. I can promise supper, and I hope a certain degree of comfort, and then people are free to take their leave in the morning—or stay on, as they wish. It's a bizarre idea to summon guests here in the depths of winter, but the navy gives me precious little choice as to the month." He was floundering; she looked ill at ease. He concluded abruptly, "I only hope you'll approve."

"Of . . . of what?" She bent to pick up her riding crop from the ground, then took the reins of the mare from the man standing beside the kennel. "Pray keep the puppies out of harm's way as we go." Then she looked at Gideon over her shoulder. "Of your . . . arrangements? They don't depend on me, surely?"

He came forward, gave her his joined hands to step into and lifted her lightly to the saddle. Then he straightened and looked up into her eyes. "My future, Mademoiselle Dalgleish, depends on one person alone."

Her hands tightened on the reins and the mare stepped backward. "I thought it was the navy . . ." Her eyes were very bright.

"Only if you say so."

"Oh, I *wish* I could speak to you!"

"Do!" He grabbed the reins of his hunter and vaulted into the saddle. "Tell me. Spare me nothing." But she wheeled the mare toward Buff House and dug in her heels to head up the hill.

Landor was lovely; Delphine wouldn't have believed that any building so unlike the dwellings she was used to in Mauritius and France could be so handsome. The manor house was a seventeenth-century gray stone pile of severe aspect comprising three stories under a single mansard roof. Inside, the decoration was restrained, with plasterwork only at doorways and cornices; the drapes and curtains were toned to go with the plain wall coverings, and the furniture alone reflected the tastes of the families who had lived there for the last two centuries—a collection formed for ease rather than ostentation. Paintings crowded the rooms, the rose-colored parquet floors creaked with the weight of deep sofas and generous ottomans, and in the music room were a pianoforte, a harpsichord and a splendid golden harp.

On being pressed, their host gave a tour of the first-floor public rooms, explaining as they went that the alterations here were structural—mainly, he remarked with a grin, to prevent the second floor falling onto the one below. "You'll be pleased to hear," he said as they finished up by the grand staircase, "that the more visible and, dare I say, lavish improvements are to the bedchambers. The servants will show you where you're housed."

As the guests began to walk upstairs, Julie Dalgleish looked out through the reception rooms toward the gardens on each side. "I recall we were promised a summerhouse, monsieur. Where do you hide it?"

"It's in that direction, madame," he said, pointing toward the back of the house. "It's halfway up the slope, with a southerly prospect, sheltered by the hill."

"It will be dark soon, Maman. Let's go to our rooms." Delphine glanced at Landor. "I look forward to seeing the summerhouse tomorrow." He gave a little bow and watched her go up the stairs.

In the bedchamber, which looked across the valley, Molly helped her dress for the evening. Delphine was acutely aware of everything that went on around her, as though the slightest events provided omens of what would happen when she and Landor talked freely at last. *I must tell him I love him, and take the consequences.*

Watching the intent, pretty face of her maid in the glass as her hair was arranged, she remembered Molly's encounter with Landor's man at Paget. "Does Ellis still attend on Sir Gideon, Molly?"

Molly's eyes brightened. "Yes, mamselle."

"And is he often obliged to take horse at midnight these days?"

"Take ship, more like. The navy disposes, Ellis says. Though he did tell me, after they got to Lisbon they went inland somewheres. Except he wouldn't tell me exact." She avoided Delphine's eye in the mirror as she added, "The secrets of war, Ellis says, are not to be bandied." *Especially not with the enemy.*

Later, in her mother's room before they went down to supper, Delphine stood looking out the window at terraced gardens bordered by chestnut trees and tinted silvery gray by the light of a half-moon. "I shall speak to him tonight, Maman. But there is still a divide between us that terrifies me."

Julie laughed. "*Chérie*, what could be more radical than the difference between man and woman? A man's feelings and desires can never be the same as a woman's. *That* is the great divide. No other comes close in magnitude. Cross it, without ever forgetting that, and you have the key to all the rest."

Delphine turned. "Do you think I can?"

"You already have."

Once they were downstairs and in the dining room, for the first time Delphine more than half suspected Landor of coercion during this visit. It was all so perfect. The meal went with military precision and smoothness. She sipped superlative wines, basked in the friendly attention of his neighbors and joined in the laughter that surged up around the table, and meanwhile the realization came of what this added up to. If she were to return his ring, she would also be rejecting the estate and the grand houses, his position in the world—the Tracey legacy. Had he invited her here so that she could weigh it all? Then she caught his eye in the midst of the gaiety and the thought flew from her head. He looked vulnerable, tense, consumed. There was too much between them for his possessions or hers to count for a feather.

As the meal drew to a close he announced that the final course would be served in the summerhouse. He smiled at the outcry as everyone was forced to abandon the table and file along the corridor toward the garden room. The insane thought of stepping out into the frigid March night held everyone silent until the rear doors were thrown open; then they all gasped. There were flambeaux lining a broad path, and on the slope the summerhouse blazed like an oriental gazebo, surrounded by braziers that shed warmth and light against its latticed railings. The octagonal building was resplendent with lanterns and hung with transparent backdrops that glowed against the black hillside: a silhouette of the Houses of Parliament beside the Thames; an impression of the Tuileries palace studded by fireworks; a tropical island scene with palms and a sailing ship. "Illuminations!" someone cried. "Landor, you have outdone yourself!"

The others crowded forward and up the slope while Delphine remained, her hand on Landor's arm, not sure whether she was expected to laugh or be gratified. "It's magic!"

He looked down at her. "I admit, it's supposed to outdo Vauxhall Gardens."

"Well, I for one like it a thousand times better." They began to follow the rest. "It's *épatant*. But if you'll forgive me . . . it doesn't seem entirely in your style."

He shrugged, then put his other hand over hers. His voice held a hint of self-mockery. "There is an English saying: 'As well be hanged for a sheep as a lamb.'"

"Oh? I've never thought of you as either, monsieur."

For some reason this made him laugh, and he couldn't stop until they reached the summerhouse. It was more spacious than the one at Thorngrove, allowing for a long table in the center spread with puddings—colorful jellies and custards that the guests could spoon from little bowls as they stood leaning against the railings, looking out into the now moonless night.

"*Comme c'est délicieux,*" Julie Dalgleish said. "A perfect contradiction. An airy summerhouse—to enjoy in the dark, in the middle of March." She looked approvingly at the illuminations, which were painted on stretched silk. "Very pretty tributes to England and France. And the third—is it meant to be Mauritius?"

"If you don't look too closely, yes. The artist is local, so his palm trees are feats of the imagination. And the ship, I'm afraid, is beyond anyone's."

"Whatever you say, it's a triumph."

Someone asked, "Remember the truly wonderful illuminations after Trafalgar?"

"I hadn't returned by then," the host said in a quelling tone.

The hint was not taken. "And the portraits of Nelson. If I saw one in London, I saw a hundred. What a time: smashing victory— appalling sorrow." Recollection caught the speaker and he said to Gideon, "Upon my word, sir, of course—you were *there*! Shining day for England."

And a hellish one for France. No one said it, but the thought suddenly crossed every mind. One of the ladies, not game to meet Delphine's eye but brave enough to speak to la Générale, said kindly, "I once met your vice admiral de Villeneuve, you know. After Trafalgar he stayed in Berkshire for quite some time, as the guest of our friend Viscount Sidmouth. A very gentlemanlike man. So depressed and so unfortunate: such a pity he died after he returned to France."

"*Vraiment?*" was the reply. "I'm better acquainted with the French army than the navy. There one hears only of victory."

Conversation resumed after this riposte, but an announcement that coffee was ready indoors perhaps came as a relief to many. There was a gradual exodus from the summerhouse, led by la Générale, who in her gentle way repented the barb she had given the Villeneuve lady, and began asking her questions about Berkshire. And then Delphine and Gideon were alone.

The Territory of Love

They would shortly be invisible to the others, for the only windows on the first floor looked out from scullery and offices, while those on the second floor belonged to the unlit picture gallery. Gideon watched her as his last unwanted guests went indoors. She leaned against the rail beside the Mauritius scene, her hair pale against a rendition of palm trees and her profile, turned toward the house, rose tinted and finely drawn against the blackness beyond. Her left hand clasped the rail, the diamonds around her wrist and the ruby on her finger sparkling in the lantern light. He stepped forward. "Do you remember the gazebo on Saint-Amour?" She turned her face to him but didn't lift her eyes. "That's when I fell in love with you. I had you trapped, but I couldn't look at you! I've loved you ever since, and there's nothing I can do about it."

Her gaze pierced his. "I can't tell you how long I've been in love with you. But once we kissed at Paget, there was no turning back for me either." The words rushed through him like wine and he took another unsteady step. He was close enough to touch her, but the expression on her face arrested him: wonder and helpless amusement. "What makes us this way?" she said with a melting smile. "Think what threw us together. Opposition. Shock. Surprise. How shall we fare without those?"

He was a hand's breadth away, and she trembled, for as always he both frightened and dangerously tempted her. Hooded against the glare from the lanterns, Landor's green eyes glittered as he looked down. "You imagine all surprise vanishes after the first kiss?"

"That I cannot know."

"Yes, you can."

On Saint-Amour and in the library at Paget, his hands had been unmerciful. Tonight, although his gaze glowed with passion, he drew her toward him with a deliberation that sent impatient desire coursing through her body. At the end of the tantalizing movement, just before her breasts touched the hardness of his chest, she flung her arms up between his, and clutched his clothes, and let out a sigh that overmastered his self-restraint and made him pull her against him with all his strength. So it was that the slow, inexorable embrace became a hot collision. She kissed him, suffocating, crushed and transported.

Her shawl slithered from her shoulders and tangled around Gideon's hands as he gripped her even more closely. Her body yielded, arching against his as he took his lips from hers and bent to kiss the hollow of her neck. Her right hand was clamped across his shoulder and he felt the bracelet graze his skin as she buried the fingers of her left hand in his hair.

This raw eagerness shook Gideon more than ever. He wanted to snatch her up, take her into the house and up the stairs to his chamber. He wanted to plunge naked with her into darkness, far from the public glare in which they had been imprisoned for so long. But all he could do was kiss her again and again, wherever his lips found her smooth, bare skin.

For Delphine, this was deeper than shock and keener than surprise—it was like a searing wind that caught her, stopped the breath in her throat, then swept on to leave her panting in his arms. She wanted to keep him close, as though at any moment they were about to be snatched away from each other, ripped apart like a living body torn in two. When he kissed her throat and the swell of her breasts she closed her eyes, then opened them again and searched his gaze, seeing in his the same desperation and yearning that made her quiver against him. "Oh," she said, "I've hurt you." She pulled his head down and pressed her lips to the graze that her diamonds had made on the side of his neck. There was the faint taste of blood on her tongue, a sharp outlet of breath across her ear, and he tightened his arms so relentlessly that her feet left the ground and she found she could not move at all.

"I love you," he said. "I can't live without you. Marry me."

Her expulsion of breath was like a laugh. "Yes! What do you think?" Her voice became strangled. "Let me stand. Let me stand." He unwound his arms somewhat and she sank onto her feet and stood with her forehead on his chest. *"Mon dieu!"* It took her a while to snatch her breath, then she pulled back, one hand twisted into his shirt front and the lace of his untied cravat. She spoke as if drunk. *"Je vous aime."*

"Vous?" He slid one hand behind her neck and tipped her face toward his. "This is formal, mademoiselle."

"Formal?!" Her gaze slid over him and herself, taking in all their dishevelment, then she said, "My parents called each other *vous* until the day my father died."

"Must I perish," he said softly, "before you will call me *tu?"*

She shivered. "You must marry me. For I have your ring, monsieur, and I won't give it back."

"Ah!" He held her against him again, but this time he didn't kiss her. Steadying her within his arms, he took quick, deep breaths as though he had smashed through obstacles to get to this point, and feared that the strength aroused to do it would now prove too great for his control. Silent, her breathing shallower than his but just as rapid, she closed her eyes and pressed one cheek to his chest, joining her impulses to its rhythmic rise and fall.

Yes, they could be one. They already were. The rest was a bagatelle.

Next afternoon, Delphine was in the countess's painting room again, this time with Landor. The countess, having selected the pose she thought best, had taken half an hour to lay in the base for the miniature, then put her oils away, smiled fondly at them both and left the room.

Betrothed in earnest: Delphine was scarcely accustomed to it yet. On hearing the news, Julie Dalgleish had laughed and then cried; the countess had cried and then laughed; and the earl, with glistening eyes, had insisted on taking Delphine down to the kennels so she could name her own puppy from the new litter.

After that, all day there had been a conspiracy to leave them alone, even amongst the guests who had believed them betrothed for months. No doubt she and Landor sent out the most potent signals—that is, if his looks while the sketch was being done were any indication. There was a festive atmosphere in both houses, and no one had yet gone home. At Landor, one group was trying out the croquet lawn and another had gone on the "blackberry walk" along the ridge at the border of the estate. At Buff House, the earl was wandering from room to room trying to gather spectators who might like an excursion to watch the villagers play a totally unseasonal game of cricket in Tisbury, and being very good-natured about it when no one could be prised from idleness.

Landor was standing with his arm around Delphine's shoulders, looking out the conservatory window to a corner of the kitchen garden. "Have you ever seen cricket?"

"No. And I don't *think* I should appreciate it as your father would like."

"Then be firm with him. He won't mind—he adores you." He turned her, his fingers warm around her arm, until they were facing into the room. "Later tonight the three of them are going to discuss the marriage settlement. I thought we'd leave them to it. Unless you have some ideas to contribute?"

She shook her head. "It's all very simple. We can each be proud of what we bring to the other. What *we* must decide is the settlement between ourselves, monsieur."

He stepped to face her, took her hands and kissed them one after the other. "About which you do have some ideas?"

"Just one."

"So have I. More than one. The first is: my name is Gideon, not monsieur." She tried, but despite having said it in her head a thousand times, it came out somewhat French. "Practice makes perfect," he murmured, and kissed her.

After a considerable interval, she made him sit on the chair where she had had her portrait drawn, and took the countess's by the table. He cocked an eyebrow, with an attempt at nonchalance. "Why so solemn?"

"We must tell each other everything. *Everything.* You must reveal all that you have ever done for England and I must confess what I've done for France. There can never be any secrets between us, or they will destroy us. What we have together is sacred, never to be broken. We must have the truth, or we can never have trust."

With lips compressed and brow lowered, finally he said, "You're speaking of the past only?"

"No! The future. Our whole lives. Confide every secret to me, and in return I swear never to tell it to another person or use it for France. And you will undertake the same for me, with respect to England."

"My God! Can we do this?"

"We cannot *not* do it. *Mon amour,* look at us, look at the lies that have bedeviled us from the first night we met. Think of the misery they have caused us. There must be no secrets, or we can never live together; we cannot marry."

"Delphine!" She trembled; it was the first time he had said her name, and he uttered it with anguish and doubt. "I haven't been given the right to take such a step. Make no mistake: in my case we would be talking of state secrets."

"And what of my case? What do you know of that, unless I tell you?"

He went pale. There was a terrible pause and she saw emotions she had hoped never to see again—hurt, jealousy and mistrust—flicker like lightning in his eyes. Then he said, "Very well. You told me at Paget that your work for France was over. But there was something you didn't tell me. You may do so now. What was Armand de Belfort doing in London last August?"

For a second she could not breathe. "*Armand?* What are you saying?"

"He was there as a liaison with the Duc de Limours and—"

"What? How on earth do you know?"

"*I* asked the question," he ground out. "Are you going to answer it?"

A pain shot through her chest and she felt stifled. She got to her feet. "You think we met? You think I *knew*? I had no idea. I haven't seen him since I left Paris."

"But you know he's in intelligence, don't you? That's obvious enough."

"He's told me nothing about what he does. Nor I him. And I have not seen him in England."

The man she loved sat looking at her as though at a stranger, his face closed. Only his eyes betrayed what had haunted them both from the moment they met; the torment of being kept in the dark by the other. He remained on the chair, rigid and implacable. She went up to him and thrust out her left hand, the ruby darting fire into his eyes. "I have not seen or communicated with Armand de Belfort since March last year. I swear it on all that's holy. If you don't believe me, take this ring back." She burst into tears.

With a wordless exclamation he leaned forward and snatched her to him, wrapping his arms around her waist and burying his head between her breasts. His arms tightened but she kept crying. She stood between his knees, with her head bent, and sobbed into his hair, "You see! You see what happens!"

She could not stop crying until he folded her down into his embrace, across his thighs, and she saw that his face was wet too, and they exchanged a long kiss, salty and punishing, which he ended by taking her head in his hands and looking deep into her eyes. "I see," he said. "I believe you. There is no other way." She nestled against him and her ragged breath slowly subsided as she felt the warmth of his touch penetrate her body. "Now," he said at last. "Let us begin. I owe you a question."

"Very well." She sat straighter, wound an arm behind his neck. She could not yet look at him. She searched around the room instead, and her eye lit upon the portrait of Napoleon. "Tell me how you got that painting."

There was the merest pause, then he said, "To explain that, I must first tell you everything I know about Napoleon's codes."

The confidences lasted through the next two days in short, intense episodes in between the periods that they devoted to his guests. What they revealed to each other was too complex, too momentous to be absorbed with any ease. At times its magnitude filled Delphine with dread. But then relief would sweep over and stimulate her mind to further inquiry and confession.

They could never alter each other's allegiances. But sometimes, when they were talking of Napoleon, as a man and as Emperor of the French, she thought that the picture she could give, of a superlative leader forging the destiny of a free people, might help Gideon to see what England's army and navy had taken up arms against. But he was still in that navy. He said once, "Our forces can't rest, *mon amour*, until Boney has been stopped. When you saw him in Paris last year, he was indulging in a rare respite; now he's getting ready to march on Poland! There'll be no end until he's crushed for good. You know, in 1805, when we just managed to turn him back from England, our prime minister Pitt looked at the map of Europe and said, 'Roll that up. It will not be wanted these ten years.'"

"Pitt is dead." She shuddered. "*He* never saw the end of it. What do you want to do, fight until 1815? What if it's 1820, 1825 . . . ?"

"No, I don't. The navy has already done its best. My duties from now on are bound to be in the Channel blockade. I know men who've been on that run, looking at empty sea for three years without a single leave ashore with their families. *I've* done what I can in this struggle, and I'm going to ask the navy to let me go. But if I'm granted discharge, never think that I don't believe in this war. It must go on—for France's sake as much as our own. Or he will lead it to ruin."

"You say France is wrong to have chosen Napoleon? Look around you. Who is there in England to match his vision and genius? Who, among all your shabby ministers vying for the favor of a senile king? And you are very much mistaken if you think our forces fight for his sake, like a set of automatons. We fight for France."

They were in the countess's inner studio at the time, and he was walking up and down by his mother's workbench. He stood looking at her with a mixture of despair and admiration, then said, "I know I can never change your loyalties. Your country deserves women and men like you. It's just . . . does *he* deserve them?" His fingers drifted amongst shavings from one of the countess's carvings that lay curled on the board. "When they fought us at Trafalgar, they were heroes. Utterly fearless, steadfast—I thought we would all sink together before one of their ships surrendered. Your admiral de Villeneuve was a Trojan, a man of absolute honor. And what did Boney do to *him*?" His eyes blazed.

"Nothing; he wasn't reprimanded and there was no retribution. Except what he visited on himself. Villeneuve was made prisoner, then exchanged. He committed suicide in France, before he even got to Paris. I know, I've seen a copy of his letter to his wife."

"He died in a locked room, of six stab wounds to the chest. Only the last was in the heart."

"I didn't know that." She went cold, then dizzy. "Why do you tell me such things?"

"Because it was murder! He was a swordsman, a naval commander." He snatched up one of countess's knives from the table and pointed it toward his chest. "So am I. What sort of a job do you think I could do with this?"

She cried out and ran at him with such speed that he barely had time to let the blade clatter to the table before he could catch her by the wrists. "For God's sake!" he said between his teeth. She wanted to scream at him in grief and outrage, but the words were tumbled together inside her. His expression changed and he pulled her to him so that her arms were trapped. He whispered, "I'm sorry. I'm sorry. This is wrong." He held her until she stopped fighting him, then sank to his knees and looked up at her, his hands around her hips. "I've been trying to convince you that Bonaparte's a monster. I've no right to do that. I don't even believe it myself. I've been trying to make us think alike and feel alike, and we never can. But we can be *true*."

She smoothed a lock of hair back from his forehead and sought the right words. "Wherever we are together is a new territory, from which no harm can come to your country or mine."

"Amen to that," he said, and she knelt to kiss him.

The next day, the last guests dispersed, the Landor manorhouse was swept, cleaned and put to rights, and dust sheets were laid over the furniture. Then, at Buff House, five people set themselves to talk of the future. The day after that, Captain Sir Gideon Landor received a letter from the Admiralty ordering him on his next voyage.

Greenwich

Gideon was standing before the altar of the parish church of Saint Alpherge, Greenwich, with his father and mother, awaiting his bride. Occupying the nave behind him were six of his ship's officers, who formed the guard of honor. It was a week to the day since he had received his sailing orders, and the *Aphrodite* left port on the morrow.

The earl was still incredulous that the wedding had been arranged with such efficacy, and as his son turned yet again toward the open church door, he whispered, "My word, when you take an idea into your head, you don't stop until you've moved heaven and earth!"

Gideon murmured, "I've had *this* idea a damned long time, and if you think I was going to wait even one more night to possess her . . ."

"Good God, sir, is this the language for a church?" Then the earl caught his son's wry look and fell silent.

Gideon had determined on the wedding the moment he read the Admiralty's summons, and had known it must take place in Greenwich, since he was ordered there at once. He had a stubborn, perhaps superstitious wish to marry Delphine in a church; and in a naval district like Greenwich, which was the scene of many a hasty marriage in the midst of leave-taking, he had foreseen little difficulty in finding a vicar to perform the ceremony. But there was the matter of his bride's religion. However, when he mentioned her supposed Catholicism, she had looked at him in amazement. "*Mon amour*, I'm the child of a lapsed Presbyterian and a freethinking woman brought up on Jean-Jacques Rousseau. How can I be anything less than atheistical?"

"The priest is prepared to accept you as Anglican—he seems very used to this kind of situation. But would that feel false to you?"

"Oh, pray don't worry on my account. I said 'atheistical,' not 'atheist.' I've come to no conclusions about the existence of God. My life has been too eventful for me to spend the proper time on that debate; I was thinking of waiting until I have children of my own."

"How reassuring." He took her hand. "Unless you have doubts on that score too?"

"Oh, no," she had said into his eyes, "none whatsoever."

She would enter the church accompanied only by Mrs. Laidlaw and a servant, and another female guest who had also promised to come: Mary Scovell, the wife of the major he had met in Frenada. Knowing that he would have very little time with Delphine while the *Aphrodite* was being readied for sea, Gideon had presented his bride and her mother to people he knew and valued in Greenwich. By chance he heard that Mary Scovell had at last been granted permission to join her husband in Portugal, and was in Greenwich settling the papers for her voyage. He had sought her out, introduced himself and the two women, and been glad to see that Delphine already liked her company. The idea of trying to turn a Parisian noblewoman into an English navy wife was ridiculous—yet if he could not reconcile Delphine in some part to the role, he was afraid that she would quickly grow resentful of the British services, and perhaps of him. Mary, an intelligent and good-humored woman with a realistic view of the armed forces and their demands, also proved an entertaining companion, and joined in Delphine's purchases for the wedding.

Gideon now had twenty-four hours before he sailed down the Thames, and he wanted to spend every second of them with Delphine. It was typical of his present life that he was ordered to sea, and his only consolation was the first—or the last—night that he was about to spend with Delphine, and the promise he had made to quit the navy if he possibly could after this voyage.

There was the crunch of iron wheels outside and he saw the Dalgleish carriage pass the door. He swallowed, his throat dry; she must love him, if she consented to join hands with him over the chasm of background and allegiances that had always yawned between them. She entered, surrounded by the little group of women, but he saw only her. She was wearing blue, and her eyes, which met his on the instant, beckoned like summer skies.

Delphine, meanwhile, as she walked down the aisle, remembered their first meeting, when she crossed the salon of the Maison Despeaux and knew that whatever wounds the lofty English lieutenant suffered from, they had been inflicted through her means. What if this marriage were another injury, one that would bring them both to danger and doom? Then she drew near enough to read the yearning in his eyes, and it was as much as she could do not to seize his hand, before the priest could utter a word, and say in the clearest English, "I take thee, Sir Gideon Landor!"

Gideon had hired three rooms on the second floor of the Temeraire Inn: the bridal chamber, a dressing room for the ladies and a generous dining room in which he and Delphine presided at a long table. After the meal, Julie Dalgleish would convey Mrs. Laidlaw and his parents home to Mayfair after the wedding feast, and the rest were dispersing to their quarters in Greenwich or to the *Aphrodite*, anchored in the Thames.

The toasts were frequent, especially amongst Gideon's officers, and Delphine had more than half a suspicion that this was because they had had their eagerness on this subject quashed for months. Mrs. Laidlaw was eloquent, and Delphine heard her say to Mrs. Scovell that she had known from the first that Sir Gideon was the very man to find a way through Mademoiselle Dalgleish's natural reluctance to love the English. "Only a military gentleman would have had the courage to persist against such scruples."

"I own there is something attractive about a man in uniform that makes him very hard to resist," Mrs. Scovell said in her collected way.

Mrs. Laidlaw said, "And what was it about your husband that swayed you when he came courting you in Yorkshire?"

"Oh, what persuades me every time, to this very day, is his Tarleton shako. He gave up his rank in the cavalry, you know, because of the expense, and joined the staff so that he could afford us a better income. The Mounted Guides have a very dashing shako, and every time I see it I feel the admiration it deserves."

Mrs. Laidlaw tipped back her head in a quick gesture that made her suddenly seem years younger, and let out a warm, appreciative laugh.

The ladies complimented Delphine on her gown, which was of blue silk, over which she had worn to the church a pelisse of the same color lined with silver fox fur. The men seconded the compliments with vague murmurs and Delphine, glancing at Gideon, recalled that he had never commented on anything she wore. Possibly he never *saw* anything she was wearing, having an eye for what was beneath. The thought brought a blush to her cheek and a glow of anticipation that he noticed at once. His hand sought hers under the table.

The presents were also discussed, particularly Gideon's from his mother—the miniature of Delphine, a fine likeness in a handsome gold frame that was handed around the table to be admired. Delphine had bought Gideon a writing case of walnut wood bound with brass. She was desolate that he should have occasion to use it so soon, but at least it guaranteed that on this voyage he would write to her!

"You haven't told us what you're giving my daughter," la Générale said to Gideon. Neither she nor his parents would be returning to Greenwich on the morrow to bid him good-bye—the melancholy privilege was all Delphine's, and the carriage would fetch her home in the afternoon when he had sailed.

"I shall take Delphine to see it tomorrow. It may be that she won't like it; it's even more probable that *you* won't like it, madame."

"You've lost us," his mother said, convinced he must be joking. "Why on earth choose a present your bride will hate on sight?"

He laughed uneasily. "I see I shall have to explain." He turned to Delphine. "It's the *Aphrodite.*" The naval men at the table looked as baffled as she. "Good Lord," he said with a grin, "not the frigate! Though you're welcome to it if the navy will part with it. No, the yacht. The Admiralty have finally made up their minds, and released her to me as a prize. It would give me a great deal of pleasure if you'd accept her. But if you'd rather I sold her, so be it, and I'll buy you something else. Jewelry . . . it's up to you."

She stared at him. "Armand's yacht."

"*Your* yacht. If you say so. On my return I thought a short cruise to Vauxhall Gardens would be in order. Then Mauritius."

Julie Dalgleish gasped and he turned to her. "Do you have any objection to being conveyed home in the *Aphrodite*? Three crew should be enough, one of them doubling as a servant." He looked at Delphine again, his gaze probing hers. "Ellis and your Molly will jump at it—they won't object to months together at a stretch. But perhaps you would? In England it's customary for bride and groom to take a journey together after the wedding. I'm forced to leave you behind tomorrow. But I shall make it up to you as soon as I can."

Delphine glanced around the board, her heart beating quickly. Only Gideon's parents looked less than happy, and it wasn't hard to guess why. "How long should we be away?"

"Six months or thereabouts. Enough time for you to put Saint-Amour to rights and for me to learn what it's like to be idle." His hand closed over hers. "We have two homes, my angel; I have a theory that we can divide our time between them. You'll tell me if I'm being fanciful."

She gave a delighted smile, and she was relieved to see that the countess was smiling too. "I suspect this is a ruse, sir, to make sure that I can never tempt you far from the sea."

"I'll go where you wish. Ask me to the ends of the earth—and I'll have everyone know, Mauritius *is* the ends of the earth—and I shall go. As long as you're with me." He brought her hand to his lips and kissed her fingers.

There were many toasts as the meal drew to a close, but the most intoxicating moment for Delphine was when she drank in the truth that whatever his navy might request, the ultimate command over his existence was hers.

*   *   *

Later it was very quiet. The Temeraire Inn was distant from the thoroughfares, in the splendid quarter formed by Greenwich's massive buildings and parks. Darkness had fallen and a chill pressed against the windowpanes, shut out by thick drapes and a cozy fire, both of which had received Molly's attention before she excused herself and left Delphine alone in the bedchamber.

They were man and wife, in name. He was hers, by promise and desire. Yet in this electric interval before he came to her, there was a whisper of fear in her mind, as though the forces arrayed against them still had power to prevail. Then he knocked on the door, and her voice, low and eager, filled the room as she bade him come in.

He was no longer in uniform. Or rather, he had removed everything military: the coat, the buckled shoes, even the stock around his neck, so that his shirt was open and she could see his bronzed throat and a shading of hair over his breastbone—dark, like his eyebrows.

She could not rise; her legs failed her. She sat before the mirror, turned toward him, and felt his gaze travel over her. He took two paces into the room. "I like what you're wearing." He said it as though automatically, his thoughts on another tack. Was he as nervous as she?

"Oh. You don't usually say so. I thought you never noticed my clothes."

"Nonsense. Your every garment is imprinted on my nervous system."

She giggled. "Surely not."

He was beside her now, and reaching out he gently pinched a fold of the nightdress between finger and thumb, at the shoulder, so that the soft muslin moved over her skin, causing a tingle across one breast. The response grew, invading her chest. He let go the embroidered fabric, and with the back of the same hand he swept her hair away from her neck, his hooded eyes gleaming as he said, "I never knew it was so long."

"It's not very. Molly brushes it too straight." It was hard to breathe; he was so close.

Then his touch was withdrawn and he moved away to sit on the white counterpane at the end of the four-poster bed. He no longer loomed. Did he know how often, in their turbulent past, he had intimidated her? He was very still, but his eyes flickered with the subtle lightning she had learned to decypher once they began to connect with their bodies as well as their minds.

He stretched out a hand, she rose and went to him and he folded her across his thighs and put his arms so lightly around her that it was like being held in a cage of taut, invisible wires. "*Mon ange*," he said. "You're too beautiful."

"Too much so to touch?" she said with a tremulous resort to teasing. "That's not true. I have bruises to prove it."

His eyes widened, then he smiled and murmured, "Really? May I see?"

"You may—" But her voice caught and she arrested his straying hand.

"Let me soothe where it hurts," he said, and his palm slid across her and began to stroke up and down her waist, steadily and smoothly, with a pressure that awakened a new warmth under her ribs, which in turn spread through her body and lit a fire in her throat, robbing her of speech. She put her fingers to the opening of his shirt and the heat she could feel on his skin seemed to rise into his eyes. She heard herself say, "What do we do next?"

"We assume the horizontal." The green eyes sparked. "Those parts of us that can."

Deliciously encircled in his arms, she managed, "And how do we do so?"

"I think, if you turn more to face me"—he gave an involuntary sound as she did so, something between a sigh and a gasp—"and then push me backward, we shall make a creditable beginning."

She was on top of him, her body adapting itself naturally to the contours of his strong frame, her mind liberated to receive the surprise and joy of this heady contact that she had dreamed of for so long. She laughed—a quick outlet of breath—and put her hands on his shoulders to draw herself up so she could gaze down into his startled eyes. He looked vulnerable, overwhelmed, but his body responded beneath her, and she reveled in her own power and his, and lowered herself to kiss him, mouthing words that he captured with lips and tongue in a language of passion that slowly, silently filled her with bliss.

They rolled sideways, and with her mouth still riveted to his, she began to tug at his shirt, trying to draw it up and run her hands over the smooth skin beneath. He laughed too, then, and pulling away, with one knee on the bed and the other foot on the floor, he yanked the shirt over his head and tossed it aside. He remained poised above her, his straight shoulders and lean waist silhouetted against the firelight, and began gently to undo the tiny buttons that fastened her nightdress down the front. She put her hands around his wrists, relishing the warmth of his touch but impeding him so that his fingers caught under one of the button loops and he laughed again, in a softer tone. She released him and undid the button below, then in a kind of frenzy, both breathing unevenly from mirth and desire, their fingers meshing and tangling in their haste, they uncovered Delphine's body to the magic of his untrammeled hands.

He pulled away only to undress himself, so swiftly that her body was still tingling as he cast himself down beside her and without thought or shame, afire with longing, she explored his body in her turn and set them both free from every restraint.

Thus they sank together into the soft shadows of the bed, and as the night wore on and firelight no longer filled the room, they voyaged through the dark—never imagining, however far they traveled, that they were going anywhere but home.

In the morning Gideon kept her in bed as long as he dared, putting off the hour when he needed to board the *Aphrodite,* and enslaved to his wife's body. It was a time of release that kept them dizzy with pleasure, driving them at one hour into reckless ardor and at another to trivial confidences and the silliest of exchanges. They didn't sleep, but she never seemed tired, only languid at times, as though in a dream. Then she would wrap her limbs around him and breathe, "Tell me this is real." Which he proved to her each time.

When they got out of bed, and dressed with slow reluctance, it was too late for him to go through the various distractions he had planned to take the edge off the parting: strolling about Greenwich; perhaps paying a call on Mary Scovell, who was due to take the coach down to Newhaven that evening; and inspecting the yacht *Aphrodite.*

So they had breakfast, which he could not face and she made a brave pretense of eating, and they walked arm in arm along the waterfront until they could see the frigate riding at anchor in the stream, with lighters and dinghies ferrying supplies and men across. Once, in the night, she had said, "I want to go with you!" By day, the knowledge that she never could was so heavy that neither of them said a word more about it.

He wondered whether she knew that captains would sometimes hold parties on board their ships before departure, with flags flapping from the yards and refreshments for the ladies arranged on the quarterdeck. She could never be one of such a party: he could not invite her to spy on one of His Majesty's vessels, and she could not wish to see the weaponry prepared for use against her countrymen. For the same reasons, she must never be a passenger on a naval vessel. Some wives sailed with their husbands, even into war—but it always took years for this permission to be granted. Army officers like Scovell suffered the same deprivations as their men, and where women were allowed on campaign, the regiment commonly drew lots so that only half a dozen wives could go abroad. Gideon remembered an embarkation at Portsmouth where one girl, rejected in the lottery, had thrown herself from the wharf into the sea after the ship cast off. Hauled aboard, half drowned, she had been permitted to sail, with only the clothes she stood up in, destitute of everything except love for her young soldier. Gideon clamped Delphine's arm to his side as he thought of it.

Out of the corner of his eye he could see a little group on the quayside: Ellis and one of the Dalgleishes' servants, who had brought his trunks to the landing steps, and Delphine's maid, Molly, in tears at the prospect of Ellis's going. Gideon slid his hand down Delphine's forearm and laced his fingers into hers, turning her away from the river. He had a desperate impulse to escape with her—but there was nowhere to go. They were stranded in the glare of midday, caught by the bustle of the port.

He took off his hat, pushed back her bonnet and kissed her deeply, shielding their faces with the hat while he crushed her to him with the other arm. She was crying, and when he tried to speak he gave one sob instead, then laid his cheek against hers, taking a long, shuddering breath. "Don't stay here. I can't bear it. It takes an age to get a ship under way; I couldn't stand to look over here and see you waiting." He drew back, replaced his hat and ran one hand over his face. The other held hers; he could feel the ruby and her wedding ring pressing into his palm.

"You want *me* to go? You want *me* to walk away?" Her eyes were still brimming, blue as a river meeting a tropic sea.

"Spare us, my angel. This will soon be over. Think of the other *Aphrodite*. Imagine us sailing home together."

She bowed her head to tie her bonnet back on, hiding her face. He beckoned Ellis, and when he was in earshot said, "Hail me the boat. Send Miss—" His breath caught. "Send my wife's servants here. They'll accompany her to the Temeraire."

In the end, because she could not move, it was he who walked away. When he looked back, from halfway across the Thames, she had gone.

Delphine lay crying on the bed at the inn. The linen had been changed and there was not a trace of him in the room—not an item of clothing, not a bright hair on the pillow, nothing. When Ellis had come in the morning to pack Gideon's things, she had noticed a penknife on the desk and pointed it out, changing her mind just too late. There was a penknife in his new writing case, so she could have kept that one. How stupid, not to have realized and snatched it as a memento. How pathetic that such small, inconsequential items should have the power to stab her to the heart.

The carriage had come for her and she had given orders for it to wait in the yard. It could wait a week, for all she cared.

It seemed impossible, after all he and she had gone through, that their one night together could ever be repeated—for it seemed illicit, wrung from fate, proscribed by two great nations. This was loneliness of the deepest kind. This was what it meant to be married. To lie alone in an empty bed, still penetrated by his touch on her skin and his voice in her ear, still hearing promises that war could rob them of the power to keep.

When she was too exhausted for more tears, she lay with one cheek on the pillow, looking through swollen eyelids at a last ray of sunshine that spanned the room from window to wainscot and swirled with motes of dust. Darkness was about to fall. La Générale and Mrs. Laidlaw would be having the fire stoked in the dining room and thinking of supper, which they would put off until her arrival. Mary Scovell would be at the coaching inn, two hours early for the post chaise, for, as she had said to Delphine, "I'd be there at dawn if need be. I've waited years for this—I'd die of the fidgets if I was anywhere else but in the yard, sitting on my box and waiting for them to fetch me." She was headed for Newhaven and the Portugal packet, which she would board as a civilian passenger, destination Lisbon.

Delphine rose, as unsteady on her feet as a sick woman. She went to the ewer, splashed water on her face and looked in the mirror, then away. She didn't recognize the haggard creature in the glass. She sat on the bed, summoning the will to return to Mrs. Laidlaw's. Not "home." As long as Gideon remained at sea, home was a dream.

There was a knock. "Come in," she said, so faintly that she had to repeat it.

It was not Molly, but the innkeeper. "Madame, there's someone downstairs who begs to see you. He's a curate, madame; I didn't catch the name of the parish, but he respectfully requests a short word. A Mr. Robinson. May I show him up?"

Was there some payment of alms that the parish of Saint Alpherge had not received for the wedding? She had cash with her, if so. "Pray tell him to step up. And have my carriage brought to the door, thank you."

She moved into the reception room and ordered Molly downstairs with the luggage. She sat by the window, looking down as darkness began to envelop the street. Then the landlord reappeared, ushered the clergyman in and bowed himself out.

Mr. Robinson was a man of middle height, dressed in clerical garb and with a hood over his head which he drew back with a flourish after the door closed. As the cloth fell from his handsome face, Delphine saw that the visitor was her cousin, Armand de Belfort.

Voyagers

Armand was cheerful and bursting with affection. He gave her no time to rise, and coming across the room with quick steps he dropped to one knee before her and snatched up one hand. "Cousin!" he said in French. "Such an age; such a deal to discuss, but in the interval—my God! The triumph! You take my breath away!" He kissed her fingers extravagantly, then with a laugh abandoned the posture, rose and swung the cloak off his shoulders to reveal the clerical clothing. Like everything he wore it became him, despite its absurdity.

"Armand!" It was all she could say as he threw the cloak over the back of one chair and took another at the table, looking at her with open enjoyment at seeing her so taken aback. "How on earth did you get here?"

"Smugglers. They landed me on the coast of Cornwall. Not cheap, but efficacious."

"How . . ." She cleared her throat. "How can you possibly pass as an Englishman?"

"I don't. I'm Canadian; my parish is supposed to be somewhere upriver from Montreal. Women are fascinated by my work among the Indians. Men are less curious. It's easy: I don't mix in high society, of course; not like you." He shook his head. "I know just what you've been up to; I was in London last year—did the Duc de Limours tell you? Did you guess?" She shook her head, her heart plummeting. *No, it took Gideon to tell me that.* "I came over to cover the duke's annual expenses and the emperor asked me to catch up with what you were doing." He gave his self-satisfied but charming smile. "I'm very close to the emperor now. He trusts me with all sorts of work. And of course I was overawed, simply overawed, by your achievements. So much that I couldn't approach you, in case I interfered with your progress. You'd stitched up Lucien Bonaparte, and Limours told me you had Ferron eating out of your hand! The emperor was beside himself when I told him. 'She's worth Limours ten times over,' he said—by then we knew about the arrests. And now you've taken care of Ferron, moved onward and upward and lo and behold, my cousin is a future countess. Married to the foremost intelligence operator in the British navy." His gaze probed hers. "Yes? I told Decaën long ago, he *has* to be in intelligence. It's written all over him."

She was trembling. "You were talking rubbish to Decaën. And then you lied to me. You *lied* to me, Armand!"

He made a pretense of striving to remember. "Ah, yes, the double agent notion." His expression changed to alarm. "Heavens, you didn't confront him with it?"

She was still shivering, with cold this time. "I did."

He let out a hiss between his teeth. "Dare I ask what he said to that?"

"He cursed you. If anger could kill, wherever you were in Paris at that moment, you would have dropped to the ground as though lightning had struck. Instead *I* had to face him. It was the worst moment of my life, and you caused it, Armand. Don't ask me to forgive you, for I never will."

He ran a hand over his face. "You didn't let on that *you're* an agent in the process?"

She thought of the library at Paget. "No." *I didn't need to, given the circumstances.*

"*Ouf.*" He sat back. "You're so beautifully placed. The emperor will be ecstatic. I'm positive Landor's a secret agent—you'll winkle it out of him in time. Meanwhile, you're in the heart of the navy, married to a man who'll be no less than an admiral one day. Perhaps you can even find out who masterminded the arrests. That's why I'm here, to see what we can discover; the people who escaped the raid are terrified there's going to be another one. Limours has no idea who it was. He's compiled a list of people who *might* have done it, but it's so long it's farcical. It even has your name on it. I ask you." He considered her, his head on one side, a curious look on his face. Perhaps he had begun to register her swollen eyes, her pallor. "How did it all happen between you and Landor? By heaven, don't tell me you're really in love with him?"

"Is that against regulations?" she snapped, straightening her back.

"Oh. I see." He nodded, as though acknowledging a slight inconvenience. "What about him? You may be the most beautiful woman in England, but, excuse me, how could he marry you?"

"He was good enough to forgive me my execrable relatives."

He didn't even flinch. The curious look was still there. "He knows you're Bonapartist; there's never been any chance of concealing that! For a fanatic like him, it's an impediment, surely?"

"The priest of Saint Alpherge didn't seem to think so yesterday." It came surging back, the moment when Gideon held her hand before the altar and slid the wedding ring onto her finger; the joyful gathering afterward; the night; this morning. Helpless tears began to run down her face. "You may tell the emperor that my loyalty is his and my heart is my husband's. He will understand."

"And if he doesn't?" Armand said softly.

"You underestimate him."

"Have you advanced this interesting concept to Sir Gideon?"

"That's my business." She dried her eyes, hiding her face for a moment in her handkerchief. She had not lied to Armand so far, but if he continued with the interrogation she would have to make some choices. To defend herself, and protect Gideon. How could this happen—how could the territory of love come under attack on the second day of her marriage? Armand was dangerous; a man without integrity or scruples, who put personal vengeance on a level with delivering a lethal strike for his country. If he ever discovered Gideon was an agent, it was just a step to linking him with the Limours arrests, and Armand's attention would turn all one way—to hunting him down. If only Gideon were in England. Instead he was sailing for Portugal and the Peninsular War. Where, as she now knew, Armand himself had been sent at least once. He could always angle to go there again.

Her cousin's cool voice reached her across the table. "What's he doing on this voyage?"

"Escorting transport ships ferrying artillery and siege equipment to Lisbon. The escort consists of three frigates including the *Aphrodite*, and Gideon's in command. It's a straight delivery of cargo but he doesn't know how long he'll be in port. The return voyage may take anything from a week to a month depending on the weather."

"Aha. Just what the vicar of Saint Alpherge told me this afternoon." She relaxed a little. She had known his question must be a test, to see how forthcoming she would be about British navy affairs. Armand had clearly been sneaking about Greenwich gathering information. He continued, "A gossipy place, Greenwich, especially amongst the clergy. Lisbon, you say? I've never gotten into Portugal; I've had very little curiosity about it. Until lately." He shrugged. "And when he gets back?"

"We're sailing to Mauritius, with Maman."

He started and his eyes narrowed. "You're not going to be much use to us there."

She flared up. "I didn't notice that *you* were much use to *us* there! It's no thanks to you that I have Saint-Amour back. You could have fought for my rights over it, but you were too busy politicking in Paris."

He shrugged. "You've done wonders on your own." His eyes widened again. "Of course. Now I see the whole picture. You secure an English marriage—and the estate stays in your hands with no need for an oath of allegiance. Congratulations. Any efforts of mine would have been superfluous. You won't be staying long on Mauritius?"

"I'm not sure; some months. Enough to be sure everything is in train. Then we'll return to Landor."

"And how is my aunt?" he said at last. "I thought of paying her a secret call but . . . what do you think?"

"No. Mrs. Laidlaw is a very clever and observant woman. And Maman has adjusted so well to English life; I'd hate her to be disturbed. She is too fond of you and Paris, Armand—please tell me you won't remind her of all that. At least until we come back from Mauritius."

"So you won't tell her you've seen me?"

"That depends on you. What would you wish me to do?"

He contemplated her for another second. "Very well; no. And whom else will you not tell?"

She rose to her feet. "I'm sorry, Armand—this is beyond me. I'm wretched and exhausted, and I can't concentrate on a thing. The carriage is waiting to take me to Berkeley Square."

"So I saw." He didn't move.

"I'm worried, for you and for me. Think how this looks. Here I am closeted with a foreigner on the day after my wedding. I have to say: I think you should go. For both our sakes."

He rose, put on the cloak and fastened it under his chin, then approached, his face alive with speculation. He took her hand. "I wonder when we shall meet again?"

After the war is over. Or never—I don't care. She nearly said it. Instead she looked into his eyes and let him see her deathly tiredness and her pain. There was no sympathy as he looked back, but she could tell that he thought he was safe to go, to achieve whatever he was out to do in London, but without her assistance. She said, "Please convey my sincerest tributes and best wishes to the emperor."

He smiled. "You are a mystery." He raised her fingers to his lips. "Take care; these are perilous times. With the Bonapartes, retribution is swift."

"I told you once before, Armand—in my family, honor is as vital to the women as to the men. I make no mystery about that."

"So be it." He released her, gave a bow and let himself out of the room.

When the door shut behind him she remained in the middle of the floor, her body frozen, her mind casting back over everything he had said. And at once it struck her: he had not asked about his yacht—his prized possession, stolen from him by Gideon in a midnight theft that had delivered him a huge slap in the face over his perfidy. Armand had not once brought up the

Aphrodite—which meant that he must know already what had become of the vessel: a navy prize handed over to Gideon, and now to her. Armand's resentment and suspicion must be enormous. She thought of the sly look he had had on his face when he said, *I've never gotten into Portugal; I've had very little curiosity about it. Until lately.* She had misjudged and botched this whole meeting.

Armand had just walked unscathed into London. Twice. Stunning proof of his talent for infiltration. And he had boasted that he was one of the emperor's favored agents. What if he decided to request a mission into Portugal? She sat down at the table and put her head in her hands. If she had not been without sleep for thirty hours and more . . . If she didn't feel more like a widow than a wife . . .

No, there were no excuses. Armand had been too cunning for her, once again. She had tried to give him the impression that her marriage to Gideon made no difference to her allegiances—but he could easily conclude that she was about to side with the British. And nothing she said to Armand could stop him hating Gideon. *She* didn't see Gideon as the enemy, but that very fact had prevented her from seeing what a demon he was in Armand's eyes. She had not confessed to Armand about the *Aphrodite*. Which exposed her, and Gideon, to his retaliation.

What would he do? Leave England as soon as possible, for he wouldn't trust her an inch now. Return to Paris—but not to receive orders from the emperor, for Napoleon wasn't there. Her mind quailed before what Armand might decide to do, on his own account but in the name of France. He was angry, frustrated and more or less free to follow his own vendetta provided he could disguise it as a mission for the ministry.

If Gideon were here, she could confide in him, assess the consequences. But if he were here, she wouldn't have this fear building at the back of her mind. She wouldn't be torn by regret that they were forced into separation. His departure had exposed her to the visit from Armand, and her dialogue with Armand had placed Gideon in danger about which he could receive no warning. She could write to him, but how could she put such issues in a letter that might be intercepted?

Her eyes hurt. Her head hurt. She crossed her arms on the table and rested her forehead on them, wondering whether she would ever sleep again. For she knew what she must do: rush down to the carriage and use it to overtake the post chaise to Newhaven. Then she must travel with Mary Scovell to the south coast, and thence to Lisbon. She belonged with Gideon. She should never have let him leave.

Gideon was pacing the quarterdeck, thinking he would grind a groove in the planking if he continued to drive himself and his officers mad in this fashion. The frigate was a thing of beauty, the crew were fit and skillful, and they were all well used to him now, so day in and day out in this favorable weather there was little for him to say to his officers. On the *Aphrodite*'s maiden voyage, when he had been brooding about Delphine and the meaningless betrothal, the lieutenants had been disconcerted by his silences. In contrast, because they knew this time why he was terse, they treated him with tact. It made him feel infinitely worse.

He had done what he had always condemned any seaman or officer for doing—he had married on the eve of a voyage. If a man loved a woman, why visit upon himself the grief of parting after just one or two nights together? If he didn't, what flimsier foundation for a rational union could he have than to make love to her for a few hours and then disappear? He felt torn in two, and there was no relief or distraction. No storms, and not even the hint of a skirmish; the French remained blockaded into their ports, and the navy's task in these waters promised to be flat and predictable until the end of the war. The only English vessels that met a little excitement these days were the warships prowling the North Atlantic and making life difficult for American merchantmen. A year ago he would have been on fire to be posted in that direction; today the idea made him shudder. If the navy refused to let him go, he must contrive some kind of command in the Indian Ocean, chasing French corsairs. He didn't care what they asked him to do—run the harbor in Port Louis, anything—as long as he could be with Delphine.

But it was hard to think ahead. His existence was desolate and the future unattainable. Delphine was to stay in Berkeley Square to await his return. He knew his parents would invite her down to Buff House, and he was confident she would go, but not for long. She would return to the London season, to the theaters, Almacks, the fashionable balls, which he had no expectation or even wish that she give up for his sake. She would shine there as always, her every look, her every word an example of feminine beauty and cultivation. If she were prostrate from misery, she would keep to the house, but once recovered, she would go forth with the same verve and the same enchanting manners that had infallibly capti-vated him—and any other male within her ambit. He trusted her; he would trust her with his life. But he wanted to be there with her, not sailing to war.

He pictured all this and cursed his fate with such savagery that he sometimes found he had uttered a sigh or a groan that was audible to whomever happened to be on duty at his side. In his cabin, he looked at her miniature for hours, in between writ-ing to her. The flotilla had not come upon any vessels sailing the return route to England, so he would send the letters in a bun-dle from Lisbon. His new writing case was full of unsealed sheets, most of which he threw out of the porthole. He wished he could write her one definitive letter to say everything he felt. But there were no words for the visceral, unceasing ache caused by separation.

In Lisbon, spring had come. The streets of the port were awash with sunlight, and flower vendors were already selling nosegays. The city had a cleansed look, reflected in the polished panels on the carriages of the Portuguese nobility and the gleaming coats of their horses—those that had escaped the requisitioning of the British and Portuguese armies that defended the country. Hope burgeoned with the soft green leaves along the avenues, for Sir Arthur Wellesley had begun the year with an élan that surpassed even the dreams of Lieutenant Colonel Colquhoun Grant. In Jan-uary, the army had captured Ciudad Rodrigo, and now everyone talked about Badajoz, the border fortress that Wellesley had begun to invest in mid-March. As soon as the cannon and siege equipment supplied by Gideon's flotilla were ashore, they disappeared on the long haul inland to the siege.

The transports that the *Aphrodite* had escorted to the port were allotted a different purpose for the return: carrying home officers and men so gravely wounded that they were out of commission, and others going on leave. Time was required for the soldiers to make it to Lisbon and for the military hospitals to process them, and Gideon's orders were to prepare for a return voyage at the end of April. Refitting the transports as hospital ships took a while, but soon he had nothing to do but wait for his departure. So he rounded up all the sailors on the *Aphrodite* who couldn't swim, found a spot on the river Tagus and had them all taught.

Ellis was appalled, for he had but one fear: getting water over his head. It was no good telling him to think of the Tagus as a rather large bath—Ellis was clean enough, but Gideon doubted he'd ever bathed in anything larger than a bucket in his life. "*Please,* sir," he ventured; "after this voyage, ain't I about to serve you as a landlubber? Ain't it about too late to try teaching me to dogpaddle?"

"Army or navy, Ellis, it's a useful talent, as many a cavalryman who's tumbled across a ford will tell you. And you're forgetting the trip to Mauritius. What if Molly falls overboard on the way? Who's going to dive in and fish her out?" This worked, and Ellis, to his own surprise, proved a strong swimmer.

Meanwhile Gideon's navy friends in Lisbon told him he was lucky to be ashore, for the armies' moves into Spain had turned Lisbon into a city of bright anticipation and social activity. They made sure that he got invitations to the grander houses of the port, but his reluctance to attend was noted by his naval commander, who must have thought he was pushing himself too hard, for he granted him a fortnight's leave—an offer he wasn't expected to refuse. It was ironic; just when he most yearned for action, he was given *carte blanche* to be idle.

Then a surprise letter came from Major George Scovell, and Gideon saw with a grin that it was in code. He hoped it was a simple one, concocted as a sly challenge on Scovell's part, and, sure enough, the presence of a few useful words *en clair* encouraged him to try cracking it straight away. The thing took him a whole afternoon to decypher and transcribe, but apart from obvious references to the Paris grand code it really contained nothing that the major might not have written to him in plain English. As entertainment, though, it worked like magic.

> Sir Gideon,
> I heard that you are here once more so cannot resist telling you of recent progress. Ciudad Rodrigo you will know about and the campaign now centers on Badajoz. You will not be surprised to learn that the method of exchange that interests us both is back in full currency. The numbers have risen from 1200 to 1400 as the participants in this region have added 200 of their own for better communication. Are you curious to see them? If you are reading this now I must conclude you have not lost your knack with such devices. We have left Frenada to come south and Marmont instead is in that vicinity with diversionary forces that we take care to ignore. If curiosity gets the better of you it would be more than a pleasure to see you at Fuente Guinaldo where we will be quartered God willing after Badajoz. Grant sends his best and asks me to tell you the coney catching on both sides of the border is superlative just now.
> Respectfully and most cordially yours
> Major G. Scovell

It was irresistible to go looking for military friends again and find out about the Badajoz campaign. It was tempting to pore over maps of the route to Fuente Guinaldo, a Spanish town just over the border, north of Badajoz but nowhere near as far away as Frenada. It was inevitable that he should picture Grant and Scovell going about their perilous and fascinating tasks, and envy them for being part of Wellesley's long-awaited push into Spain. In his inquiries around town he learned that a few wagonloads of weapons that he himself had brought into the country had rolled out a few days before, for delivery to Fuente Guinaldo. That clinched it. He set Ellis the task of securing horses and rounded up the other necessities himself. It would give him a sense of completion to ride into Fuente Guinaldo with the new arms from England; to hear Grant's stories from over the border; to see the grand code finally unravel under Scovell's keen analysis. It would be his last action in a war that he had promised to turn his back on, and it offered a fit ending to one part of his existence, before he found a new life with Delphine. When he rode out of Lisbon he was almost cheerful again, for the first time since he had left her.

Delphine arrived in Lisbon on the eighth of April. There had been no mishap on the journey to Newhaven or the voyage itself; she always traveled well at sea, and Mary Scovell was a kind and friendly companion. If it were not for these hopeful signs, Delphine would have had nothing to counter the sense of doom that overtook her after Armand's disappearance from the Greenwich inn. She had been desperately overtired, and catching up with the post chaise had taken two hours, a period of panic followed by an attempt to sleep at last, which wasn't easy in the jolting vehicle. In Newhaven she had had to acquire more funds for the voyage, and there at least she had a ready solution—she paid a call on a representative of her London banker and convinced him to take her diamond bracelet as security for the cash she needed. The next task had been harder: writing to her mother with a fuller letter of explanation than the hasty note she had sent home with the Dalgleish carriage.

Only on board ship had she had time, if not peace and quiet, to contemplate what she was doing. There were secrets she could not share with Mary, who believed she was taking this plunge into the unknown for love—and envied her for it. "It's what I've always wanted to do myself," the older woman said wistfully, "and never been able." But there were many questions to which Mary had answers—where to go on their arrival in Lisbon, whom to approach in order to locate Gideon—and Delphine was grateful for her good sense and her help. Otherwise it would have been a lonely voyage, with only Molly beside her.

For Mary, the demands of the army were almost second nature. She was not only married to an officer—her brother, also a major, was with the Third Dragoons in the Peninsula. Mary took charge when they landed, insisting they go straight to the pre-arranged lodgings. They were escorted by army personnel and Delphine was impressed by their politeness and efficiency, and even more so by the city itself, as they left the docks and pene-trated into the grand avenues and thoroughfares.

A gigantic earthquake had leveled all of Lisbon a half century before, and everything she saw had been built since then: the public palaces, the port authority and ministry buildings and the vast mansions of the wealthy elite. The architecture would have been almost too grand without the lively, sometimes extravagant touches of decoration that revealed the national character. Del-phine gripped the side of the gig as it bounced across the cobbles of a square, held a wide-brimmed hat to her head with the other hand, and looked about with a sudden lift of the heart. She had not been able to spy the *Aphrodite* in the crowded port, but she had a thrilling certainty that Gideon had arrived. Somewhere in the city he was going about his duties, quite unaware that she had come to seek him out. She had imagined the meeting in a thou-sand different ways. She could predict shock, surprise, disarray, even a little disapproval. But afterward, when the confidences were over . . . She gave a sigh of longing.

"You're impatient," Mary said. "So am I! But there'll be a note from George waiting, and just as soon as I know what's what, we can make inquiries about Sir Gideon. I'll come with you, with pleasure."

"If your husband is here, I won't intrude for a minute. I'll take myself off to—"

"He won't be," Mary said. "He has to cross Portugal to get here. His leave begins today and he calculates that on the eleventh he'll report into town. So the eleventh it will be. George is the most correct, the most scrupulous man alive." She caught Delphine's eye and her cheeks grew rosy. "Does that sound dull? To someone of your sophistication, no doubt it does. But I can tell you—if your husband shows half the faithful devotion that George has shown to me, you will be a lucky woman."

"Dull? That's not in the least what I was thinking!" It was true—Delphine had been remembering what Gideon had told her about Scovell's genius with codes. She imagined Scovell as quiet, clever and confident, with ironic humor in his smile. She had an urge to share this notion with Mary—but Mary knew only that Gideon and her husband had met, and not what they had worked on together. Delphine even wondered whether Mary was aware precisely what her husband did on Wellesley's staff; she certainly gave no indication of it.

The accommodation proved clean and comfortable, and a letter from George Scovell kept the color in Mary's cheeks for the rest of the afternoon. Later, when they were unpacked and refreshed, the ladies set themselves to finding facts. They learned three, of major importance, all in one blow.

The news had just come in: Wellesley's army had smashed its way through the high walls of Badajoz and taken the town in an unprecedented orgy of drunkenness, murder, pillage and rape. Discipline was not one of the features of this triumph, but it was victory nonetheless.

The navy was able to tell them that Captain Sir Gideon Landor, his voyage of duty completed, had left Lisbon to spend a fortnight's leave in the British-occupied village of Fuente Guinaldo, beyond the border.

The army kindly advised the ladies that if they wanted to learn any more, they should await the arrival of Major George Scovell, who was heading from the battle zone into Lisbon at all possible speed.

Prisoners of War

Lieutenant Colonel Colquhoun Grant was experiencing a level of comfort that he had not enjoyed in years. He was invited to a fine dinner, and his uniform, travel stained and creased from his bivouacking on hard ground, had at his host's command been taken away and transformed with much care and polish. He had had a day of leisure in which to anticipate this evening; to rehearse topics of conversation and dredge up his social skills, which had had little use of late amongst the bandits, *guerrilleros* and peasants of the high sierras. But he kept coming up against the same obstacle: disbelief. In his line of work, he had always known how likely it was that he would be captured, but when it happened, he could scarcely get his brain to comprehend it. It was not until eight o'clock on the tenth of April 1812, when he was escorted into a dining room in Sabugal, Portugal, that he fully admitted to himself that he was a prisoner of the French. It was not until he took his place at the table opposite his smiling host, General Marmont, Duke of Ragusa, that he realized the finality of his situation.

Yet the facts were brutal enough. Overtaken by French cavalry in a valley near the border, he and his two companions had dismounted and tried to slip away through woods, without success. One man was wounded and brought to the ground, while Grant and the other were subdued. One of these, who wore plain clothes, was executed at once, with a bullet to the back of the head.

It was this scene that Grant recalled as he sat opposite Marmont, examining the regular features, the slightly boyish roundness of chin, the fashionably cropped dark hair and thick-lashed eyes. What a difference between a living face and a dead one: it took only seconds for a man who had been companion, sparring partner, guide and friend to become a distorted figure of scorched flesh and spilled blood. Grant wasn't bitter—there could be no bitterness about losing one round of a contest he had entered with open eyes—but he was oppressed by the scent of death that seemed part of this setting. He was untouched, but his head ached as though someone were holding a pistol jammed against his temple.

"I'm confident of the wines, for we brought them with us," Marmont was saying in French, "and the game—generally it's good around here. The roast is young boar, killed the day before yesterday. I have a fancy," he said, turning to the French officers at the table but really aiming the joke at Grant, "that the pork tastes better in Portugal than it does in Spain. Have you found that?"

"I ride across the border with such tedious regularity, monseigneur, that I confess it has ceased to mean much to me. I would guess it doesn't mean much to the pigs either."

Marmont gave a quick laugh and cut a neat wedge out of the little *pâté en croûte* on his plate. "You're not claiming your presence in our midst was some kind of mistake, Lieutenant Colonel? A little absence of mind?"

Grant felt no amusement. "We knew you'd penetrated back into this area, but we couldn't be sure exactly where."

"So you came looking."

"Nor could we be sure exactly why."

A disagreeable look came over his host's smooth face. "We were forced to test an extremely foolish theory. A theory that was not mine. We were asked to push into northern Portugal and make enough mischief to lure your commander in chief northward, hence distracting him from Badajoz. I at once explained to the illustrious architects of this theory that Wellesley would have none of it." Marmont pushed his plate away. "Witness the result, for who was it that came forward to challenge my marauders on the Beira Plateau? Your party of three. Brave, but scarcely sufficient."

Grant said, "What's next, now we have Badajoz?"

Marmont shrugged. "Finally, I shall be able to withdraw. Beginning tomorrow. We're moving to Salamanca, and so are you."

"What about—"

"The wounded man? He too."

Grant shook his head. The first course was being cleared from the table, and an empty crystal glass rang as the immaculate sleeve of a military servant brushed against it. "He can't sit a horse—he can't even raise his head. If you move him, he'll die. You couldn't transport him tomorrow; I doubt if you could even do it next week."

There was a shuffle of feet and someone brought in a covered tureen and set it in the middle of the table. Grant tried to get his mind to focus. What had he just said? If Marmont left without the prisoner, would he place a guard on him or just leave him to die? There was a third alternative that started a shiver at the base of Grant's spine: leave him dead. How scrupulous was the man on the other side of the table?

Marmont was ambitious. Like the other French commanders, he resented being in Spain, neglected by Bonaparte and cut off from the glory of more glamorous campaigns. Marmont, avid to salvage something from the stalemate in the Peninsula, was rumored to have his eye on the throne of Portugal. There were a number of ways he might bring this within his grasp, none of them compatible with loyalty or integrity.

The silver dome was removed from the tureen and a fragrant cloud of steam rose and spread over the table. Through it, Grant saw Marmont narrow his eyes. "Lieutenant Colonel, tomorrow you will bid farewell to Portugal. From Salamanca I shall arrange your transfer to Paris. You must accustom yourself to conversations like this along the way—and I cannot guarantee they will all be in refined company." As the suckling pig was being carved in front of him, he leaned forward with an almost benevolent air. There was an implication that Grant didn't miss: *Oblige us now and we will pave your Paris journey with whatever safeguards we think you deserve.* "I congratulate you. On your French, your Spanish, your elusiveness—do you know how long we have been trying to intercept you?" Marmont flicked his fingers, as though all differences between himself and Grant were irrelevant. "Let's talk about strategy. What an interesting subject your commander in chief has turned out to be! How little I suspected it when he first landed in Portugal. A man of patience and method; I confess, when I sit down to read one of his dispatches, I bring no less concentration to it than I would if it came from the emperor."

Grant felt the other officers start at this and allowed himself a wry grin. He was clever, Marmont. How many of Wellesley's dispatches had he really captured? Nothing to compare with the pile of decrypted French messages that Scovell and he between them had been able to deliver to Wellesley. But it wouldn't hurt to play to this air of confidence. "You might say there are similarities, monseigneur, between Sir Arthur Wellesley's case and your own. He is far from the capital, and his country must depend for success on his considerable military talents. The struggle here is not so much between nations as between generals. In such a situation, the enemy resolves itself into another keen and intelligent mind at work on the other side of the border."

Marmont took the flattery as his due. "My opinion of his tactics improves monthly. What will he do now? Advance toward us, that's obvious—but has he finished with Philippon?"

"What is your opinion of Philippon?" It was an invitation for Marmont to express contempt for the general who had lost Badajoz.

Marmont was not deflected. "Wellesley likes to isolate our armies, *if he can,* and that is when he strikes. It worked at Badajoz." A thin smile. "He'll find Salamanca another proposition entirely. But no doubt he'll try to cut us off on the way?"

Grant smiled without reply. Through the last courses, the meal proceeded in the same fashion: polite fencing, guarded speculation, charged silences. The officers contributed little, for Marmont liked to preside. He showed few signs of frustration at extracting so little out of Grant, but all of a sudden, while the dried fruit platter was being emptied, he sketched a gesture over the board with his paring knife.

"It's fortunate for you, monsieur, that you have that piece of red across your shoulders; if you hadn't, I'd have hung you on a gallows twenty feet high."

"Wouldn't a bullet in the head have done as well?"

Conversation languished after that. Grant felt drained. At the end, before he was escorted back to the village in which he was being held, he gave his parole, pledging not to try to escape on the way to Salamanca. There was no hope of that anyway, since he would be on the march with Marmont's whole bloody army. And he had an ulterior motive; if he cooperated at this stage, Marmont was more likely to deal humanely with the gravely wounded officer who had been captured with him.

It was an hour's ride to the village, back toward the Spanish border, and despite his pledge they bound his hands and led his horse, taking no chances. His brain was too tired to know whether he should have given his parole, but it was a question of timing; there was a possibility that they would keep him in Salamanca until the British laid siege to it. Then, if all went well, he would merely have to sit tight and wait for release.

In the one-room hut where they were holding him, he asked for a candle and another canteen of water and sat on his mattress with his cloak wrapped around him, listening to the painful, irregular breathing of the man lying on the other mattress at his side: Sir Gideon Landor.

It was a cool night, but Grant could see that Landor was still burning with fever. The bullet that had felled him during the pursuit had gone in beside the spine and worked its way up through to the breast, just under the collarbone. A French surgeon had been able to pry it out and dress the wounds, but the reaction that followed was so severe that Grant feared the worst: damage to the lung, and infection. What he'd told Marmont was true— Landor could not be moved in this state. But if he were left behind without medical care, he might die anyway.

He was startled when Landor whispered, "What happened?"

Grant turned. "Marmont asked me a long list of questions and I gave just as many useless replies." He waited, but Landor showed no reaction apart from a strange glitter in his half-open eyes. "They're moving me with them to Salamanca. They're leaving you here under guard. Marmont asked me, 'What's a British officer *in naval uniform* doing on this plateau?' When they think you can take it, they'll haul you after them and start questioning you. I wish I could be around to keep you company, old man, but I've given my parole and they're moving me on."

There was no answer. After a while, Grant made Landor drink some water, then extinguished the candle and stretched out.

Some time later, in the blackness, he heard the quick, uncertain voice again. "Delphine."

"What!"

"Be careful. It's all in code."

When Major George Scovell arrived in Lisbon from Badajoz, Delphine discovered he had not yet been anywhere near Fuente Guinaldo, but he could confirm that Sir Gideon Landor was installed there as a guest of a Lieutenant Colonel Colquhoun Grant. "Our forces are pushing north from Badajoz, and I'm posted to Fuente Guinaldo directly my leave's over. By the time I get up there Sir Gideon will be on his way back, and we'll probably be able to snatch all of five minutes' conversation on the road. When does the army ever arrange things for our convenience? Answer: only once every three years." He glanced at his wife with a warm, intimate smile. The three of them were sitting in a place called the Grotto on the fashionable Largo de São Paolo; he and Mary were holding hands under the table.

The major's happiness at being with his wife was touching, and Delphine tried not to intrude on it. The three of them often sallied forth together in the evenings, for Delphine received invitations to soirées and balls from the navy, and there were army suppers to which Scovell loved to take Mary, but during the day Delphine left them to their own devices.

She was still haunted by dread; the spring days dragged, and she struggled to fill them. One task was shopping, for she had only the clothes she had brought from Landor to Greenwich during the week of her wedding. Molly required outfitting too, and Delphine took her along on visits to milliners of high and low degree. For herself, she ordered two new gowns, a riding habit and some soft leather boots, which were ready within days. Lisbon was dedicated to finery; the town was crammed with outfitters displaying fabrics, hats, military accoutrements and brilliantly decorated uniforms in their shop windows.

On foot, she explored the mysterious alleyways of the Bairro Alta district and let Molly choose a straw hat with a red ribbon, the product of a village in the hills outside town that also specialized in woven baskets, one of which Molly bought herself, to complete the ensemble. "Do you think Ellis will like this, my lady?" she asked, her black eyes shining beneath the brim and her hands on the waist of a new full skirt with deep flounces.

"Please, Molly, you must remember to address me as madame. Our family sets no store by titles." She smiled. "Ellis will think you a perfect picture. If someone were to do your portrait now, not a soul could guess you're a Londoner."

"I've no mind to look as native as that," Molly sniffed, undoing the ribbon.

"Why not? Don't you think Ellis must already be chewing garlic and eating sausage off the point of a knife?" When Molly gaped at her, appalled, she laughed and said, "Keep the hat, do. I've a mind to wander in the Chiado market. We must see if we can find any cherries."

That evening their little party had no engagements. There was a narrow balcony off the apartment, and as the sun went down the three of them sat in chairs brought from indoors to line the railing, and looked down on a humble street where older people had carried their own chairs out onto the pavements and were watching boys and girls play up and down the cobbles in the dusk. Shrill voices darted up between the high stone walls to mingle with the thin cries of swifts that swooped across the rooftops. With the westerly sun gilding a clear sky beyond the port, it almost seemed like a summer evening.

Scovell, ever attentive, had the idea of sending out to see whether they could buy any ices, and while he was inside Delphine turned to Mary and examined her neat profile. "Don't you wish you could go with the major to Fuente Guinaldo?"

Mary kept her gaze on the families below. There was no surprise; of course she had been thinking about it, every day. "I'm supposed to wait until the army's gotten back to the north for the winter. Scovell thinks they'll be spending it in Frenada, where they were last year."

"What are his quarters going to be like in Fuente Guinaldo? Could you share them? Could you find a room with a family? It's a real town, not a village like Frenada."

There was a silence, broken only by the cries of children and birds. At last Mary turned her head. "I know what you're thinking. Would they say me nay, if I arrived there with George? Well, I suspect they wouldn't. They need him too much just now to take umbrage about my turning up. To be honest, after the first fuss I hardly think they'd notice." She said despairingly, "But it's not about what *I* wish. George has his orders and I can't compromise his career. He's made too many sacrifices for us already."

"Don't you think in his heart he wants you with him?" Delphine said. "When Gideon left, we both knew it was wrong. Everything will be wrong until I find him again. I can't help it; I'm afraid. I feel as if I need to find him right now, this instant, to prevent something dreadful from happening."

"War, madame," said Scovell's level voice behind her, "does terrible things to us all."

Mary Scovell got to her feet as he walked out onto the balcony, and Delphine could see she was worried he might have heard what she had said. Delphine felt a pang that this loving, resourceful woman had come all the way to Portugal only to be separated yet again from her husband. And, as if that were not enough, both man and wife were made to feel guilty for resenting it! "Mrs. Scovell," she said softly, "will it hurt to speak your heart? Among friends, can't you say what you wish?"

It was a gamble, the kind of question that might have made Mary angry and the major unhappy. But to her amazement, after a moment's hesitation Mary straightened and said, looking into her husband's eyes, "George, I want to go with you."

It was said with gentle simplicity, and the major put out his hand to take his wife's. "I shall do my best, Mary. My very best."

Tears misted Delphine's eyes and she took a few steps back into the apartment and left the two together. She stood quite still, letting sweet expectation steal down like balm into the region where she hid her innermost fears. Now there was hope. Journey's end beckoned. In a few days, she could be with Gideon.

Able Seaman Ellis was having a last drink outside the largest inn on the main plaza of Fuente Guinaldo. In fact he was having a last bottle—for if he got enough wine in him before he left this god-forsaken town, he might just jettison his hard-won control and dap a cobblestone through the window of the mayor's house where Sir Arthur sodding Wellesley was quartered, and do the same for Sir Henry bloody Hardinge, wherever he happened to be laying his empty aristocratic head tonight.

Who'd choose to be in the army? Who'd slog for years through these blessed mountains, knocking the Frenchies out of one fortress after another, only to trudge back across the same hard ground to sit on your arse under a blasted tree somewhere and wait for them to do the same to you? Who'd sign up under commanders like these, that sent men to their deaths as they would beaters to a partridge shoot, as though there was nothing to account for when it was all over except what was in the bag?

Hardinge had not shown the least alarm when Grant and Sir Gideon failed to return from reconnaissance—"Grant had gone missing a hundred times before and always come in"—and he had not turned a hair until Sir Gideon's riderless horse made its way back to the stables. It was a day before Hardinge ordered another scout into the area to see what he could learn, and by that time the trail was as cold as death. The man found a Spanish agent—Grant's companion, Leon—lying in a gully with his brains blown out. There was more blood nearby, and enough hoofprints to suggest a cavalry unit. The peasants said the French had moved off the Beira Plateau, leaving nothing behind.

And that, as far as Hardinge was concerned, was that. You sent your scouts out, and if they were clever fellows like Grant, they generally came home with a full bag. If you were unlucky, and one day they didn't get home, it was devilish bad luck. Now, as likely as not, the French had him, and unless he was exchanged he was going to be of no use to you until the end of the war.

Ellis took a long pull on the wine. Was he judging Hardinge too harshly? Hell, no. There'd been volunteers enough to make up a party to go after them, with himself at the top of the list, but the officers had been categorical—no pursuit, no attempt at recovery, no risk. Now the issue was closed. Further information had since trickled in: the French had taken two prisoners, one wounded, and they were on their way to Salamanca.

A number of officers, not all unsympathetic, had given Able Seaman Ellis to understand that his presence was inappropriate in Fuente Guinaldo. He had one reply to this: he took orders from Captain Sir Gideon Landor of His Majesty's Navy; he would be staying on until the final day of the captain's leave, in the lodgings provided and paid for by the captain, and if anyone tried to prevent him from doing his duty, he'd soon show them how the navy went about its business.

And now it had come, the final day. Here he was, surrounded by redcoats with not a thought in their heads except swallowing their next meal and then piling into bed. Wellesley's heroes, sated with the wine and women they'd gorged themselves on at Badajoz, weighed down with the booty they'd pillaged from the fortress, had buried their companions and then staggered up here to Fuente Guinaldo to sleep it all off. What did the loss of two scouts matter in the midst of that? Ellis raised his bottle and peered into the dark, syrupy wine of last summer. "Sod them all," he muttered.

If Major Scovell had been here, it might have been different. Grant was Scovell's eyes in the region, and he brought home the intercepted messages from the French. Scovell would be devastated to lose Grant, and he was the only one of all these boneheaded army officers who knew the true caliber of Sir Gideon Landor. Scovell would understand. He would know the twisted feeling Ellis had in his gut as he looked out across the plaza, hating Fuente Guinaldo. Sleepy, slow, glutted—the town that never gave a curse.

He heard the sound of hooves approaching and watched as the first of the riders came into view: a Mounted Guide as escort, and behind him a young Portuguese woman riding a mule sidesaddle, her full skirt spread over its crupper, and the black eyes in her pretty face gleaming with curiosity as she looked about her from under a straw hat. Ellis slammed the bottle down on the table and leaped to his feet. "Molly!"

She turned, and across the plaza their eyes met. Then the rest of the party came up behind her, and Ellis at once recognized two of them: Major Scovell and Miss Dalgleish—that is, Lady Landor. His first impulse was to dash toward them. He took a few steps across the plaza—then he stopped. The twist in his gut tightened, for he could see the wonder and delight on her face, the hope in her eyes, the smile on her lips that included him in the radiant greeting she had been saving for Sir Gideon. She didn't know.

Ellis had a duty to perform. He went forward, came to attention, bowed to Lady Landor and saluted Major Scovell. The major began to help her ladyship dismount, so Ellis took Molly by the waist and swung her down off the mule. Molly looked shy, then happy, then puzzled. Holding on to her hat with one hand and smoothing her skirt with the other, she examined his face for a second before saying in a low voice, "Ellis, what's wrong?"

He couldn't answer; he was looking at Lady Landor, who had descended from the horse and was standing with one hand against its neck and the other stretched out a little toward him, as though seeking support from the very person who was about to deal her the worst harm. She was such a quick creature, you could light tinder with the sparks that came off her. She had a way of darting a glance at you that opened up a bit of blue sky. So Molly said. But she couldn't summon any of that today. "Ellis," she said. "Tell me." She was as pale as porcelain.

"He's taken, your ladyship. The French have him. Wounded or not—I can't say."

She moaned, her hand slipped down the horse's smooth neck, and she sank to the ground, so swiftly that Major Scovell was just in time to prevent her head from striking the cobblestones.

Ellis got down on his knees at her side, while the major cursed under his breath, Molly gave a shriek and the other lady, still on horseback, rounded on the Mounted Guard and cried, "Good heavens, please, will someone go for assistance?"

Something was choking Ellis. *The French have him.* He'd said that—to her! What heavy weapons words could be. He put one hand over his eyes to hide the tears.

Fuente Guinaldo

Gideon could hear, and make sense of what he heard, more or less. There were men moving about as usual in the little place they'd chosen to hold him. And horses, their hooves scraping on stone in a yard—they were keeping the mounts outside, so there must be no stables in this huddle of buildings. It consisted of two farmhouses and their outbuildings, from which they must have banished the peasants, for he heard no Portuguese spoken during the long days. They were all cavalry, then, the Frenchmen left behind to guard him.

He could see, but there was little to be gained by that. For a long time he'd had no idea of his surroundings; they'd changed so much, swelling and shrinking as fever shuddered and burst in his brain. As it retreated, the hut reformed itself around him: timber roof covered with uneven tiles, rough walls and an earthen floor that smelled of the cows, pigs and poultry that it had housed, and of the hay piled against the wall behind his mattress. He was so weak when the fever broke that for an incalculable time he lay staring at the walls until he felt part of them. He had no personality, no thoughts, no existence beyond a thread of consciousness that linked him for hours with the slow progress of a sunbeam through a gap in the tiles and along the surface of a wall. As it picked out sparks of mica in the pitted stone, he would fix his eyes on each one until it winked out, then seek another as the beam moved on. By such minute advances did he go on living.

Now he had reached another stage. He had begun to learn what kind of trap they had him in, and his sense of self had returned, along with pain that was like a battering ram. One thing he could not tell was how long Grant had been gone. He knew he'd been here, because of the incoherent memory of his voice in the dark. But that was all. So Gideon couldn't tell how long ago he'd been shot, either, though he remembered the event with hideous clarity. Just as he recalled the execution of Leon.

That particular nightmare had swollen and taken over his brain, extending through the time when they'd slung him over a horse and then into this hut, and dominating the period when he lay pinned to the floor by agony and confusion. Images, words, had collided in his head. He'd been obsessed with the name of Fuente Guinaldo, which kept repeating itself like a demonic refrain. The letters of "Leon" were contained in Fuente Guinaldo, and they burned in front of him, four red letters picked out in a strange banner stretched before his eyes, blotting out everything else.

Even now he had to shift position, despite his body's protest, to break the fixation. Gritting his teeth, he rolled onto his side and levered himself into a sitting position. It was time for an experiment. Breathing shallowly, he analyzed the pain in his chest. He'd known as soon as the bullet hit him that if a lung was punctured low down he would sooner or later succumb. Higher, and he stood a chance. He just had to assume that he had escaped the point of no return. The fever had gone and he was able to eat and drink: now for a few more daring physical feats. He got to his knees, then crawled off the mattress and over to the wall, scuffing through the straw. He cursed inwardly at the noise and tried to move more quietly, but as he rose to his feet, propping himself against the stones, he let out an involuntary groan.

No one came, however. Impatient though they might be to get the hell out of here, they had their routines, and judging by the way the light angled under the eaves, he had half an hour or so to amuse himself before they brought the evening meal.

He edged around the walls toward the window fashioned in the southerly side of the hut—a gap plugged with ill-fitting shutters held in place by a heavy wooden bar on the outside.

He could stand; he could just walk, which meant he could sit a horse. But he couldn't let them know that yet. At least, not until he was strong enough to sit a runaway horse going like the devil back to Fuente Guinaldo. They were four guarding him: a young lieutenant, who put up a good front but must resent being left behind on guard when everyone else was marching to Salamanca. A sergeant, a grizzled old soldier who'd seen a lot and didn't think much of officers. And two others, also cavalry, at present employed on picket duty, and no doubt loathing it as beneath their dignity. All itching to sling him on a horse and take off to Spain.

He peered through the holes around the shutters. There was a kind of lane directly outside, between the hut and the farmhouses, which were windowless on this side. These buildings were separated by a narrow gap, and he could see along it and through an untidy vegetable garden, across a dirt yard and into a sloping field, where the view was cut off by a wood. How far to the trees, over the bare ground? Fifty yards, near enough. Running down it—supposing one could run—would present an open invitation for another bullet in the back. And he'd have to get through the shutters first, which he could only do by sliding something between them and knocking the bar up and out of the slots at each side. His sword would have been handy, but of course they'd taken that, along with the belt for good measure.

He didn't go near the door in case they saw movement. They had no one placed outside it, but he fancied the sergeant who did sentry duty was posted across from it inside the back of one farmhouse, in the kitchen, from which Gideon sometimes heard the scrape of a chair, the thud of crockery meeting a table, the rattle of pot lids. No talk, though—no one addressed whoever was preparing the meals, possibly an unwilling peasant.

He leaned his forehead against the shutters, getting a narrow view of the wood. All roads were closed to him now, except the one to Salamanca. And it was his fault. What had possessed him to go on that foray with Grant? Some last vestige of adventure seeking that he had not been able to confess to Delphine or himself? Whatever it was, he had risked his future and hers, and lost. He had put his shoulder once more to the great machine of war and it had taken him bodily in. It would grind him up and spit him out somewhere, months or years hence, in an exchange of prisoners.

He went back to the mattress, every sinew dying for rest and every particle of his mind rebelling against it. But there was no choice. Fate and his own mistakes had brought him back to the same predicament he'd been in when he first met Delphine— he was a prisoner of the French. He scraped some straw under the head of the mattress, each movement sending a lance of pain through his chest. He had tried every position and the discomfort was equal whichever way, so he lowered himself onto his back. It felt as though he were leaning against a marlinspike. *Tant pis,* he could see his captors the moment they came through the door, and take glimpses through the gap between door and wall. He could hardly move but he could at least observe.

But he closed his eyes and thought of Delphine. Of the way she had wept after they had tried to work things out, and failed; when she cried, *You see what happens?* He remembered snatching her into his arms, as though they were alone in midocean and would drown if he let her go. But he had let her go.

On Delphine's second day in Fuente Guinaldo, she received an invitation to dine with Sir Arthur Wellesley and his staff in the evening, including Major Scovell and Mary. Scovell had ex- plained what a privilege it was, and he clearly wanted her to ac- cept. It wasn't hard to see why: since he had escorted the intriguing Lady Landor to headquarters he had been forgiven the unexpected presence of his wife.

Delphine felt very differently. It angered her, now that Gideon was lost, to discover that the commander in chief suddenly wished to see her at his table. Was it cynical of her to imagine that Wellesley's real motive was to grill her about Napoleon? He knew her origins—everyone knew about such things in this revolting little world. She would make an interesting focus for their meal, and during it they could question her in the subtle, urbane fash- ion they employed with their French captives. Meanwhile, she could not use the opportunity to plead for a rescue party to seek out Gideon and Grant—the official assessment said that Grant was in Salamanca or on the way there, and there was nothing to be done about it.

In midmorning she stood in her inn chamber looking at her two new evening dresses from Lisbon that Molly, in some excitement about the event, had spread on the bed for inspection. Delphine felt sick; she had struggled with nausea and tears ever since the appalling moment in the plaza the day before. She had come to, and the first thing she had seen was that Ellis was crying. At once she thought he had lied, and Gideon was dead, and she broke into hysterical weeping. Before Mary, Molly or Scovell, Ellis guessed her terror and took control of himself in order to help her. She had seen how attached he must be to Gideon, and from that moment she felt a bond of trust and affection with him.

Molly said, "Which would you like me to prepare, madame, the blue or the *eau de nil*?"

Delphine shook her head. "Would you go and find Ellis for me? He's been asking around this morning, to find out what word's come in."

Molly went off with a will and Delphine leaned beside the window looking down into the plaza. Three officers came out of the mayor's house and down the steps to where some horses were being held. By their appearance, they must be going hunting. Sure enough, a moment later a tall figure, similarly dressed, came briskly down the steps and mounted a large brown hunter. She knew the commander in chief did this every second day, charging about after any game his party could start from the boulder-strewn highlands. With a heart like a stone, she watched him say a few words to the aides, then wheel his horse and clatter away. As he went by under her window, she saw the flash of a glance upward and realized he had known she was there. Her lip curled and she drew back. In that moment, she made up her mind.

Armand de Belfort was thoroughly enjoying himself on this trip into Spain. In his youth he had served here in the regulars, and though he had had his share of action and glory, he'd always felt a strong resentment at taking orders from officers who were unequal to him in intelligence. His time as captain of militia under Decaën in Mauritius had been even more frustrating. He shuddered now at the thought of what his pride had had to endure when he was in uniform. By contrast, what magnificent opportunities opened up to one in the direct service of the emperor!

Armand's knowledge of Spain and his position in the Ministry of Marine and War meant that he was a natural choice as liaison to Madrid and the generals, and he had already been to the Peninsula on two missions, the first to Madrid and the second to Marmont and the Army of Portugal. This third visit was to Marshal Soult, who led the French in the south. Soult was the only commander who did not as yet have the grand code, and to complete Napoleon's communication system in Spain, he must receive it. Armand traveled fast and light on the quickest route south toward Soult, heading for the French-held bridge across the Tagus at Almarez, the sole strategic gateway to the Estramadura and Soult.

From Salamanca, Armand had taken a surly but reliable Spaniard as guide, and they were both mounted on nimble horses used to the terrain. No one in the French forces knew what Armand carried in the satchel wedged into his saddle bag, and the enemy stood no chance of laying eyes on it either: the pages of the code were impregnated with a flammable substance, and if trouble threatened, Armand had only to discharge his pistol into the papers and they would go up in flames.

On the way out of Salamanca he had fallen in with Marmont again and gotten a gentlemanly, not to say enthusiastic, reception. A few minutes' conversation on the road (the duke was eager to reach the city) gave him Marmont's latest opinions on Philippon and Soult (contemptuous) and the news that two English intelligence agents had been captured. The name of the first meant nothing to Armand but that of the second made him exclaim in sheer pleasure. "Landor! What, in *uniform*. What as? The man's not army, you know—you could have shot him on the spot!"

"I'm afraid not. He was in naval dress and gave his rank as captain."

"Good God. Where is he?" Armand had twisted in the saddle, examining Marmont's entourage as though he were about to see his nemesis tied to a horse and ripe for retribution.

"He was wounded, not fit to travel. I've left him on the other side of the border in a place called Arosa with orders to bring him on here next week. You know of the man? This is excellent news; we've gotten nothing out of him yet. What the hell was he doing with Grant?"

Armand could not stop grinning. "Damned if I know. But I hope you'll give me leave to find out?"

Marmont smiled back. "With pleasure. You'll be kind enough to put it in writing and give it to Lieutenant Angelou to bring on to me. With the prisoner. The intact prisoner."

Armand controlled his features and gave a correct military salute, which contrasted nicely, he thought, with his elegant traveling clothes. "I have some experience in interrogation, monseigneur. The prisoner's health is in no danger from me. But I guarantee to cause some damage to his peace of mind."

Marmont's soft laughter echoed in Armand's head as he rode along a cattle track in the lee of a ridge. He wasn't keen on the fact that Arosa was over the Portuguese border, but then again it wasn't really out of his route, for the bridge at Almarez was only days away across country. *Landor.* Wonderful, wonderful. He couldn't wait.

"A bandit called Jeronimo Saornil came in this morning," Ellis was saying. "He sells information. He's been well paid in silver by Hardinge so he talked to me for free. He has no English but his French is fine. He's from the north, Valladolid way, but he's been down here more than once and into Portugal too. He knows Sir Gideon—he met him once, somewhere near the Agueda."

Delphine said quickly, "When?"

Ellis shook his head. "Last time." He looked at Delphine hard and she knew he was trying to work out how much Gideon might have told her about his work. Then she saw him give up the attempt—there was too much at stake for caution now. "In the new year, madame. He didn't take me with him—I wish he had, so I'd know the terrain. But Saornil does."

"What else does he know?"

Ellis looked reluctant. Reluctant to tell her more, or reluctant to hope? Then he said, "Saornil spoke to a couple of families that have been chased out of a place called Arosa, across the plateau on the Portuguese side. It's no more than a couple of farmhouses on a crossroads. He says there are French cavalry there and they've a wounded prisoner that the army left behind when Marmont moved back into Spain. We've no troops up there and they know how to deal with the peasants. They must think themselves safe there for a few days at least. I don't know, madame, but what are the chances it's Sir Gideon they're holding?"

Delphine didn't answer. She couldn't. She sat silent in front of the dressing table; Ellis was standing in the middle of the room so he could not be heard outside it, and Molly was by the door, on guard. Finally she said, "Saornil is still here?"

"He was on his way, but I told him it would profit him to wait half an hour."

"You did well." Delphine sat very straight, twisting the Landor ruby round her finger. She said to Molly, "You'll lay out my riding habit and boots, if you please."

Molly started but obeyed, while Delphine addressed Ellis in quiet, earnest tones. "I'm French, Ellis."

"Yes, madame," he said woodenly.

"I'm riding across country from Spain to join my husband, who is a French officer. I'm traveling with a guide, and an armed servant leading a packhorse."

"Madame?"

"The army is not where I was told they'd be; I'm left behind and lost and I need to rest and ask after my husband. They won't turn me away." She took another breath and said into the stunned silence, "If I pay Saornil enough, will he take us to Arosa?"

"He'll take me, but he won't do more than that. He has a reputation to protect."

"He'll take *us*, Ellis."

He shook his head. "Excuse me, madame, but can you see Sir Gideon allowing me to guide you into that sort of danger?"

"Ellis," she said urgently, "they are *my people*. I'm a civilian and a patriot. There is no danger to me and never will be. It's you I worry about. If you do this for me, I'll be turning you into a spy."

"You won't be the first, madame."

It meant acceptance, against all the odds, and she could have embraced him. Instead they discussed the details. Saornil would bring them within sight of the village, avoiding the pickets, then head back into Spain. Ellis would be armed but not Delphine— he had the right to defend himself, but she would never harm a compatriot. Having declared herself to the French in the little hamlet, she must find her own solution and her own time for extracting Gideon by stealth. The strong, swift horse that carried the packs would be Gideon's mount when they left. If that proved impossible, Delphine insisted that she would stay with Gideon, even if it meant going to occupied Salamanca. "Even," she said wryly to Ellis, "if it means telling the truth." If that was necessary, Ellis would slip away and return to Fuente Guinaldo, and Molly, and finally England. She said, "If it turns out that way, I may not return until the end of the war."

Delphine said nothing to Mary and Scovell; they would find out soon enough. She left Molly to await the inquiries about her absence from Wellesley's dinner, and quitted Fuente Guinaldo, with Ellis riding as her groom, in the direction taken by the commander in chief, as though she had a fancy to observe the hunt. Once beyond the town, they swung across country to rendezvous with Saornil, who led the packhorse. They would bivouac only once en route, for Saornil said they were less than two days from Arosa.

Lieutenant Angelou was paying a visit to his prisoner. It was a cool afternoon and black clouds hung low over the ranges. There was a scent of moisture in the crisp spring air and the young lieutenant was longing for the warmth and bustle and companionship of Salamanca. He was ambitious, and eager to perform this task well, but he had no superior officers here to impress with his efficiency, and one did not get mentioned in dispatches for herding prisoners about the country. His only hope of distinction would be to convey to Salamanca not just Landor, but some piece of information he'd been able to prise out of him. At the moment this looked no more likely than when they'd laid him out senseless in the hut. There was an improvement, however, that Landor tried to conceal, but which betrayed itself in his satirical green gaze. He sat propped against a hay bale, having claimed he could not get to his feet, but declaring himself ready for conversation if the lieutenant so desired. Angelou, struggling against a strange feeling of intimidation, said in French, "The sergeant tells me you're healing well. When he changed the dressings today, he saw the wounds are knitting."

"Really? Then no doubt he's right. I'm grateful for his attentions. He's an old soldier of great experience."

There was the faintest emphasis on the last two words, suggesting a comparison offensive to Angelou. He drew himself up a little. "I judge you fit to ride a horse. We leave tomorrow." To his glee Angelou detected a dampening of the spirits. The journey to Salamanca would be acutely painful for the prisoner, and he might well fear more torture in the city. Was there a chance of loosening his tongue with a little bribery—better treatment, a longer stay in Arosa? "I'm glad to see you so much mended. I should like to invite you to dine with me this evening. The company," he bowed, "you may of course regret. But I can promise the meal will be superior to the food we've been obliged to give you of late. Will you allow me to offer you some amends this evening? Along with an excellent rosé?"

There was a moment's silence, then the prisoner drew in his long legs and shifted slowly to his haunches and thence to his feet; one did not after all respond to a gentleman's invitation sitting down. A muscle along his lean jaw tightened as he rose, a mute signal of what it cost him to stand. There was a hard line between his brows as he looked at Angelou. "Thank you. I accept. On one condition." Angelou tensed, suddenly furious, imagining himself condemned to a whole deadly meal in which he wouldn't be able to pose a single question. Sir Gideon went on, "Who serves us, the sergeant or the cook?"

"The cook?" Angelou exclaimed. "The cook's an idiot Portuguese. The sergeant serves."

"Pray tell him not to pull the cork until we're at table. The local rosé is temperamental—it's not advisable to let it breathe too long."

Angelou found himself smiling. "Agreed. Excellent. I look forward to the pleasure of your company, monsieur." He was still smiling as he shut the door of the hut behind him and let the bar fall across it with a gratifying thud. Whatever benefit the meal might afford, he had achieved one result already—he had brought the prisoner to his feet.

Angelou was not ashamed of what he could put on the table that evening. A lamb butchered the day before would be the focus of the meal, and he spent an hour or two chivying the cook and the sergeant about the rest of it. He even sent the sergeant into the hut with shaving gear and had him wait and watch while the English captain spruced himself up. Then, just as the sun was about to go down across the border, there was a shout and the sergeant came to him at the double, catching him in the olive orchard behind the houses.

"*Mon lieutenant,* Legros has a party in charge. A lady and her servant. He's made them halt at the bottom of the hill. Requesting your orders."

"A *lady*?" Angelou strode around to the yard and looked down the track that formed one arm of the crossroads of Arosa. A lady all right: slender, in a black riding habit and hat with a veil. He stared at them. "The servant's armed to the teeth. What's their business?"

"She's French, and looking for her husband, *mon lieutenant.* He's in our forces it seems—a general, I'd say, if her looks are anything to go by. The servant's armed for protection against the Spanish and the Portuguese, he says; he's given Legros no trouble. But Legros has told him they're coming no nearer without your say-so."

"Gendreaux?" Angelou looked uphill toward the spot where he'd placed the other sentry, who had a view eastward. "Any signal from him? This could be a distraction; I'll have no lack of vigilance."

The sergeant shook his head. "He gave the all-clear not five minutes ago, *mon lieutenant.*"

"Good. Go back to your post in the kitchen. Watch that cook—tell him I'll have no nonsense from him or he'll go the way of the roast lamb."

Angelou entered the house, buckled on his sword, straightened his uniform and put on his hat, then proceeded down the gentle slope to the waiting group, which formed a bizarre sight in this savage landscape where of late he'd seen only travel-worn soldiery and swarthy peasants. The lady was a blonde, with the palest skin to match, and she sat her horse like an aristocrat taking an afternoon ride in a park. As he strode closer he could see that the eyes examining him through the veil were very blue. She was racked with tension and fear; the carbine in Legros's hand no doubt had something to do with that. The servant was behind her, holding the reins of his own mount and the packhorse—two pieces of rather expensive horseflesh, Angelou noted, despite their present functions. A second string for the husband once they met up? Legros had got the servant to fasten his weapons onto the packs, which improved Angelou's confidence as he came to a halt, swept off his hat and gave a bow. "Madame, I'm Lieutenant Angelou of the *chasseurs à cheval*, commanding Arosa. May I respectfully beg to know your name and your purpose?"

He saw her eyes widen when he mentioned the chasseurs—she recognized his splendid green-and-red uniform decorated with lace and aiguillettes, and knew the prestige of the crack light cavalry to which he belonged. A military wife then. Her voice was very low and not quite steady. "I'm Madame de Belfort. I'm traveling to rejoin my husband, Armand de Belfort. Do you know of him?"

The name meant nothing to Angelou. "Which regiment does he command, madame?"

"He—he is connected with the army but has no command. He is in Spain on military business and I'm here to rejoin him. I expected to meet him in Salamanca, then I was told he had crossed into Portugal, and now I find—I think he is with General Marmont in that direction . . ." She pointed east with a trembling hand, her voice dissolved and two tears rolled down her perfect cheeks under the veil.

Angelou was horrified. "Excuse me, madame, but I'm astonished that you should be traveling in these circumstances. Could not your husband have provided an escort of more substance? Better still, should he not rendezvous with you in the safety of a town?"

She gave a little sob, then pressed her gloved hand over eyes and veil for a second. She murmured, almost too low for him to hear, "He doesn't know I'm looking for him."

"Ah." The situation took on another color in Angelou's mind. He could not tell whether she wore a wedding ring, but an enormous ruby glowed on a finger of her gloved hand. It was more than possible that she was the gentleman's mistress. Whichever she was, mistress or wife, the gentleman would feel nothing but gratitude for anyone who brought her to him.

Delphine struggled meanwhile with tears of exhaustion and panic. The journey had been grueling, for she had never in her life spent so long in the saddle, and the terrain was daunting. When Saornil had finally brought them within sight of Arosa, taken his payment in silver and then melted away into the uplands, she had felt abandoned. Any confidence in her plans had disappeared at the thought of what she had to face. Ellis had warned her that they would be challenged by the pickets, but when the cavalryman roared at them and leveled his carbine at Ellis's chest, she had nearly screamed. She hated weapons—of any kind, anywhere. She was appalled at herself for dragging Ellis amongst French cavalry. Here they were in the midst of a war, and she had not even the excuse of knowing that Gideon was being held in the tiny collection of buildings up ahead.

She heard herself cry, "I want . . . my husband!"

The young lieutenant stepped closer and took her horse's reins. "Madame, it's my great pleasure to offer you our protection. We have accommodation at your disposal, and we're moving on tomorrow morning, across the border, in the direction of Salamanca. I shall be honored—delighted—to give you safe passage to the city."

Relief swamped her, then a new kind of alarm. "You are very good, monsieur." As her horse moved forward she twisted in the saddle to catch Ellis's eye. He nodded grimly and twitched the reins of his two horses, ignoring the brute with the carbine.

"Legros!" said the lieutenant over his shoulder. "Back to your post."

Delphine's voice was still shaky as she said, really wanting to know, "Do you have many sentries posted?"

"Two: that fellow and another to the east—ample in this position." She must still look nervous, for with an admiring glance he said, "You need have no fear at night. They're recalled to the house and take turns on watch, patrolling the perimeter. We are here to guard an English prisoner, madame, but don't concern yourself on that score either. He's wounded—no danger to a soul."

She could scarcely say it. "Who is he?"

The lieutenant shrugged. "All he's vouchsafed so far is his name and rank. I've been hoping to tempt a little more out of him, and in fact I've invited him to a very good meal tonight— better than he has had in many a month, I'll be bound." He looked up again into her startled face. "A civilized evening can do wonders in this situation. May I be so bold as to hope you'll honor me with your company? Do not hesitate on account of the prisoner; he speaks French, his manners are irreproachable and I'll vouch he's a gentleman in his own country."

She wanted to shriek, "Give me his *name!*"

The lieutenant looked so young. Fine boned, with a lean, fit body, and somewhat shy, despite the air of authority. He said, "May I ask what your husband's business is with Marshal Marmont?"

She had given Armand's name for two reasons. To begin with, it had seemed more plausible to use a real name that might mean something to the army in the region. Second, and more important, if Armand was in the area when she pronounced it she would find out at once. It was the one relief of this awful day that there had not been a flicker on Lieutenant Angelou's face when she said it. "Monsieur de Belfort is in the Ministry of War and Marine. I'm not at liberty to tell you his mission, lieutenant, but his passport is signed by the emperor." They halted by the yard where a makeshift barrier shut in five horses surrounded by piles of hay. One mount would be for the prisoner. So she and Ellis had four men to deal with. Where was the other: inside one of the houses? She smiled down at the lieutenant as he put up his hands to help her from the horse. "I remember the *chasseurs à cheval* from the parades in Paris. You form part of the Imperial Guard. The emperor is extremely proud of you."

Something in her tone arrested him. "You . . . you know him, madame?"

"I do. And he has my loyalty, forever." She was touched by the awe and reverence in his upturned face. Tears trembled in her voice again as she said, "And I see he has yours."

Arosa

Gideon lay cursing as darkness fell. Another bloody lot! He'd heard them come up the rise—at least three horses—and dismount on the far side, outside the yard, just too far away for him to distinguish anything from the voices. One sounded like the lieutenant's. There was a masculine grunt from someone else, and the lighter tones of either an adolescent or a woman. If he was lucky, they'd simply be peons brought up here to help with the lieutenant's idea of an elegant repast. If he wasn't, it was another little contingent of cavalry.

They were all indoors now, and he could hear nothing because the farmhouse walls were so thick. No doubt the group would be housed in the unused building for the night while the lieutenant remained in his own quarters. No one extra seemed to have joined the cook in the kitchen, whose voice one never heard anyway. Not even the sergeant, on guard as usual, could bully the person into conversation.

Gideon got up quietly and went to the far wall of the hut. Settling his shoulders against the stones, he watched through the narrow gap between the door and its frame. Light from the kitchen spilled across the ground and through the gap, but the slender beam stopped halfway across the floor of the hut. He was confident that he could not be seen by the sergeant, but he himself could see everything that went on in the vertical segment of the kitchen open to his gaze. Unfortunately, despite the extra activities in the two houses, tonight was no different from any other. He had not laid eyes on the cook yet, and it seemed he was never going to. The sergeant, sustained by the bread, olives and some kind of tipple that always sat beside him on the table, sat staring out toward the hut. He was sent out on the dot to recall the sentries, but soon returned.

Then, suddenly, Gideon got his reward. The cook came across behind the sergeant to fetch something from the other end of the kitchen and Gideon got a good look at him. Jet-black hair tied back off his face with a bandanna, revealing long black eyes and a hooked nose. It took two seconds of recall—he'd seen him with Leon! The man had come with Leon to the rendezvous with Colquhoun Grant by the Agueda River. In the night, on Gideon's first foray into Spain. He took a deep breath, ignoring the pain under his ribs. He had an ally in the enemy camp.

And then the miracle happened. Another man came strolling into view, making the sergeant jump. There was a gruff exchange, and the stranger was told to get the hell out of his line of sight. Undeterred, the man leaned one shoulder against the kitchen doorway so that Gideon could see the back of his head and part of his square frame, and tried getting the sergeant into conversation.

Ellis. It was Ellis. The surprise was so great that Gideon felt himself go faint. He slid down the wall onto his haunches and fought to clear his head, avid not to miss a syllable pronounced by that rounded, pleasant, Guernsey-accented voice.

"And what might you be up to?" the sergeant demanded.

The reply was cheerful. "Reconnaissance, my friend. Rumor has it there's a well somewhere. I'm to bring fresh water to madame."

Madame? Gideon sat down on the floor, his forehead on his knees. So the voice he'd heard earlier was indeed female. This was insane. Impossible. Ellis, posing as the servant to a lady. A French lady, clearly, at present enjoying the lieutenant's hospitality. His heart began to pound. He couldn't hear anything; he could scarcely think. Dazed, he lifted his head and looked toward the light. He could see the point of Ellis's shoulder and an incoherent blaze beyond, out of which the sergeant replied, "You've come the wrong way. The well's back there, down to your left under the trees. Announce your presence, though, or Legros might shoot your arse off by mistake."

"Who've you got in there?" Ellis gestured over his shoulder with his thumb.

"None of your business."

"Madame's not too happy about him, I can tell you. Sets a great value on security, does madame. Quite right too if you saw the stuff she travels with. I don't need to tell you how wealthy she is. Just take a glimpse at the ruby she wears—size of a rock."

For Gideon, this was like the fever again. He was hallucinating. Ellis, four-square outside his door, spinning him clues—none of this was happening.

"Damned if I care," the sergeant said. "You think I fancy carting her to Salamanca, rubies or no rubies? You can do all the fetching and carrying you like, my *friend.* Just don't get in my way. I've enough to do without that."

Ellis laughed. "Let's continue this after dinner, shall we? When we're both at our leisure." Then he was gone, his last clue hanging in the air like the echo of some sweet melody. It was a dream. Gideon leaned his head back against the wall, praying never to awaken.

Oddly enough, Delphine thought of Molly when she donned the blue gown for supper. Molly preferred it to the *eau de nil.* A pity, since Delphine would have to split it up the sides if they managed to grab the horses for their escape, as she would be riding bareback. It was only by thinking of such practicalities that she could arm herself for the meal, for she had not discovered who the prisoner was. Ellis, apologetic after his own failure to do so, was still optimistic. "It has to be Sir Gideon, madame. I'm ready to proceed as planned. You give the signal: I take care of the sentry on patrol. The other's asleep, so I shan't need to tangle with him."

"You're sure you can manage it?"

"I've handled sentries before, madame. I think you can guess where."

"The sergeant in the kitchen?"

"I'll have to play that as it comes. But the cook's a vicious-looking Portuguese, and none too keen on what he's being asked to do. If he tried to stand in my way I'd be a bit surprised."

"Lieutenant Angelou—" her throat contracted.

He considered her with compassion. "We all take our chances." Suddenly he stretched forward his right hand; then he dropped it and turned on his heel, embarrassed at offering comfort unasked, and left the room.

She got dressed with slow care, selecting items from the bed onto which she had tipped her belongings from the pack. There was no mirror in the spartan room the lieutenant had had made ready for her. There was no dresser or stool either—just an empty chest in a corner. She was in the simplest environment she had ever stepped into—as stark as a prison cell.

The dining room was in the other farmhouse, a slightly larger, three-roomed dwelling commandeered by the lieutenant. He had had the front room cleared for the meal and it held just an uncovered table, which must have been dragged through from the kitchen. Candles provided a glow and threw the corners of the room into merciful dimness. The smells that drifted in from the kitchen behind were appetizing, and someone had ripped up a bunch of spring flowers and thrust them into an earthenware mug on the table. The lieutenant, resplendent in the flattering candlelight, offered her wine as clear as rose water.

He was courteous and deferential. She was tolerant and unbearably tense. He pulled out the best chair for her, and she sat facing the door. He took the head of the table and asked her questions about Paris, which she answered in full, keeping him entertained. She didn't want to ask him about his campaigns or the war.

There were no servants. The sergeant, whom she had not laid eyes on, was at his post in the kitchen. The lieutenant explained that he would serve at table once he had escorted the prisoner to the room. "I shall have to ask you to forget Paris at that point," he said with a smile. "Forget Madrid also, and Salamanca. Rusticity, madame, cannot show its colors more clearly to you than it will tonight. But I stand by the quality of the food."

And then the prisoner arrived. There was a loud knock at the door, the invisible sergeant pulled it back, and in the half darkness outside, standing on the beaten earth that formed the only doorstep, was a man in navy blue uniform. Gideon.

She rose, nearly tipping over her chair. She clasped her hands over her midriff, holding herself in. She could not help her eyes meeting his, signaling relief, love and yearning as he stepped across the threshold. He was more prepared than she was, but for a second his eyes engulfed her with the sea green that she remembered, and she felt too breathless and dizzy to stand. Then he turned to the lieutenant, bowed and submitted to the introductions. After that he could not look at her until he sat down.

Gideon, meanwhile, felt all his forces fail him except one. His desire to touch her was so imperious that his sinews knotted with the effort to sit still. She looked bereft, rigid as a china figurine on the other side of the table. A figurine with eyes like jewels.

He broke the gaze, looked down, tried to think. "I'm sorry but I didn't catch your name, madame. Forgive me."

"Belfort, monsieur. My husband is Armand de Belfort, of the Ministry of Marine and War in Paris." His hands on the table were unmoving but he was trembling inside. Things had stopped making sense. He heard her words this time, but they had no meaning. It was as though she were speaking in code. She filled the silence with her low, musical, heartbreaking voice. "He was supposed to be in Spain on a mission. I believed he'd come across the border, so I followed. But it seems he is not here, and I was mistaken. Armand is not here. I'm alone."

He understood then. He raised his head just as the lieutenant put in politely, "Madame, never feel you are alone while the *chasseurs à cheval* are with you." He turned to Gideon. "We have the honor of escorting Madame de Belfort to Salamanca. I look forward to many occasions like this along the way. I'll make the journey as comfortable as possible for both of you. Meanwhile"—he snapped his fingers—"allow me to offer you the soup."

Delphine leaned forward, scanning Gideon fearfully: the pale face, the heavy-lidded eyes, the stiff way he sat. "But tell me, monsieur, are you able to ride?"

"Alongside you, madame? Anywhere."

Angelou smiled at this gallant opener and looked at her gratefully. Delphine had the idea—hardly surprising, with her knowledge of Gideon—that the lieutenant had found his prisoner unforthcoming. It would help if she could show how a feminine influence might soften Captain Landor's attitude to the French.

The soup was excellent, and laced with garlic. "You don't mind the taste?" she said to Captain Landor. "It must be so very different from what you eat on board ship."

He seemed to catch her ruse at once. "The table of a navy frigate, madame, is the last place to boast of. The food in Portugal and Spain is ambrosia by comparison. When the *Venus* put into port in March, I went straight off to indulge myself at the Grotto on the Largo São Paolo—do you know it?"

"Yes, I—" She stopped, colored and laughed. "That is, I've heard of it. My husband once told me, when peace comes to Portugal and Spain, he will bring me on a visit to Lisbon, and then to Andalusia. How long would it take us, if we were to sail right around the coast of the peninsula?"

They continued like this all through the meal, with Gideon dropping tidbits that enchanted Angelou. But he was tiring, and it tore at Delphine's heart. What if he became too weak for them to pull off the escape? He ate little, all his concentration being on her. She was astonished that the lieutenant didn't notice the intensity of the way they talked to each other—but perhaps he did, and judged it favorable to his own plans. He was young and unsophisticated; it must please him to host a meal that showed such signs of success despite the bizarre collection of people around the table.

The last course consisted of plump cherries, halved, stoned and marinated in a concoction of honey and vinegar. It was served with a fresh white cheese that was as soft as cream. She said, "You have done wonders, lieutenant. In England, I believe this would be the time for the ladies to withdraw. Can I confess how much I should prefer to stay? But Captain Landor, now—you look as if you can't wait to retire. Don't allow me to be selfish."

He took the hint; it seemed physically impossible for him to do otherwise. After polite good nights and compliments on the meal, the sergeant escorted Gideon to the hut, returned to clear the table and went back to his vigil in the kitchen.

Delphine, battered by the tensions of the evening, accepted a last thimbleful of rosé from the lieutenant. "I regret," he said, "I can offer you no coffee. Civilization has yet to reach these parts."

"One wouldn't have thought so tonight, monsieur. May I ask you a question?" He nodded, his eyes bright, curious and without suspicion. "What is an English naval officer doing in northern Portugal, so near the Spanish border?"

"I wish I knew, madame."

"It seems so odd. Perhaps he came looking for a relative in the English army and he won't speak in case he lets fall the position of his regiment." The lieutenant gave a dismissive smile at this and she pushed on. "Or he is a spy. Except, who ever heard of navy intelligence operating on land? Or, he is here because of a woman."

Angelou laughed. "Now that, madame, never occurred to me!"

"Why not? You know the little piece of wisdom: *Cherchez la femme.* Might the captain have been here before, during the siege of Ciudad Rodrigo?"

"I'm not sure I follow you."

"It's just—if there is a woman involved, she must be Portuguese or Spanish. When you rejoin the army in Salamanca, your agents may have something to say on the matter. You may be able to locate the woman, take her into custody. If I'm right, that is just the kind of coercion that would work on Captain Landor. Especially since he has risked his life to be with her."

He laughed again. "We don't even know if this woman exists, madame!"

"No. Indeed. Would you like me to find out, tonight?"

He stared at her. "Tonight?"

"Why not? Why shouldn't I pay the captain a short visit of concern? I could inquire about his health and see if there are some small comforts I can provide. I think he and I established a certain basis of sympathy at your table, lieutenant. It was natural, given the ambience you provided. It seems a pity for me to retire without seeing whether he might confide in me a little more. Only with your kind permission, of course. I shall follow your lead."

He was titillated, intrigued, but he frowned. "The sergeant must be present. I cannot expose you to danger."

"Danger! Monsieur, he could scarcely hold up his head! No, I must be alone with him. That is the way to build trust. I should so love to assist you. I was alone, friendless—and you rescued me. Let me repay you; let me be of service to you in my trivial way."

She knew he would say yes, and he did it with a toast. "I propose: to the ladies. Heaven help us all when they decide to wage war."

"You cannot expect me to drink to that, monsieur! Let me propose another. To the emperor!"

Together they raised their glasses and drank the last drops of rosé.

Gideon was leaning against the wall opposite the door when the sergeant let her in. He had heard her approach: he was waiting for her, every nerve quickened. She had difficulty speaking while the soldier hung around, gazing at them both with dour suspicion as though he guessed what they were about. Then, finally, the door closed.

They stepped forward and into each other's arms. For a moment, Delphine thought he would slip through her grasp and fall, for they touched each other with such desperate care, as though they were made of glass and might shatter with the force of a true embrace. But their lips met with the same crushing ardor that they had felt on their wedding night. "I love you," he said. "I love you. How did you manage this? What are you *doing* here?"

She drew back a little, her voice husky as she said, "Where are you hurt?"

"Through the chest, but it's no problem. I can ride, I can do anything. Why are you *here*?"

"It was Armand. He frightened me. He came to see me the day you left. I don't know where he is now, but he terrified me. I had to see you, be with you." She could not squeeze him in her arms so she clutched the woolen cloth of his uniform, pulling him to her.

"Belfort?" he said in amazement.

"I'll tell you later. Please, we *must go.*"

"What's happening?" His hands were on each side of her face, but he glanced aside at the door.

"Ellis is taking care of the sentry. Then he'll creep to the yard and bridle our horses."

His gaze returned to hers, a hard line between his brows. "Won't the lieutenant hear? Where's the yard in relation to him?"

"On the other side of the house."

"What about the sergeant?"

"When I leave you, I'll go into the kitchen to speak to him. I'll draw him out of sight and Ellis will release you. When I join you at the yard, we leave."

"I won't do it. It's too dangerous for you."

Then all of a sudden they heard loud male voices and the thud of hooves. "Oh, God," Delphine said.

He laid two fingers across her lips and whispered, "Angel, listen—it's from the east, the direction of the border. Someone else is arriving. Two horses."

"In the dark?"

"They were lost, maybe, and saw the lights."

"But there was no challenge."

"Then Ellis has already done his work."

"Oh, God," she said again, "what do we do now?"

At that moment it began to rain, so copiously it was like a tropical downpour. Heavy drops drummed on the tiles above and splashed into the dry earth around the hut, drowning out all other noise. "We'll have to wait," he said in her ear. "Let them settle in, whoever they are." His hands slid down over her breasts, the roughened fingertips catching in the silk, their warmth penetrating to her quivering skin. "You were sent to woo me, *mon ange.* Let us pray no one comes to interrupt us."

"You still speak French to me," she whispered, her throat tight. "I thought you never would again, after what they've done to you." Then her lips sought his and he responded with a sound that she interpreted with intoxicating ease.

*   *   *

Armand de Belfort was dizzy with relief when he reached Arosa. The last few of hours of his journey had been diabolical. Not long after a midday meal in a godforsaken village, he had succumbed to the horrors of the local cuisine and had to dismount from his horse with a pain in his bowels that sent him running to the side of the track again and again under the sardonic eye of his Spanish guide. When these shaming bouts were over, rain overtook them and turned the upland tracks into mudslides that made the horses cautious and slow. The light failed, the clouds came down and dumped even more rain, and Armand had to sling the satchel with the code in it over his shoulder and pull his riding cloak across to make sure it stayed dry, while the water streamed through his hair and down his neck.

Exhausted, and sick to death of his companion, Armand also had to contend with the likelihood of coming upon pickets unawares when they reached Arosa, and being shot by a startled sentry. Near the hamlet he ordered his guide to light a flambeau to announce their presence, but in the rain and the dark they actually reached the place without being challenged. He was here, nonetheless. And locked somewhere in the huddle of dwellings was a prisoner called Landor. Armand was about to find out whether all this hardship had been worthwhile.

Suddenly a man in uniform appeared at the open door of one of the houses, a pistol in one hand and drawn sword in the other. And Armand remembered what to do. The hauteur he had polished in Paris moved into operation, and in a few minutes he had asserted his authority and claimed due deference. The guide was sent around the buildings to a yard to unsaddle the horses. Armand was invited by Lieutenant Angelou into the front room of the house, where there was a rustic table, onto which Armand slid his loaded pistol.

"Monsieur, may I take your cloak?" Armand ignored the lieutenant, pulled it off himself, shook it and laid it across the back of a chair. Outside, the squall began to ease, though rain still pattered on the roof. "If I may view your papers, monsieur?"

Armand held the safe conduct from Napoleon tucked into the breast of his coat. He always enjoyed watching people's faces as

they saw the curt message, the seal and the signature. This time
the effect was dramatic. "Monsieur de Belfort! I . . ." There was a
long moment during which doubt, perplexity and a strange kind
of nervousness crossed the lieutenant's fine-boned face. "I have
the honor to inform you that your wife is here in Arosa."

Armand, holding out his hand, gave a quick laugh. "Now, that,
lieutenant, is the last thing I'd expect anyone to say to me! You're
mistaken. The document, if you please."

The lieutenant relinquished it, but his embarrassment increased. "The lady left no room for mistake, monsieur. She gave
her husband's name as Armand de Belfort."

Armand, his amusement gone, was about to make another sarcastic retort when something inside his head turned silently over,
like a finely honed piece of clockwork. He began to fold the
paper. "Describe her, if you please."

"A very . . . elegant lady. Indeed, exquisite, if I may be permitted to say so. She has fair hair, fair skin and blue eyes. She arrived
today and requested an escort to Salamanca, which I considered
it my duty—and my pleasure—to guarantee."

Armand's dizziness began to return. "You're not telling me she
was traveling alone?"

"Madame was accompanied by an armed servant. I've made
the house next door available to madame tonight."

There was something about the way the lieutenant said
"madame" that indicated a certain lack of credulity. Armand had
just denied that his wife was on the Peninsula—he could not
blame the lieutenant for conjecturing that the lady was his mistress. The lady! She *had* to be Delphine. If he were not so tired,
he would find it delicious. He left the satchel over his shoulder
and the cloak on the chair, and picked up the pistol. "Kindly escort me to her door."

The lieutenant remained by the table. After a moment's debate with himself, he said, "We are guarding an English prisoner
in Arosa, monsieur."

"I know. What's that got to do with it?" At the lieutenant's surprise he said impatiently, "Sir Gideon Landor. The Duke of Ra-

gusa has specifically asked me to question him. I repeat, where is my wife?"

The lieutenant's eyes showed a new kind of apprehension and curiosity. "Madame is with the gentleman. The three of us dined together this evening. Afterward, she was good enough to suggest that a private conversation would perhaps—"

"Enough." Armand felt almost as furious as a jealous husband or lover. "You'll stay here, out of my sight, and you can remove that look from your face. This isn't private; it's the emperor's business, and I take full responsibility. Where is the prisoner?"

The lieutenant gestured over his shoulder. "Behind the house, in the hut. If you really . . . I suggest you go through the kitchen; you take that door, then turn right. The rain—"

There was intense anticipation on the lieutenant's face as Armand strode by, but he wouldn't interfere. Why should he? The results would be entertaining enough, and they were now out of his hands.

Armand walked from the room into a kind of alcove, then turned and barged into the kitchen where two men looked up, startled. The lieutenant's voice rang out: "Sergeant! Open the prisoner's door at once."

A cavalry sergeant rose from the chair near the door, glowered at Armand, then stepped across the gap between the two buildings, lifted a bar from the door of the hut and swung it inward. And there they were.

They had the unmistakable look of a couple surprised in dalliance. The heightened color, the unsteadiness, as though they had just sprung apart. The amazement; the deep alarm. Aiming the pistol at Delphine, Armand shot a triumphant glance at Landor. "*Mon dieu,* what an age it is since we were all together. Don't you hate unfinished business?"

The Code Revealed

For Delphine, after the first stunning shock, it was the return of the nightmare. She looked at Armand and knew defeat. She had been mad to twist and turn and try to find a way for her and Gideon to escape the war; they were all enmeshed in it, and none more so than the man in civilian clothes who was just now pointing a gun at her breast. "Armand," she said, "I love him. He is my husband. When they take him to Salamanca, they may take me too."

"Oh, no, it's not as simple as that." Armand wasn't looking at her. His hand with the gun was steady, but his eyes were fixed on Gideon. "What kind of cretin would let you live after capturing you in *naval uniform*? It's too ludicrous for words. The rules of warfare don't begin to provide a definition for your sort of insanity."

Gideon gave a grunt of contempt. "Since when did you care about rules, Belfort? Let alone honor."

"Prepare yourself for execution," Armand said coolly. Delphine made a start toward him and he said, "Or would you prefer her to go first?"

Gideon's heart thudded and he clenched his fists, willing himself not to react hastily. He was standing only two paces away from Belfort, but he found it hard to read his expression, for the light from the kitchen was behind his head. Meanwhile Gideon could see just what was happening in the room beyond. The Portuguese cook, the friend and associate of Leon, had moved to stand behind the sergeant, who was in his chair again, looking on with a scowl. Gideon suddenly guessed how important it was to keep Belfort talking. "What? My wife is a Bonapartist—always was, always will be. How do you think that makes me feel, Belfort?"

The cook stepped closer to the sergeant. In his right hand was the broad-bladed knife with which he had carved up the lamb.

Belfort replied with a sneer, "A Bonapartist with an English husband, an English title, and a plantation that supplies the British catering corps on Ile de France. Where's the patriotism in that, *ma cousine?*"

With a glance of supplication, Gideon begged Delphine to answer—it didn't matter what she said as long as she kept Belfort's attention. She didn't have the same line of sight as Gideon, so mercifully she could not see what was going on in the kitchen. Perplexed and trembling, she found her voice, while out of the corner of his eye Gideon watched the inexorable scene play itself out in the rectangle of light behind Belfort's slim figure.

"I'm French, Armand, and I have French allegiances." The cook put his left hand across the sergeant's mouth and jerked the head back. "But my country cannot choose whom I will love." The carving knife swept over the sergeant's throat, then slashed back across it in a silver arc edged with scarlet. "Nor can it condemn me because Ile de France was invaded." The cook let the sergeant's head slump forward onto his red, sodden chest, and wiped the knife blade on the thick cloth of the cavalry coat. Then, silent as a ghost within the veil of rain, he crept up to Armand de Belfort.

Delphine gasped as he came into view. When the man's brown hand clamped itself across Armand's mouth his eyes jerked back in his skull. In the same second, Gideon put himself between Delphine and the pistol and lifted it out of Belfort's fingers. "Wait," he growled to the Portuguese, still in French, "Leave him to me." The man shrugged and at the same time tightened his hold on Armand, who was so off balance that he needed the support of his captor's strong, stocky body to stay upright. "Inside," Gideon said, "out of sight." Armand must have forbidden the lieutenant to appear, but he was bound to do so soon.

The cook pulled Armand into the hut, hauling him crabwise so that he stumbled, his face caught in a rictus of fear as the knife grazed his throat. Delphine moved back out of their way, which brought her within view of the kitchen. The sergeant in his chair appeared like a sentinel at the corner of her vision, and she shrank back—and then she registered how still and crumpled he was. And saw the blood. Then Ellis appeared in the doorway, blocking her view of the house behind. "Sir?"

"Ellis," Gideon said, as though they were resuming a conversation over waistcoats or boots. "The sentries?"

"One's still asleep and the other . . . received a little help in that direction, sir." Then his eye fell on Armand and he pursed his lips as though to let out a whistle of approbation.

"The guide who came with Belfort?"

"Inside out of the rain, sir. Too busy getting into shelter to notice me. Probably being questioned by the lieutenant."

Delphine shivered as she looked at Armand. The knife was still at his throat and his face was contorted by fear, but he collected himself enough to say, "There are four of them. They'll shoot you down before you've gone a yard. Call the lieutenant and parley— it's your only hope."

The Portuguese snarled and the blade pressed inward. Delphine gasped and Gideon said, "Release him." There was indecision in the cook's face, but then his eye fell on the carbine that Ellis swung forward off his shoulder. He opened his hands and moved back.

Armand's legs began to fail him, he staggered and was about to fall, and he took a quick step sideways to recover. Gideon hit him under the chin, with a powerful punch that snapped his head back and sent him crashing against the stone wall next to the closed shutters of the window. There was a crack, and Armand collapsed to the floor and lay still.

Gideon gave a groan and doubled over with his arms wrapped across his chest, struggling to breathe, his eyes closed and his face gray. Delphine went to him but she was afraid to touch him, for the pain he endured was etched in his face. After a moment he opened his eyes and whispered, "Forgive me, *mon ange*. I've wanted to do that for a very long time." He stood straighter and said, "Go. Check that he's alive."

She approached Armand with the same shrinking terror that would have gripped her if she had had to go near the dead sergeant. He looked so pale, so broken, and it was as though she alone had brought him to this catastrophe. But when she put her fingers against his neck she could feel that his skin was warm and a pulse beat strongly beneath. "He's alive."

"Beg pardon, sir—" came Ellis's voice.

Gideon's cut across it. "Take his bag. Can you pull it from under him?"

Her skin crawled as she tried to get the satchel over Armand's head, and without a word the Portuguese came forward and helped her. Once the satchel came free she slipped it over her head and across her chest so that it rested on her hip. Then she held out her hand for the carving knife.

It took a moment for the Portuguese to respond. With speculation in his black eyes he glanced from Armand's insensible body to her face, until with a grimace of sardonic humor and admiration he handed the knife over.

Silence fell in the hut. Then Delphine bent and carefully slit the sides of her gown from knee to hem. The only sound was from the scattered raindrops on the roof and the long, keen blade as it parted the silk. When she was done, she handed it back. The Portuguese stood weighing it in his hand and looking at Gideon, who raised one eyebrow and nodded toward the kitchen. "An eye for an eye . . . you've taken that. You're coming with us?" A moment slid by, then the Portuguese shrugged again and nodded. "Good. Ellis, we'll follow you. The horses, if you please."

"And always at blighted midnight," Ellis murmured as he turned to go.

Delphine was astonished at the horses' agility as they thundered away from Arosa. Ellis led, having committed the route to memory as they approached in the daylight. The cavalrymen could not follow, for the yard was open and the other horses had burst free as well, though the hay would call them back in an hour or two when they got tired of blundering about in the rain. Someone fired a shot, however, just as she reached the foot of the slope, and her back stiffened, but next second her mount swerved onto the track into the woods, where they went in single file—Ellis in

front, the Portuguese behind him, then herself and Gideon. "I'm
riding behind you, my darling," he'd whispered as he helped her
to mount. "I'm not losing you now."

She bit her lip when the shot rang out, and the taste of blood
stayed on her tongue. She crouched up on the horse's shoulders,
her legs tucked back around its wet, warm sides, and kept her
eyes half-closed against the spatters of mud flung back from the
hooves in front. They were riding bareback, jolting and slipping
as the horses plunged into the darkness. Behind her, Gideon was
riding the heavy creature they had used as a packhorse; for Delphine, the sound of its harsh breathing heightened the urgency
of their flight. And she was terrified that Gideon wouldn't be
strong enough to stay on its back for hour after hour. She willed
him to shout an order for Ellis to stop, take stock—but there
wasn't a word from behind her, and she could not even turn
around to see how he was faring, or she would fall off. Armand's
satchel thumped against her hip and she wondered what was inside it. Was it worth carrying something that might be soaked by
the rain? Yet it must be supremely important, for Armand had obviously kept it with him at every moment.

At last Ellis put up his hand and they all came to a halt, the
horses jostling one another in a narrow cutting leading down to
a stream. Gideon leaned over his horse's neck, taking great gasping breaths, and Ellis addressed the Portuguese.

"We're going southeast. In Portugal for half of the journey,
the rest in Spain. Do you know your way from here?" He
pointed to a sheep track that wound along beside the stream.
"That's the direction of Sabugal." The Portuguese nodded; it
was all the farewell they got. He dug his boot into his horse's
side and whirled away from them. For a while they could hear
the thud and splash of hooves as he rode off into the gloom at
a rapid trot. "Thank God he's gone," Ellis said, "with his inces-
sant chatter."

Delphine brought her horse alongside Gideon's and put her
hand over his where it was tangled in the horse's mane. He raised
his head, then brought up his other hand to caress her cheek,
across the streaks of mud on her skin. "Brava! Can you stand an-

other hour of this? Changing direction through the stream will help, and the rain may wash out the evidence after that. I can't see them pursuing us this far anyway—or they might meet the army before we do."

Delphine didn't want him to talk. She leaned across and closed the pale lips with her own.

Ellis said behind her, "I agree, sir. Another hour, at a decent speed, and we can stop the rest of the night."

Delphine released Gideon, with reluctance, and leaned toward Ellis. "Wasn't there one little village on the way?"

"No, madame, you're thinking of that poxy place—beg pardon—outside Fuente Guinaldo. We won't get that far. But there's a tor I remember, no more than an hour away, with a great pile of boulders that'll give us shelter and a good vantage. And we might as well keep going while this rain holds. When I'm soaked to the skin I'd as soon be on the move."

So they left, splashing across the stream and up over a rise that returned them toward the plateau. The rain stopped eventually, clearing the air and making the contours of the land more visible. There was one more waterway to cross, swollen with the spring melt, that came up to the stomach of Ellis's horse when he pushed unhesitatingly across.

Gideon examined it. "Can you manage?" he said to Delphine. "We'll go in together and I'll stay downstream. Give me the bag if you like."

She shook her head. He looked beyond exhaustion, as though another ounce of weight would bring him to the ground. And she had not made up her mind about what she had stolen from Armand. Did love give her the right to keep it, or would she sully her own honor by handing it to the English?

She put her horse into the water, swinging the bag out of the way, onto the upstream side, as Gideon joined her. The larger, heavier horse provided a bulwark that gave her mount more confidence, but she could feel it shivering as the swift water roiled against its flanks, sucked at her feet and plastered her gown against her calves. Armand's papers from Paris were perhaps by now beyond recognition. Would it matter if the satchel dropped from her shoulder and drowned, never to be recovered? Gideon wouldn't even see or feel it go.

The horses drove forward, Gideon leaning over with a hand on her mount's bridle to keep it looking ahead so it could see Ellis's horse waiting safely on the other side. She could let the emperor's secrets slip through her fingers, without remorse. She had the right, and the perfect excuse.

The horses were huffing with fright but their strong legs sliced through the buffeting water and their hooves found a footing near the bank. With a powerful surge, Delphine's mount prepared to heave itself up, and the strap of the satchel slipped off her shoulder and caught in the crook of her elbow. She brought her hands forward, into the horse's mane, and urged it on. Then she and Gideon were on the bank beside Ellis, their horses quivering with the effort and water streaming from their sides. Delphine reached across, took the strap of the satchel and hooked it back over her head. The sodden leather made a rough, hard bar between her breasts.

"Well done, madame," Ellis said.

She avoided his eye.

Without Ellis, Gideon could not have hoped to find his way back to Fuente Guinaldo. He was certain of never having come this way before; the route he had taken with Grant and Leon had been different. This shortcut was known only to the bandit Saornil, and now to Able Seaman Ellis, who rode ahead across the plateau with the stolen French carbine over his shoulder and a bandolier across his broad chest.

And beside Gideon rode the woman who had saved him. When they'd burst into that first insane gallop from Arosa, tears had choked him. He had wept in disbelief, gratitude and love— and prayed she wouldn't turn to see. Now the disbelief had gone, but so had his resources. They were safe; he could assure her of that. They would reach Fuente Guinaldo. But not tonight, and it made sense to stop at this vantage point that Ellis had lined up. His only concern was making it there, before the fire in his chest consumed the last of his strength.

Somewhere, they had crossed back into Spain, and a wash of rosy light along the ragged horizon announced the dawn. Ellis pointed ahead, to where a massive silhouette loomed against the sky. "There, sir! The tor!"

Gideon looked at Delphine. There was more fatigue on her face than relief, but she smiled back. She was caked in mud, her gown clung to her like the flimsy fabric on a Greek statue and her damp hair had come down around her shoulders, but the kingfisher dart of her glance was as true to the mark as it would have been in a crowded ballroom. "Rest and reconnaissance, *mon capitaine?*"

"For you, madame, anything."

When they finally got to the tor and dismounted, Gideon found he could not stand, so Delphine stayed with him and the horses in a little gully while Ellis climbed farther up to have a look about. Gideon sat with his head on his knees and Delphine's hand on the nape of his neck, beyond speech and almost beyond consciousness.

But after a while there was the muffled sound of cursing, with a lilt to it that brought Gideon's head up. "My word, sir," Ellis said when he came back into view. "It's better than I thought."

"There's shelter?" Resigned to the climb, Gideon got slowly to his feet.

"A cave! And I don't know who uses it—shepherds or bandits—but someone does. The catering's not royal, but there's a fire-place and a stack of dry wood, and a few blankets. Not of the cleanest but they're not damp, either."

"Capital, Ellis. Lead the way."

On the way through the rocks Gideon took the satchel from Delphine as they helped each other up. She seemed pitifully frag-ile all of a sudden, as though all her sparkling vitality had been washed away, never to return.

In the cave, Ellis lit the fire, shook out the blankets and then left to reconnoiter the surroundings while Gideon and Delphine stripped, piled their clothes by the fire and then found a place where they could sit side by side, wrapped in rugs, looking out over the crackling flames toward the lightening sky.

Before Ellis returned, Gideon kissed her. She had cleaned her face with her wet gown, and rubbed at her hair with a corner of a blanket, and against his lips she felt smooth and fresh, like a child after a dip in a river. Tenderness overcame him, making his voice break as he said, *"Ma vie."*

"My life."

Also before Ellis came back, Gideon undid the flap of Belfort's satchel and opened it. It was stuffed with papers that were damp on the sides, but had otherwise been protected by the thick, polished leather and an inner sleeve of oiled paper.

From the first glance, there was no mistake. "The code!" Delphine said.

He laid some of the sheets out on the dry earth floor, near enough to the fire for the light to flicker across their surfaces and reveal the carefully drawn grids, the neat lines of lettering. "The whole thing," he said. "Decryption and encryption. This is it. This is Scovell's pot of gold."

"Straight from the devil's lair."

He turned on his haunches to look at her. "How much did he show you?"

"Armand? *Nothing.* I never knew he had anything to do with it!"

"No. Bonaparte."

"One simulated page, no more."

He noticed that she didn't draw near to look at the real thing. She was crouched with her arms about her knees, her blue eyes enormous and expressionless in her white face. She was denying him her thoughts. Concealing the impulses of her heart. Again. Trying to hide her loyalties—the link from childhood and the dawn of principle that bound her to France and the emperor.

Slowly Gideon gathered the papers together until he held the whole precious sheaf in his fingers. They rustled slightly, for his hands were unsteady. A pulse beat fast in his temple and he clenched his jaw, looking down at the key to French strategy that Wellesley coveted, that Scovell had been seeking all year.

Without looking at Delphine, he said, "You know your cousin; he'll never admit he lost this to us. He'll claim he destroyed it in a moment of danger." He paused a moment, then continued

firmly, "In a few weeks, a few months, we'll march against Salamanca. We'll take it. And before we do, Scovell will have the code.
He'll crack it wide open, and the French will never know we have
it. I trust Scovell; he knows his business. The code will be England's."

Then he stretched out his hands and threw it into the flames.

When the sun came up they were all asleep. Delphine awoke first.
She was curled into Gideon's back, and out of the corner of her
eye she could see the landscape spread below them in great
swathes of gray and brown, dotted by patches of lichen and spiky
grasses in fresher shades of green. She crooked one elbow beneath her, lifted her face above Gideon's shoulder and saw a wisp
of smoke curl up from the fireplace into the cool, dry air of the
cave. Beyond, at the arch of stone, Ellis stirred, his hand tighten-
ing on the stock of the carbine that lay at his side.

She was stiff and bruised, and the blanket rasped against her
skin, but happiness glowed in every limb, as powerful as the rising
sun.

She laid her head against Gideon's temple, listening to his
steady breathing and relishing his warmth against her cheek. He
opened his eyes and twisted in her arms, laughing softly despite
the pain and the rough entanglement of their coverings.

She slipped one arm beneath his neck and buried her fingers
in his tousled hair. "Welcome to the new day, *mon amour.*"

He kissed her as though it would never end.

HISTORICAL NOTE

Sir Gideon Landor owes his existence to an explorer, surveyor and naval commander: it was the ordeal of Captain Matthew Flinders on Mauritius that provided the situation for the hero of this novel. Flinders's health may have been undermined by his long captivity, for he lived only a few days beyond the 1814 publication of the book on which he was laboring in Nassau Street when Delphine and Julie Dalgleish went to visit him in 1811.

Somehow each of my novels to date has ended with a major battle, but this is the exception, since what fascinated me was the suspenseful period *before* the British campaign that led to victory at Salamanca in July 1812. It was Napoleon Bonaparte's own policies—deploying his armies widely, taking no personal part in the war, bypassing his brother Joseph and failing to prevent rivalry amongst his commanders—that opened the gaps in French strategy that Wellesley (later the Duke of Wellington) exploited with such skill. Equally, it was the distances between the French corps, and Bonaparte's remoteness from Madrid, that made the development of the Grand Paris Cypher necessary.

The guiding spirit of this book is Major George Scovell, whose dedicated work in the quartermaster general's department eventually gave Wellington the key to French intentions in the Peninsula and facilitated the string of victories that would banish France's armies from Spain. Using his genius for languages and mathematics, and documents gleaned by Hardinge's intelligence officers, Scovell mastered the French regional codes and then cracked the Grand Paris Cypher itself, mere months after it first came into use in Spain—despite its being the most complex code hitherto known. (Armand de Belfort's mission, incidentally, is plausible, for Marshal Soult was in fact the last commander to receive the cypher, after Badajoz.)

I have taken just one liberty with what we know of George Scovell: his wife Mary did not go with him to Fuente Guinaldo after his Lisbon leave in April 1812; she had to wait until the army returned to Frenada for the winter. She was the only officer's wife in the village, and the couple's home provided comfort and entertainment for fellow officers during the cold months before the campaigns of the new year.

Both survived the war. Like many of Wellington's old nonaristocratic campaigners, George Scovell was somewhat neglected by the duke in later life, but he reached the rank of full general and in 1829 was appointed lieutenant governor of the Royal Military College at Sandhurst. He was buried there in 1861, alongside Mary, who predeceased him at the age of eighty. They left no children, and Scovell wrote no memoirs, but he carefully preserved his records and tables. These have in very recent years received the attention they deserve, and scholarship has resurrected a fascinating character in the history of warfare.

Lieutenant Colonel Colquhoun Grant was taken from Salamanca to Paris as a prisoner of war, but managed to escape and make his way back to England. Readers of my novel *The Chase* will know that this intrepid man went on to play a part in the Battle of Waterloo in 1815.

Lucien Bonaparte returned to France with his family after Napoleon's abdication in 1814, and supported the emperor's claims during his return to power, but after his defeat Lucien retired to Italy, where the pope created him Prince of Canino.

The little King of Rome (Napoleon II) saw his father for the last time in 1814 and thereafter lived in Austria, where he died without issue at the age of twenty-one.

Mauritius was not to be French again, but its inhabitants created a style of living that became a graceful blend of French *savoir vivre* and English resourcefulness, enhanced by the lively influences from India and Africa that make the island nation unique.

ACKNOWLEDGMENTS

It was after reading *The Life of Matthew Flinders,* by Miriam Estensen, that I conceived the idea for this novel. It would not have taken its present shape without the brilliant work by Mark Urban, *The Man Who Broke Napoleon's Codes: The Story of George Scovell,* which is also a highly readable history of the Peninsular War. Two fine books on espionage formed part of my reading: *Most Secret and Confidential: Intelligence in the Age of Nelson,* by Steven E. Maffeo, and *Secret Service: British Agents in France 1792–1815,* by Elizabeth Sparrow.

I would like to thank my mother—the only person who reads my novels in installments—my father and my husband for their unfailing support and advice.

And I gratefully acknowledge the encouragement that our dear friends Eric and Patricia Tracey have always given me, with the hope that they will not object to Gideon's home occupying their lovely environs in Wiltshire.

If you found *The Code of Love* thrilling,
then you will love Cheryl Sawyer's
next romantic work of historical fiction,

The Winter Prince

on sale in April 2007.
Read on for a sneak peek. . . .

It is the twenty-third of October, 1642, after the Battle of Edge-hill, and King Charles the First and his cavaliers have just beaten the army of Parliament. It is the beginning of the English Civil War, the bitter struggle between the monarch and his Puritan Parliament. Tonight the king's General of the Horse, his nephew Prince Rupert, has just led the cavaliers to victory against the parliamentarian Earl of Essex.

It was very cold, and Rupert was momentarily alone, leaning against the trunk of a tree and looking down the slope across the bivouacs and cooking fires to the muffled plain below, where the burial parties had stopped working because the night was too black.

He was thinking of what he and the king's army had done, what they might have done, what he would do tomorrow. They had blown open the road to London; they might have cost Essex more men if the light had not failed; and tomorrow he would harass and torment the earl's regiments in retreat and see if he could snatch more of the baggage train.

He was unscathed but exhausted, and along with his raw regret for the men who had been killed, a fierce glow of victory filled his chest.

He thought further ahead: to the king's triumphant return to the palace of Whitehall in London, to the homecoming of the queen, to peace with parliament and the resumption of the cultivated court that gathered around the royal family, whose refinement and sweetness meant more to his future and his dreams than he would ever have conceived.

He thought about Mary Villiers, the Duchess of Richmond. Months ago, in the courtyard of the Wassenaer Hof in the Hague, he had begged for her friendship, yet the moment she gave him her hand, he realized he could never be her friend, except in name. Ever since, he had been wrestling with what this meant.

But he knew, tonight, how it would be. The Duchess of Richmond would return, and walk into his life again, never to escape. He could not touch her, he could not have her, because she was his friend's wife—and because she told her husband everything. And the world everything. But against all these odds he would conquer her and win her love. He would have her heart and soul, as she had his.

Ever since Mary had come back to the king's new capital at Oxford, her husband had been convinced that they two and Prince Rupert were destined to be friends—and the prince did not refuse his kind offices. Prince Rupert might be absent every day and sometimes a night or two from Oxford, but his quarters were in the city, at hardly any distance from their own, and in the first week they dined together twice, with no formality—a note from James arrived each time during the day, forewarning Mary, and she commanded meals that could be eaten late if necessary, when both men dragged themselves away from their duties and arrived to eat in the comfortable private chamber, closeted away and eager to talk of other matters.

She found herself able to smile naturally and give the prince a friend's greeting. He treated her with warmth and respect, and she found ways to tease him once more and make him smile back. She had an excuse to spend hours in his company—did she have the right to yearn for more? And while he talked to James, she had time to observe him. She found delight in letting her gaze travel over his strong face and tall body, as she might look at a dearly loved painting. Yet out of guilt, or discretion, or to assist a gratification of the senses that she had never known herself capable of, she rationed these effects. On his second visit, she chose to study one part of him alone. Irresistibly, it was his mouth.

It was chiseled and firm, with the upward tilt at the corners that she knew how to turn into a smile. Under the lower lip was a dint of shadow that made the whole shape of the mouth look willful, even arrogant. There was a cleft in his determined chin, and although she could tell he shaved every morning, within the cleft the blue shadow that darkened on his face during the day deepened into a distinct line. She sat silent with her gaze caressing his mouth, and imagined running one fingertip down over the contours of his lips, to the little hollow underneath and into the cleft below. While his eyes were turned away, she could do this. She could touch him, as she had never wanted to touch a man before.

The fourth time he came to her home, she was there alone. He was shown into the great chamber, and when she rose to greet him, she felt confusion and a deep inner response. He seemed in too much haste, however, to notice her reaction. Clad in a buff coat and a black suit under an enormous greatcoat, with his sword buckled on and leather gauntlets on his hands, he was clearly on his way out to the garrisons, and looked as though he had no time to linger.

He bowed, smiled and said, "Forgive the intrusion. But I promised to drop this off for your husband." He held out a worn-looking book bound loosely in calf leather.

She took it and instinctively held it to her without looking at it, her hands folding over the book to clasp it to her midriff. Then she felt embarrassed, opened her hands and the book, and looked down. It was a battered copy of *Militarie Instructions for the Cavall'rie* by John Cruso. She looked up to find Prince Rupert watching her intently. Mary was thinking only that with his book in her hands she now possessed one more item of his along with the handkerchief he had given her in the Wassenaer Hof. She could never let anyone, least of all him, know how she treasured it.

Misinterpreting her silence, he said firmly, "It wasn't my idea; the duke asked if he could borrow a manual on the use of cavalry. He may keep it; as you may imagine, I know every line and picture." When she still did not reply, he continued, "His interest is theoretical. I hope you do not think I would ever encourage him to become an officer or to be involved in the army any more than he . . . You cannot think that of me?"

"No," she said. "No, never. That was not what I thought."

But he held out his hand, palm open, and shook his dark hair back over his shoulders in an impatient gesture. "Perhaps you would like me to take it back?"

"No!" Afraid of losing the book, she stepped away quickly and placed it on a dresser at the side of the room. "It is most kind of you. James is something of a student of strategy, as you know, but he is not versed in tactics. He will find this fascinating. And when would you like it returned?"

"As I said, he may keep it," he said softly. He stepped forward, and the expression in his dark eyes changed as he looked down at her. She felt all the power of his gaze, as though until this moment, for all the time they had known each other, he had been keeping it in reserve.

She must protect herself. With an attempt at her usual tone she said, "Do you have a large library of military books? And where on earth do you store them?"

"I have books of every kind, kept in several places, Oxford included." He smiled into her eyes. "I don't flatter myself I have anything that would interest your elevated mind. But if there is aught I can bring you—books or anything else—you have only to ask."

"Thank you," she said brightly. "I know your largesse. I already have something of yours, if you remember?"

By another change in his eyes she saw he did remember. In every detail. But he did not speak for a moment and neither could she. What had possessed her to mention the handkerchief? Now she must at all costs conceal the dangerous value it held for her.

She took a deep breath. "Of course, that too was a loan. You must tell me at once if you would like it back. Delft lace, if I recall, and the finest linen."

He looked at her as if she had done him an injury. He frowned, took a small step back and glanced at her sidelong. "Pray return it, madam, if that is important to you. For myself . . ." Then he bit his lip and looked at the floor.

She was lost; the conversation had gone beyond her horizon,

and she must bring it back to a navigable channel. In the same playful tone she said, "Oh, I'm not sure I can part with it, when I recall the unique spirit in which it was given. You remember the moment—you had us all in fits. When you handed it to me, I was in tears of laughter. But let us agree: you may have it back when I provoke the same in you. Laughter, or tears, or both together."

His expression darkened still more and his voice took on a deeper note. Facing her, he said, "Laughter is ever your territory, madame. As for my tears—you command them at any time." Then he gave her a low bow and immediately left the room.

She remained looking after him, transfixed.

His tears? What did he mean? She shivered and put a hand on the dresser to steady herself. There was only one interpretation, and with the intensity of his gaze he had meant her to know it. She stayed there for a moment longer, taking it in.

Then she went to the window and looked down in time to see him emerge from the doorway. His officers were a little way up the street, mounted and in a group. The men's heads turned, but Rupert ignored them and stopped in the road. His tall figure was a straight black line against the gray stones, but his head was bent. He was thinking. She held onto the window frame, afraid that he would turn and look up, but unable to move away. He regretted what he had said or done, or he wanted to make himself clearer—either way, she could tell he was debating whether to turn and come back. But suddenly he replaced his broad-brimmed hat, so she could not see his face, joined his men and mounted his black stallion, and they all clattered off down the street.

She sank onto the carved chest under the window and held onto the sill with one hand. She commanded his feelings. He loved her.

Rupert spent the morning riding across fog-bound country to inspect the work at the water mills on the rivers, where gunpowder maker William Baber was setting up production. Talking with Baber in the dark expanse of the big Thames mill, standing on the riverside where coopers labored with timber and iron to make barrels for the powder, or riding east for miles through farmland and villages to the second mill on the Isis, his mind kept coming back to what he had just said to Mary Villiers.

Thinking of it was like succumbing to vertigo. His campaign for her heart and soul had begun—but without any planning. Nothing could have been further from his intention when he paid her that fleeting visit; all he had wanted was an excuse to see her without Richmond by, to watch her face as she bestowed a smile of greeting on him alone. All he had wished for was a harmless, stolen pleasure to begin his day.

But she had given him an opening, and he had stepped straight into it. There was no going back; he had no desire to go back.

She had directed the conversation with her usual skill, but there had been that flicker of alarm in her eyes over the handkerchief. She did not want to give it back to him; it was as though in her mind she was clasping it to her, just as she had held the book. In that moment of confusion and alarm she had retreated, and so had been forced to bring out her sharpest weapon—she had teased him. At once, without forethought, he had come out with his riposte.

It was all in the open now. The battle lines were drawn. She knew he loved her and she need not think he would try to conceal it any longer. Except from her husband and the world.

He had no idea about her feelings, for the altercation over the handkerchief was a trifle; it might mean nothing at all. He was not going to make the mistake of underestimating his opponent's powers of resistance. And at the very same time, at the thought of her, all his own defenses collapsed and desire overtook him so strongly that he could hardly see, or ride, or pick his way forward through the misty countryside.

Yes, his campaign had begun. She must not guess that she was at present the victor on all points.

In her first years, New Zealander **Cheryl Sawyer** lived just a few steps from the sea, and her favorite places, whether they be Caribbean islands or coastal towns on the Pacific rim, are still within sight and sound of an ocean. She has two master's degrees with honors in French and English literature, and her career has included teaching, publishing, and writing. After a year's travel researching and writing in Europe, the USA, and Costa Rica, she is now living and working in the harbor city of Sydney, Australia. Her Web site is www.cherylsawyer.com.